T R A I N

A novel inspired by hidden history
Danny M. Cohen

Published in partnership with
UNSILENCE PROJECT

TRAIN

A novel inspired by hidden history
Danny M. Cohen

Suitable for age 13 and up

Published in partnership with *Unsilence Project*

Visit www.unsilence.org to access educational programming created to accompany this novel.

This is a work of fiction based on historical events. All characters portrayed in this novel are either fictitious or are used fictitiously.

www.dannymcohen.com

Artwork by Ava Kadishson Schieber
Cover design by Sergio Gutiérrez-Montero

ISBN 978-1-5055-6045-9

Manufacturing information for this book can be found on the final page.

For Miriam Esperanza

GRATITUDE

With the encouragement and help of so many incredible people, a series of short stories became entwined and grew into this, my first novel.

It was my mentor, Phyllis Lassner, who pulled me into the world of Holocaust literature; thank you for providing me with those first kicks of encouragement to give voice to the marginalized and silenced narratives of history. And thank you to my academic advisor, Brian Reiser, for helping me to build the foundations and frameworks for my research. Throughout the writing process, artist and poet Ava Kadishson Schieber inspired me to be a better writer and not take myself too seriously; and I'm so grateful to you for the gift of your artwork that accompanies this book.

This book would not be possible without the vital research of Holocaust and genocide scholars. The contents of these pages build on and are inspired by the works of a number of historians, especially Doris Bergen, Henry Friedlander, Geoffrey Giles, Jud Newborn, Patricia Pientka, and Nathan Stoltzfus. I also thank the anonymous contributors of the publications and online encyclopedia of the United States Holocaust Memorial Museum.

Thank you to my editor, Christa Desir, for your brilliant honesty and contagious joy for what we do. Thank you to my copy-editor, Dahlia Adler, for your shrewd insights and meticulous work. And thank you to Sergio Gutiérrez-Montero for your support and for giving your time and talent to design this book's cover.

I'm so grateful for the invaluable feedback I received throughout the writing process. To Alexandra Benjamin, Jason Braier, Jeff Dritz, Ira Dym, and Amanda Sinai for your terrific advice. And to Jenna Brager, Julia Eksner, Beth Healey, Sara Levy, Mia Spiro, Alexis Storch, and Kelley H. Szany for your critique and guidance, grounded in your expertise in Holocaust, genocide, and human rights scholarship. To Adi Bloom, Amy Braier, Emma Gordon, Alison Gross, Greg Lanier, Jennifer Loeb, Aron Kandinov, and Stacey Mann for your professional insights and brilliant ideas. To Melanie R. Flaxer, Claire Goodrich, Jennifer Herr, and Anne Xie for your honest suggestions. To Clare Biggs, Rachelle L. Cherkasov, Sarah Levine, Jennifer Nielsen, and Ellen Rago for helping me to think carefully about young readers.

Thank you to Ilana Hutchinson for your endless excitement and so many unforgettable conversations. And thank you to Liz Lassner for stepping into the story, then staying for the entire ride.

Thank you to my wonderful friends and family—close to home and half a world away—for your encouragement and enthusiasm.

Thank you to my parents for giving me the support and resilience to be myself and achieve my dreams.

Finally, thank you to my daughter, Miriam, for inspiring me to tell stories, and to my husband, Bernard, for your limitless patience and willingness to always listen. I love you.

TRAIN

CONTENTS

THE THIEF

Tsura

They'll never know we were here.

No sound. No impression in the hardened mud. Tsura had learned to keep her head below the brick walls of the city. To become the shadows and sidestep the light. She could recite each route by heart. Over railway lines and through private gardens, across main roads and public parks. But some checkpoints were impossible to avoid.

A crowd had gathered close to the U-Bahn station. Two young soldiers blocked the entrance.

"What's going on?" Tsura asked them.

"The train station is closed," one soldier said. He held out his gloved hand. "Papers?"

Tsura handed over her identity documents for inspection. "What happened?"

"Someone fell on the tracks."

"Why are you dressed like a man?" the second soldier asked, rifle at his side.

Tsura pointed at the sleeves of his jacket, which didn't even reach his wrists. "Why are you dressed like a schoolboy?"

The other soldier laughed. As he unfolded and checked her papers, his grin widened. "Nice to meet you, Greta. We share a birthday."

"Lucky me," Tsura said. Her fake smile matched her false identity.

The soldiers sniggered as she walked away.

"I know what I'd do with her."

"She likes you," the other said.

Tsura shivered with disgust. *Nazi scum.*

Through the city, she moved against the winter morning wind that slipped between her neck and turned-up collar. The woolen overcoat hid the curves of her breasts, and her hair stayed tucked tight into a flat cap. She looked like a man and felt stronger for it. The sense of danger thrilled her and the familiarity of the damp corners was calming, yet Tsura remained wary of what lurked nearby, of being discovered.

Behind rows of houses, she crouched by a fence.

She watched Seraph approach. Seraph—a code name, of course—with her short fair hair and skinny frame, pulled a revolver from her pocket. "Here. It's loaded," Seraph warned.

Tsura's pulse quickened. *She managed to pull it off.* Tsura had never held a gun before and she was already in control. Testing the weight of the weapon, Tsura felt it become part of her as the distant clattering of a train on its tracks, like whisperings through walls, took her to thoughts of her imprisoned family. Through hidden voices and faded screams, her people pleaded, *Tell our stories.* The wheels of their words moved on rails that until that moment had dragged Tsura along but now filled her with momentum. Tsura had assumed her fateful position—she was the engine now, and the carriages she pulled were her responsibility.

She slid the revolver into her overcoat and led Seraph onto a local street. "The documents. When will they be ready?" Tsura asked, keeping her voice to just above a whisper.

"We're working on them. I just need those photographs."

"I owe you," Tsura said, and she meant it. Seraph hadn't had much time to prepare the forged identity documents, and Tsura was grateful.

The young women stepped out onto the side streets toward Seraph's home in Berlin's affluent Schöneberg neighborhood. In the dim light, factory workers trudged away from the closed train station.

"So, did you hear?" Seraph asked.

"What?"

"Gestapo. Another *Aktion* soon," Seraph whispered.

"Round-ups? Who?"

"More Jews. By the end of the weekend, they'll be gone from the city."

As she absorbed Seraph's words, her deep hate for Hitler's henchmen grew. Waves of muted rage summoned painful memories and Tsura bit down hard along the cracks in her lips, frightened that the Nazi plan for the Jews of Berlin also included the Roma—her people.

Tsura wanted to walk in silence, but Seraph continued to chatter. "Are the papers for someone in your family?"

"No. Someone else."

Alexander

The morning air froze in Alex's throat and his boots hit the ground hard as he tripped over the crisscrossing tram tracks set into the cobblestones. He passed the uniformed soldiers on the streets. *Don't look at them.* Walking too fast or too timidly would raise suspicion. He kept his eyes on the pavement and his hands in his coat pockets, touching old crumbs, shivering with nerves. Graying buildings and barren trees stood over him. Leafless branches pointed at him. Rows of flags—red, black, white—billowed overhead against Berlin's sky. As if the entire city knew his secret.

The shop stood almost hidden between the grander stone buildings. Jangling bells above signaled his arrival and startled the old man behind the counter.

"Paul Voeske sent me," Alex said, his stomach in knots.

"You came here alone?"

Alex nodded. "You take photographs, right?"

The old shopkeeper bowed his head at the teenager. "Follow me."

Alex squeezed through the narrow aisles between pieces of furniture pushed up against shelves and cabinets filled with ornaments and crockery. The room was bursting, from the overlapping rugs on the creaking wooden floor up to the mismatched dust-covered chandeliers hanging from the tin ceiling.

In the back room, Alex put on a jacket and tie and sat for the camera. Shoulders square, clean-shaven, chin forward. Sweat collected on his forehead as he waited for the shopkeeper to give him instructions. They both knew they were breaking the law. With unsteady hands, Alex smoothed down his hair.

"Keep still, please." The old man moved quickly and began to hum an unfamiliar song as he adjusted the camera stand. The camera flashed. Then once more.

Alex felt older than seventeen. He resembled his father and imagined himself bald like him one day.

"Please wait in the front," the shopkeeper said.

Alex removed the borrowed tie and suit jacket and threw on his coat and cap. His face still burned with worry, and he returned to the front of the shop, which was packed with trinkets and treasures. Perhaps he'd discover the perfect birthday gift for Ruti.

Searching dusty bookshelves along the far wall, below the volumes on history, anatomy, and music, Alex found a small group of books on travel. A London guidebook or British map would have been perfect, but there were only books on German architecture and German railways and maps of Austria. *They must've burned all the good stuff.* As he snaked through the aisles, one object caught his attention.

A miniature porcelain train sat locked behind grimy glass. The front engine and each of the five matching carriages had been brushed with a distinct tone of ivory glaze. The wheels and crankshafts were decorated with silver leaf. Each carriage was intricate and unique, and was connected by an elegant silver hook to a tiny silver hoop on the rear of the next. Silver paint framed its miniature white windows, and the details of the carriage doors, including the locks, were carved perfectly into the ceramic. But the most striking piece was the train engine itself, painted an ivory matte. Its furnace, valves, and driver's cab were covered in silver leaf and its thin white porcelain chimney was perfect in its simplicity. Alex knew Ruti would love it, and not just because her big brother picked it out.

The shopkeeper returned, his wary eyes fixed on the street outside. "You can come back for the photographs at the end of the workday. And please, not a word to anyone, or I'll be shot." The man's smile erased the sting of his words.

As Alex anticipated holding the black-and-white images, ready to be added to false documents, his stomach growled with both hunger and apprehension.

Alex pointed to the porcelain train. "How much is this?"

The old man peered over his thick glasses and reached up to unlock the cabinet door. He gestured for Alex to pick up the ornament and, once more, hummed his pretty tune.

Alex's thumb and forefinger unhooked the train engine from the sequence of carriages. A small paper tag, resting on the glass beneath the ornament, stated what he thought was a more-than-fair price. He held the engine in his palm. Its chimney had broken off once but was now carefully fixed with glue. He placed the engine back on the shelf and examined its five carriages, detaching and checking them one by one. He discovered fractures along the sides of the first and fifth carriages. Even with its imperfections, the train was beautiful.

"Could you wrap it? It's a gift."

With his wrinkled hands, the shopkeeper scooped up the six train pieces and carried them over to the counter. The old man continued to hum his melody as he placed the porcelain train into a small wooden box and wrapped the box in brown paper.

"Thank you," Alex said. He handed over crumpled bank notes for the photographs and train, tucked the wrapped box beneath his arm, and stepped out onto the street. He squinted at the sunlight and pulled down his flat cap as his breath left his mouth in a cloud of vapor like cigarette smoke.

His younger sister, Ruti, had collected porcelain ornaments for years. Alex knew she'd love the tiny train and she'd love his treasure hunt that would lead her to find it. But his satisfaction was followed by hollow guilt. *Ruti will cry tonight when she finds me gone.* He pictured Mother and Father crying, too. If only he could give them a proper goodbye. If only he weren't leaving the day before his sister's birthday. But this was Alex's only chance to escape Germany. By tomorrow night, he'd be far from Berlin. Far from the lifeless trees and iron-cold factories. Far from the frozen cobblestones and the buildings with their swastika banners. And far from the passersby who could only stare at the yellow star sewn to his coat.

Ruth

The light fell through the stained glass windows of the cathedral and sparkled across the lenses of Ruth's glasses, making her squint.

Mama stepped out of the confession box on the opposite side of the vast space. "Ruti!" she called out across the rows of wooden pews. Ruth's nickname echoed up the pillars into the domed roof. "Your turn."

Every year, Mama brought her here. The twenty-sixth of February. The day before Ruth's birthday. Earlier, walking into the cathedral, Ruth had whined that she hated confession. And Mama had reminded Ruth that birthdays were new beginnings. It was 1943 and the war could be over soon, Mama had whispered, so there was even more reason to make amends and repent for their sins.

The confession box was dark and smelled of musty wood. As Ruth closed the curtain, she forgot the list of sins she'd prepared to recite. *I'd rather be at school.*

"Good morning, my child," Father von Wegburg said through the wooden lattice.

Ruth knelt and stared back at his silhouette, trying to make out the features of his face. She adjusted her glasses.

"Are you all right?" he asked after a few moments of silence.

Ruth tried to keep a straight face. "Oh, I'm fine. Thank you."

"You may share whatever is on your mind. There are no secrets from the Lord, for He has already seen what we have done."

Ruth pictured herself standing on the kitchen countertop, in her winter nightgown with its hand-stitched leaves and flowers, reaching to open a cupboard and finding the cake Mama had made for her. The number *15* had been piped over white cream icing. "I found my birthday cake. I woke up early when my family was still sleeping."

"Looking for a cake is no sin," Father von Wegburg said.

She wanted to laugh. If Mama knew what she'd said, she would have either scolded Ruth for mocking the Catholic Church or chuckled along. Ruth continued, "I tasted the icing. I shouldn't have. But I couldn't help it."

"In that case, you might be guilty of gluttony."

Ruth nearly snorted.

"Is there anything else you need to confess?" Father von Wegburg asked, sounding as if he was smiling, too.

Ruth should have been admitting to a small list of transgressions, she knew. Earlier that week, when her teacher asked Ruth to share her views on the justifications of Germany's war, she hadn't told the truth. *Nobody can speak the truth anymore.* "There's nothing else."

"Say two Hail Marys," Father von Wegburg told her. "And have a pleasant birthday."

When she stepped out of the confession box, Mama was kneeling at one of the pews.

"How do you feel?" Mama asked Ruth when they walked outside.

Ruth suppressed a grin. "Hungry."

"What do you fancy for lunch?"

"Something hot."

Against the cloudy sky, the dome and cross of St. Hedwig's Cathedral stood proudly, just like Mama. It was the way she carried herself that made her so beautiful. Mama wore her hat not because it kept her warm in the February weather, but because it suited her. Their gloves on, Mama linked her arm with hers and, as they followed the arc of the street, Ruth mimicked her mother's elegant posture. They had the same green eyes and the same healthy light-brown hair, but while Ruth's was tied into a single braid, Mama's was pinned perfectly into a bun at the back, like the scoop of ice cream Ruth was hoping would accompany her birthday cake.

Ruth couldn't wait to tell Elise about her cake confession. They'd have a good laugh about it. Ruth hadn't seen her best friend in days. Since the beginning of the year, with her father fighting in the war, Elise was constantly running errands for her mother, and was always cancelling their plans.

But Ruth would see her this evening, and she couldn't wait. Every year, Elise stayed over for Ruth's birthday. After a special dinner, the girls would whisper in Ruth's room for hours, gossiping about boys and shrieking at the nighttime sounds of scurrying mice beneath the floorboards. And then they'd wake up—on Ruth's birthday—for breakfast, gifts, and Alexander's annual treasure hunt. And delicious cake, of course.

E*lise*

I always ruin everything. Elise practiced how to break the news to Ruth. Mother wanted Elise at home. She wouldn't be able to stay over as they'd planned, so they'd have to celebrate tomorrow, instead.

As Elise left the League meeting, she avoided a proper goodbye with the other girls. Hurrying to the door, she threw her pink coat over her brown Girls' League climbing jacket. She stuffed her neckerchief and beret into her bag and put on her woolen scarf and warmer hat. Her uniform was hidden completely.

"Enjoy your weekend, Elise," one of the League leaders called out.

Not bothering to reply, Elise headed north toward Hackescher Market. Brittle weeds reached out to her through the cracks in the pavement.

Today had been like any other day. Elise had been up at dawn. She'd washed the floors and prepared boiled potatoes and fish for her mother. Then school. Mathematics in the morning. Writing after lunchtime. In Girls' League later in the afternoon, they'd practiced their embroidery and sang their usual pledges to the Führer—their leader, Adolf Hitler—and the Fatherland.

Hackescher Market on Friday afternoons was always bustling, with its rows of red brick arches on one side of the square and a line of food stalls along the promenade. Orange juice and butter had already sold out. Mother wouldn't be pleased. Elise used her ration card to buy potatoes, a tin of pickled fish, canned vegetables, a little sugar. Since autumn, the citizens of Berlin had been surprised to see food rations increase—a sign of Germany's victories, the newspapers reported.

The women and old men working the stands wore thick scarves and hats. They announced their wares, but not as cheerily as they once had. In wartime, it's not easy to be proud, Elise's mother once said. But Elise knew that wasn't strictly true. The girls in the League couldn't have been prouder. The leaders taught them how to chant and sing. And how to think. *We are the future mothers of the Reich.* Their Führer would be victorious. Their grandchildren would lead the new world.

Elise looked down at her coat. Its soft pink material and off-white trim were elegant, but even with her League jacket underneath, it wasn't warm enough. She'd have to switch it for her old overcoat.

As she passed the fish stall, Elise turned toward the dark corners and vacant arches along the brick structure. Carved panels and pretty windows stood out against Berlin's sky, while the illegal traders worked in the shadows below. Trading without ration cards wasn't allowed, but it was common and easy. The traders ignored the policemen on patrol, who paid little attention in return.

As Elise passed the opening of a courtyard, she heard someone yelp in pain. Around the corner, two people were scuffling. She held her satchel close. Her eyes locked on the scene. A man a few years older than Elise, with unshaven, grubby pale skin and dark hair, had his back against the brick wall. An African boy pressed his hand against the young man's pale throat. Elise recognized the boy—he stood out, since almost all people in Berlin were fair-skinned. She'd seen him in the market before. He was younger than her, maybe twelve or thirteen. *Keep away from him*, Mother had said. Elise's leaders in the Girls' League had warned them about Africans. *Thieves.* The Jews had brought them to Germany to poison and weaken the superior German race.

"Give it to me!" the African boy shouted, and he kicked at the young man's shins.

The African is robbing him. She had an urge to intervene. Or get help. With his hands around a heavy bag, the young man pushed and punched the African boy away. When the boy turned his eyes toward Elise, she held her breath. Her stomach spun. She wanted to turn and run, but her feet were firmly in place.

The boy punched the young man's stomach and pulled down on the bag's strap, which cut into the young man's neck, and he grimaced in pain. Elise wanted to fling herself toward the boy, to dig her nails into his dark skin. Her eyes caught the silver flash of a knife, its handle clutched by the boy's fist, the blade pointing at the scruffy young man's throat. Elise gasped. Her sudden sound, like a choked scream, startled them both, and the boy turned, giving the young man the chance to grab and twist the boy's wrist. The African boy screamed out and released the knife, which fell and landed by Elise's foot. She looked down at its razor-sharp edge.

"Pick it up!" the young man yelled at her, his arm now pinning the African boy against the wall.

"No! Girl, that's mine!" the thief shouted.

Elise wanted to pick up the blade. But she felt paralyzed. The young man turned and jabbed his fist hard into the boy's shoulder. While the African thief yelped and winced in agony, the young man reached for the knife. Then he stood, arm outstretched, holding the blade to the thief's neck. For a moment, the young man backed off. Then he lunged forward and slammed his fist into the thief's ribs. With a howl, the boy doubled over.

The young man slipped the knife into his coat and turned to Elise. "Come on."

In her head, Elise heard the voices of her League leaders. *Black blood is a danger to our race.* "Should we call the police?"

"No. Leave him. Let's go."

They ran into Hackescher Market. Their shoulders and bags bashed into the crowd. The young man ran fast, ahead of Elise. But she kept up, even with her satchel of food. They scurried like cats between the stalls and carts and traced a perfect route through the busy cobblestoned streets. If her brother, Viktor, were there, he would have screamed in delight. He would have turned to shoot his make-believe gun at the boy trying to catch them. A soldier in battle.

Slowing down to a fast walk, Elise glanced behind her to make sure they'd lost the thief. They turned onto Rosenstrasse and ducked into another courtyard off the main road. Out of breath, she faced the young man.

"Thanks," he said.

"For what?" She felt lightheaded, in part because he was extremely good-looking.

"You saved me. And my bag. You distracted him."

The young man wore a long, gray coat. A flat charcoal-colored cap almost covered his eyes. Earlier, in the rush of everything, he had seemed grubby, but as he adjusted his cap, his thick dark hair fell neatly over his ears and partly over his face, making him look clean and respectable, and now somewhat younger, too. He was a little older than Elise, but definitely no older than eighteen.

"Did he hurt you?" she asked, pointing at his throat.

"Nah," he said, his knuckles touching his neck, grazed by the bag's strap.

As he laughed, his face creased into dimples and Elise noticed his chipped side tooth. *He's not from a good family.* If Mother had known Elise had been involved in a fight with a black boy and his knife, Elise would have received a lecture about setting a poor example for little Viktor.

"Smoke?" he asked, filling her awkward silence.

He reached into his coat and pulled out an almost empty packet of cigarettes. As he held them toward her, Elise studied his thin forearm. She shook her head. She'd never been offered a cigarette before. He took a cigarette for himself, lit it, inhaled deeply, and blew smoke up into the air.

"I'm Elise. As in Beethoven," she blurted out.

She cringed with embarrassment. Referencing Beethoven was something her father would have done. She was blushing; she could feel it. The young man's smile was infectious and she admitted almost aloud that he was handsome. For a moment, Elise thought about asking to see the knife in his pocket. She wanted to hold it and stare at her reflection in its blade.

"Where do you live?" she asked, not quite believing her own confidence.

"Here and there."

She let out a short squeaky laugh.

He reached into his bag. "Here you go." He took out a packet of biscuits, the fancier kind Elise had loved as a little girl.

She shook her head.

"Go on. Take it."

Elise reached out her hand. He was staring down at her coat sleeve that was pulled up a few inches so her forearm was exposed, revealing the scratches on her skin.

"Thank you," she mumbled. She took the biscuits and pulled her arm away.

"See you around." Then he disappeared into the crowd.

As Elise turned back onto Rosenstrasse in the direction of Ruth's home, she placed the packet of biscuits into her satchel, next to her Girls' League books and the food she'd bought. She could feel the red fading from her face. *I told him my name, but he didn't tell me his.*

Marko

I'm lucky as hell. The little girl with stringy hair and spotty skin— Marko's little helper—had appeared from nowhere.

Opening a compartment on the side of the heavy bag, Marko almost cheered when he found an old wristwatch. Straight away, he put it on. He'd never worn a watch before. Marko laughed to himself. If the black kid hadn't pulled out a knife, Marko would've felt sorry for the scrawny wretch.

About fifteen minutes earlier, Marko had been walking through Hackescher market. A commotion had broken out in front of a market stall after a middle-aged woman was accused of stealing produce. Marko had seen the woman before; she roamed the alleyways and stalls around Hackescher, collecting only the best quality wares in an oversized bag. Some market sellers ignored her. Others were happy to trade, and the woman would swap one item at a time. Accusing her of stealing, a market seller had alerted a policeman. As two guards held her wrists, she'd cried and pleaded. She hadn't done anything wrong. But the Nazi policemen had dragged her away. When Marko spotted her bag on the street, he'd pushed through the crowd. But the woman was long gone. He'd planned to keep her bag for himself and sell whatever was inside.

By the time he'd reached the market stall, the bag had disappeared. That's when he'd seen the black kid with the woman's bag on his back. Feeling cheated, he'd followed the kid into an alley and confronted him. He'd seen the bag first, Marko told him, and suggested they split the contents. But the kid had refused and put up a good fight, but in the end, Marko had been stronger.

On a quiet side street, Marko kneeled and opened the bag's main compartment. Below fresh produce and orange juice, he discovered bars of chocolate, packs of cigarettes, bottles of wines and liquors. *Perfect.* He would give the perishable foods to old Duerr and leave Berlin on her good side. He'd gift some of the chocolate to Kizzy, his little cousin. And it wouldn't be hard to sell the rest.

Getting across the city on foot would take an hour. Catching the U-Bahn would mean switching train lines. Marko checked his new watch. It looked expensive, so he tucked it under his sleeve. Opting to walk, lugging the bag, he moved fast. His neck was scratched, but it was no big deal.

West on Reinhard Street, Marko passed the new air raid shelter, a massive structure with tiny windows that made the government look weak after the air raids a few months before. The idea of Hitler losing the war amused Marko, and he purposely walked close to a Nazi guard, who shot him a look of contempt. Marko felt like punching his bastard face.

"What?" Marko dared to say. Then he spat on the ground and kept going.

Kizzy

There were things nobody knew about Kizzy. She wanted to live on a ship for a few months and travel the world. She dreamed of learning to tame and ride a horse. One day, she'd try beekeeping; she wanted to see up close the honeycombs inside the hives. *Or maybe I'll be a nurse.*

"Your tea's ready," Kizzy called out.

Climbing the stairs, she balanced a heavy tray—full teapot, cup and saucer, bread and honey.

As usual, Professor Duerr's room reeked of stale smoke. The old woman was sitting up in bed, napping, with a half-full packet of cigarettes next to her. Now and again, when the woman wasn't looking, Kizzy would take a cigarette or two.

She set the tray down on the bedside table.

"Frau Professor?"

Kizzy nudged her arm. Professor Duerr didn't move and, quickly, Kizzy stuffed a handful of the cigarettes into the pocket of her pinafore dress. She was about to tiptoe away when she saw a line of saliva hanging between the old woman's chin and nightgown.

"Frau Professor?"

Leaning over the old woman, Kizzy grabbed and shook her shoulders. Nothing. Minutes earlier, Professor Duerr had called out to the girl to make her some food. Kizzy tapped the old woman's face, and panic filled her head and gut as she wondered if her guardian was dead.

"Frau Professor, wake up!"

Remembering an old trick her cousin Tsura had taught her, Kizzy looked around Professor Duerr's cluttered bedroom. Piles of clothes covered every surface, empty cigarette packets here and there. Kizzy found the hand mirror she was looking for. She lifted the old woman's forehead and, with the other hand, held the mirror below Professor Duerr's nose. The mirror fogged up. *She's breathing.* Kizzy breathed, too.

"Frau Professor! It's me!"

Kizzy tapped the old woman's face, a little harder than before, but Professor Duerr sat there, slumped forward, away from her pillows, her face down to one side. *What's wrong with her?*

Kizzy poured tea into the cup on the bedside table. With a spoon, she forced some of the warm liquid into the old woman's mouth. The tea spilled back out and onto the bed sheets. *I've gotta get help.*

Kizzy bolted down the stairs, found Professor Duerr's house key on the kitchen worktop, and threw on her coat.

Outside, Kizzy pulled on her hat. Its thick light-blue wool covered her ears, keeping out the icy air.

The idea of taking an underground train filled Kizzy with fear. She'd never traveled by U-Bahn on her own. So instead she ran south, over the river and toward the western edge of the Tiergarten. Kizzy held the key in her pocket and pictured the poor old woman, her guardian, slumped over in bed. Kizzy needed to find Tsura.

G O

Tsura

Their footsteps light, Tsura and Seraph climbed the ornate iron staircase inside Seraph's elegant apartment building. The weight of the new revolver inside her coat pocket made Tsura think of Gestapo officers swarming the streets of Berlin, relentless in their hunt to catch their inferior prey. Guards and soldiers had checked and double-checked Tsura's falsified papers dozens of times. To most, she went by the name Greta Voeske. *Greta would make a great member of the Nazi party.* Tsura longed for her other self to penetrate the government's core, to corrode from within. Before they could grasp her plot, Greta would suffocate them, beat each Nazi with her bare Romani hands, each crying out for mercy just as her family cried, just as they'd beaten Father and her uncles, just as they'd taunted Mother and Aunt Marie. Through Greta's eyes, Tsura saw the blood of revenge pouring over the Nazis' boots, the beautiful souls of her people looking down.

But that was only a fantasy. It was early 1943 and the political climate was more repressive than ever. Since the Gestapo's recent clamp down on student resistance groups, Tsura and her peers had been inspired and, for now, silenced. Only a few still dared to pass out anti-Nazi leaflets. In the middle of the night, Tsura and Seraph would scamper across the cityscape to plaster up illegal anti-Nazi posters on Berlin's buildings and billboard pillars. Occasionally, Tsura helped to ferry the Nazis' targets—mostly political opponents of the government—from hiding place to hiding place, risking her freedom and life to smuggle food and information between the darkened corners of Hitler's capital. Others, braver still, sabotaged trucks and cars, smuggling weapons and explosives. But even they couldn't prevent the round-ups. More families torn apart. More pain. More killing.

Six flights of stairs up, Seraph tapped out the password on the door. Wolf let the young women inside. He was unshaven as usual and, despite the warmth of Seraph's apartment, still in his coat and gloves. Tsura hadn't seen him in days.

Seraph pulled Wolf close and kissed him on the mouth. "Wolf, your boots," she whined and slapped him hard on the arm.

Wolf shrugged and sneered at Tsura. Behind Seraph's back, Tsura smiled at him. Then she locked the door and kept her boots on, too—always ready to run—while Seraph plunged her bare feet into the plush blue rug.

In the living room, Seraph poured hot coffee before leaning into Wolf and repeating the rumors. "Sounds like they'll be arresting more Jews this weekend."

As Seraph lit her cigarette, Wolf's eyes burned with fury.

"When are we leaving for Marzahn?" Tsura asked.

"In a few days. I'm still organizing a vehicle," Seraph explained.

"That could be too late. What's the delay?"

"Trucks don't fall from the sky" was Seraph's retort, and Tsura ignored her.

Rastplatz Marzahn, a Nazi encampment on the outskirts of the city, separated the so-called Aryan population of Berlin from the government's Roma prisoners. Its rundown caravans, guarded by police, held women, children, and a handful of men, including Tsura's mother and aunt. The government's choice to refer to the

Marzahn camp as a resting spot—*Rastplatz*—as if the Roma families had chosen to move there, was both insulting and frightening.

Tsura took out the revolver from her pocket, turning it in her hand. "So where did you get this?" she asked Seraph.

Seraph laughed. "I've become a gun smuggler."

"I thought you were a pacifist," Wolf said and he rolled his eyes at Tsura.

Seraph took out her own gun and waved it carelessly in Wolf's face.

"Careful with that," Wolf snapped.

"I suppose violence is necessary sometimes," Seraph said and she put the pistol away. "I've never hurt a fly and I'd only kill if I had no choice."

Wolf ignored his girlfriend's ramblings. With his gloved hand, he took the revolver from Tsura and, pointing the gun at the floor, he looked her in the eyes, indicating she should pay attention. He drew back the release and imitated pulling the trigger.

Seraph was still talking. "Guns are for cowards," she sighed.

When they heard a knock on the door, Seraph became silent. Eyes wide, Tsura stood, taking the revolver back from Wolf. Without a sound, Tsura and Wolf moved across the room and stepped into an alcove behind a tall mahogany cabinet, out of sight. Wolf took out his pistol. Any anxiety Tsura should have felt had been replaced by the comfort her new gun provided, and she wondered if she'd need to use it. The tapping turned into their password. *Someone who knows us.* Seraph unlocked and opened the door, gesturing for the visitor to step inside.

"Is Greta Voeske here?"

"What's your name?" Seraph asked.

"Franziska."

At the sound of the familiar voice, Tsura dropped the gun back into her coat. As Seraph closed the door, Tsura stepped out from the alcove, astonished to see her little cousin Kizzy. Just as Tsura used her false name, Greta, Kizzy was using her own false name, Franziska. Tsura smiled. She'd taught Kizzy well. Even in the dim light, Kizzy's tangled hair and rosy skin sparkled under her crocheted hat, a hand-me-down, the exact same blue winter hat Tsura had worn when she was Kizzy's age.

"What's wrong? How did you find me?" Tsura asked. She was both troubled and entirely amazed to see Kizzy. She must have followed them, somehow. And she knew their code. *Kizzy and I are family, for sure.*

Kizzy glared at Wolf's gun. Wolf stared back, seemingly confused as to how and why this thirteen-year-old had tracked them down.

"This is my Kizzy," Tsura declared.

As soon as Tsura used Kizzy's real name, she could see her cousin relax. Seraph and Wolf could be trusted. But Wolf scowled at Tsura, angry she'd allowed herself to be followed.

"She's my little cousin," Tsura explained.

"Not so little," Kizzy said.

Seraph nodded while Wolf continued to sulk. They walked into the kitchen, leaving Kizzy and Tsura alone.

Tsura felt bad for patronizing her. *You're my little cousin, but you're no longer a child,* she wanted to say out loud. While Tsura was impressed that her cousin had found the apartment, she could tell from Kizzy's worried expression that this impromptu visit was serious.

Kizzy was still breathing heavily. "It's Duerr. I think she's dying."

"How bad is it?"

Kizzy shook her head.

Images of Professor Duerr collapsed on the kitchen floor or slumped over in her reading chair blocked words from leaving Tsura's throat. *Everything's different now.* The old woman had chosen the wrong day to die. "Wait here."

The kitchen was filled with cigarette smoke. The scratches in the wooden table matched the lines on Wolf's head as he inhaled his tobacco and listened intently to the wireless, tuned into the forbidden news reports. Seraph nodded as the voice of a British reporter, speaking in German, reviewed the implications of the Soviet's recent victory at Stalingrad.

Seraph clapped and looked up at Tsura. "Did you hear that? The Nazis will lose the war. What did—"

"I have to go," Tsura interrupted. "I need to take care of something."

Seraph exhaled quickly. "Fine. But I need the photographs by seven o'clock."

Tsura would need to change the carefully laid plans. "I'll see you by seven. But I'll get you the photographs later tonight."

Surrounded by his clouds of cigarette smoke, Wolf appeared to be hypnotized by the radio, but Tsura could tell he was listening to the conversation.

"I'll see you later," Tsura said, looking at him.

Without looking up, Wolf nodded.

On the echoing stairwell, Kizzy knew to keep silent. She didn't speak until the two cousins stepped out into the wintery afternoon.

Kizzy laughed. "Surprised I found you?"

Tsura narrowed her eyes. "You're in trouble, Kizz."

When Kizzy saw Tsura was smirking, she grinned, too.

Tsura watched her beautiful cousin walk half a step ahead. The sight of Kizzy's maturing features, her shoulders determined, leading them to Kizzy's home, filled Tsura's heart with pride and her stomach with dread. *You're not a little girl any more, Kizzy Lange.* It was then Tsura knew what she had to do. She ignored the ball of sadness creeping its way from her chest toward her throat. Kizzy didn't know—not yet—that in a few hours she and Tsura would be saying goodbye to one another, perhaps for many years.

Alexander

Alex's house was empty. As he'd expected, he wouldn't have a chance to say goodbye to his parents and sister.

He had no choice but to leave. The floodwaters of National Socialism were rising. *I'm a Jew on Hitler's list.* His stepmother and stepsister, Ruti—both Catholic—were safe. But Alex worried for Father, who'd soon be the last Jew remaining in their family. *I should stay at home, where I belong.* Yet Alex felt an obligation to escape the impending flood. He imagined himself at the coast, a failing world behind him, as he boarded his ark to London. To abandon the people he loved the most was better than drowning.

In the kitchen, Alex chewed down leftovers—Mother's roasted potatoes, yesterday's stew, some bread with butter. As he ate, he saw the marks of his family everywhere. Father's slippers rested neatly beneath the kitchen table. Mother's cookbooks with her recipe notes sticking out from their pages were piled on the wooden countertop. The wall calendar had Ruti's birthday circled in hand-drawn flowers.

For the last time, Alex walked upstairs to his room. Just as he had climbed the stairs at the factory earlier that afternoon, every step felt heavy. Today, while he prepared to leave Berlin, each act was a goodbye to everything he knew—to his routines, his family, his home.

He dropped Ruti's gift on his bed. Its brown paper cover was crisp and waiting to be unwrapped. Next to the gift box, Alex spread out his overcoat as if dressing an invisible man. From the edge of his bed, he looked down at the yellow star. Alex fell back onto the quilt and trailed through the list of tasks he couldn't forget. He needed to pack and write letters to his parents and sister. He had already planted some of the clues leading to Ruti's birthday prize, but he needed to hide the rest. He took hold of his coat's sleeve. Alex and the invisible man lay still, staring up through the window to Berlin's afternoon sky. Against the gray, the empty tree branches swayed in the winter wind, as though waving goodbye. *This is really happening,* Alex said to the man in his overcoat.

The man whispered, *Don't worry.*

Alex found Father's small suitcase and filled it with shirts, socks, underwear. He remembered soap, a razor, a small towel, his toothbrush. At his desk, Alex watched the street below, the reassurance of the familiar view echoing the comforts of his bedroom. His pencils and notepads lined up on the desk reminded him of the hours he'd spent writing about his ambitions. He'd be a cartographer and give public lectures on geology and the science of map making. The map book on his desk and the framed world map on his bedroom wall reminded Alex of the journey ahead, full of exciting possibilities.

He ripped two sheets of paper from a notebook and began to write a summary of what had happened.

> *Dearest Mama and Papa,*
> *I have some exciting news, an opportunity I couldn't pass. I know you'll both understand. This morning at the brewery, my colleague pulled me aside with some urgent news. A chance to get out of Berlin…*

In the letter, Alex didn't mention how he had made excuses to his supervisor. How, on his workmate's recommendation, he'd headed to an antique shop in the city where an old man had taken his photograph. But he mentioned the chance to acquire false papers. He kept the letter upbeat, focusing on his chance to escape. Both Father and Mother would be pleased, he knew.

Fighting back tears, Alex ended the letter to his parents and began to write to Ruti. The handwritten farewell would accompany her hidden gift.

> *Happy fifteenth birthday to my favorite (and only) little sister.*
> *I'm so sorry to be missing your celebration, but I'm thinking of you… By now, Mama and Papa would have told you everything… I wish I could take you with me, Ruti… Make sure you work hard in school. I know you will. And look after our crazy parents…*

He stared at the notes on his desk, the cryptic puzzles of Ruti's birthday treasure hunt waiting to be hidden.

When he read the first puzzle again, a better idea hit him. He shredded the original clue into pieces and dropped it into the wastepaper basket beneath his desk. On a blank piece of notepaper, he rewrote the new first clue, ensuring its prose was purposely unclear. He folded Ruti's goodbye letter and tucked it inside the brown paper of the gift box.

He placed the letter to his parents on his desk next to Ruti's new first treasure hunt clue and his house keys, which he no longer needed.

Leaning over the invisible man in his black winter overcoat, Alex lifted a corner of the yellow star. The stitches snapped as he ripped it off, leaving no mark on the woolen fabric. He put on his coat and flat cap, then dropped the yellow patch into the top drawer of his bedside table and hid the remaining treasure hunt clues around the house. In Ruti's bedroom, he rummaged through her art box and found a piece of white chalk. Suitcase in hand and Ruti's boxed porcelain train under his arm, Alex said goodbye to the paintings and photographs lining the walls of his family's home. The framed portrait of his grandmother seemed to whisper a blessing for his safe escape.

Alex found a shovel from the gardening tools by the kitchen door. He used Ruti's chalk to write his final clue and hid her train in the spot he'd been planning. All Alex had left to do was pick up his developed photographs and take them to the meeting place. Walking away from home, he filled the February air with clouds of his breath.

Alex's family home stood close to rail tracks in the western corner of the old Friedrichshain district. As a child, Alex would run through Berlin's neighborhoods with his friends, jump aboard the city tram, and head to a park to play ball. Now, as in old times, he had no yellow star. When he'd worn the Jewish patch on his coat, the same people who had once called him charming and given him treats had gawked at him from afar. Alex had become used to it.

Now, he worried that the empty space on his chest was visible to the passersby. He implored the city to remind them of who he used to be. He walked by old apartment blocks, with their sloped roofs and iron balconies. His family had lived in Berlin for generations. Carved monuments stared back at him, just as they had when he was a boy. The red, black, and white of the Nazi banners flying from silent buildings reminded Alex of Father's family—his cousins, aunts, uncles, and grandfather—sent away to the labor camps. The black crooked lines of each swastika flag pointed to the distant corners of Hitler's new world.

The bells on the shop door jangled and the old man appeared from the back room. "Good timing. I was about to close for the day." Through the clutter of furniture and ornaments, the shopkeeper kept his eyes on the street. Then he reached into his waistcoat pocket and handed Alex two developed photographs.

Alex stared down at the two small black-and-white images. In the suit and tie, Alex didn't look like himself. *This is how strangers will see me.*

Alex turned to leave. "Thank you."

The old man gave a heavy sigh, making Alex stop. "You need to be more careful, young man."

A chill ran across Alex's neck. "Why?"

"You didn't barter for the porcelain train. You must stand up for yourself. Especially in wartime." The man pointed to a box of old coins and buttons on a shelf. "Go on, choose one for yourself."

Surprised by the man's integrity, Alex rummaged around and picked up what he first thought was a small coin bearing the imprint of a soldier's helmet and crossing swords.

"It's steel," the shopkeeper explained. "A medal from Germany's first war, awarded to an injured trench soldier, most likely. And now it's yours."

Alex paused. Then he dropped the medal into his trouser pocket and the photographs into the inside pocket of his coat.

"Thank you for everything."

On the main road, Alex's stomach jumped into his chest when he saw a small group of Nazi guards walking toward him. *If they ask to see my papers, I'm dead.* Alex crossed the street and kept his eyes on his feet. He dared not look up.

Like a crackling radio being tuned in for the early evening broadcast, their voices sharpened through the haze of Alex's thoughts.

"Jewish dog," one guard yelled, as the others laughed along.

Alex found it difficult to catch his breath. *How do they know I'm a Jew?* He looked up. The insults had been aimed at somebody else. At first, he didn't want to look back, but he couldn't help himself. A woman and man walked arm in arm, their yellow patches glowing against the cloudy afternoon. Alex choked when he recognized them both, and he spun his head forward, hoping they hadn't seen his face. He quickened his pace.

Alex turned left onto a quiet side street and glanced back. The Nazi guards were out of sight, but the Jewish man and young woman were following him, their winter shoes shuffling on the cold cobblestones. Alex wanted to turn and tell them to leave him alone. But they kept up, whispering behind him. *They know I saw them.*

Then the man called out. "Alexander? Alexander Broden."

Checking every direction, ensuring he couldn't be seen, Alex stopped and turned, nodding for Lea and her father to approach.

Lea Federman and her father were Alex's colleagues. They stepped away from the street to join Alex in the shaded stone doorway of an apartment building. Lea's dark-brown hair folded where it hit her thin shoulders. Her gloved hands held onto her elbows to keep herself warm. She stared at the breast of Alex's coat—where the yellow star used to be. But she said nothing.

"Where are you headed?" Mr. Federman asked.

"Home," Alex lied.

The man's eyes were bloodshot, exhausted from the long workday. He stood hunched over, just as he did on the brewery's factory floor while his daughter worked in the office. Alex would sometimes say hello to Lea when he collected his delivery schedule and she would smile while her colleagues giggled at their exchanges. Lea was also seventeen, but extremely shy.

"Have you heard the warnings?" Mr. Federman asked in a whisper.

Alex shook his head and stepped back into the doorway's dark corner, his back against the frozen stone. He couldn't be seen talking to people with yellow stars. "I have to go."

He was taken aback when the usually silent Lea began to talk. "Before the end of work today, we heard rumors of more round-ups." Her voice was soft and full of fear.

There were always rumors of an imminent Nazi *Aktion*. Sometimes the speculations were true. Often they weren't.

"I haven't heard anything," Alex said truthfully.

Mr. Federman looked relieved. Lea was about to speak again when they heard the marching of boots on the street. More Nazi guards. Alex grabbed the door handle of the building and slipped inside, pulling Lea and her father with him. Without a sound, Alex closed the door to the dark tiled hallway they were now standing in, his finger against his lips to tell them to keep quiet.

Alex could see they were startled. The whites of Lea's eyes were fixed on his, wondering why he was hiding. Her father's eyes were now closed, as if awaiting execution. Alex clenched his fists, hoping that the people outside—Nazi soldiers, police, or Gestapo—didn't see them. The smell of the brewery lingered on Mr. Federman's clothes.

Alex heard them walking fast, away from the building now, their trudging fading into the distance as they hid behind the wooden door.

"We need to get home," Mr. Federman said to Lea, "or your mother will start to worry."

Lea nodded at her father, then turned to Alex. "Are you going into hiding?" she asked.

Alex remained silent.

Then Lea leaned forward on tiptoes and, in the dark hallway, kissed his cheek. "Please, be safe," she whispered, and she and her father disappeared into the late afternoon.

If the circumstances had been different, Lea Federman might have been Alex's girlfriend.

Ruth

Ruth loved birthdays. But sometimes she built them up too much.

"Ruth, I'm so sorry."

While Elise stared at the ground, Ruth tried to stay cheery. "Don't worry. We'll celebrate tomorrow."

Sitting on the step outside her house, Ruth wanted to tell Elise to stay for their sleepover, but she dropped the topic. A packet of delicious biscuits, an early birthday gift from Elise, sat on the step between them, marking the end of their short party. Against her spotty skin and messy fair hair, Elise's pink coat made her look washed-out and ill. Elise had once been a happier person, but everything had changed. This was the first year in as long as Ruth could remember that Elise Edelhoff, her closest friend, wouldn't be sleeping over for her birthday. Elise hadn't mentioned her mother, but her friend was needed at home, Ruth knew. Elise would miss a good dinner, and the gifts, and Mama's cake, and leftovers for breakfast.

"You'll still have fun," Elise said.

"Just me and my parents." Ruth laughed. "How incredibly boring is that?"

"And Alex."

As much as Ruth adored her brother, her birthday dinner would now be an anti-climax. With only Alexander and their parents, tonight would be no different from any other Friday. Ruth usually blew out her candles and opened her gifts with Elise by her side. Last year when Ruth turned fourteen, Alexander had rewarded her with a set of tiny ceramic cats to add to her collection of ornaments. And while Papa raised a toast in his daughter's honor, Mama disapproved as Ruth and Elise stuffed their mouths with too many slices of cake and cackled away about how they'd grow up to be fat old women.

"Please save me from my family," Ruth whined.

Elise said nothing and Ruth immediately felt embarrassed that she was complaining. Ruth pushed her glasses into place. "I didn't mean that."

Everything had changed so much in one year. Elise had new obligations. Elise's father was fighting the Soviets on the Eastern front. Mrs. Edelhoff never left their house. Almost every day, Elise would rush through Berlin's markets and then head home to cook and clean and even repair anything that needed fixing. Ruth felt terrible for her best friend. As Ruth's mother often said, the longer Germany's war lasted, the more difficult life would become. The war was now into its third year.

"It's getting cold. I should go," Elise said.

Ruth leaned in for a hug. "See you in the morning."

Elise stood up and reached into the pocket of her pink coat. Between her fingers, a folded piece of paper fluttered in the February wind. "I was supposed to give this to you tonight, when you asked me for it."

Ruth's nickname and the word *"Freund"*—friend—was written on the outside of the paper. Nobody called her Ruti except for Alexander and her parents. Immediately, Ruth knew that the paper was part of Alexander's birthday treasure hunt, created especially for her. She unfolded it.

"Ruth Broden! What are you doing?"

"It's just a silly riddle," Ruth said.

"But you'll ruin your brother's game."

Ruth grinned and tugged on her best friend's coat sleeve. "If you can't stay for dinner, you can help me find my gift."

Ruth read Alexander's clue.

Three circles
In blue fabric
Provide comfort and discretion

Ruth's glasses fogged up when they walked from the cold into the warmth of her home. They dropped their overcoats onto the chair in the hallway and Ruth rushed into the living room.

"Blue fabric," Ruth said out loud.

Elise tutted with disapproval but she seemed amused. "Ruth, don't! Your brother planned it all out for you. You have to start from the beginning."

Ignoring Elise, Ruth read the treasure hunt clue again. She knew she was spoiling Alexander's game. Her brother usually gave Ruth the first riddle in the chain himself. But she couldn't resist. *Blue fabrics. Comfort.* "Cushions!"

"You're so funny," Elise said. She was smiling, with her arms folded across her Girl's League uniform. That brown jacket and ugly skirt. Ruth had once found Elise's Nazi uniform frightening. Over time, fear had been replaced by discomfort.

Again, Ruth read Alexander's riddle. She was sure it referred to the circular swirling lilac patterns of the armchair pillows and matching curtains. She lifted each cushion and checked around the windows. No notes in sight. The previous year, Alexander had buried one of his clues down the back of the sofa. Ruth checked there, too. *Three circles.* The word "discretion" made her think of her bedroom.

"Upstairs?" Elise said, letting out a giggle, and she raced Ruth to the top of the staircase.

Ruth joined her on the landing and sighed. Ruth loved her brother, but his riddles and childish treasure hunt games were becoming tiring. "I'll be fifteen tomorrow. Alexander needs to stop making these for me."

"Oh, Ruth, shut up," Elise said with a smirk. "It's fun."

Elise was right, of course, and Ruth read the clue again.

"What does it say?" Elise asked.

Ruth raised her eyebrows, folded the note into her hand, and pretended to scold her friend. "So now you want to play along?" Then she poked her tongue out, which made Elise chuckle.

Ruth checked in the drawers of her bedroom dresser, rummaging through her blouses and undershirts. She found what she was looking for—some lavender ribbons she often used to tie back her plaited hair. But there was no note there. She checked the piles of clothes scattered about on her floor and bed.

Elise stood at Ruth's dressing table, as she often did, admiring Ruth's collection of ceramic figurines. She picked up a porcelain boy and girl in traditional German dress. Ruth's parents had bought her the piece for her tenth birthday, when her hobby was at its peak. While she still liked the figures and tiny objects, Ruth knew they were just knick-knacks. *Alexander's prize will be another piece of porcelain, I bet.* She worried she'd be disappointed. She was secretly hoping for some jewelry or new clothes.

Still, Ruth felt compelled to solve the puzzle in her hand. "Follow me."

Unlike Ruth's bedroom, everything in her brother's room was in its place. Alexander's bed was made. His floor was clear of clutter. His desk and bookshelves were neatly organized, and a map of the world hung, framed and dusted, above his bed.

"What are you looking for?" Elise asked.

Part of Ruth wanted to solve the riddle alone. "I haven't figured it out." She opened the doors of her brother's wardrobe and rummaged through his shirts. Ruth pulled out a blue shirt to check its pocket and sleeves. Nothing. "Don't just stand there, Elise. Check the dresser."

Elise beamed. "Okay. But I'm not touching your brother's underwear."

"That's it!" Ruth squealed, forgetting to be unimpressed by her brother's game. "Move!" she boomed and she comically bumped Elise out of the way. Then she pulled open the top drawer of Alexander's dresser and picked up a pair of his underwear.

"Disgusting!" Elise howled.

Ruth tugged at the waistband, the largest of its three circular openings. "Alexander has one pair of blue underwear." Ruth knew this because she helped Mama with the laundry. It was just like Alexander to make her touch his disgusting undergarments.

Elise winced and wiggled her fingers, as if preparing to reach into a sewer. Then she grabbed the corner of a pair of long johns and threw them in Ruth's face. Ruth screamed and fell back onto Alexander's bed, and they both cackled with laughter.

"The Underwear Man!" Elise said and she burst into hysterics.

"Yes!" Ruth screamed. The infamous Underwear Man was a neighborhood legend, a grouchy middle-aged gentleman known for screaming at children who dared to wander into his front garden. He earned his namesake because he was rarely seen wearing trousers. Ruth and Elise had never met him until, one weekend afternoon, a few years earlier, they'd spotted him in the street and were completely astonished that he was wearing his underwear on his head.

Wrapping Alexander's clean long johns around her hair, Ruth blew out her cheeks, pretending to be fat and round. She furrowed her forehead and shouted in a deep voice, "Get out! Get out! Get out of my shrubs!" Then she couldn't make any more words, only fits of giggles. Rolling back onto Alexander's bed, she held her stomach in pain.

Elise was crying with laughter now and they lay there, side by side, snorting and cackling until they could just about manage to speak.

Ruth took in a deep breath. "So funny."

"What do you think happened to him?" Elise said, rubbing her eyes.

Ruth stopped laughing. "I think he died."

In silence, they stared up at the ceiling.

"I wonder what he wore when they buried him," Ruth said and she started to giggle again.

But Elise didn't laugh. She furrowed her eyebrows, disapproving of Ruth's tasteless joke. Then she stood and approached the dresser. "Ruth, you were right."

Ruth removed her brother's long johns from her head and joined Elise by the open drawer. There, between the blue fabric and the drawer's base, was the next treasure hunt clue. "Ruti" was written along the top, over the word "Unterwäsche"—underwear.

Ruth's fingers quickly opened the folded paper. Her eyes skimmed the next puzzle.

Embroidered leaves
On winter branches
Good night, Ruti
Stay warm

"What does it say?" Elise asked.

Good night. "Check around his bed," Ruth said.

The image of leaves and branches led Ruth to look out to the street, remembering how one year Alexander had managed to hide one treasure hunt clue on a windowsill outside. She walked over to his desk and pulled at the window's handle. When a gust of cold wind filled the room, a pile of papers blew onto the floor. Ruth checked the windowsill. She looked at the trees outside her house. Nothing. She shut the window and bent down to pick up the papers.

"I've never touched one before," Elise mumbled. She was standing by Alexander's bedside table, an object in her hand.

"What's that?" Ruth asked. She walked over to Elise, who held a single yellow star—frayed edges, threads hanging from its corners. Against Elise's brown Nazi League jacket, the flash of gold startled Ruth, as if the two should never touch.

"*Jude.*" Ruth read aloud the word printed in black ink. *Jew.*

"Hitler is sick in the head," Elise blurted out.

Ruth stared at Elise, who stared down at the yellow patch of fabric. Ruth was surprised to hear such an explicit, forbidden opinion from her best friend.

"I hate these things," Ruth said, taking the yellow star from Elise.

Alexander and Papa wore Stars of David all the time. They had to. Ruth held the rough and flimsy material and recalled the cross of St. Hedwig's Cathedral pointing into the sky that morning. She remembered seeing Papa and her brother wearing the stars for the first time, just a year or so ago. They'd been forced to wear them and Ruth said she wanted one on her coat, too, in protest. Papa called her innocent—a euphemism for naïve—and said he was glad Mama and Ruth weren't Jewish. Wearing the star was dangerous. But Ruth didn't see them as unsafe—just reminders that Papa was her stepfather and Alexander was her stepbrother. Before the stars came along, she'd liked forgetting that.

Elise let out a small gasp. Ruth turned to see Elise on her knees, by Alexander's desk.

"Ruth," she said, almost whispering. She held a piece of paper.

Ruth thought it was another treasure hunt clue, at first, but Elise was gawking at her, with her eyes ready to pop.

"What?" Ruth grabbed the paper.

> *Dear Mama, dear Papa,*
> *I have some exciting news, an opportunity...*

She skipped to the end of the letter.

> *...and I promise to be in touch as soon as I can. My only regret is that I couldn't say goodbye to you in person. I'll be thinking of you, every day.*
> *All my deepest, fondest love.*
> *Alexander*

Ruth looked at the yellow star still in her hand. "Oh God. He's gone."

Elise

I'm bad luck. It was typical that Elise would be around for a sad moment like this. On the floor, both on their knees, Elise and Ruth read through Alex's letter. *I can't be here,* she almost said aloud. She didn't want to see the flood of Ruth's tears that was about to begin.

Ruth's hand covered her words. "I can't believe this."

"Lots of Jews escape or go into hiding," Elise reminded her. It wasn't safe for the Jews anymore. Everyone knew that.

Ruth began to sob. "No, I can't believe he didn't tell us."

In her dark blue flannel dress and white stockings, Ruth's mousey brown hair was neatly braided and her green eyes were shining with fresh tears through her perfectly fitting glasses. Ruth looked like a painting. Elise looked down at herself. Compared to Ruth, she was a mess. Her skin was blotchy and her hair was like straw. Not enough nutrients, her father would have said.

Ruth picked up a set of keys from Alex's desk and cried harder. Elise wanted to put her arms around her best friend, but she stopped herself. Instead, she scooped up the scattered papers from the floor and dropped them back onto Alex's desk.

The sound of the door downstairs was followed by the cheery voice of Mrs. Broden. "Ruti!"

"Mama, we're upstairs," Ruth called back, her voice shaking.

Elise edged toward the door. "I have to get home."

Taking in loud, deep breaths to calm herself, Ruth led Elise downstairs, the letter in one hand and the yellow star in the other.

Tying her apron, Mrs. Broden walked out of the kitchen. "Wash your hands. You can help set the table."

"Elise can't stay," Ruth said.

Mrs. Broden nodded, as if expecting that. It had been over a month since Elise had last stayed for dinner. There had been a time when she'd eaten with Ruth and her family every other day.

As Elise put on her coat, Ruth held out the letter to her mother, along with Alex's keys and the yellow fabric.

Mrs. Broden's hair was pinned back away from the soft makeup on her cheeks. "God," she whispered. Elise could see that she was about to burst into tears, too.

I need to leave. "See you in the morning," Elise said to Ruth.

Elise put her arms around her best friend. She had planned to tell Ruth about the fight in the market and how she'd saved the handsome young man. But it was trivial now.

"Thanks again for the biscuits," Ruth said as Elise stepped into the front garden.

Her satchel at her side, Elise hunched her shoulders against the wind. In the last few days, the temperature had dropped. She reminded herself to switch her pink coat for her heavy coat starting tomorrow. Walking north, away from Ruth's home, Elise felt a sense of relief. She usually begrudged her mother and her endless list of chores. This time, Elise was glad to have a reason to leave. She wondered whether she should cancel her plans for tomorrow, too. With Alex gone, Ruth's birthday would be a long slog.

In Elise's head, her little brother, Viktor, walked by her side, his silky blond hair blowing in the breeze. She remembered that she'd missed visiting him on his birthday. That year, Viktor had spent his birthday alone. When their father said Elise wasn't allowed to see him, she'd cried in her bedroom for hours. Elise pictured herself laughing upstairs in Alex's bedroom. She remembered The Underwear Man and she tried to smile. Despite the sadness of Alex's sudden departure, Elise knew she needed to be with Ruth on her birthday weekend. *I'm a terrible friend.*

Behind her, the trains on their tracks rattled like machine guns. So many of the men were gone, fighting in the war, including her father. Among the faces of pedestrians on their way home from work, Elise searched for him. She pretended he was returning to Berlin as a surprise. Viktor walked next to her, his thin fingers grabbing onto her sleeve. Elise shook the thought of Viktor from her head and instead forced herself to picture the handsome young man from the market—his unshaven face, his dark hair. *His knife.*

Marko

From the end of the street, Marko spotted his cousin's frizzy hair. Kizzy was out front, smoking. In her pinafore dress, no coat, no hat. *She'll catch a cold,* Marko worried, but he stopped himself from saying aloud anything that would sound considerate.

Kizzy looked up and threw down the smoke. "Where've you been, you idiot?" she yelled.

She was always giving him a hard time, and he played along. "What the hell is that?" Marko said, pointing to the still-glowing cigarette on the ground. Marko picked it up, took a deep hit, and blew smoke at Kizzy's face, hoping for a reaction.

"It's Duerr. She's dying," Kizzy said.

"What're you talking about?"

Professor Duerr was stronger than Marko. There was no way she was sick. He took another hit of the cigarette and flicked it into the street.

"Tsura's here," Kizzy said.

Marko followed Kizzy upstairs, still in his coat and cap. The professor's room reeked of stale cigarettes. Duerr was in her bed, eyes shut, looking half-dead.

Tsura, Marko's older sister, sat at the old woman's bedside in her overcoat, her hair hidden in her cap, no makeup, clunky boots.

"What happened?" Marko asked. He put his bag on the floor.

"I told you," Kizzy shouted.

When Duerr let out a slurping sound, Kizzy shut her mouth.

"Kizzy came to find me. Duerr had some kind of seizure," Tsura explained to her brother.

Kizzy smirked. "Hear that, Marko-baby? I found Tsura."

"You have to get her to the hospital. Take her to Charité," Tsura said to Marko.

No chance. There was no way Marko would be changing his plans.

Professor Duerr was Marko and Kizzy's guardian. She'd been looking after Marko and Kizzy—her sweet little Gypsies, as she put it—for years. Tsura too, at one point. A favor to their parents. The old woman had been a university teacher. Duerr had cooked their meals, mended and washed their clothes. And now she was sick. But that Marko and Tsura had an obligation to care for the old woman was only half the problem; they were now responsible for their younger cousin, Kizzy, too.

Marko pulled up his sleeve to look at his new watch. He didn't have enough time to take Duerr to the hospital.

"You take her," Marko said to Tsura.

Tsura shook her head. "Too much to do."

Marko's sister was always busy. Her so-called work usually had something to do with fighting the Nazi regime. But Tsura rarely shared the details.

Marko leaned in so Kizzy couldn't hear. "I can't do it, sis. I've got stuff, too."

"No need to whisper, Marko-baby. Tsura told me everything," Kizzy said.

Marko glared at Tsura and she nodded. "I told Kizzy to pack her bag."

Holy hell. "Pack?" Marko shouted. He felt sick. Kizzy would be leaving Berlin with him. *This can't be happening.*

Duerr's fat body was slumped over in bed. A heap. Marko suddenly resented the old woman. If only she'd stayed well for one more day.

"Kizz, find some blankets," Tsura said.

Kizzy, always listening to Tsura, left the room.

"Pack her bags?" Marko said through clenched teeth.

"Don't argue. Kizzy can't stay here now."

Duerr's double chin was wet. She was drooling like a baby. Marko thought about getting across the border with Kizzy in tow.

"It's too dangerous," he said. And he meant it. It would be one thing if he was arrested, but the thought of little Kizzy getting caught filled Marko with dread.

Tsura scowled. "Kizzy can't stay with me. There's no other solution."

"I can't believe this!"

"She's our family." Tsura's eyes popped.

Marko's sister made him crazy sometimes. It was impossible to argue with her.

"You're taking Duerr to the hospital," Tsura said.

"No."

Tsura crossed her arms and raised her voice. "What else do you suggest, Marko?"

"We'll leave Duerr here."

"After everything she's done for you?"

Marko felt stupid for suggesting it. It had lost him the argument and he knew he'd have to go to the damn hospital after all.

"Take Duerr and I'll meet you later," Tsura said.

Marko let out a huff of resignation. "I'm not gonna let you forget this."

Tsura reached for a stack of papers on Duerr's table.

"What's all that?" Marko asked.

His sister held out some old documents—Duerr's identity cards, used ration books, old photographs. "You'll need these," Tsura said. She picked up Duerr's coat and stuffed the papers inside.

There were some photographs still on Duerr's table—Marko, Tsura, and Kizzy as kids. In one portrait picture, Kizzy looked the same but younger. Their little cousin was thirteen now.

"Marko, I'll help to get her downstairs, but then I have to go. And I can't meet you at eight any more. I'll see you at midnight instead."

"Fine."

"Friedrichshain Park. Western corner. By the fountain," Tsura said.

"Okay." Marko repeated the time and location in his head to make himself remember.

An hour earlier, escaping Germany had felt thrilling. Now Marko had to leave Berlin with Kizzy. It wasn't going to work.

"You really told Kizzy everything?" Marko asked.

"Not everything."

Duerr was heavy. Marko and Tsura moved the old woman so she was sitting up in bed. She gurgled, but her eyes stayed shut. They pushed Duerr's arms in her coat-sleeves and swung her legs down. She smelled like she'd wet herself and Marko wanted to puke. Their hands in her armpits, they lugged her onto the landing. Kizzy was at the bottom of the staircase with a wheelchair.

"What the hell?" Marko laughed.

"Tsura found it," Kizzy said with a grin.

Tsura was smiling, too. "Don't ask."

Together, Marko and Tsura half-carried, half-dragged the old woman down the stairs and dropped her into the chair. Kizzy placed a blanket over her legs.

Moving quickly, Marko fetched his bag from upstairs. He opened it in the kitchen and placed the fresh produce on the table—eggs, butter, orange juice. He kept the rest—bottles of wines, cheeses, tins of spreads, jams, boxes of cigarettes, chocolate. He swung the bag onto his shoulder and headed back to the hallway.

"I have to go," Tsura said.

Tsura never stayed for long. She buttoned Duerr's coat and kissed her wrinkled cheek. Kizzy was unusually quiet. With the new plans, it meant that Kizzy would probably never see Professor Duerr again. And, in a few hours, Marko would be saying goodbye to his sister. His stomach flipped and he swallowed hard at the thought.

"Leave her outside the hospital," Tsura told Marko. Her voice was steady, as though she didn't feel anything toward the old woman. "And if anyone asks, you found her in the street."

"Found her?" Kizzy coughed.

"Shut up," Marko snapped, fighting a pang of sadness. His little cousin didn't understand.

Kizzy crossed her arms. "Idiot."

"See you later, sis," Marko said to Tsura, and he elbowed Kizzy playfully in her shoulder.

Kizzy let out a yelp of pain, obviously exaggerating. "He hurt me!"

Tsura laughed at their squabbling. "Kizz, while Marko's out, make yourself some dinner," she said and kissed her little cousin on the forehead. Then she turned to her brother. "I'll see you later." Tsura pulled her cap down and left through the kitchen door.

It was just Marko and Kizzy now. And the unconscious old woman. Marko hung his bag, which was now a little lighter, on the wheelchair's handles. He needed a solution, and quick. There was no way he could take Kizzy with him, out of Germany. She was too young. And she'd be in the way. *I'll find her somewhere safe to live.* He lifted his sleeve and checked the time. "I'll be back late. Eat something, then get to bed."

"You got a watch?" Kizzy said, sounding surprised and jealous.

"Please shut up." Marko didn't mean to sound so harsh. But inside he was panicking and trying to figure out what the hell to do.

Kizzy lurched her face forward. "I hate you, Marko!" Then she put her arms around Duerr's shoulders and whispered, "Goodbye."

Marko stared down at Duerr and let out a loud, frustrated sigh. Then he noticed Kizzy's nasty brown coat and her ugly blue hat on the floor in the corner. *Yes.* Marko almost cheered out loud at his own genius.

Kizzy

Kizzy's teeth rattled in the evening air. She was only wearing her thin pinafore. And she wanted to burst into tears; she'd never see her kind, old guardian again. Her chest burned with sorrow and an unexplainable regret. She turned away.

"Kizzy," Marko said.

"What?"

"I need to get her down the steps. Grab her legs."

Looking at Professor Duerr made Kizzy want to cry. "Do it yourself," she snapped back at Marko.

"Please. I need your help. And put your coat on. It's freezing."

Kizzy almost grinned. Embarrassed and suspicious that her cousin seemed to care she was cold, Kizzy crossed her arms.

"Will you just help me?" Marko snapped.

Kizzy poked out her tongue. "Fine." She stepped back inside and put on her coat and hat, pulling the wool over her ears so she didn't have to listen to Marko's nonsense. She helped him get Professor Duerr down the steps outside. While Kizzy steered the chair, Marko held the old woman's legs. The wheelchair was shaking and the professor's head knocked against the handle, hard.

"What're you doing?" Marko barked.

"It's not me!"

"Stupid kid," he muttered.

"Oh, grow up, Marko!" *I'm not a kid anymore,* Kizzy wanted to scream. She was already thirteen, but Marko still treated her like a baby. He'd smoked when he was Kizzy's age, but now he said she was too young for that. Marko and Tsura were brother and sister, but they couldn't have been more different. They looked like siblings, with their dark hair and slim frames. And they were almost the same height. But Tsura was serious and brave and treated Kizzy like a grown-up.

Months ago, curious about where Tsura disappeared to, Kizzy had followed her to an apartment in Berlin's Bavarian Quarter. Kizzy had hidden in the stairwell, one floor down. Tsura had tapped out a code on the door and Kizzy had made sure to remember it. Earlier, inside the apartment, Tsura had seemed impressed and proud that Kizzy had found her, trying to get help for Professor Duerr. Tsura didn't even tell Kizzy to keep the door code secret. *Tsura trusts me.*

Marko, on the other hand, didn't trust Kizzy with anything. *He's an idiot.* And now Kizzy had to leave Berlin with him. They'd argue the whole time, but Kizzy was excited for the journey. She wondered where they'd go. Maybe they were leaving Germany altogether. Kizzy and Marko would travel by train, but she hoped she'd have a chance to travel by boat, too. She'd see the ocean. They'd settle in the countryside and Kizzy would learn to ride horses. She'd get to know different towns and villages and use her real name, rather than Franziska.

As Kizzy pushed the wheelchair down the front step, the old woman's head continued to jolt.

"Frau Professor?" Kizzy said, in case they'd knocked her conscious.

Professor Duerr didn't respond. When Kizzy pushed the chair again, the wheels buckled.

"Kizzy. Stop. Now."

Marko dropped Professor Duerr's legs, pushed his cousin aside, and took over Kizzy's job, ready to push the chair. As the footrests had broken off, Kizzy now had to lift and carry the woman's blanket-wrapped feet so they didn't drag. The shaking wheels continued all the same. Her cousin's ugly face was driving Kizzy nuts, so she turned her back to him and walked in front of the chair with Professor Duerr's legs under her arms.

When they reached the pavement, Kizzy adjusted the professor's blanket. *I'll never see her again.* Kizzy wanted to cry. But not in front of Marko. If she did that, he'd have the chance to make fun of her for weeks. The old woman was slumped in her chair. Kizzy put her hand on Professor Duerr's shoulder to push her upright, but she flopped back down like an old ragdoll.

Kizzy whispered into the unconscious old woman's ear, "Frau Professor. I have to say goodbye now, okay? Thanks for keeping us safe." Kizzy kissed her silver hair and turned toward the house.

"Kizzy, wait."

"What?" Kizzy shouted at Marko, her teeth together, holding back tears.

"Do me a favor, Kizz."

"No."

"Take her to the hospital for me. I've gotta go."

"Go?" *What's Marko talking about?*

"You've got a key, right?"

He had to be joking. Kizzy touched Professor Duerr's key, still in her coat pocket.

"Tsura said to take her to Charité. It's that way," Marko said, pointing along the street.

"Are you kidding? I can't take her on my own!" Kizzy's voice cracked and echoed against the buildings.

Marko hung his bag on his shoulder.

"Where're you going, Marko? You can't leave us. Charité isn't close. She'll freeze to death!"

Marko walked back to the front door of the professor's house, pulling it shut. He was serious. Before Kizzy could speak, he reached into his bag. "Here." He was holding out a jar of jam. Real, good-quality jam with an official seal. "It's yours."

Marko smiled with half his face. He was up to something. And it was something big. He'd never given away good stuff before, especially not to Kizzy. She took the jam jar and dropped it into her coat pocket. It was heavy and pulled her coat down on one side.

"Take her to the hospital. Please, Kizz."

Suddenly her annoying cousin was pretending to be sweet. He never said please. And he never called her Kizz. He called her things like Fränzi, the irritating name he used when he wanted to wind her up. He was definitely desperate.

"Why?" she asked.

"Thanks, Kizz!"

"I'm not taking her." Kizzy reached for the house key and walked up the steps to the door.

Marko groaned. "We should've left her upstairs."

Kizzy pictured Professor Duerr, dead at home, just because Marko refused to help. "You're so horrible."

"Look, I really need you to do this." He was serious now.

Secretly, Kizzy was surprised he trusted her. Kizzy didn't really mind taking Professor Duerr to the hospital. Kizzy would pretend not to know her. The idea was exciting. "Fine. But you're gonna pay me back for this."

Marko grinned. "Whatever you want."

Idiot. Kizzy was determined to come up with something really disgusting. Cleaning her room or doing her laundry was too easy. She'd think of a chore Marko would hate.

Marko pushed the wheelchair along the street. He kept checking his new watch, showing off as usual. The sky was thick black and covered in stars. The temperature had dropped even more.

"What do I tell the hospital?"

"Nothing. Just leave her there," was Marko's bright idea.

"I know that, idiot. I mean, if someone asks."

"Like Tsura said, you found her on the street."

All they had was one another, Professor Duerr had told Kizzy many times. The old woman wasn't family by blood. She was an old friend of Marko and Tsura's parents, and she risked her life to keep them safe. Leaving the professor at a hospital where she would probably die alone felt like a terrible thing to do. Kizzy's throat tightened. She couldn't speak.

"You don't know her, okay?" Marko said.

Kizzy ignored her cousin. The professor had loved Kizzy so much. She'd shouted at Kizzy sometimes, and told her tales of her old husband and stories about Kizzy's Romani family, and made jokes to cheer Kizzy up when she was unwell.

"Kizzy. Are you listening? This is serious."

"Yes, I know!" Kizzy couldn't help shouting.

Marko stared at Kizzy, but she refused to look at him. *He doesn't trust me. He thinks I don't know what's going on in Berlin. In Europe.* Kizzy didn't understand everything, but she knew if they didn't get Professor Duerr medical treatment, she'd die. Kizzy understood why she had to pretend the old woman was a stranger. If the authorities found out the professor had helped Gypsies, they'd all be in trouble. And Kizzy knew what it meant to be Roma. They were loathed. Feared. To the Nazis, they were thieves. And if not thieves, vermin. The government called them *Zigeuner.* It meant "don't touch," Tsura once said. Kizzy remembered resting her head on her mother's shoulder, on Mama's long dark hair, as Mama recited fairy tales and fables. Kizzy wondered if storybook princesses hated their storybook cousins as much as she hated Marko. And if witches hated little hungry children as much as the Nazis hated the Romani.

See, Marko. I know stuff, Kizzy wanted to shout. Kizzy knew the government had arrested Papa and sent him away. She knew the big questions everyone asked. She knew about the encampment in Marzahn, where Mama and Aunt Jaelle were imprisoned. Tsura often talked to Kizzy about their people and how the Roma should've been fighting back. Tsura told Kizzy her plans and plots, and stories about heroines and ghosts. Real ghosts. And Tsura asked Kizzy her opinions. Not like Marko, the ignorant buffoon. What Marko didn't want to understand was that, while she didn't know everything, Kizzy was only thirteen and already knew too much.

Bells from a church tower in the distance made Marko halt. Kizzy dropped the professor's legs onto the cobblestones and the old woman let out a whimper.

"She said something!" Kizzy said with a gasp. "Frau Professor?"

Marko checked his watch for the millionth time. "Okay, I'm off."

"You're leaving? Now?"

Marko didn't answer. Kizzy hated him for making her do this. She should've said no. She didn't want Marko to abandon them out there. Two minutes earlier, the idea hadn't seemed so bad. Kizzy would take the professor to the hospital then come home. Kizzy had wanted the responsibility. But now, with the idea of being alone with all the streetlights switched off, she wasn't so sure.

"I can't push the chair on my own," Kizzy said. She preferred for Marko to think of her as physically weak than to know she was nervous.

"I'll see you at home," Marko said.

"The chair's too heavy. She'll die out here. I can't do it!" Kizzy had to get Marko to stay. She worried about not finding the hospital. *What if the wheelchair breaks?*

Marko exhaled an impatient sigh.

"I'm not an idiot, you know," Kizzy said. "I worked it all out way before Tsura told me. I knew we were leaving Berlin."

"Keep your voice down," Marko snapped back.

"I figured it out. You and Tsura. All the whispering. It was obvious."

"You're such a whining baby."

Kizzy ignored the comment. She crossed her arms and smiled smugly. "We're leaving Germany, right?"

"Kizzy! Everyone can hear!"

There was nobody around. Marko was making a fuss for nothing. Kizzy decided not to respond to his pointless shouting. She was amazed that she'd guessed everything right.

"When were you gonna tell me?" she asked.

"Shut it."

The wheels on the chair screeched along the stones as Marko pulled the chair, backward now, to the pavement. Professor Duerr's feet dragged and Kizzy could see how rolling the chair backwards would've been much easier all along. The freezing wind smacked her face. Her woolen hat had slipped up. She pulled it back down to cover her ears and the back of her neck.

"You're horrible!" Kizzy shouted at Marko, wanting him to stay.

"And actually, you're staying in Berlin." Marko's tone was harsh.

"No, I'm not."

"Didn't Tsura say? I was leaving Berlin without you. Then Duerr got ill and Tsura wanted me to take you, too. But there's no way that's happening."

Kizzy stayed quiet. She hated her cousin more than ever.

Marko laughed. "See, Kizzy, you don't know everything. You didn't figure it out."

Her cousin was trying to get her angry and it was working. She wanted to punch him hard. "Fine!" she shouted. "Leave me in Berlin. Then I won't have to stare at your irritating face."

Marko ignored her. *He's bluffing.*

"Where will I stay?" Kizzy asked, knowing she couldn't stay in the professor's house. There was nowhere for her to go.

"Don't know," Marko said. He paused, appearing to think things through.

"You don't know?" Kizzy gave him a smug grin.

Marko's expression changed from annoyed to concerned. "Kizzy, we'll talk later. I'll figure it out. I've already got an idea where you can stay. But right now, I'm late. Take Duerr. Then come straight home. And make sure your bag's ready. We'll need to leave first thing."

Kizzy hated it when Marko talked to her like he was her parent. "Fine." She let out a breath of defeat. "But you definitely owe me."

Marko stood over the professor. He didn't touch her. He said nothing. Not even a goodbye. Kizzy wanted to cry for them. *He might never see her again.* Then Marko reached into his bag. "Here." He took out a whole bar of chocolate.

Real chocolate! "Where did you get that?" Kizzy squealed in delight, forgetting she hated his guts. She snatched the chocolate bar from him without a second thought and dropped it into her pocket, the jar of good jam in the other.

"I'm going. Don't do anything stupid, okay?" Marko said and started to walk away. Then he pointed at his backside—their secret for code for "kiss this."

"Idiot!" she called out. Even though she'd never ever admit it, Kizzy found Marko kind of funny.

Marko now out of sight, Kizzy looked down at Professor Duerr in her rickety wheelchair. Her head and arm had dropped to the side and Kizzy worried the chair would topple over. Propping the professor upright, Kizzy put the old woman's arms inside the seat by her sides and tucked in the blankets to hold in her legs and feet. Kizzy pulled the wheelchair backward—a lot easier than forward—letting the professor's feet drag. Professor Duerr made more groaning sounds. With her hands growing numb from the cold, Kizzy considered giving up and leaving the old teacher out there. Someone would find her. Then Kizzy shook the idea from her head. *I've gotta get her somewhere safe.* If the woman was dying, she deserved to be more comfortable. Professor Duerr made more sounds. When Kizzy stopped the wheelchair and leaned toward her, she saw the woman's wrinkled fingers begin to move.

"Frau Professor?"

Duerr groaned again. Her eyes twitched, but they stayed closed.

"It's me—Kizzy. I'm taking you to the hospital."

The woman's frail whimper gave Kizzy instant energy to keep going.

The roads twisted, empty and dark. The starlight pointed the way. After half an hour of trudging and stopping and trudging again, pulling the wheelchair backwards all the way, Kizzy was sure she'd taken a wrong turn. Her worry faded when she recalled the route to Charité Hospital. Kizzy was hungry, but she resisted the chocolate and jam in her pockets. Blackout shades covered the windows of the buildings they passed. Kizzy listened to her shoes shuffle on the uneven ground. Above her head, the empty branches of tall trees looked like the thin fingers of storybook witches. Other girls her age would have been frightened, and the journey seemed to be taking forever, but Kizzy was enjoying being outside. For once, she was in charge.

When Kizzy arrived at the Charité Hospital complex, it was the sight of two policemen that scared her. As she walked up to the entrance, the policemen, neither much older than Marko, stared at Kizzy dragging the wheelchair along. They said nothing. One of them opened the hospital door, assuming Kizzy wanted to take the old woman inside.

"I found her," Kizzy said.

The policemen gawked at her.

"Should I just leave her here?" Kizzy tried her best to sound childlike.

"Who is she?" the taller policeman asked.

Kizzy shrugged. "I think she fell asleep in the street. I found her, so I brought her here."

The tall policeman nodded. "You did the right thing." He reached for the wheelchair's handle and gave Kizzy a nod, permission to leave.

That was easy. Ignoring the cramp of sadness in her gut, she turned to walk away.

But the second policeman called out, "Girl, what's your name?"

Kizzy's false documents with her photograph were in her coat pocket, folded and ready to be shown. Kizzy almost smiled when she told them her well-practiced lie. "Franziska Scholz."

"Your papers," the short policeman demanded.

Kizzy reached into her pocket, happy with herself that the rehearsals with Tsura were paying off. He looked over the document and then stared at Kizzy.

"Why are you outside so late?" he asked as he handed her papers back.

Kizzy put the documents back into her pocket, wondering what to say. Her stomach turned. Her hunger disappeared. She didn't have an answer prepared. *Why am I out here?* As soon as she found herself hesitating, she knew she was in big trouble. "I found her near my home. And it's not that late."

"Where's home?"

"I live with my auntie."

"How old are you, girl?"

"Thirteen."

Kizzy could feel herself tremble, in her stomach and in her throat. She wished she could have said eleven, or even ten, but her false papers told the truth.

"You shouldn't be out here alone," the taller policeman said.

Kizzy nodded and tried to look thankful for the advice.

The short guard—Kizzy hated him now—stared at her with his medals. "What have you been up to?"

"Nothing."

Kizzy wished Marko were standing right there with her. As much of an idiot as he was, he would've known what to say. Or, even better, Tsura. *Tsura would know what to do.*

The policemen looked confused. In her head, Kizzy kicked herself. Why would a thirteen-year-old be out at night, alone? Why didn't she have this figured out?

Kizzy looked at the ground. "I'm sorry. I won't do it again."

The taller guard stepped forward and bent down in front of Professor Duerr. When he slapped her face—either to wake her or just for fun—the old woman groaned. He hit her again, harder, which made Kizzy flinch. Professor Duerr started to drool.

"She needs a medic," the policeman said.

"Can I go now? My aunt will be worried," Kizzy said in a babyish voice.

The young men looked at each other.

"We'll have to complete a report," the shorter guard mumbled.

Why did Marko make me do this? When Professor Duerr made more noises, Kizzy and the policemen all stopped to listen. *She's saying something.* Kizzy wanted to put her arms around the professor and tell her she'd be okay. But she just stood there. Helpless. *Professor Duerr is a stranger.*

Slowly, with her head still hanging, the professor opened her eyes and Kizzy's heart jumped. Professor Duerr was going to be okay. But then Kizzy was frightened. *She mustn't see me.* Kizzy took a small step back. She couldn't say a thing. No words of comfort. *She's a stranger. I found her.*

The tall policeman bent down again. "Woman, what's your name?" He spoke slowly with kindness in his voice.

Professor Duerr looked at him, her head hung to the side. She mumbled again, her speech dragging. Tears came to Kizzy's eyes. When the professor turned her neck and looked right at her, Kizzy took another small step back.

"Your name?" the policeman asked again.

With a half-smile from only one side of her drooping mouth, the professor spoke, clearly. "My Kizzy."

Kizzy felt faint.

Professor Duerr lifted her shaking hand toward Kizzy.

"Do you know her?" the taller policeman asked.

"No." Kizzy laughed as if to find it funny that the woman was confused. "She thinks I'm someone else."

As Kizzy spoke, the tall policeman crouched in front of the professor, reached into the old woman's coat, and pulled out her documents. Kizzy held her breath as he examined the papers.

"Liar!" he blurted out.

"What is it?" the other policeman asked.

"Her house address is the same as yours." He looked genuinely betrayed that Kizzy hadn't told them the truth.

I have to run. Kizzy turned, but a hand came down on her shoulder. Kizzy tried to pull away, but there was no point.

Professor Duerr let out a feeble cough. "My Kizzy," she said again. And then she mumbled something else before closing her eyes.

The tall policeman squeezed Kizzy's shoulder hard. "What did she call you?" He asked not because he hadn't understood but because he wanted to humiliate Kizzy even more.

"I don't know," Kizzy lied.

The policeman raised his gloved hand and brought it down onto Kizzy's face. She was too shocked to make a sound.

"What did she call you?"

Kizzy stood with her mouth hanging open, unable to speak. He lifted his hand again.

"*Zigeunerchen,*" Kizzy repeated. *She called me her little Gypsy girl.*

As if Kizzy had stayed silent, or because she hadn't, his hand landed harder against her face. This time she screamed. Her cheek stung in the freezing air. The short policeman pushed Professor Duerr and her wheelchair through the hospital doors. The tall policeman, the one who had seemed kind, reached for Kizzy's neck and grabbed the terrified girl by the ends of her frizzy hair.

I DARE YOU

Tsura

Seraph and Tsura had a running joke that Wolf couldn't live without radio news reports. As he always did, he sat at the shabby kitchen table, turning the dial on the stolen wireless. Tsura sat opposite him, waiting for Seraph to return and drowning in thoughts of Nazi round-ups. It was quite possible, Tsura calculated, that the Roma would be on the Gestapo's deportation lists, along with the Jews.

A replayed excerpt from a BBC news report on Stalingrad began. Listening to any foreign radio broadcasts had been outlawed years ago. But this was how they remained informed. This was how they kept themselves hopeful. The BBC reports were in German, and to Tsura, the journalist, in his smooth, commanding voice, was talking directly to her. The news was usually positive. Two weeks earlier, the British and their allies had reported the capture of another eight Nazi generals and forty-five thousand German troops. The Soviets' victory at Stalingrad was humiliating for Hitler and his government.

Wolf laughed at the broadcast, despite it being old news. "This is the beginning of the end."

Tsura hoped he was right.

The rattling of keys in the lock announced Seraph's return. "I'm back," she called out to them. Seraph joined Tsura and Wolf in the kitchen, unbuttoned her coat, and kissed Wolf on the mouth. "Change of plans," she said, a little out of breath. "Nazi raids are confirmed. We're heading to Marzahn in a few hours."

Marzahn. The name of the internment camp filled Tsura with rage, and she quelled a shout. "Tonight? We don't have everything we need." Yet Tsura had been waiting months for this moment.

Seraph reached into her pocket. "Another gift for you." She handed Tsura a pair of binoculars.

Holding its black casing, admiring its bronze trim, Tsura let out a laugh of disbelief. "How did you get these?" She held the binoculars to her eyes to test them out.

"Don't sound so surprised," Seraph said with a scowl. Then she looked at Wolf. "I got us a special vehicle, too." Seraph winked as she said it.

"What do you mean?" Tsura asked.

Seraph grinned and said nothing.

"Knowing Seraph, we'll be traveling by circus truck," Wolf said. It didn't sound like he was joking.

Seraph pulled hard on Wolf's dark hair, then pecked him another kiss. "You'll have to wait and see." Seraph always talked with a smile and a carefree tone. She leaned against Wolf, kissing him, her hands on his face, as if they weren't in the middle of a war. Tsura watched Wolf pull away from his girlfriend before kissing her. Despite his seriousness, Tsura found Wolf amusing. She especially liked watching Seraph try his patience. There had been a time when Tsura was jealous of Seraph. But she'd given up on those weak emotions. There were more important matters to worry about.

Tsura stood. "I have to be somewhere. I'll meet you at twelve thirty. Pick me up."

"Where?" Wolf asked.

A map of Berlin appeared in her head. Tsura pictured the area around Friedrichshain Park. "Greifswalder Street. On the corner of Danziger." She closed the door behind her.

Collar up against the wind, Tsura slipped into the side streets.

Marzahn. The thought of driving to the Nazi encampment filled Tsura with purpose and reminded her of the gun in her pocket—and now the binoculars in the other. The government had chosen the quiet town of Marzahn, on the rural outskirts of Berlin, as its compound for Roma and Sinti people. Tsura's entire family had lived there once. Mother and Aunt Marie were still its prisoners and there was now a chance she'd see them in only a few hours.

She pictured the Marzahn guards in their uniforms. Tsura had never shot a gun, but she was prepared to kill if necessary. Imagining her family held captive at Marzahn led Tsura to thoughts of Kizzy and Marko. She felt bad for her brother. Having Kizzy accompany him on his journey would be a burden. But if their little cousin were to stay in Berlin with Tsura, Kizzy would be in even more danger. *Marko will learn to live with it.* They all had to make sacrifices.

Alexander

Ruti must be so upset. The thought of his sister and parents racked with worry over his unplanned departure distracted Alex from his fear of being caught.

As the red sunset moved through the black winter clouds, facing northwest toward the factories of Prenzlauer Berg, Alex traced his past. The suitcase in his hand was conspicuous, but he took each stride with his chin up, face to the wind. He was glad to be leaving Germany, but he didn't want to leave his Berlin.

He recalled the excitement of school holidays as a boy. In summertime, they visited Hamburg in the North and stayed with Mother's family. In winter, they headed south to Father's family in Leipzig. During those times away, Alex was always homesick.

He had followed these streets all his life. His most vivid image from childhood was of holding Father's hand as they walked to church for the first time. Father had warned Alex to behave himself—not because they'd be visiting a church, but because the single father wanted to make a decent impression on his bride-to-be. The young woman had a baby, too. Every sound in the sanctuary echoed. Somehow baby Ruti knew not to cry in that place. Hypnotized by the statue of Jesus nailed to his cross, Alex had sat through the service in silence. When Ruti's mother said *Amen*, Alex looked up at his father for permission to participate. Father shook his head and they both said nothing.

After Father and Ruti's mother were married, the new family attended a few church services. The people around them noticed how Alex and his father stood with their mouths closed as everyone else recited the Catholic prayers and stayed in their seats when the congregation received communion.

Back at home, with the sermons from the Christian Bible fresh in their memories, Father had introduced Alex to German translations of Jewish prayer books and stories from the Books of Moses. Alex would sit in the dining room, reading the tales of Miriam, Naomi, David, Jonathan. The story of Noah became his favorite and he imagined himself on the ark, surrounded by his family, safe from the floodwaters.

By the time Alex was twelve, that biblical fantasy of escape had turned into a real objective. Some older boys had approached him after Sunday service. They called his family swindlers and liars—typical Jews, they said. His mother and sister were Christians, Alex told them. Jesus was Jewish, too. The older boys were hypocrites. They hated Alex, yet they worshiped the Jewish Son of God. The contradiction was frightening. Alex would fall asleep, every night, imagining his secret escape.

Alex wondered where those boys were today. Fighting in Hitler's war, most likely. Forced to say goodbye to their families, too.

Alex walked in the direction of his work and wished he could ride the train as he once had. The Nazis' laws were absurd. The government had banned Jews from using most forms of transport, even in winter. Only Jews who lived far from their work could apply for special licenses to use public transit. Father worked for Siemens in the west of the city. The factory was over an hour's walk from home, so Father was permitted to commute by city train, only to break his back on the production line.

A decade earlier, the new laws introduced by the Nazi Party had forced Alex's father to give up working as a civil servant, all because he was a Jew. Alex had been seven years old. When Father was assigned a job assembling electrical equipment for the German military, the irony became his running joke. *Adolf Hitler hates the Jews, but he can't run the country without us.*

When Alex was old enough, the authorities assigned him to a factory job, too, working at a brewery in Prenzlauer Berg, not far from their house. Alex had expected free beer tastings and laughs all day. But he was sent to the finance office. The work was tedious. Thankfully, after a few months, the management had agreed to demote him to deliveries.

Under the darkening sky, Alex's pulse began to race.

He met Marko in the spot they'd planned, twenty minutes south of the brewery in the back gardens near the park. Alex's boots crunched the gravel ground and Marko, with his back against a brick wall, looked up. Alex clutched his small suitcase and his heart pounded. *This is really happening.* Marko's flat cap pushed his black hair over one side of his forehead and his hands were hidden in the pockets of his thin coat.

"Look at you, Broden! You're an Aryan now." Marko laughed and pointed to Alex's coat where the yellow star used to be. He punched Alex's shoulder and tapped his face.

"I have my photographs," Alex said with a grin. He was eager to tell Marko about the antiques dealer. Then he noticed a scratch on Marko's neck. "What happened?"

"Nothing." Marko inched toward Alex.

"Not here."

Marko's smile disappeared and he let out a sigh.

"What's the matter?" Alex asked.

"It's Kizzy. We need a new plan."

Ruth

This was all for the best. Since Mama had come home, Ruth had been crying on and off. Alexander was gone, but his attempt to escape Germany had been coming for some time. As Ruth helped to prepare dinner, Mama wiped her hands on her apron and put her arms around her daughter.

Ruth cried into her shoulder. "Where's Papa?" *What if Papa's gone, too?*

"He'll be home soon, I'm sure," Mama said.

Ruth cried even more as she set the table for what was supposed to be her birthday dinner. She wished Elise were with her. Her best friend would have understood what Ruth was going through.

She heard the key in the door. "Papa!" Ruth ran to him with tears streaming down her face.

"What is it?" he asked.

She could barely speak. Clutching Alexander's goodbye letter, Mama walked out of the kitchen. Still in his coat and hat, Papa read the note.

"Did you know?" Ruth asked.

"No," he said. He paused and exhaled. "But it's good your brother has taken this chance."

Papa's words calmed her, but his face was covered with sadness. He looked at the dining table set for four. "Let's eat in the kitchen, shall we?"

Her birthday celebration had been cancelled.

As they took their seats, Ruth stared at Alexander's empty chair.

"There's some good news," Mama said, trying to sound cheery. "A letter from Papa's cousins in Chicago."

Mama handed him an envelope and he read parts of the letter aloud. "The children are studying hard at school... They talk about you all often... I've been promoted to head of accounts at a fancy department store." Papa chuckled. "From selling shoes in the Fatherland to head of accounts in America!"

Papa's cousins had left Berlin five years earlier, before the round-ups of Jewish families. They were lucky to get out of Germany when they did. There had been a time when Hitler wanted all Jews out. Sponsorship was the only way, and they had connections in Chicago. Every evening after Ruth went to bed, her parents and Alexander would talk in the kitchen. They didn't know that Ruth was sitting at the top of the stairs, listening to every word.

But Hitler changed his mind. The Jews had to stay. America, France, and Britain were no longer options, and the remaining members of Papa's family were trapped. Soon came the violence, then the round-ups, and then Poland and the war. Ruth's Jewish grandfather on Papa's side was among the first to be deported to the labor camps.

After dinner each night, from the top of the stairs, Ruth would listen to the terrible stories Alexander and Papa had heard at work. More trains to the East. Then came the rumors of mass murders. Rumors only lead to panic, Papa would say. Mama disagreed. *Rumors are the children of truth.*

Mama carried the pot of soup to the table. "First, let's say a prayer," Mama suggested. "We pray for Alexander—"

A loud knocking on the front door made Ruth gasp. With a terrified look, Mama gestured for her to hush. Papa's eyes were panicked. Then Mama pointed for Papa to run upstairs. Ruth wanted to scream, but she managed to stay calm and quiet, just as they'd practiced. *More round-ups.* Nazi officers with a list, weeding out anyone with Jewish blood. Alexander had left just in time.

Papa bolted up the stairs while Mama walked slowly to the door. Ruth stayed in the kitchen. She knew Papa was climbing into one of the bedroom cupboards, covering himself with a blanket. Just months ago, Papa and Alexander had scurried through the house, trying out different hiding spots. Under a bed was too obvious. Crawling up into the attic took too long. They'd cleared a cupboard in each bedroom to clamber into quickly. Mama had timed them. She'd scolded them for being too slow. They had to find their hiding places faster. In the worst scenario, they had to be ready to jump from a back window and run.

Fists were knocking on the front door again. From the hallway, Mama let out a shriek.

"Mama!" Without hesitation, Ruth ran into the hallway.

She saw his flat cap first. Then his coat. Ruth almost shouted and laughed out loud to see Alexander and Mama with their arms around each other. But she stopped herself when she saw a young man standing next to them. He was around Alexander's age. No older than nineteen and slightly shorter than Alexander. The man's black hair and unshaven face made Ruth feel wary. He looked like a grown street kid, with his coat unbuttoned, his hands in his trouser pockets.

"Sam!" Mama called for Ruth's father to come downstairs. "I'm so relieved it's you," Mama said to Alexander.

"Ruti!" Alexander's face lit up when he saw his sister.

With no words, she threw her arms around him, the top of her head hitting his chin.

When Papa saw it was Alexander, he almost tripped down the staircase. But he and Mama were unusually quiet. Their eyes were fixed on the stranger.

Alexander introduced him. "This is Paul. He works with me at the brewery."

Paul smiled broadly. "Good to meet you, Herr Broden, Frau Broden." The formality of his greeting didn't match his informal tone and stance.

"Hello, Paul." Papa extended his hand. Mama nodded her head. Ruth's parents were obviously nervous.

"Don't worry," Ruth's brother said. "Paul's helping me leave Berlin."

"He is?" Mama said.

"It's fine," Paul said, looking at Alexander. "They can call me Marko."

Ruth said nothing, trying to follow each revelation.

"What do you mean you're helping?" Papa asked with suspicion in his voice.

At first, Alexander hesitated. "I'll explain," he said.

Ruth could feel the tension in the air disappear. Marko was Jewish, she guessed, living in hiding under a false name.

"This is my sister, Ruti," Alexander said to Marko, his arm around her shoulder.

"Ruth," she corrected him. When people called her Ruti, it made her feel like a six-year-old. She'd always thought that people old enough to introduce themselves should be called by their given names.

"Nice to meet you," Marko said to Ruth, taking off his hat. His smile exposed a broken side tooth. Ruth saw dimples appear on each side of his mouth. He wasn't so scary now.

"Let's move to the dining room," Papa suggested.

With a grin, Ruth carried her plate. Her birthday had been restored.

"I can't stay long," Marko said to his hosts.

"But I can stay until around eleven," Alexander told them with a sad smile. "Maybe eleven thirty."

Ruth's heart filled. She'd have her brother all evening. And although he was leaving, she was so grateful they'd get to have a proper goodbye.

"Wait," Mama said when Alexander began to eat. "We thank God for sustaining us through this war."

Alexander twisted his face at Ruth—he was as confused as she was. Mama never prayed before eating.

When she finished her prayer, Papa stood and opened the sideboard cupboard. "Now, where are they?" He took out a silver wine cup and a bottle of sweet brandy.

Ruth hadn't seen the cup in years. When they were children, she and Alexander would get into trouble for playing with the precious cup and its matching candleholder and egg-shaped spice box.

Ruth and her brother rolled their eyes.

"It's Friday night—Shabbat," Papa said and placed his hand on Alexander's shoulder. "And my son's farewell supper."

A cramp of sadness crawled into Ruth's throat. Alexander had come home for his final meal.

Papa hadn't celebrated the Jewish Sabbath in years, but still he recited the Hebrew prayer without stumbling. "And we're celebrating Ruti's birthday," Papa said with a wink. "Fifteen! Can you believe it?"

Ruth was trying not to cry. But she giggled when Mama piled on Alexander's plate a month's worth of food.

"Don't be shy," Mama said to Marko, pointing at the roasted potatoes.

"So where're you heading?" Ruth asked her brother.

"London."

"And when are you leaving?" Papa added.

"On the morning train," Marko said.

Papa nodded. "Good." Some of Papa's family lived in London. "And Marko, you're going with him?"

"No," Alexander said, glancing at Marko.

Her brother wasn't telling them the full story. Ruth could tell. She bit into a piece of meat and waited for Papa to object to her brother's plan and question his short answers.

"We need to ask you something," Alexander continued, addressing his parents. His voice was raised now.

"It's my cousin, Kizzy," Marko said, his mouth full of potatoes. "I gotta find somewhere for her to stay. Our guardian—she's sick."

Ruth swallowed her food. "Your cousin—How old is she?" Ruth asked, excited at the idea.

"Thirteen. You'll like her." Marko smiled. Ruth was about to respond, excitedly, but Marko turned away and continued to explain his predicament. "Kizzy has false papers. She goes by Franziska. Or Fränzi, if you wanna wind her up. She's clean and polite. There's nowhere else for her to go."

False papers.

Papa leaned forward. "Her papers are forged?" he asked, as if reading Ruth's mind.

Ruth's head spun with possible explanations. *Marko's family is Jewish for sure, like Papa and Alexander.*

Marko stood and reached into his trouser pocket. "Here." He slid his identity documents across the white tablecloth. Mama examined them for a few seconds before handing them to Papa.

"Paul Voeske," Papa read aloud. "What's your real family name?"

"Lange. In Berlin for two generations."

"You're Jewish on your mother's side?

Marko stood and returned his papers to his trouser pocket. He sat back down and paused before speaking. "We're Romani."

Ruth sat quietly, startled by his disclosure. She'd never met a Gypsy before. She was surprised how Marko looked like a real German, with his black hair and broad shoulders. Then she checked herself. *We're all real Germans.*

Papa huffed and shook his head. "Taking in a Romani girl is too dangerous. I'm very sorry, but we can't help you."

Alex turned to his mother. "Please. Hear what he has to say."

"My father and uncles were all sent to the camps." Marko said. He caught Ruth's stare and spoke as if only telling the story to her. "Just before the Olympics, nearly eight years ago, they rounded up most of the Roma—the Sinti people too—and sent us to Rastplatz Marzahn on the edge of Berlin. It's a guarded camp."

Ruth's parents tut-tutted their tongues. It seemed they didn't know any of this. "A camp in Marzahn?" Mama asked.

Marko kept talking. "My father got us out. His friend—Frau Professor Doktor Duerr—looked after me, and my sister, and Kizzy, our cousin. Then the Nazi bastards sent the men away and refused to let the people in the Marzahn camp leave. My mother and my aunt are still there." Marko's voice was angry.

Papa continued to shake his head. "I understand. Believe me. And I want to help. But I can't put my family in danger." He gestured toward Ruth as he said it.

Mama stood and tapped Ruth on the arm, suggesting she help in the kitchen. As Ruth followed her mother, she could hear Papa telling Marko about the Broden family. Papa's father had died in a Nazi labor camp. The Nazis had deported the Jews to the East. His cousins and aunts and uncles, all gone. If it weren't for Ruth and her mother—both Catholics—Papa and Alexander would have been deported, too. The intermarried Jewish families had been left untouched, for now.

From the kitchen, Ruth could hear parts of the conversation.

"Then you understand!" Marko yelled.

Ruth's eyes bulged at the thought of a stranger—a dinner guest—shouting at Papa. Marko was determined to change Papa's mind. Ruth imagined having Marko's cousin Kizzy stay with them. The idea was exciting. And comforting, too. With Alexander leaving, Ruth was about to become an only child. "Mama, Kizzy can share my room."

Mama shook her head. "That's very sweet, but you heard your father."

Ruth imagined herself living with only her parents. She couldn't picture not having Alexander around. And then there was Elise. Ruth hardly saw her best friend these days. "Kizzy can keep me company. While Alexander's in London. It'll give me someone to talk to."

Ruth's mother didn't reply. Ruth wasn't going to get her way. She carried the refilled dish of potatoes back to the dining room. Marko and Papa were still arguing.

"I get to decide what I do in my house," Papa said, almost shouting.

"Look." Marko pounded on the table and the glasses and cutlery rattled. "I'm helping your son. He'll have papers by the morning and he'll get out of Germany by tomorrow night. He'll be in London by next week. I need somewhere for my cousin, starting tomorrow morning—people like you to keep her safe."

Ruth could tell Papa was growing angry. Her father didn't respond well to blunt pressure. Before he could shout back at Marko, Ruth spoke up. "Papa, imagine if it was me." She'd surprised herself with her outburst.

As soon as Papa looked up, his eyes softened.

"She's right," Mama said and pushed the potatoes toward Alexander.

Papa let out a heavy sigh, defeated. Then he gave Marko a nod.

Marko didn't smile or thank them, but there was appreciation across his face. "I'll bring Kizzy here at dawn."

Ruth kept quiet. She knew better than to make a fuss. Inside, she was thrilled. *I'll be her big sister.* Ruth loved the idea of Marko's little cousin arriving on her birthday. But when she remembered Elise would be visiting in the morning, too, Ruth foresaw a problem. "What do we tell Elise?" She imagined Mrs. Edelhoff, Elise's mother, making a stink.

Her parents gave each other a look of surprise.

"Tell Elise the truth," Alexander said.

"No, no, no," Papa said.

Mama leaned forward, her eyes on Papa. "If anyone asks, Kizzy is our distant cousin from Hamburg."

"Franziska. Her name must be Franziska. And I'm Paul," Marko reminded them.

The issue was settled.

Ruth was full of questions. "What's Franziska like?"

"She's a brat," Marko said. Then he smiled. "No, she's a good kid. She just thinks she's already grown up."

"She can help open my gifts." Ruth grinned, hinting at her parents.

Alexander leaned in. "And she'll help you with your treasure hunt. Did you figure out your first clue?"

"The one Elise gave me?"

Ruth's brother gave her a confused stare. "No. Your first clue was next to my letter. In my room."

Ruth stood to head upstairs. "Finish eating first," Mama said, and Ruth sat back down.

"What does Franziska look like?" Ruth asked Marko, trying to picture her.

"Like my sister. And my sister looks like me."

"We look so different," Ruth said, gesturing at Alexander and stating the obvious. "Nobody believes he's my brother."

Mama laughed. "Last summer, one of Sam's colleagues thought Ruth was Alexander's girlfriend," she told Marko.

Alexander laughed along. "It's a true story."

"It was disgusting!" Ruth squealed.

People were always surprised to hear that Alexander and Ruth were siblings. Ruth had straight light-brown hair, freckles dusted her button nose and round cheeks, and thick glasses framed her green eyes. Alexander's hair and features were dark, his eyes were a grayish brown, he was naturally slim, and his chin was square. Whenever they explained they weren't biologically related, people seemed relieved.

They finished dinner and Ruth's parents began to clear the table.

"Wait here," Alexander said to Ruth with a wink.

Ruth knew he was fetching her first treasure hunt clue. Marko followed Alexander upstairs.

As the clock in the hallway chimed ten, Ruth helped Mama carry the dirty plates to the kitchen. Papa was standing at the sink, talking about his first wife—Alexander's mother—who'd been Jewish, too. Once, Papa had explained how, if she hadn't died, they would've been deported with all the other Jewish families. Ruth found it strange to hear him talk like that. As if it was lucky Alexander's mother was dead.

Ruth's thoughts took her to her own biological father. She had asked Mama about him a few times and Mama had promised to tell Ruth about him one day. But she never did.

"Call your brother and Marko from upstairs, would you?" Mama instructed.

Ruth knew it was Mama's ploy to prepare dessert. *My birthday cake!*

As Ruth climbed the stairs, she had a terrific idea.

Alexander and Marko didn't see Ruth in the hallway. They talked, in hushed voices, side by side, on the end of Alexander's bed. To Ruth, they seemed unlikely friends. Alexander was clean-cut, his hair combed, clean-shaven, well spoken. Marko was badly spoken. He didn't seem to care what he looked like with his scruffy unshaven face and disheveled hair. They were looking through Alexander's map book, probably checking Alexander's escape route out of Germany.

Before telling them to come downstairs, Ruth sneaked into her parents' bedroom. She opened Mama's jewelry box and found what she was looking for. Then she headed back out onto the landing.

"—for Ruti," she heard Alexander say to Marko. Ruth stayed out of sight, peering at them through the crack between the door and its frame. It was hard to make out what they were saying. But Ruth caught some of their words. "You go... I'll leave later... meeting Tsura at midnight..." Alexander said.

Struggling to hear, Ruth heard Marko say, "She doesn't know."

Ruth had never heard the name Tsura before. For one thing, it was unusual. *Why is my brother meeting someone called Tsura at midnight?* Ruth instinctively began to decipher their secretive conversation. She wondered what Tsura didn't know. And whether Tsura was a friend. Or Marko's girlfriend. Or even Alexander's girlfriend. Alexander never told his sister about that kind of thing. Ruth wondered if Tsura was helping Alexander escape. Or if she was some kind of spy. Was Tsura a false name, like Franziska and Paul?

Through the gap between the door and the frame, Ruth watched Alexander stand and reach into his trouser pocket before passing something to Marko. There was a small object in the palm of his hand. Alexander was talking, but Ruth couldn't hear. Whatever Marko was now holding, he looked at it for a moment and put it into his pocket. Alexander jumped when he saw Ruth walking into the room, as if he'd been caught. Ruth wanted to ask Alexander about Tsura and what he'd just given to Marko, but Marko's expression was serious. Whatever they were talking about was a secret.

"Time for cake," Ruth said in a singsong voice.

"Sounds good."

Downstairs, Mama had placed Ruth's birthday cake at the center of the table. It was the large, white cake Ruth had found earlier in the morning, with *15* written in icing, now with a candle on top. Papa began to sing "Happy Birthday" and Mama, Alexander, and Marko joined in. Ruth closed her eyes, ready to blow out the flame.

"Make a wish," Papa reminded her.

She paused, her hands together, the piece of jewelry she was holding still hidden. Ruth considered making the same wish she'd made last year and the year before—for the war to come to an end before her next birthday. But last year's wish hadn't come true. *Why bother wasting it?* Instead, she made a wish for Alexander, for him to reach London safely. She opened her eyes to her family's applause and fixed her gaze on her brother, who stared back, as if he knew she'd given up her wish for him.

They managed to get through more than half the cake before Marko stood to leave. "Thanks for everything, Frau Broden, Herr Broden." He grabbed his coat from the back of the dining room chair and checked his watch. "I've gotta go."

Papa stood up. "Marko, you're welcome to visit Franziska any time."

"Thanks."

"Papa, you have to call him Paul," Ruth said and grinned at Marko. She felt happy she'd be seeing him again.

"Bye, Ruti," Marko said.

She half-frowned, half-smiled at him. "Ruth."

"Okay." He winked. Then, as he left the room, he called out, "Happy birthday, Ruti. Enjoy your day."

Marko's teasing made Ruth like him even more, and she wondered why Alexander hadn't introduced Marko to them until now. Alexander saw Marko to the door while Ruth helped herself to more cake.

When Alexander returned from the hallway, Papa let out a loud sigh. "Can that boy be trusted?" he asked, referring to Marko.

"Without a doubt," Alexander said and Ruth believed him.

Mama opened a bottle of red wine and poured four full glasses. "To my beautiful children," she said, raising her glass, and they all took sips of wine.

With sweet cake mixed with bitter wine in her throat, Ruth turned to Alexander. "I had an idea."

She passed him the piece of jewelry she'd stolen from Mama's dressing table, a cross Mama had inherited from Ruth's grandfather. "It'll keep you safe. If they suspect you're Jewish, just show them this."

Alexander held the cross between his thumb and finger. "Thank you."

"You're a little genius," Mama said as Alexander secured the chain around his neck and tucked the cross into his shirt.

The evening went too quickly and, before Ruth knew it, Alexander was by the back door, in his coat and clutching his small suitcase. Mama was already crying.

"I need to go," Alexander said, his voice breaking. "What's Papa doing?"

Moments earlier, Papa had disappeared upstairs.

"Alexander, be honest with us," Mama said. "Will the false papers be convincing? Does Marko know what he's doing?"

"Paul," Ruth said. Then a flood of questions filled her head, too. "And what about money? And where will you stay? Your English is terrible. How will you understand anything in London?"

Alexander waited for Ruth to finish. "It's all taken care of. And, yes, I can trust him."

Ruth almost asked her brother about the object he'd given Marko and why he was meeting someone called Tsura at midnight.

Mama wiped her eyes with her sleeve. "God will provide everything, just as He has throughout this war."

Alexander rolled his eyes at his sister and put on his hat. Ruth tried hard not to burst into tears.

"Please, be safe," Mama said as she kissed him goodbye for the fiftieth time.

Alexander hugged his sister tight. "Happy birthday." Then he reached into his coat pocket and pulled out a piece of paper. He gave Ruth a folded note, with "Ruti" written on its front. It was the start of her treasure hunt. She'd forgotten about it. "Don't read it until the morning," he said and kissed Ruth's cheek, now sticky with drying tears.

"I won't." Ruth didn't tell him she'd already followed two clues.

"I found it!" Papa called out from the staircase.

When Ruth saw her father holding his own overcoat, she gasped. "Papa! You're leaving, too?"

"No, no," Papa said with a kind smile. He turned to Alexander. "Take off your coat." Papa was holding his expensive coat, heavy and warm. The one he used to wear. The one he could never bring himself to adorn with a degrading yellow star. Papa had worn it when he had been a member of the German elite; when he, a Jew, had held an honorable position in Berlin society; when he'd lived without having to fear for his son's life.

Alexander was hesitant. "Papa—"

Papa shook his head. "It's fine, this coat belongs to another time."

Alexander removed his coat, passing it to Mama, and Papa draped his heavier overcoat over Alexander's shoulders. He buttoned it up for Alexander, as if Ruth's brother were a child on his way to school. Then he put his arms around his son, holding him for the last time. Ruth wiped the tears from her face.

"Goodbye," Alexander said and took a deep breath. He opened the door. Icy air filled the kitchen. He picked up his suitcase and stepped outside.

After saying goodnight to her parents, Ruth climbed the stairs to her bedroom, her chest aching and throat sore from crying too much. Sitting on her bed, still in her day clothes, she held Alexander's folded first clue. *I'll wait until morning to read it, until my birthday.* After all, she needed something to look forward to. As Ruth untangled her braid, the curled edges of the notepaper persuaded her to unfold it, to read her brother's words.

If you want to count to ten
Follow the carriages, one by one
Now find the girl on the hill

Reading the note made Ruth feel worse. *Alexander should be here.* Every year, as she'd discovered each puzzle, her brother would stand right next to her, trying not to give anything away. Sometimes he'd offer a hint, but she would always decline. Then, after a few hours of thinking, Ruth would give in and Alexander would help, but only a little.

This time, Ruth already knew the answer to the first puzzle. The girl on the hill was Elise. Her best friend's house, just north of Ruth's home, stood on one of the highest streets in the city. Papa called her family the watch guards of Berlin.

Ruth looked down at the paper in her hand. She'd solved the first clue and Elise had already given her the second, which had led her to Alexander's underwear drawer. On Ruth's nightstand was the third puzzle—the one she'd found just before Elise had discovered Alexander's goodbye letter, about staying warm and embroidered leaves on branches.

Thoughts of Alexander carefully putting together her treasure hunt made Ruth want to cry again. She lifted her pillow and removed her nightclothes from underneath. A small piece of paper fell to the floor, "Ruti" and the word "*Nachthemd*"—nightgown—on the front. With her nightgown in her hand, she touched the hand-embroidered flowers, twigs, and leaves along the collar and hem. Finding the next clue, completely by accident, made Ruth feel happier. It was as if Alexander was with her. He must have known she'd find it at bedtime. Ruth opened the note to read the next riddle. It was a childish game, but she made herself a promise. *As long as I solve the treasure hunt, Alexander will be safe.* But this riddle was baffling.

Her place of birth

As she undressed, the words circled her head. It was such a short clue. She couldn't figure it out. Ruth's tiredness hit. She would sleep on it and continue the hunt in the morning. Climbing into bed, resting her glasses on her nightstand, Ruth looked around her room. Her ceramic ornaments made strange shapes in the blurry darkness.

Her dressing gown hanging on the back of her wardrobe door looked like a ghost.

Ruth remembered her birthday wish. Her chest filled with excitement at the thought of Marko's cousin Kizzy arriving in just a few hours—*Paul's cousin, Franziska*, Ruth corrected herself. As sleep came, shadows across the wall turned into an image of her brother at the border, a Nazi officer checking his papers, discovering that Alexander was Jewish. The papers fell to the floor.

Ruth forced her mind back to Alexander's puzzle.

She stared up at the dark bedroom ceiling. She imagined how much more comforting this would have been had Elise been with her, sleeping over as they'd planned. But Ruth would see her in the morning. Elise would understand what she was feeling. Ruth's best friend had had to say goodbye to her brother, too. *It's better Elise isn't here.* As Ruth's eyes fell closed, she thought about Elise and little Viktor—and the typhus—and then back to Alexander. Ruth was lucky. *At least my brother is alive.*

Elise

Nothing worked anymore. The clock on her father's desk was broken, but Elise knew it must have been around midnight.

All the way from Ruth's home, Elise had thought about the handsome young man in the market, with his grazed neck and messy hair, and how she'd saved him and his bag from that African boy and his knife. While preparing dinner, she had thought about how she'd blushed when the young man talked to her. And all through her meal, as Elise's mother sat in silence, Elise had laughed at his offer of a cigarette. But Elise didn't mention him. That would only have led to questions and one of Mother's lecture about strangers.

For three years, since her brother Viktor had died, Elise's mother had been ill. She was grieving, the doctors had said. And then Elise's father had left to fight in the war. Mother barely talked now. If she wasn't in bed, she was stuck in her armchair in the front room. Every day, Elise would return home to cook and clean. At mealtimes, Mother rarely asked questions about Elise's day. She never asked about Elise's schoolwork or her time at the Girls' League. And she didn't ask about Elise's friends. They listened to music on the wireless. Whenever the news reports came on, Elise would hold her breath and wait for new information about the soldiers on the eastern front. But Mother always instructed Elise to turn the dial.

That evening, she hadn't asked about Ruth, and Elise hadn't mentioned Ruth's birthday or her gift of fancy biscuits. Mother would only have been angry that Elise hadn't brought the biscuits home.

Elise had helped her mother to bed and was now sitting, still in her League uniform, at Father's desk by the kitchen. Attempting to catch up on homework, she was distracted by the blackout curtains in front of her. Images filled her head of the back garden behind it, empty and dead in the winter. Last summer, before Father left to fight in the war, he'd tended to the garden and fixed things around the house. Since the air raid bombings last year, blackout shades had become mandatory. Berlin had to stay hidden in darkness.

Elise opened the desk drawer and pulled out a small pile of letters and papers, some from Father that he'd sent them over the last few months, and some from Viktor, from years ago, when he was sent away. She flicked through them, reading words and sentences, beginnings and endings.

Her hands found Father's letter opener and she touched its blunt blade with each finger. Just as she sat in her brown League climbing jacket, Elise pictured Father in his uniform, writing his letters home, his hands illuminated by lamplight, the other soldiers in their bunks fast asleep, like Mother upstairs.

Words called to Elise from their pages. She knew what she was about to read, as she'd read them before. She couldn't resist. An old letter from little Viktor found its way into her hand, his voice clear in her head.

... Elise... I can see nice trees out the window... Today I had strawberry jam. Elise, you love strawberries... The nurse is very pretty to me... Visit soon...

She never did visit him.

After he died, Elise had listened through the wall to the sounds of Father crying himself to sleep every night for weeks. The doctor's report had listed typhus as the cause of Viktor's death, but that had been a lie. Father's sobs had turned to screams of rage.

With the silver letter opener against her skin, Elise stared at the dull fabric of the blackout curtain. A noise—someone moving outside—startled her. She turned off the desk lamp and moved the blackout curtain aside. From the darkness of the kitchen, she leaned toward the window. Elise jolted back when she saw the heads of two people standing behind the garden wall to her left, both wearing flat caps. She couldn't see their faces. One of them was facing her house, blocked by the other.

A shiver rushed through her when she thought about who they might be. Criminals. Policemen. Spies. People trying to escape the Gestapo.

Elise had become accustomed to the noises at night. Father had told her to pay no attention. That's what happened in wartime, Mother always said. But Elise couldn't ignore the shouts and screams. She'd never been scared; they'd just always interested her.

Her hand on the curtain, Elise leaned over Father's desk, watching the two figures. Each appeared to be whispering. And waiting. Members of the resistance, perhaps. Fools, Mother would have said, risking their lives for nothing. Father would have called them traitors. But he wouldn't have called the police.

Elise was hypnotized. Their heads were so close, whispering so intently. She watched as a hand moved up to the other person's head. *They're kissing.*

Immediately, Elise moved away from the desk and ran upstairs. While Mother snored from her bed, Elise walked across the landing. Compared to the rest of the house, the room she walked into was cold. But from there she had a much better view down to the gardens and side alleys, especially as their house stood at one of the highest points of Berlin. Sometimes, as she looked out across the rooftops, Elise thought of herself as a maturing spinster locked in a tower by her mother, unable to leave and barred from the world. Just an observer.

She rested her forehead against the windowpane. Standing in the darkness, she looked down at the two strangers behind the garden wall. One of them was turned away from the house, but now Elise could see the other face clearly. She gasped. *It's Alex Broden.* Ruth's brother was talking now, and smiling. Then he leaned forward and his face was blocked again. She had just caught Alex kissing. She couldn't see the girl's face—she was facing the other way. All Elise could see were the girl's shoulders, her coat collar pulled up to the edge of her flat cap.

Since when does Alex Broden have a girlfriend? She wondered whether Ruth knew. Surely Ruth would have told her; Elise's best friend was unable to keep secrets for very long. She wished Ruth were standing beside her.

Earlier, when Elise had found Alex's farewell letter, Ruth had been so upset that he'd left home without a sendoff. And now he was right here, behind Elise's home. Elise wondered if Alex and his girlfriend were escaping Berlin together. *Or maybe they're saying goodbye.*

Alex stood with his arms around the girl. Animated as he spoke, smiling, he appeared relaxed. Elise still couldn't see his girlfriend's face. Elise's eyes followed them as they began to walk away. Moments later, they were out of sight.

Elise couldn't wait to tell Ruth what she'd seen. Knowing Ruth, she would giggle and be horribly annoying with excitement and ask Elise to repeat the story over and over again.

Elise stared down through the windowpane. Her own brother appeared in her mind. Viktor's light-blue eyes were brilliant against the reflection in the glass.

Marko

Marko grabbed Alex's hand, leading him through the private gardens. He pulled Alex against a wall to kiss him. The back of Marko's cap scraped the bricks. Alex kissed him back.

"I missed you, Broden," Marko said.

Alex stepped back. "Your sister's waiting."

"Don't care."

Alex tugged Marko's arm to get going. Marko loved being alone with Alex. From now on, that was what it would feel like. *Every day.*

On the street, they couldn't hold hands. It was too dangerous. They were on the western edge of Friedrichshain Park, not far from the concrete military tower. Walking into the park, it was hard to see between the trees. In the pitch black, Marko wanted to kiss him again. But Tsura was lurking somewhere, waiting. She had no idea about her brother and Alex.

They climbed over the high wall into the garden. Marko helped Alex over, then he followed. Tsura wasn't there yet.

Alex smiled at their surroundings. "When I was little, my parents brought Ruti and me here all the time."

It was like nothing Marko had ever seen. Stone arches made a half circle around a large pool. In the water and along its edge, statues of kids' story characters stood on stone platforms.

Alex pointed them out, as if introducing them to Marko. "Gretel. Hansel. There's Cinderella. That's Snow White."

But Marko wasn't looking at the statues. He was watching Alex. Earlier in Alex's bedroom, he'd told Marko about this place. About the statues and their stories.

Alex jumped when Tsura stepped out from behind the stone arches in her long coat, her cap pulled down to her eyes.

"You're late," she snapped at Marko.

"Sorry," Alex said. He was always too polite. "We went through the back gardens, behind the houses. It was safer that way."

Tsura narrowed her eyes. "You must be Alex."

"Broden, this is Tsura. Sis, this is Broden."

Tsura and Alex smiled at each other. Marko was happy they were finally meeting.

Tsura looked over her shoulder. "This way."

Alex followed Tsura without hesitation. Marko was skeptical, walking slowly behind them. "Where are you going?"

Tsura spoke as she guided them toward the back of the fountain. "Keep your eyes open. Soldiers on Greifswalder Street. They're everywhere."

"Yes, sis," Marko groaned. He doubted Nazi soldiers would be patrolling a children's garden. Tsura liked to pretend she was in charge. Marko looked up at one of the statues along the water's edge. A wild dog with its tongue hanging out looked up at a little girl holding a stone basket. *Red Riding Hood.*

Tsura stepped around the row of pillars, leading Marko and Alex into the shadows. "Your papers will be ready by the morning," she told Alex.

Marko felt a rush. Everything was working out.

"So we don't need the back-up plan?" Alex asked.

Tsura seemed startled. "Back-up plan?"

"Your brother wanted us to join the Hitler Youth. He wanted to wear those Nazi shorts."

Tsura laughed, which was a rare occurrence. It was the first time they'd met, just to say goodbye.

Marko put down his bag and leaned against the low wall. The stone felt cold through his trousers. Alex stayed standing next to his suitcase, staring through the pillars at the statues around the fountain. Marko followed his gaze. It was as if the fairy tale characters were once alive and now all stuck in place. "They're giving me the creeps."

"So, did you leave Duerr at the hospital?" Tsura asked him.

For a split second, caught off guard, Marko didn't answer. "Left her outside," Marko lied. He didn't mention leaving the old woman with Kizzy. He pictured his cousin pushing Duerr's wheelchair. He hoped to hell it went okay. *Kizzy's at home, asleep,* he reassured himself.

"Did the hospital staff ask any questions?"

"No," Marko said. Then he changed the subject. "Sis, we've got an idea—for Kizzy." He looked at Alex, encouraging him to tell Tsura the new plan. There was more of a chance she'd listen to Alex.

"We talked to my parents. It's all arranged. Your cousin will stay with my family."

"Kizzy will stay with them," Marko repeated. "Great, right?"

Alex continued, "Franziska will share—"

"No," Tsura interrupted, her eyes on her brother. "People will notice. And they're Jews."

"Only my father is Jewish. His wife—my stepmother—and my stepsister are Catholic," Alex explained.

Tsura frowned. "No."

Marko was prepared for the argument. "Look, sis. Kizzy won't be safe with us. Broden's parents agreed. She goes there tomorrow. They're expecting her."

"I don't like it."

She's so bleeding stubborn. His sister never trusted his ideas. "You can take her yourself, if you like. You can meet them."

"My parents are good people. She'll be safe," Alex added.

Marko went in for the kill. "Safer than she'd be with you." He said it to get a reaction from Tsura.

But she didn't bite. "Remind me how you two know each other," Tsura said, more quietly now, looking at Alex. Tsura knew how they'd met. She was testing him.

"We met last year. Marko started at the brewery just after me."

"What did you do at the brewery?" Tsura asked him.

"I worked in the office. The work was dull, so I asked to switch to deliveries." Alex was leaving out key parts of the story.

"Sis, I told you all this." Marko tapped his foot in frustration. Marko had told Tsura about Alex, months before. They were close friends, he'd said. He'd failed to mention that Alex was his boyfriend. Tsura had been talking about getting Marko out of Germany—out of Europe. With Roma men being deported to the work camps, and Aryan men being sent to fight, it wasn't safe. Not even with false papers. Marko had asked Tsura to help Alex, too. She'd said no at first. But when Marko told her that Alex was a Jewish guy his age, Tsura started to come around. Marko made the case that traveling alone would be difficult. Tsura agreed, eventually. She always listened to Marko in the end.

"So Kizzy can stay with his family?" Marko asked.

Tsura paused, then nodded. Marko tried not to grin too widely. It would be him and Alex. Just them. Like they'd planned.

Tsura turned to Alex. "Give me your photographs. I'll see you both in a few hours. At Duerr's place."

Alex reached into his pocket. He patted himself down. "No. No!"

"What is it?" Marko asked.

"My coat. My photographs!"

Tsura put her finger to her lips. "Keep your voices down. What's the matter?"

"In my coat. My father. We swapped coats." Alex grabbed his own coat collar. "This is my father's coat." He kicked the ground and hit his forehead with his wrists.

"What the hell?" Marko said, trying not to shout. *Our plan is dead.* Alex needed his photographs. Marko wanted to punch something.

"We still have time," Tsura said. "Alex, go home. Meet us in the morning with your photographs at Putlitz Street Train Station. Be there by seven in the morning."

"Okay," Alex said. Judging by the panicked look on his face, Alex would've agreed to anything.

"Broden, I'll come with you," Marko said. Then he turned to his sister. "Meet you at Duerr's place."

"Fine. Duerr's. Just before seven."

"Where're you going?" Marko asked her.

Tsura narrowed her eyes at Alex. It was clear she didn't trust him yet. "I'll be up all night."

Alex shot Marko a look, wondering where she was heading.

Marko laughed. "She never sleeps."

Marko thought about needing sleep. Alex would stay with him tonight. It would be the first time he'd see where Marko lived, just like when Marko saw Alex's home earlier, for the first time. *Perfect.*

"Stay alert. They're rounding up Jews this weekend." Tsura looked at Alex as she said it.

"Raids? When?" Alex asked. He swallowed hard and bit down on his lip. "How do you know that?"

Marko rolled his eyes. "She knows everything."

"Shut up, Marko." Tsura punched his arm.

Tsura was a pain, but she was great. And she really did know everything. Marko knew she'd get Alex his papers. *She'll get us on that train.* It was good they were heading back to Alex's home. "We can warn your father about the raids."

Alex looked frightened. He stared at the ground, then up at Marko. "Maybe we'll bring my father with us."

"No," Tsura snapped. "He doesn't have the right papers."

Marko glared at Tsura in surprise. "His father agreed to help Kizzy."

Tsura puffed out her cheeks in resignation. "Only if he has nowhere to go. I could find somewhere for him to hide."

"Thank you," Alex said with a heavy sigh.

Marko winked at him, then turned to his sister. "What time's the train?"

"Nine thirty." Tsura stood up, getting ready to leave. "But we'll be cutting it fine. I'll meet you at Duerr's by seven. Then I'll have to run with the photographs to get your papers. Then I'll meet you at Anhalter station at nine. Okay?"

"Okay."

The nine-thirty train. Anhalter station. Marko repeated it all in his head. Alex was getting his papers. He wondered what fake name Alex would be given.

"Hey," Marko said. He opened the main compartment of his new bag filled with wines and cigarettes and fancy foods. "Look what I found."

"Only Marko," Tsura mocked.

Marko looked at Alex. "After dinner, I tried to sell it in the market."

"What else do you have?" Tsura asked.

Marko rummaged through the bag. Cheeses and pâté. Wines and booze and cigarettes. Caviar. Real coffee, real chocolate. He remembered the chocolate he'd given to Kizzy. She'd probably eaten it already. Alex and Tsura crouched down and picked up some of the items.

"This is incredible," Alex said.

"Oh, I got this, too," Marko said, pulling out his new knife. He held it up, proudly.

Alex looked alarmed. "What's that for?"

"Might need it."

"My brother, the thief," Tsura said and scowled.

"I didn't steal this stuff," Marko protested. "It belonged to a woman. She was arrested."

"Good meeting you," Tsura said to Alex, clearly not believing a word Marko was saying.

Alex flashed his handsome smile. "You too."

Tsura pushed her hair into her hat. Sometimes she looked more like Marko's brother than his sister. They watched her disappear away from the fountain, into the trees.

Marko looked down at his new watch. It was him and Alex now, with hours before their train. Still crouching, Alex leaned his back against the wall. His yellow star was gone. *We're leaving Berlin.*

"Why are you smiling?" Alex asked.

His knees on the dirt ground, facing Alex, Marko reached into his pocket. He took out the steel medal that Alex had given to him earlier in his bedroom. Scraping his fingernails on the medal's edge, Marko looked left and right. Only the strange fairy tale statues through the pillars could see them. Marko kissed him. Alex's skin was cold.

"We should go," Alex whispered, his mouth on Marko's mouth.

Just a few more hours and they'd be on the train leaving Germany together. It was perfect. Marko planned it out in his head.

They'd sleep side by side, for the first time. Marko kissed Alex again. He wanted to kiss Alex all night. Marko pictured them as old men together, in some big city. London. New York.

"I'm sorry about Frau Duerr," Alex said, standing up.

"Duerr? She's old. She's as good as dead." Marko closed his bag and stood, too.

Alex frowned at Marko's harsh words.

"You look good without your star, Broden," Marko said, tapping Alex's collar.

"What's that supposed to mean?"

"I don't know," Marko said and wanted to laugh.

Alex grabbed his boyfriend's hand as Marko swung his heavy bag onto his back. Alex carried his suitcase, leading Marko along the edge of the fountain, passing the statues that seemed to watch them knowingly. They headed back south, toward Alex's home.

As they walked, Alex chuckled. "I'll say goodbye to my family all over again. Ruti will be happy."

"They'll be sick of seeing you," Marko joked.

Alex seemed worried about his younger sister. It reminded Marko to feel guilty for sending Kizzy to the hospital with Duerr. With a bar of chocolate and a jar of jam.

"Kizzy's gonna be happy I'm gone," Marko said.

"Ruti will keep an eye on her."

They walked away from the park and onto Frieden Street, shoulders close, almost touching. The only people in sight. Just for the hell of it, Marko pulled Alex to a stop. Marko leaned in, wanting to kiss him, but they weren't in the side streets anymore. Marko placed his hand on Alex's chest—his yellow badge of honor missing. Alex let out a cloud of breath into the icy air, his mouth turned up at the side.

Marko shivered. "I dare you," he said.

Alex kissed Marko on the mouth. Marko's stubble scratched against his chin.

Alex let out a gasp. Marko opened his eyes. Alex was staring forward.

"What?" Marko said, spinning around.

A Nazi officer stood across the street, with polished boots and dead-straight blond hair under his Nazi helmet. He wasn't much older than them. Nineteen at most.

"He saw us," Alex whispered.

Marko was ready to run. But the Nazi just stood there. They were close to the Nazi Flak Tower. Marko wanted to kick himself. He lowered his voice, speaking to Alex while barely moving his lips. "If I bolt, stay close, okay?"

"Okay."

The Nazi was standing across the street, his back to the park, glaring at them with his white-gold hair like an actor in a film Marko once saw. The Nazi smiled, lifted his hand, pointed two fingers at his eyes, then pointed the same fingers at Marko and Alex. Then the Nazi grabbed himself below the belt.

"What the hell?"

"What do we do?" Alex whispered.

When the officer pulled a whistle from his top pocket, Marko shouted. "Go!"

The Nazi's whistle pierced the quiet of the night. With their bags, they sprinted. Marko was right behind Alex. The sounds of boots on the road behind them made Marko run faster. Voices of three, maybe four soldiers. *Bastards.* But as some of the voices faded into the distance, Marko could tell one soldier was still chasing them. Alex led Marko back up the street. West to the city center, away from Alex's home. They didn't say a word. They were running too fast. A pulse raced through Marko. He laughed, his feet hitting the pavestones hard. He almost tripped. They turned a corner. Still running fast. The boots behind them were waning. But Marko kept up his pace. More corners.

Alex was trailing now. "You okay?" Marko asked as they ran. The idea of Alex hurt or caught made Marko feel sick. He didn't want to think about it. Alex ran faster and he turned toward the river. Marko pulled on Alex's arm. "No. This way." Marko led Alex away from the checkpoints.

Street after street. Corners. Jumping curbs. The soldier was far behind, but wasn't giving up. Building after building and across the river. Bags in their hands. Into an alley. *Bad idea.* Alex threw his suitcase over a wall. Marko couldn't throw his bag—the bottles of wine would smash. The bag on his back, Marko gripped Alex's arm, smiling at him, and they helped each other up and over. Alex grabbed his suitcase and they kept running through the alleys and gardens. Marko looked at Alex and laughed again.

Alex shot Marko a look like he was crazy. "What's funny?"

Marko was laughing. He couldn't help it. They ran by buildings that looked empty. Alex turned toward the main street, but when Marko saw an open window, he grabbed Alex's shoulder. "In here!"

They threw their bags inside and jumped into the basement of an abandoned shop. Boots hitting the street were getting closer again. In the corner of the dark basement, Alex found a door. They bounded up four, maybe five staircases, to the roof. Marko leaned on Alex as, together, they pushed the roof-hatch open. They scampered across the rooftops, around chimneys, and jumped from the building onto another roof. They stopped.

"We lost him," Alex said, out of breath.

"That was your fault."

"Definitely yours."

By that point, they were both laughing. They found an entrance into the building below and ducked into the doorway. Into the shadows. Hidden. They were safe. Face-to-face.

Kizzy

Kizzy's face stung from the policeman's slap. It was after midnight and she was with Professor Duerr in an examination room inside Charité Hospital. The professor sat slumped sideways in her wheelchair by Kizzy's side, sleeping again. *I should be sleeping, too.*

Kizzy felt grubby against the clean white tiles and metal table. Professor Duerr reeked of urine.

In Kizzy's pocket, the jar of dark red jam that Marko had given her weighed down the side of her coat. Kizzy took out the jar, forced open the lid and, using her fingers, tasted the rich berry mixture. It made her feel slightly better. She thought about Marko's chocolate bar in her other pocket, but decided to save it. Who knew how long she'd be there.

Kizzy tapped the old woman's shoulder.

"Frau Professor?"

Professor Duerr groaned.

"Here," Kizzy said and pushed some jam into the woman's mouth. The professor's eyes were still closed, but her mouth moved a little and she seemed to be eating. Then the woman was still again in her chair, breathing lightly.

I should've been home by now. Kizzy worried what Tsura would say. If Tsura had been there, she would have told Kizzy to run. She had to get out. She had her false documents. She wondered if she'd be able to trick someone into letting her leave. But the door was locked and a nurse was keeping guard. How did she get herself arrested? How did she not have a plan? *This is all Marko's fault.*

The doctors would turn Kizzy over to the Nazis and she'd be sent to the camp for the Roma in Marzahn. The thought made Kizzy feel better. *At least I'll join Mama.* She thought about her mother and Aunt Jaelle—Tsura and Marko's mother—inside the Marzahn camp, close by.

When they were younger, Tsura had told Kizzy stories about their family and taught her some of the traditional Romani dances and songs. But Kizzy couldn't remember them now. Tsura talked about the camp, too. Tsura had visited Marzahn many times to check up on their mothers and cousins and old friends, returning with stories that were usually sad. Not enough food. Dirty. Freezing in winter; in the summer, rampant with disease. The idea of Marzahn was frightening.

Kizzy, Tsura, and Marko were lucky the professor had agreed to take them in. Mocking the Nazis' derogatory slurs, the woman called them her little Gypsies. And she was right. They were hers. They quickly belonged to the professor and the professor belonged to them.

Kizzy loved having Tsura as a kind of sister. But when Tsura was old enough, she'd moved out. Now she lived with that man and woman in that apartment. Kizzy and Marko didn't see Tsura much. She was busy, working against the government.

Without realizing it, Kizzy had finished all of the jam. She put the empty glass jar on the floor and wiped her mouth with her coat sleeve. She felt sick. Too warm now, Kizzy took off her woolen hat and stuffed it into her coat pocket, revealing her wiry hair.

A while later, the door opened. The nurse who had been keeping an eye on Kizzy entered the room. Two other women, also in hospital uniforms, followed her.

"There she is," the nurse said, pointing to Professor Duerr.

"Please, nurse," Kizzy said, trying her best to sound like a sweet little girl. "Can we have something to drink?"

"Keep quiet!" the nurse barked and reached into Professor Duerr's coat pocket for her identity papers. When they started to remove the professor's clothes, Kizzy looked away.

"Oh no," one of the medics said.

A foul smell filled the room—Professor Duerr had messed her underwear.

Kizzy stared at the professor. Her coat was open. Her dress and bra ripped, breasts exposed.

"Look." One of the women pointed to the professor's mouth. "She's been coughing up blood."

"No—" Kizzy tried to explain.

"I said, be quiet, girl!" the nurse screamed.

It wasn't blood; it was jam.

As Kizzy was about to pick up the empty jar from the floor, the nurse slapped Professor Duerr's face hard with the back of her hand. "Wake up, old woman!"

Professor Duerr made a small sound, a quiet howl of pain, and the nurse seemed satisfied. "Take her away," she said.

Within moments, the two police guards from outside appeared. Professor Duerr was still half naked as the five of them huddled together, whispering.

"Zigeuner," Kizzy heard one of the policemen say.

The tall officer seized Kizzy by her coat.

"Frau Professor!"

But it was too late. Kizzy was now in the corridor and the room slammed shut with the three medics and Professor Duerr still inside.

As the guards marched Kizzy along the hallway, she didn't struggle. Her heart felt as if it would explode into her lungs.

"Where are you taking me?" she dared to ask.

The guards didn't reply.

Kizzy tried to stay calm. She thought about Papa, sent away to work for the government in this horrible war. For a moment, Kizzy hoped they'd send her to join him. *He'll take care of me.* Otherwise, she'd be sent to Mama in Marzahn. Either way, it wasn't so bad.

Kizzy was facing a door. The guard unlocked it to reveal another examination room, with a medical table and a wooden chair. A small metal bed in the corner stood against the shiny tiled floor and walls. When Kizzy saw that the room was windowless, she remembered what Tsura told her to say if she ever got caught.

"I'm pureblood. *Zigeuner,* pureblood."

Pureblooded Gypsies, Tsura had told Kizzy many times, were protected by law. They weren't the same as *Mischlinge*—mixedbloods.

"You'll sleep in here for the night," the tall policeman said, pointing at the metal bed.

"No. Please. Don't leave me here. My aunt—I really do have an aunt. I have to get home to her. Please. I'm scared of being alone!" Kizzy was saying anything now. She was desperate.

They closed the door and locked it from the outside.

"No! I'm pureblood!" she screamed, knowing they could hear her. She threw herself at the door and pounded her fists against it, again and again, until they hurt. "Please. Please!"

She could hear the guards' boots on the corridor fade as they walked away.

Dropping onto the metal bed, Kizzy started to cry. She hugged herself and tasted real tears mixed with Marko's berry jam. *Where's Marko? Where's Tsura? Marko left me on my own.* Thinking about her cousins made Kizzy cry harder. Tsura wouldn't cry, Kizzy knew. But Tsura was older. *I'm only thirteen.*

MARZAHN

Tsura

The powdery smell of raw potatoes filled Tsura's head.

"Wake up," Seraph said.

Tsura forced her eyes open. "I'm awake." She had fallen asleep for a moment and her instinct was to check the gun in her coat pocket.

"Is this the right road?"

Tsura checked their surroundings. "Yes, this is the way. Keep going."

The road out of Berlin was smooth, but as they neared the edges of the city, the van shivered and jolted. Tsura rested her head on the van's interior wall, sacks of potatoes all around them. Wolf slept beside her. To Tsura, Wolf and Marko looked alike, both unshaven, dark hair. But Wolf was responsible, determined, focused, while Marko was carefree and immature. *If Marko put his mind to it, he could be like Wolf.*

The calm sounds of the trickling water at the Fairy Tales Fountain lingered in Tsura's immediate memory. She had been there before as a young girl with Mother. Tsura remembered the arches and white stone pillars. And the elegant limestone statues, recalling the children's stories with which every German girl and boy grew up. Transported back to that time filled Tsura with peace, memories of a better life for her family. Meeting her brother's friend, Alex, was calming, too. He seemed levelheaded and sensible. Leaving Berlin with Alex would keep Marko out of trouble. But in the dark hours of the night, when a vague recollection came to her, Tsura's unease swept over her again; the Fairy Tale Fountain had been built decades earlier as a memorial to dead German children killed by an epidemic. Tsura placed her hand on her lower stomach and pushed away a painful childhood memory.

"I wish I could drive all the time," Seraph said, hands on the wheel, gun on her knee. "I'd love it. Honestly. My father taught me how, you know."

Seraph couldn't stop talking. Tonight, she was either nervous or trying to keep herself awake.

Seraph was talking about Marzahn now. "I'd never heard of Marzahn 'til I met you. Nobody knows about it. Am I right? I'm right."

"They choose to ignore it," Tsura said, breaking Seraph's babbling. The Nazi encampments for Roma and Sinti people were unfamiliar to most Germans.

"Tell me about Rastplatz Marzahn again," Seraph said.

"The Olympic Games were coming to Berlin—" Tsura began, as if reciting a practiced speech.

But Seraph wasn't listening; she hummed snippets of songs under her breath. Tsura wondered how she and Seraph had become friends. Tsura disliked her more than anyone she had ever known. Of course, there were times when Seraph would talk constantly about avenging the incarceration of her family. It was what she and Tsura had in common. But that was all.

Tsura turned her eyes to Wolf, who was still asleep. Despite Seraph and Wolf's love affair, they couldn't have been more different. While Seraph didn't know how to shut up, Wolf was usually silent, always deep in thought. Asleep, his boot tapped the van's wall with each jolt, his coat like a blanket, his head tucked down. Tsura continued the story in her head.

Adolf Hitler could be tamed, Tsura's parents had said, a belief stolen from radio announcers. The world's leaders had presumed diplomacy would keep Hitler's government under control. It was 1936. Tsura was twelve and Marko was ten, old enough to remember it all. Their cousins, Kizzy and Samuel, were too small. Kizzy was a sweet six-year-old and Samuel, Kizzy's baby brother, was still crawling. While the world descended on Berlin for the Olympic Games, Hitler spent his time creating a grand illusion.

The city came alive again. With the eyes of the world on Germany, their lives seemed safer. Tsura's grandmother prepared a small celebratory meal at her home in Charlottenburg, close to Berlin's center. The whole family gathered to raise toasts to their people, to the hope that the toxic anti-Roma atmosphere in the German capital would be somehow swept away by international peacekeepers. At the very least, they hoped the wide spotlight pointed at the Olympic stage would expose the Nazis' hatred for the Roma people. The world would listen.

Then came the eviction notices. The Romani community was part of Hitler's magic trick; the Games were to be picture-perfect and that meant no Gypsies in sight. Tsura could remember the Nazi police pointing their guns at her and Marko, ripping them from their home, away from the city, dragging Aunt Marie by her beautiful hair, beating Father and their uncles. While the adults cried, baby Samuel and Kizzy remained quiet. The Nazis forced Tsura's family to the edge of the city. No chance to say farewell to their friends. Father didn't say goodbye to his colleagues at the clothing factory where he'd worked for sixteen years.

At least they were together, they told themselves. The encampment in Marzahn stood in an open field, between a cemetery and a sewage dump. Tsura's Aunt Marie—Kizzy's mother—always the one to make light of the worst, once warned them to not confuse the two; she had no intention of being laid to rest in rotting waste. Aunt Marie also poked fun at the irony of their living conditions.

Tsura's great-grandparents had been lifelong travelers. But her grandparents had shaken off their nomadic traditions and settled the family in Berlin. They'd taken on a typical German name. They were proud city-dwellers. Yet there they were, back in caravans, just like that. They made these kinds of jokes as people fell ill, but before the deaths. After the deaths, it was difficult to joke about anything.

The conditions of Marzahn worsened. Within days, there were a few hundred inhabitants—the Roma from across Berlin, all forced into old caravans and huts, packed in like tins of smoked fish, refugees on the edge of their own city with two toilets for the entire camp. No running water. No electricity. Guards roamed the field and kept its perimeter secure. The closest village was a fast fifteen-minute walk away. The prisoners saved their crumbs, rationed their rations, cooked spoiled vegetables. They burned rotten scraps and washed them down with boiled rainwater. Sinti Germans were brought to Marzahn, too. The government saw the Romani and Sinti peoples as the same. They were all simply *Zigeuner*, regardless of heritage.

The summer Olympics came and went, but the Nazis still kept watch. The news that they were permanent prisoners at Marzahn hit them hard. A rumor spread that the encampment had been part of the government's plan for two years. When the autumn chill settled in, some fell ill, first the elderly, then the youngest children. Malnutrition and cross-contamination led to sickness. The very old and very young were the worst affected. First, Tsura's grandmother. Then Kizzy. And then Samuel. All very sick.

Tsura's grandmother died in January 1937. Baby Samuel's health deteriorated quickly and he died two weeks later. Samuel's death was shocking, especially for the adults, but they were too focused on sick little Kizzy to grieve.

They breathed a collective sigh of relief when Kizzy's health improved. Time dragged on. Another year passed. They became accustomed to the disease and the dying and the exhaustion. Some of the women in the camp even became pregnant and gave birth to healthy babies. They had hope. They all adjusted. The Nazis worked them hard at factories and warehouses back in the city, even the teenagers. Traveling into the city for work every morning made Tsura feel somewhat free. Even though they had to return to the stinking encampment each night, life became tolerable. They had a routine.

In 1938, another horror hit. Tsura was older now. One early evening, traveling back from the city to the camp, she and the adults heard rumors that the Nazis were to send Romani and Sinti men, including boys old enough to work, to labor camps.

Their parents were terrified for Marko—he was now a teenager, too. They organized for Kizzy, Marko, and Tsura to move back to Berlin. They would live with an old, trusted family friend, Frau Professor Doktor Duerr, a retired German academic and one of the first female professors in Germany. They would pass for Aryans, Father was sure. Their hair was almost black but, compared to many in the Roma community, they were fair-skinned. Somehow, forged papers with forged Nazi stamps were arranged and, suddenly, Tsura, Marko, and Kizzy were real Aryans with new boring names and ration cards.

The morning Tsura was taken to Duerr's home was the last time she saw her father. Kizzy had held Tsura's hand tight. Days later, Tsura's father and uncle, along with most other men and teenage boys in the Marzahn encampment, were sent to Nazi camps. Marko had been saved.

Professor Duerr found the youngsters new clothes and fed them well. Kizzy, Marko, and Tsura grew stronger. They heard from their mothers now and again through short written notes containing updates and promises that one day they would be reunited. Then the notes stopped. The encampment had been closed off. Tsura, now a young woman, traveled to Marzahn. She didn't dare approach the guards. As Tsura stood at a distance, her stomach knotted at the thought of Mother and Aunt Marie so close by.

Tsura went back to the city. Reluctantly, Duerr gave her the addresses of old friends and kind neighbors of her family, people who knew Tsura as a child. One lead led to another and she found herself visiting a small apartment in the city.

Seraph had opened the door, dressed in slim trousers and a waistcoat. A student at Humboldt University, she participated in a secret political student group organized by a young Austrian woman, also a student at the university.

Seraph was not her real name. It was her pseudonym, denoting purity and pacifism. She was helping to distribute anti-Nazi flyers to encourage non-violent resistance. She passed on information and helped dissidents connect with one another. Seraph claimed links to other resistance groups, but Tsura got the sense she was embellishing the truth. When the student group broke up, since its activities were becoming too dangerous, Seraph began to work alone, offering her home as a meeting place for other dissidents.

Tsura had wondered how Seraph could afford an apartment in such a fancy building. Seraph had pointed to missing light fixtures, and empty spaces where expensive furniture had once stood. Her family had been wealthy, Seraph had explained, but Nazi soldiers had stolen everything of value. Years earlier, the Gestapo had arrested Seraph's father as an intellectual with the wrong political leanings and sent him to the infamous concentration camp at Dachau, just north of Munich. Seraph's mother was arrested in 1940, for much the same reasons, and sent to the Ravensbrück camp, north of Berlin.

Even though she was all talk, spending time with Seraph was like drinking a tonic. Her apartment became Tsura's home and she spent hours there, along with other students and runaways who drifted in and out, listening to music old and new, taking in Seraph's stories, and always, eventually, discussing politics and the war. Tsura suggested they bomb Gestapo buildings and shared her fantasies of executing Nazi officers. But Seraph shook her head at any ideas of violence and revenge. Tsura talked about getting into the camp in Marzahn to rescue her mother and aunt and others, even killing the guards and helping the entire camp escape. Tsura checked in with Marko and Kizzy now and again, telling them she was working against the Nazis. But, really, it was all still fantasy. Until Wolf arrived in 1942.

Wolf was different. Quiet, serious, rarely animated. While Tsura had her own bedroom in Seraph's spacious apartment, newcomers would sleep on the floor in the living room. But within days, Wolf was sharing Seraph's bed. Their sudden romance accentuated Seraph's childish side; she was always flirting and giggling around him. Tsura could tell how Wolf didn't like Seraph's immaturity. He rarely talked to Seraph—at least not in front of others—but he allowed her to hang on his arm, her hands up his shirt, his permanent shadow.

Wolf rarely initiated a conversation. But he would listen to their ideas and anti-government plots and tell them how to turn them into reality. Sabotaging the Gestapo offices would involve finding explosives. Wolf knew how to get them and he knew someone who would help to rig them up. Executing prominent officers would be extremely difficult and too risky, but not impossible. Wolf knew people. He could obtain weapons. There was always a way, he would tell them, his face unsmiling.

Tsura had talked to Wolf about the Marzahn camp, the Romani people, her family. Wolf never mentioned specifics about his past. He'd confided in her that his family was gone and would never return, lost to the Nazi regime. She'd asked him how he'd come to call himself Wolf. He had taken his name from the flag of one of the tribes of Israel, he'd explained. Wolf was a Jew. Then he changed the subject.

When Tsura had suggested they go to the Marzahn encampment to rescue her mother and aunt, Wolf had ridiculed the idea as impossible. Tsura had argued with him. She'd cited tales of successful escapes and rescues from Nazi prisons and camps across the Reich, including a rumor of an escape from the Marzahn camp. They at least had to try. Just before Christmas, Tsura convinced them to help organize a clandestine excursion to Marzahn to observe the guards and check the camp's perimeters—nothing else. Reluctantly, Wolf agreed to explore the idea. Tsura became impassioned and focused. They would go in the dead of night. Seraph, forced by Tsura to be useful for a change, hatched a plan to find them a truck. Still, Wolf was skeptical and Tsura argued back. But when Wolf suggested they get their hands on weapons and explosives, Tsura listened to his concerns.

By the turn of the new year, Wolf announced he could obtain three guns. Small explosives, too. If Wolf were able to cause a small explosion close by, as a diversion, the camp guards would be forced to investigate and the boundaries of the camp would be safer for Tsura and Seraph to penetrate. If necessary, if they found themselves in danger, they'd shoot a guard or two. Quietly, slowly, the plan fueled Tsura's fantasies of revenge.

But the Nazi crackdown tightened and their scheme was put on hold. They heard rumors of the Gestapo seeking out dissenting student groups. People were arrested. Even executed. It was too risky.

Now the plan was back on. Their objectives were to count the number of nighttime guards and inspect the encampment's perimeter. Seraph had already learned the route and Wolf had an idea of where to plant the explosives. It was Seraph's idea to use a delivery vehicle, in case they were stopped and searched. Tsura and Wolf laughed when Seraph drove up in a borrowed van full of potatoes. They could take a couple of handfuls of potatoes each, Seraph had said. Nobody would notice.

As they approached the road that led to Marzahn, Tsura imagined herself, gun in hand, leading Mother and Aunt Marie out of the camp. She would tell them to run, and she pictured their friends behind them. But, in the face of gunfire, Tsura knew the women would panic and throw themselves over their children. Tsura recalled her mother's caution, her mother's permission for Tsura to escape the camp. *If we keep our children too close, we'll suffocate them with fear.*

"Stop here."

Seraph brought the van to a steady halt.

Tsura elbowed Wolf in the arm and he opened his eyes. Tsura pointed to the left. "Welcome to Marzahn."

Tsura led them along the twisting road. The caravans would soon fall into view. Staying close to the thick bushes that ran along the pavement, Tsura led them over the hedgerow, backs arched, heads bowed. On their knees, they looked over the frost-covered hedge. In the distance, the Marzahn encampment stared at Tsura through the night air, calling out the secrets it held. She removed the binoculars from her pocket. She could make out the camp's perimeter. As her eyes adjusted to the equipment, she counted three uniformed guards, two sitting on wooden chairs, one standing. One of the seated men appeared to be asleep. The other two chatted, distracted. Tsura could see the guards' rifles, held by their sides. Hopping from foot to foot, the men appeared to be cold and tired. *Better for us.* She led Wolf and Seraph to the edge of the bushes.

"It's one on one," Tsura whispered. "Take a look." She passed the binoculars to Wolf.

"Don't be crazy," Wolf said, his black eyebrows furrowed, as he passed the binoculars to Seraph.

Tsura felt a rush of boldness move through her core. She removed her pistol from her coat and turned it in her hand. "Why not?"

Seraph, atypically, said nothing.

Tsura's heart pumped hard inside her chest. Mother was close. "I say we shoot them. I'll talk to them. Pretend to be lost. I'll make them turn their backs and you'll approach from behind."

"You're kidding, right?" Wolf said with a smirk.

When Tsura said nothing, Wolf lost his smile and placed his hand on Tsura's wrist. "We haven't thought this through. There are more guards inside the camp, I guarantee it. We should leave."

"No!" Tsura snapped, keeping her voice low. "My mother is in there."

Wolf said nothing. *He understands.*

Tsura returned her gun to her coat and removed her cap. Her thick dark hair fell below her shoulders and Seraph let out a laugh at her unfamiliar appearance.

"What are you doing?" Wolf asked.

Tsura smoothed down her long hair. She almost smiled at him, but harsh words found their way from her mouth. "You always forget I'm a woman." Embarrassment swelled in her chest. *Why did I say that?*

Under other circumstances, Seraph would have teased Tsura for such an odd outburst.

"We won't shoot them," Tsura said. "Unless something goes wrong." She turned to Seraph. "Aim for the Nazis, not at me."

Seraph let out a quiet chuckle, as if Tsura was joking. Wolf frowned, knowing she wasn't.

She stood up and Seraph let out a muffled gasp.

"Tsura!" Wolf whispered.

But Tsura, with her hair down, was already walking toward the camp. Her fingers in her pocket clutched the gun. It took a good minute before Tsura could distinguish the faces of the guards. One of them had his hand on a rifle. In his other, he held what looked like a bottle of cheap branntwein.

As she approached, she saw him stumble and sway. *He's drunk.* They could see Tsura approach. One of the seated guards stood up. The third remained asleep.

"Excuse me," Tsura called out cheerily.

Without much care, the drunk guard lifted his rifle with one hand and pointed it vaguely in Tsura's direction. A swell of dread rose from her stomach. The drunk was a little older and had more military badges than the others.

"Can we help you?" he slurred.

Tsura kept her distance and forced a smile. *Don't sound afraid.* "Is the cemetery this way?"

"At this time of night?" the drunk guard asked.

Tsura took her hands out from her pockets, leaving the gun inside. "It's an anniversary. I've been walking for hours. To visit the dead."

She could hear the truth within her lies. She remembered baby Samuel and the other dead prisoners of Marzahn. Her eyes became fixed on the drunkard's face. *I should kill him.*

The drunk guard lowered his rifle. "Go home." He slurred his words, but he said them kindly.

"Women shouldn't be out at this time," the younger guard added. His words were a warning. Almost a threat.

"What is this place?" Tsura asked, nodding toward the caravans behind them.

They seemed taken aback by her blunt question. The drunk hesitated. "It's a military base."

Liar. Tsura concealed her rage and continued her improvised façade. "There are too many dead soldiers."

As she spoke, she stepped along the pathway. The guards turned to face her, their backs now to the bushes where Wolf and Seraph were waiting. The third guard was still asleep.

"My dead Germans need to be remembered. Is the cemetery this way?" she asked, knowing that it was.

"Along the path," the drunk guard said. In his eyes, Tsura sensed pity. He probably suspected she was a young widow, or perhaps a little cracked.

Tsura heard voices to her right, coming from inside the encampment. Footsteps in the gravel and dirt. Half a dozen policemen walked slowly toward them. More guards. More rifles. And, it seemed, more drunks. For a moment, Tsura couldn't breathe. Her body trembled. She wondered if Wolf and Seraph could see the crowd of guards through the binoculars.

The guards at the front of the pack approached. "Got yourself some late-night fun?" one jeered at the drunk.

I need to leave here. Tsura turned back in the direction she'd come from. "Good night."

"Wait," the drunken guard said. "The cemetery's that way."

As the group of soldiers approached, the drunk stepped forward and gripped her wrist, just as Wolf had done minutes earlier. "I'll take you there."

Tsura glanced back. Seraph and Wolf were out of sight. They wouldn't have dared to approach so many police guards. She was alone now and she turned toward the cemetery, the drunken guard walking in her shadow. The group of guards jeered behind them.

"You two need some privacy?" one called out.

"Did he find a prostitute?" another asked over their laughter.

The gun in Tsura's pocket tapped against her thigh. *I'm trapped.* Taking the deepest of breaths, she considered running from him. "Thank you for escorting me," she said to the drunk.

"I'm your tour guide," he said to her, now by her side.

Their boots crunched the gravel as they strolled away from the camp.

"How old are you?" he asked.

"Nineteen. Why?"

"What's your name?"

Tsura wondered if he knew her mother. *She knows him, I bet.* "I'm Greta." Tsura was well practiced at introducing herself with the false name stated in her identification papers. "And you?"

"Wilhelm. Friends call me Wim. I'm twenty-four."

"You look older," she said.

Wim sneered, then chuckled. "You'd look older, too, with my job."

Tsura forced a laugh. "Guarding an army base in the middle of nowhere?"

"It's good having someone to talk with, Greta," he said with branntwein on his breath.

She could see the dirt beneath his fingernails. Inside, Tsura screamed at the thought of her family, so close by, suffering. Freezing. Starving to death.

"Where're you from?" Tsura asked him.

"Grew up in Munich. Moved here last year."

Tsura felt sick. "There's a lot happening at this base?"

Wim shook his head. "Not much. But it's good being near Berlin. It's where the decisions get made. Never thought I'd work in law enforcement."

You're loathsome, Tsura wanted to say. "What did you want to be?" she asked.

Wim took a swig of branntwein. "An athlete. A builder. Maybe a businessman." His words were filled with pride but his tone was of disappointment and shame.

"Maybe you'll get the chance. When the war ends."

"If it ends," he said, sadly. "What grave are you here to see?"

She hesitated. "It sounds strange, but I don't know. I'm not crazy, if that's what you're thinking." Her fear had subsided. Wim was no threat. He was weak.

"Are you married?" he asked. "I bet you've got a fiancé fighting on the front."

Tsura pictured Kizzy's baby brother, Samuel, and other members of their extended family. "I know too many dead Germans."

"You're nineteen," Wim said. "Time for you to find a good man to marry." When Tsura said nothing, he continued. "I've got a wife. And two young boys. But they're back in Munich. It's lonely here. I'm just a guard, but I want my sons to be whatever they want. I'm fighting for them."

Fighting my mother? The constant pull of the gun in Tsura's coat pocket found its way to her throat and, with a hard gulp, she swallowed her profanities. "Don't you spend time with the other soldiers? Why are you lonely?" she asked.

"I prefer keeping to myself." Wim swigged more branntwein.

The caravans were far behind them. Tsura thought about how easily she could shoot him dead—or, even better, shoot him in the groin. *He'd die slowly or be ruined for life.*

"That was quite the party," she said, referring to the group of policemen. "Do you all get together like that every night?"

"It's the weekend. During the week, overnight, it's just five or six or us."

"At the entire military base?" Tsura asked.

"That's right, including my boss."

Tsura made a mental note of the vital information.

"What do you do here?" Wim asked as they arrived at the cemetery.

"I talk to them," Tsura said, staring out at the field of gravestones.

Wim sat on the ground, close to the path. "Some of my friends are dead, too. My age." He drew a mouthful from his bottle. "How did you hear about this cemetery?"

"I stumbled on this place long ago," she said truthfully and watched his reaction.

He nodded and stared out at the graveyard.

Tsura remembered the men of her family. She could barely recall their faces. "So many dead."

As he drank from his bottle, Wim coughed and spluttered. "Some people deserve to die." He spat on the ground.

"Who?" she asked, almost shouting, willing him to give her a reason to shoot him on the spot. The Communists, the Jews, the Gypsies, she waited for him to say. But he said nothing. He just drank from his bottomless jar.

"Let's go," Tsura said.

He tried to stand, but he fell. He laughed out loud. "Help me up." He held out his arm.

Tsura ignored him and began to walk back to the encampment, back to Wolf and Seraph. Back to the other police guards. She could hear Wim stumble behind her.

"Stop walking," he said.

But she refused to listen. When he ran up to her and grabbed at her coat, she became irritated and pulled away.

"Greta, you're beautiful." Almost falling over his own feet, Wim ran across her path, forcing Tsura to halt. As if drinking water, he took another gulp of his branntwein. He held out his arm, the neck of the glass bottle close to her face. She could smell the alcohol. "Take off your clothes," he said.

Fear rose to her throat. She had underestimated this man. Her instinct was to step back, but that would make her appear weak. She took a step forward. Her hand in her pocket, Tsura unlocked her gun's release. "If I undress, will you tell your wife?"

Her question made Wim lean back, his eyes filling with regret.

"I said, take off your clothes," he ordered again, but this time with uncertainty. Then he pushed the neck of the bottle against her overcoat, attempting to pry open its buttons.

Trying her best to hide her dread, Tsura flashed a hint of a smile and then sighed. "Not tonight."

She was ready to shoot him dead. But she hoped it wouldn't come to that. At least not yet. A dead soldier at Marzahn tonight would spoil any possible attempts to break into the camp at a later date, however far-fetched such a plan might have been. Her fingers around her hidden gun, she used her other hand to shove the bottle away.

"I'll visit again. I enjoyed talking to you," she said.

"I'd like that." Wim appeared to be salivating. He lowered his arm and moved aside to allow her to walk.

Tsura breathed out with relief. She needed more information. "Tell me. What do you do at this base?"

"It's not an army base," Wim admitted. "It's a prisoner camp." His words spilled out like fresh blood.

The other guards were in sight now and Tsura's anxiety surfaced again, this time in her stomach. "What kind of prisoners?"

Wim stopped on the road, sharing his secrets away from the other men. "They keep *Zigeuner* here." He said "they," rather than "we," as if he had nothing to do with it.

"Gypsies? Really?" Tsura asked.

"They say the Gypsies spread disease. I heard they're magicians. They say they kidnap German children."

Tsura kept quiet, allowing him to continue.

"The Gypsies made the nails that held Jesus to the cross. The Jews killed the Son of God. But the *Zigeuner* made it possible. That's what they say."

You don't know me. You don't know my family. She expected to feel a profound hatred for the man. Instead, she pitied his ignorance. "How many prisoners do you have?"

"There's a few hundred left. Most of the men are gone. Mostly women and children now."

A sharp pain pierced her chest. As they walked toward the other guards, Tsura wondered if Mother and Aunt Marie—Kizzy's mother—were still there. Were they even alive? If she were to scream their names, would they hear?

"The women and children—what will you do with them?" she asked. Her pity for Wim transformed again into disgust.

"We're waiting for orders. They'll probably send them East, into Poland, on the trains."

His words hit Tsura hard. She knew what that meant. She'd heard the rumors of killing camps for the Jews. *They're murdering us too?* "Trains? When?"

"No idea. Soon, probably."

At first, his drunken state prevented him from finding his pocket. When his hand emerged from inside his coat, Tsura could see he was clutching a photograph. Wim held it out for her to look.

Tsura took the photograph from him. "This is your family?"

"Yes."

The woman in the center of the black-and-white image had been caught in a laugh, the waves of her hair folding neatly just above her shoulders. Wim, in a jacket and tie and seemingly sober, was seated, his smiling eyes staring at his wife. A little boy with dark limp hair sat on Wim's lap and frowned into the camera's lens. Wim's wife cradled a baby in her arm.

"How old are your children?" Tsura asked.

Wim took back the photograph. "I miss my boys more than I miss my wife. It's an old picture. Peter will be five this summer. Hans is turning three."

As Tsura and Wim approached the other policemen, the men laughed and jeered.

"Did you feel her breasts?" one guard asked.

The guard who'd been asleep was now awake and laughing along with the others.

Tsura's dread intensified as the crowd of guards stared right at her. She feared and despised them all.

"This is my friend, Greta." Wim said. "She visits the graves of dead German soldiers."

Their laughter stopped. Some guards looked down at the ground. That she was relying on Wim to protect her made Tsura feel anxious. Finding the courage to speak, Tsura looked at Wim. "Goodbye, Wilhelm." And she began to walk away.

Wim followed her along the gravel path. "Greta, wait! You're going home now?"

"Yes."

"I want to see you again. I work the night shift. I'm here from seven in the evening until five every morning."

Seven, Tsura repeated to herself. "Always drinking?" she asked.

He shrugged. In another place, Wim would have been a good-looking man with a soft smile and kind, brown eyes. Here, he was someone else. Assuming she was still alive, Tsura's mother was close by, asleep and starving in her frozen Marzahn cabin.

As Tsura walked away, she wanted to scream out to the sky. She implored the clouds to open, for rain or snow to wash her skin.

Seraph and Wolf were in the front seat of the van. Seraph was asleep, her head on Wolf's shoulder as he watched the road. When Wolf saw Tsura, he nudged his girlfriend and she opened her eyes with a jolt. They both seemed relieved Tsura had returned apparently unharmed. Without a word, Tsura climbed into the van, the chalky stench of potatoes filling her throat.

"Are you okay?" Seraph asked, holding out the binoculars.

Wolf scowled at Tsura. "What did you find out?"

"Just drive."

Tsura had information to share. But she couldn't talk. Not yet. As they started their short journey back toward the city, the rocking of the vehicle sent Tsura deep into her thoughts. Her family was dying, Wim had said. Soon to be sent on trains to the East. *The world will be rid of us Roma altogether.* She held her wrist against her stomach and pushed away a painful memory, but the stifled thought forced its way to the surface of Tsura's conscious. The regime had tried other methods to quell the Romani population: before deportation, internment; before internment, forced sterilization. Tsura would never be able to have children. The Nazis had made sure of that. In her mind, she walked to Mother, asleep on her bunk. *I've come for you. For our people. I'd have children, if I could. I'd teach them the Romani ways.* The future of her family depended on Marko and Kizzy. The idea strengthened her. If she couldn't give Mother grandchildren, the very least she could do was to fight for their freedom, fight to help her brother and to protect her little cousin.

Tsura fell asleep within minutes and the half-hour journey was over in what felt like moments.

"Tsura." Wolf shook her awake and tapped her face.

Tsura struggled to open her eyes. Something was wrong. "What is it?"

Seraph was panicked. She gripped the steering wheel with both hands. "We had to take a detour," she muttered. The van was parked on an empty side street. The dark windows of the brick buildings around them stared into the night. "We're lost!"

"Roadblocks," Wolf said, clearly more calm than Seraph. "Gestapo, everywhere."

Tsura was shaken by Wolf's words. "You didn't wake me?" The distant rumbling of engines and wheels on the street forced them into silence.

"Get out," Wolf said.

Seraph threw open the van door and the three of them jumped down. The freezing air and the prospect of an impending chase woke Tsura fully. Seraph ran and crouched behind a wall. Wolf grabbed Tsura's arm to follow. From where they were hiding, the sound of vehicles grew louder and what looked like a furniture truck turned the corner onto the road. The truck stopped and two Nazi soldiers climbed out. Tsura, Wolf, and a frightened Seraph kept their heads behind the wall, out of sight.

"The engine's hot," said one of the soldiers, inspecting the van.

Tsura reached into her coat for her handgun, but Wolf grabbed her forearm and shook his head. There were more sounds of wheels on gravel and three more trucks arrived. Seraph led Tsura and Wolf away from the street and they disappeared into the shadows.

"We didn't get our potatoes," Seraph whined as they scurried away.

Both Wolf and Tsura laughed. Seraph's out-of-place complaint was calming. Checking her surroundings, Tsura had an idea of where in the city they were. Soon, it would be daylight. She needed to return to Duerr's home to collect Alex's photographs. Tsura led them along the side of a grocery store, away from the main streets.

"I'll see you at the apartment in a couple of hours," she told Wolf. "You'll have the documents, right?"

"Not a chance," Wolf said.

Tsura knew he was right. Obtaining false papers tonight would be impossible now. They had to keep out of sight—for a few days, at least. Marko wouldn't be happy. He would need to leave Berlin alone, without Alex. There was no other way.

"I have to return to Marzahn," Tsura announced.

Wolf slammed his boot against the brick wall. "Stop this, Tsura. Tonight, you went too far. You nearly got yourself killed."

Tsura clenched her fists. "They're putting them on trains. Any day now. That's what the Nazi told me. Trains to Poland, Wolf. Understand?"

She watched Wolf swallow hard and become silent.

"I have to go back there."

"You've got some kind of plan?" Seraph asked her.

Tsura nodded and folded her arms. "There are fewer guards during the week. Just five or six. I have to go back. We'll go over everything first. Wolf, please, if it were—"

"Monday night," Wolf blurted out.

Tsura paused with surprise. "This Monday?"

Wolf nodded.

Knowing he wasn't happy, Tsura suppressed a smile. "Monday. After sundown. I'll see you at the apartment and we'll talk it through."

Seraph took Wolf by the arm, leading him away.

Alone, fading in and out of Berlin's streets, Tsura could hear rumbling trucks in the distance. In her head, she could still hear Wim's slurred words. It was now close to five a.m. A new wave of Nazi round-ups had begun.

Alexander

Stretched across two mattresses pushed together against the wall, Alex rested his head on Marko's shoulder. They hadn't slept at all. The soldier had seen them kissing, but they'd managed to lose him.

Alex shook his head. "How could we have been so stupid?"

Thankfully, Marko had figured out where they were and led them to their hiding place, an abandoned basement Marko had discovered months ago, close to Motzstrasse, south of the Tiergarten. Even though they'd been coming here since early autumn, Alex still found this part of the city confusing. He wondered if professional cartographers needed to recall every aspect of the terrains they drew. *Maybe I'll create puzzles for a living.*

"One day, I'll write all this down," Alex said.

Marko kissed Alex's forehead. "Even that?"

Especially that.

Marko had found the old mattresses, too. They were certain the building had been an old bar or restaurant. And this had been a wine cellar. This was their first time here at night. In the near darkness, the shadows of the empty wine barrels stacked along the back wall made repeated sharp patterns on the plaster. Through the rusting barred window close to the low ceiling, they could see the street. Buildings and leafless trees stood silent against Berlin's night sky.

Marko laughed, his fingers on Alex's coat buttons. "Broden. This coat! You—"

"Leave me alone," Alex said, knowing Marko was teasing.

When Father had given Alex his expensive overcoat, Alex had felt like Joseph, the youngest and favorite son of Jacob the Jewish patriarch. When Alex had realized he'd forgotten his photographs in his other coat's pocket, he felt as though he'd betrayed his family.

Marko drummed his knuckles on the cellar's cold wall. Pieces of plaster cracked and fell to the damp floor. Then he took out the soldier's medal from his pocket. Marko sat up and scraped the medal's edge against the cracking plaster. Alex squinted through the darkness at Marko's carvings on the wall, the letters "M" and "A."

"If we get separated, we meet here," Marko said.

The idea of being separated from Marko filled Alex's gut with dread. "But that won't—" Marko kissed his mouth. Alex pulled away to continue. "After we leave Berlin, if we lose each other, find the Broden family in London. Find any synagogue and they'll help you. Tell my family you know my father. Give them his name and tell them you know me."

"That I'm your boyfriend?" Marko said.

"Don't joke."

Lea Federman would have been shocked if she knew about Alex and Marko. Their colleagues in the brewery office made jokes about Lea and Alex marrying one day. If Alex were different, if he had any interest in women, Lea would have been his girlfriend and eventually his wife. Here with Marko, the idea was ridiculous. *Marko is my future.*

"In London, where're we gonna live?" Marko asked.

"With my cousins. Or our own place."

"I can't speak English."

"Neither can I," Alex said. They lay staring at the basement ceiling. "But we'll study. And learn professions."

Marko smiled his broad, scruffy smile. "Study?" A smudge of dirt sat across his forehead. His black hair smelled of cigarettes and fell perfectly over his ears.

Alex imagined himself older. "Fine. I'll make maps. You'll stay at home."

"Doing what all day?"

Marko lifted himself up with one arm and leaned over to kiss Alex along his jawline. His shirt collar was open and Alex could make out the graze above his collarbone. Alex pressed his knuckles against the scrape on Marko's neck and kissed him back. Even though the concrete floor was damp, even though the wine cellar in the darkness resembled a prison cell, Alex wished he and Marko could stay there like that until they were old and frail and forgetful.

"I liked the prayer your father did," Marko said.

Alex let out a chuckle combined with a yawn. "That Hebrew blessing? We don't usually do that. He's not religious."

He rested his head on Alex's arm. "My family too." Marko's voice became distant. "I kind of remember, years ago, whenever we had visitors, my parents and all the adults sang songs in some strange language. They only did all that when their old Romani friends were visiting. People are funny."

Alex let out a sound of agreement. He was drifting off to sleep.

"Your father's name is Sam, right?" Marko asked.

"Yes. Samuel."

"My cousin—Kizzy's little brother—" Marko spoke with hesitation. "He had that name, too."

Alex opened his eyes. "He died?" Marko rarely talked about his family.

Marko nodded, puffed out his cheeks, and let out a heavy sigh. "Look at this," he said, sounding upbeat now. Marko pulled up his shirtsleeve to show off a watch. Its leather strap was black, maybe dark-brown, its round face white with a silver frame.

"I love it," Marko said.

"Where did you get it?"

Marko grinned and gestured to his bag on the floor. "I found it."

Alex sat up, his eyes narrowing. He remembered Tsura's accusation that Marko had stolen the bag.

"I'm not a thief, Broden! God! Just because I'm a Gypsy—"

"No! Marko, I'm sorry— I wasn't suggesting—"

But Marko was smirking and he planted a kiss on Alex's mouth. "We'll sell it all. But not the watch."

Alex nodded at Marko's idea. They needed the money for their journey. Side by side, Marko pulled Alex toward him. "We won't get separated," Marko said.

Alex remembered the contingency around his neck. "Look at this." He reached under his shirt collar for his new chain and cross.

"What the hell, Broden!" Marko held the cross between his finger and thumb.

"It was my step-grandfather's. It was Ruti's idea."

"She's nice, your sister," Marko said.

"I feel bad for missing her birthday," Alex said. He imagined Ruti at home crying over his disappearance. "But I got her a great gift."

"Those puzzles?" Marko asked.

Alex had told him about the treasure hunt. If Marko hadn't sent him to that antique dealer for the photographs, Alex would never have found Ruti's prize.

"I found it in that shop. It's a tiny train engine, plus five carriages. All made of porcelain. It's beautiful."

"My folks had an ornament like that," Marko said. Then he placed his hand on Alex's wrist and traced inside Alex's coat sleeve and along Alex's forearm. "Are you cold?"

Alex shook his head. With Marko, he didn't feel cold at all.

"Franziska and Ruti will be good friends," Alex said. He felt glad they'd figured out a solution for Kizzy. Kizzy would become part of his family.

"I hope she got home okay," Marko said.

The rumble of a vehicle on the street made Marko leap up toward the window. Alex jumped to his feet too and stood behind him, his chest against Marko's back, feeling protected. From basement level, they could see the lower part of what looked like two trucks, and the boots and legs of a small group of Nazi soldiers, maybe half a dozen. An uncomfortable swelling of heat rushed through Alex's veins and through his neck and face. *Round-ups. Tsura was right.* Alex had to get home. He had to get the photographs and warn Father. They'd bring Father to the wine cellar. He'd go into hiding. Or maybe he'd leave Berlin, too, somehow. Marko's sister would help. Alex slipped the cross back into his shirt.

Marko's head jolted. "Look."

Alex stepped forward, his shoulder to Marko's shoulder. Through the barred window, the soldiers were now out of sight. Then a crash of glass. Broken windows across the street. They couldn't see around the trucks. For a moment, the street was silent. Then distant screams. The soldiers were shouting at each other, then shouting at someone else. More feet, more legs, more boots, moving quickly. *Civilians.*

"Jews?" Alex whispered.

Marko placed his hand on Alex's back. "Probably."

The shouts grew louder. The feet approached their hiding place. Alex stepped back into the darkness, suddenly terrified they'd be found, his hand on Marko's neck to pull him away from the window. Marko held onto Alex's hand and joined him in the shadows. They could still see the people on the street. One man's legs in his pajamas, a woman in her nightgown, more shouting. The guards guided the civilians—Alex counted five of them—onto one of the trucks. The soldiers climbed up and they drove away.

Marko turned, his dark eyes studying his wristwatch. "We've gotta go." Alex's wrist in his rough hand, Marko led him to the door.

But Alex's gut told him to stay away from his family's house. *Maybe we should run, forget the photographs.* Then he thought about his parents and Ruti. He had one more chance to see them. To warn Father. Marko pulled up his collar, pushing the thin fabric against his grazed neck. Still hidden, Alex leaned in and kissed Marko's chapped lips. Marko returned the kiss, his short beard rough against Alex's shaven face.

The street was clear. When Marko opened the door, the icy air hit them. Alex understood the risk Marko was taking for him. *I'd do the same in return.* Slowly, over these months, Marko had become all Alex could think about. Alex loved Ruti and his parents with all his heart, but Marko was different. This was new. He wanted Marko. Alex didn't need anything else.

The raids had begun before sunrise. The whole city was asleep, which Alex was sure was no coincidence on the part of the authorities. Bags in hand, glancing across the street, he and Marko could see that the doors of the apartment building opposite were wide open. Whoever had been taken—Jews, Communists, pacifists—they were now on their way to one of the many Nazi labor camps. Or worse, if the rumors were true.

As the young men walked east toward Alex's home, they kept on the side streets as much as possible, Marko in front. Each time they heard vehicles on the road, they stepped into a doorway, out of sight. They climbed over hedges, through back gardens and walled alleyways. Every step, Alex expected to be seen, anticipating another truck, another Nazi soldier around each corner.

They stood on the western edge of the Friedrichshain neighborhood. Alex's street was two minutes away. They needed to meet Tsura by seven in the Moabit neighborhood and Alex worried it would now take longer to get there with the Gestapo swarming the streets. "We don't have much time."

"We're fine," Marko replied.

"Wait here."

"I'll come with you."

"No. Stay behind the houses. Outside is safer."

Marko nodded. "Be quick."

They dared not kiss—not again, not out in the open.

Alex held out his suitcase. "Take this." As Marko grabbed Alex's case, their fingers touched. Marko's hands were so cold.

"Here," Alex said and took off his father's coat.

"I'm fine."

"Marko, you're freezing."

"Paul," Marko said with a wink. Quickly, they exchanged coats. Marko shivered and fastened the fancy buttons. The dark, rich fabric of the coat made Marko look less disheveled. The collar sat high, covering the scratch on his neck.

"Paul never suited you."

Marko laughed, eyes shining. "You look good in my clothes, Broden."

Alex grinned. "Marko Lange." Wearing Marko's shabby coat felt good. "They did this in ancient times."

"Did what?"

"Exchanged cloaks."

Marko looked at him, puzzled.

"It's a great story," Alex called out as he walked away.

In Marko's thin coat, even the two-minute walk to his house became difficult. Instinctively, he checked the coat's inside and outside pockets. They were all empty and the coat's lining was thin and torn. Alex wondered how Marko could tolerate the cold. Alex added a step to his plan. Not only would he fetch his photographs, but he'd switch Marko's coat for another.

The silence of the early morning was broken by sounds of more trucks in the distance. As much as Alex wanted to sit and talk with his parents and Ruti, he wouldn't be able to stay for long. He tapped on the windowpane and heard someone coming to the door.

"Mama—"

"Are you okay?" Mother threw herself at him, her arms open.

"Wake Papa. Quickly."

"He's at work. He left a while ago."

Oh God. "Already? My coat—I—"

Mother was smiling. In her long nightgown, she closed the door, stepped over to the hallway telephone table, and picked up his two photographs. "Look what I found."

A breath of air tumbled from Alex's throat. "Thank you!"

She smiled at him and touched his face.

Alex held the small photographs in his hand. "I need to go. But we need to warn Papa."

Her smile broke. "Why?"

Alex tried to sound calm, for her sake. "Round-ups. We have to let him know. There's somewhere he can hide."

"You go. I'll call your father at the factory." Taking Alex's wrists, she kissed his hands and held him again. "Go safely."

As she picked up the telephone receiver to call Alex's father at work, she didn't notice a piece of paper falling to the floor. It was one of Ruti's birthday treasure hunt clues, with one of Alex's key words written across the front. Alex picked it up and slipped it inside mother's telephone number book, making sure the note was visible. He discarded the idea of heading upstairs to wake Ruti on her birthday and wish her a final farewell.

Looking around, Alex spotted his coat—the one in which he'd left his photographs—folded over a chair in the dining room. But fists on the front door startled him. He spun to face Mama. She dropped the phone receiver and, saying nothing, pointed for Alex to run upstairs. His heart in his throat, Alex ran, treading as lightly as he could. Two, three stairs at a time. Behind him, the door rattled again.

"Just a second!" Mother called out, her voice calm and slow.

By the time Alex reached the upstairs landing, strange voices were filling the downstairs hallway. "Turn on the lights," a man's voice demanded. "Where is Samuel Broden?"

They're looking for Papa. Alex rushed into Ruti's room, making no sound, closing her door behind him, the photographs in his hand. *I shouldn't be here. God, Marko's outside.*

"Ruti," he said in a panicked whisper.

Ruti looked up at him, bleary eyed. "Alexander! What's—"

He held his finger to his lips. "Pretend to sleep."

The loud voices were on the staircase now.

With her hand, Ruti covered her mouth. As she threw the blankets over herself, Alex dropped to the floor and crawled under his sister's bed, Marko's coat on his back.

Ruth

This is a rehearsal, Ruth told herself, but she knew it wasn't. She'd been half-awake for a few minutes, listening to Mama talking to someone downstairs. It had sounded like Alexander, but Ruth had thought her mind was playing tricks. She'd been imagining all sorts of things. Alexander was returning as a birthday surprise, she'd told herself. Or he was no longer leaving Berlin. But when she saw

Alexander's panicked eyes, Ruth knew something awful was happening.

Her eyes were closed tight, heart thumping.

She heard her door open. "You, girl. Get downstairs!" a man shouted at her from the doorway.

She pretended to wake with a jolt. She didn't need to pretend to be terrified. As she followed the soldier's orders, she purposely let the blanket hang over the side of the mattress so it touched the carpet and covered the gap between the floor and her bed. Barefoot in front of the Nazi soldiers, Ruth realized she'd left her glasses on her nightstand. At that same moment, she heard the lightest rustle of bedsheets behind her.

"I can't see. I need my glasses. Okay? I'll be just one second, okay? I'm really sorry." Ruth rambled and spoke loudly to hide the sounds Alexander was making.

"Be quick!" one of the soldiers yelled.

Ruth returned into the darkness, to her nightstand. As she put on her glasses, she almost gasped to see the edge of her bedsheet hanging from the wardrobe's top shelf. Alexander had climbed inside, just as he'd practiced. She took her dressing gown from the hook on her wardrobe and nudged its door closed, the bedsheet now out of sight.

Walking out of her room, Ruth trembled. *Alexander shouldn't be here. Why did he come back?* More Nazi officers were at the bottom of the staircase. Mama stood next to them and Ruth ran down the stairs and into her arms.

Mama combed Ruth's hair with her fingertips. "It'll be okay," Mama whispered. With Alexander hiding in her bedroom, Ruth didn't believe her for a second.

One officer held a pile of papers—a list. "Where is Samuel Broden?" His voice boomed, loud and scratchy.

Mama began to speak. "He was—"

"I was talking to the girl," the Nazi snapped. He glared at Ruth. "Where is your stepfather?"

Ruth shivered and shook her head. If Papa wasn't at home, he must have already left for the factory. Unless he was hiding, too. "Maybe at work?" Ruth blurted out.

"And where is Alexander Broden? He's your stepbrother, correct?"

Ruth couldn't catch her breath.

"Oh, don't be shy," the Nazi said in a sinister tone.

"Yes, he's my brother."

Her parents had said this might happen one day. They would round up the last of the Jews and few Germans would object. When she turned to look at Mama, the officer grabbed Ruth's face, forcing her to stare forward. His hand was hot. His palms and face were covered in sweat. *Only an overfed Nazi pig would be sweating in February.* Ruth prayed she wouldn't give anything away. She hoped her answer wouldn't contradict what Mama had already told them.

"Where is Alexander Broden?"

At first, she struggled to speak. "At work, too, maybe?"

"Why are you unsure?" the pig asked.

"Because I just woke up," Ruth snapped, surprising herself with her confidence.

A yelp from upstairs made Ruth jump. *Alexander!* Boots appeared at the top of the staircase. When she saw her brother— behind a soldier and in front of another—she let out a shriek and Mama dug her nails into Ruth's arm. *They found him.*

"Dear God!" Mama shouted.

Alexander looked at his sister and mother as the Gestapo officers marched him down.

"Hiding in the girl's room," one of the soldiers reported to the officer in charge.

"This is your brother?" the pig asked.

Alexander stood at the foot of the stairs. "No. Voeske. I'm Paul Voeske," he lied.

Ruth gulped a mouthful of air.

Before the Nazi could respond, Mama stepped away from Ruth. "Under this roof?" she shouted at her daughter. Mama's arms were flying. At first, Ruth didn't understand. "Never in my life. Never! Ruth Broden, you should be ashamed of yourself." Mama seemed genuinely angry. She turned to Alexander. "You too, Paul! Never in my life. Just wait until your parents hear about this. I swear, Paul Voeske. You will never, ever set foot in my house again!"

"Mama, I'm sorry," Ruth said, playing along.

"What is all this?" the fat pig demanded.

"He's—" Ruth purposely hesitated and pretended to be embarrassed. "He's my boyfriend."

With a look of disgust, Mama began to shout again. "What will everyone say? I am so ashamed!" She looked at the fat Nazi officer. "What would you do if your daughter had boys creeping around your home in the middle of the night? Sharing a bed. Doing God knows what!" She looked at Ruth again. "I don't know what else to say. I should throttle you."

The Nazi was staring at Mama. "If my daughter behaved like a prostitute, I'd teach her a lesson and beat the life out of the boy." The fat officer stepped toward Ruth's brother. "Trousers down," he yelled at Alexander.

Alexander looked startled.

"Do it!" the Nazi said.

As Alexander unbuckled his belt, Ruth looked away. Mama averted her eyes, too. Ruth knew what they were doing. They were checking to see if Alexander was a Jew, to see if he was circumcised. They did that sometimes, Papa once said. Now Ruth knew he hadn't been joking.

Alexander yelped. He was doubled-over, his trousers and underwear around his knees, his shirt hanging over his naked thighs. Ruth looked away again. Her brother was coughing and moaning in pain.

The Nazi pig stepped toward Mama. He raised his arm toward Ruth. His hand missed her face and his palm landed hard on Mama's head. He pulled hard at her hair. "Liars are worse than whores," he said.

"Don't touch her!" Ruth screamed, throwing her arms around Mama's neck and pushing the Nazi away.

Ruth looked back at Alexander. He was holding his trousers up and staring at the floor.

Mama shouted again. "I'm a German mother, and this my son! As Christians, you should be ashamed. My husband and I worked for the old government. My father fought in the Great War. They were patriots. I have true German blood!"

With a sneer on his sweating face, the pig nodded to an officer to march Alexander outside. His hands behind his back, Alexander's shirt was a mess, his belt undone. His face and eyes were red.

"Everything will be okay," Mama said to Alexander, her voice resolute. Then she turned to the Nazi, her voice softened now. "Please. You don't have to do this."

Tears were stuck in Ruth's throat and a tingling moved across her skin, as if she were floating above the hallway floor.

"I'll be fine," Alexander said with a tone of defeat.

Two officers dragged Alexander toward what looked like a removal truck.

"Samuel Broden," the fat pig said. "Search every room. If the boy was hiding, then his Jew father is hiding, too."

The officers climbed the staircase.

"Mama!"

"Your Papa's at the factory," Mama whispered, dousing Ruth's worst fears.

She and her mother listened and flinched as the soldiers overturned furniture. Cupboards emptied. Crashing and more crashing.

Both in their nightgowns and robes, both in bare feet, Mama led Ruth into the dining room and they sat at the table, saying nothing, holding each other's arms. Despite her composure, Mama was trembling.

"Ruti, don't let them see you're frightened. They want to see us terrified."

The soldiers returned from upstairs. When the Gestapo pig walked into the dining room and dropped Alexander's torn-off yellow star on the table in front of them, Ruth felt sick.

"We'll find every Jew in the end."

Ruth felt faint as Mama stood, her head held up, looking at him in the eyes. She grabbed Ruth's arm, pulling her up to stand, too. Inside, Ruth was shaking.

"You should be fearful of what the Lord has in store for you," Mama said.

With both hands, the pig grabbed Mama's chest. Ruth looked away.

"A good German woman shouldn't be sharing a bed with a Jew. Or raising a Jewish child."

Ruth wanted to scream. She wanted to scratch his eyes out.

"I could teach you the proper ways of the Fatherland." Then he looked down at her daughter and reached toward Ruth.

"Don't touch me!" Ruth said and her spit landed on the collar of his uniform.

The man laughed and pulled his arm away. Then he left and walked out into the street without closing the front door.

They listened to the truck drive away. The Nazis were gone. Alexander with them.

Ruth felt a surge of defiance. Standing up from the table and confronting the Gestapo pig had given her a rush of boldness. "We have to call the factory and warn Papa."

Mama ran to the telephone.

The house was wrecked, furniture pulled away from the walls, cupboards opened, a chair overturned, smashed ornaments. The cold wind blew in from the street.

"Nobody's answering," Mama said, putting down the telephone. She closed the front door and tried calling again.

Ruth walked over to pick up some books from the floor. In the doorway between the hallway and the living room, she found Mama's telephone number book. As she was about to return it to the entry table, she noticed a piece of paper hanging out from its pages.

Ruth's heart leapt and she wanted to burst into tears. She pulled out the notepaper to read "Ruti" and the word "*Telefon.*"

Her head was spinning. Her brother had been arrested. Ruth remembered the third clue she'd found the night before—to find a woman's birthplace. But this clue, hidden inside Mama's telephone number book, was from another part of the treasure hunt.

In a daze, Ruth found herself opening the paper to reveal Alexander's riddle inside.

Hidden in rose petals
With white piping
A pickpocket in reverse

She folded the note closed.

Then she saw the broken pieces of a glass ashtray around her bare feet. She stood still, staring down, wondering if she'd cut herself. "Mama!" Ruth wanted to run to her, to hold her, but tiny shards of glass surrounded them.

"Ruti, don't move. I'll get the broom."

"Why did Alexander come back?" Ruth asked.

"Your brother forgot his photographs," Mama explained as she swept the shards of glass away from Ruth's feet. She stopped sweeping and put her hand to her mouth. "I don't know what to do."

They'd rehearsed many times for the round-ups, but never for an arrest.

Still clutching Alexander's treasure hunt note and Mama's book of telephone numbers, Ruth held out the book and a plan of action fell from her mouth. "Here. Call Papa's friends. His coworkers, from the factory. Call their families. Maybe someone will know what's going on."

Mama grabbed Ruth's face and kissed her between the eyes. "You're an angel. Everything will be okay. You'll see." Mama sounded sure.

But Ruth found her mother's promise difficult to believe. They'd lost too many people over the years. Papa's parents, his friends, her aunts and uncles, and Viktor, Elise's brother.

Mama opened her telephone book and dialed a number. "It's me, Annett... Yes, I know. I'm sorry... Listen, my son was just arrested... Yes, Alexander... I know... Yes, I think they're going from house to house... Thank you... Have you heard from your family?... No, no... Yes, do that... Okay, call your sister and call me back if her husband was taken, too... Okay. Bye... Yes, yes. Bye."

Then she made another call. And another. Calling her friends. Telling them to call others. She explained everything all over again.

In between conversations, she gave Ruth a commentary on what she was finding out. So-and-so's husband wasn't at work, but the Gestapo came to their home. So-and-so's wife couldn't stop crying. One family was fine but was in search of a place to hide. So-and-so's husband was missing. Someone's husband had been arrested on the street. Another Christian woman's Jewish children had been taken.

When Mama put down the telephone, her hands were in fists.

"We should eat something," Ruth said, even though she wasn't hungry.

Ruth's mother led the way toward the kitchen.

"Mama, where were you born?" Ruth blurted out, wondering if the answer would help her solve one of Alexander's riddle.

Mama turned to her daughter, her eyebrows furrowed. "Hamburg. You know that. Why?"

"Never mind," Ruth said and burst into tears.

Standing by the staircase with their arms around one other, Ruth sobbed as she pictured Alexander on the Nazi truck, all alone. It was February the twenty-seventh, 1943. Ruth would remember her fifteenth birthday forever.

"For the rest of my life, my birthday will be the anniversary for all this."

Mama took in a deep breath. "Oh, my darling." She paused then spoke again. "You know, Ruti, in wartime, everyone's birthday turns into a commemoration of something so sad."

Elise

Unsure if it was midday or the dead of night, Elise stared up at thousands of fighter jets that swarmed the sky, weaving in and out of black clouds. She and Viktor stood in the middle of the city. Painted boxes and wooden crates fell and crashed around them. As one box hit the street, it spilled building blocks and dolls across the cobblestones. Soon the road was littered with toy bears and paper planes. Elise was horrified Viktor would be seen.

"Get inside," she told him.

Her brother protested.

"They'll find you. You'll be safe inside."

Her brother climbed into the painted toy box.

"Don't make a sound," she said.

"Elise."

"I told you to be quiet."

Viktor sat inside the crate, his knees at his chest, staring up at his sister. His cloudy blue eyes reflected the flocks of aircraft above their heads.

"Elise! Elise Edelhoff!" Viktor shouted now.

Elise held the crate's lid in the air and brought it down toward his fair head.

She opened her eyes with a jolt.

Mother stood over her, yelling her name. A dim orange glow through the branches of a tree outside made patterns on Elise's bedcovers and across the scratches on her forearm. Elise quickly slipped her arm under the sheets.

"Elise, time to make breakfast," Mother said and shuffled out of the room.

Elise climbed out of bed. Exhausted, she put on her long stockings, winter skirt, blouse, and sweater.

Downstairs, mother sat at the kitchen table in silence. Elise cooked up some pancakes with jam and sugar.

"Too sweet for me," her mother complained.

In Elise's head, Viktor sat at the kitchen table, singing to himself as he once had.

It had been over three years since Viktor had died. The news had come suddenly. There had been an outbreak of typhus at the hospital, the official report had said. Many weeks later, Father found out the truth.

For the first few months, her mother's depression was to be expected, everyone said. Having a child die was the hardest thing a parent could face. Elise's father would pick her up from school and they'd come home to find her mother collapsed on the bathroom floor, crying and shrieking. She'd scream at nighttime, too. Once, one of their neighbors complained that her mother's screaming was keeping her family awake. Father told the woman to mind her own business, as if her children's crying didn't disturb them every night, he'd snapped. After that, their awful neighbor never talked to Elise's family.

Mother didn't get any better. She refused to leave the house. She didn't clean. She didn't cook. Father and Elise took care of the housework. They'd buy food and cook it together, trying different recipes, different ways of cooking the same ingredients. On the weekends, when her mother slept for most of the day, Father would tell Elise stories from when he was a boy, and they'd play board games. When her mother woke up, Elise went to her bedroom while her parents argued. Father screamed at her mother. She needed to pull herself together. She had a home to keep. A daughter to raise, he would shout. Elise's mother didn't argue back, which made her father angrier.

Last year, when Father was called up to fight in the war, Elise had told him she couldn't care for her mother on her own. He was sorry, he'd said, but on the day he left, he'd seemed relieved to be leaving. When he'd hugged his wife goodbye, he'd said nothing.

Elise forced down a few bites of the sweetened pancakes. "I'm going out," she announced.

Mother didn't bother asking where.

Elise left her pink coat on its hook. She put on her warm Girl's League jacket and her heavier, uglier coat over the top.

Outside, the brisk morning was bright. At a fast pace, the walk to Ruth's home took just under twenty minutes.

Ruth opened the front door, wearing her robe over her nightdress.

"Happy birthday!"

Ruth didn't smile back. Behind her glasses, her eyes were puffy. Her cheeks were blotchy and red.

"It's my brother," Ruth said.

"Alex?" Elise's mind jumped to last night—how she'd spied on Alex kissing his girlfriend.

Ruth had been crying. "It's so terrible."

Elise wanted to tell Ruth what she saw, but Ruth's serious tone and bloodshot eyes kept Elise from chattering. Elise stepped inside Ruth's house and closed the door.

Mrs. Broden was standing in the hallway, also in her dressing gown, talking on the telephone. She nodded at Elise, but didn't smile.

"What's wrong?"

"They took him," Ruth said.

"What?"

"The Gestapo. Alexander's gone. He was supposed to be leaving Berlin. But he came back. And they found him."

Elise was confused. Alexander had already left. She'd seen his goodbye letter. She'd seen him behind her house. Elise could only think about Viktor. *What happened to me will happen to Ruth.*

"Papa's at work. Mama's been calling around to find out information," Ruth explained.

Mrs. Broden glanced at them, her hair pinned back, making her colorless face look stern. Ruth sat on the bottom stair. Thumbing the pages of her small address book, Mrs. Broden made another call. Ruth's hands were shaking, touching her face. Elise wanted to ask her if she was okay, but that was a useless question.

When Mrs. Broden let out a small gasp, Ruth jumped to her feet. "Mama, what is it?"

Mrs. Broden looked at her daughter, her hand covering her mouth, and she spoke into the telephone. "I'm coming over right now."

"What's happened?" Ruth was on the verge of tears.

"Goodbye." Mrs. Broden put down the phone. "The Gestapo raided the factory."

Elise watched Ruth's reaction.

"They took Papa?" Ruth cried out.

"All the Jewish workers were taken away," Mrs. Broden explained. She began thinking aloud, calmly. "There must've been something like thirty or forty Jews at the factory. Maybe more."

Elise stayed quiet, observing. Ruth's mother was a strong woman. Not like Elise's mother, at home doing nothing. The women had been friends once. Not best friends like Ruth and Elise, but they'd been close.

Mrs. Broden made another call. "It's me again... The factory was raided... Yes... You heard? Tell me..."

Ruth started to sob.

As Mrs. Broden listened and nodded to new information, she reached out for Ruth's hand. Then Mrs. Broden ended the call. "I'm heading out. To East Friedrichshain." The neighborhood was a fifteen-minute walk away.

"We're coming with you," Ruth said.

Mrs. Broden shook her head. "You're staying here."

"Please, Mama. They can't do anything to us. We're not Jewish."

Viktor wasn't Jewish, Elise wanted to interject. The government could do anything it wanted, just as it was responsible for Viktor's death.

Mrs. Broden got dressed. She dropped her telephone book into her handbag and opened the front door. Ruth and Elise stood in the doorway.

"When will you be back?" Ruth asked.

"I don't know. Before dark, I promise." She kissed her daughter on the forehead. "Now get inside. Stay warm." The door clicked closed.

With streaming eyes, Ruth took a seat on the bottom step of the staircase.

"Stop crying," Elise said.

Ruth glared at Elise as if she were being insensitive, as if Elise didn't understand. But Elise kept her mouth shut. She refused to tell Ruth she'd be okay because, if this were anything like what happened to little Viktor, nothing would ever be okay for Ruth again.

Marko

From the shadows, Marko had heard the truck approach Alex's street. He'd wanted to stay, to somehow warn Alex, but every part of him had known to run.

With his bag and Alex's conspicuous suitcase, he needed to stay out of sight. The U-Bahn trains would be too dangerous, so he lugged the suitcase and bag and walked fast across the city, east to northwest. His throat and lungs stung from the cold air. Marko needed to find Tsura. His sister always knew what to do. He didn't stop until he arrived at Duerr's place. The lights were off. The sun was almost up. In the kitchen, dirty pots and plates were stacked on the counter. He swigged the orange juice he'd left there yesterday.

No sign of Tsura. Marko threw his cap and coat on the armchair and walked quietly upstairs, not wanting to wake Kizzy. Tiredness hit him. In the bathroom, he took off his shirt and stared in the mirror at the start of a beard. Above his waist, he wore only his new watch. His body looked healthy, but his face looked like hell. He turned on the tap and held his head under the ice-cold water, spraying the mirror. He grabbed some soap and washed his neck, chest, and under his arms. Soaked.

A noise downstairs made him hold his breath. *My knife. Damn it.* It was in his coat, on the armchair in the living room. Footsteps on the staircase. He needed to hide.

"Kizz? Marko?" It was Tsura's voice.

Marko let out a breath of relief. "Up here."

His sister, in her overcoat and cap, reached the landing. She frowned, looking at him without his shirt. "You're not eating enough."

"It's Alex—" Marko said.

But Tsura wasn't listening. "Is Kizzy all packed?"

"She's still sleeping," Marko said.

"Listen, Marko, I'm sorry, but I don't have the papers for your friend. You and Kizzy will need to—" Tsura stopped talking.

Marko joined his sister in the doorway of Kizzy's bedroom. Kizzy's bed was made. Then he knew. *I told her to come right back.* He'd left Kizzy with Duerr out on the street, but she hadn't come home. *Something went wrong.* He didn't bother drying himself. He ran into Kizzy's room and jumped down to the floor to check under the bedframe. Cold water dripped from his head. He opened her cupboard. Maybe she was hiding. "Kizzy!"

"Kizzy!" Tsura screamed out. "Where did she go?" she shouted at Marko.

Tsura checked Duerr's room while Marko checked his bedroom, pulling his bedframe away from the wall.

"Kizzy! It's us!"

They checked inside and behind every wardrobe.

"She's not up here."

They ran downstairs. "Marko, when did you last see her?"

I left her on the street was the truth, but Marko couldn't tell his sister that. Marko's head was pounding. He'd sent her to the hospital. "I don't know. I got home just now. I saw her last night, when you were here."

"You just got home?"

"I was with Broden. We got chased. He made it home and I waited outside, but I heard the trucks and I ran straight here. I think

Broden was arrested." Marko still couldn't be sure what had happened to Alex. He hoped to hell the trucks weren't for him. And now Kizzy was missing. *She never came home.* He'd sent her with Duerr, alone, and his gut began to ache with the realization of what he'd done.

"Kizzy!"

Room to room, Tsura checked where Marko checked. And Marko checked where Tsura checked. Marko looked in the kitchen cabinets Kizzy could have fitted into. He pushed the sideboard from the wall. Duerr's china plates crashed inside.

Tsura returned to the upper floor and Marko followed. She stood at Kizzy's dresser, rummaging through Kizzy's belongings.

"What're you doing?"

"Maybe she left. I'm checking her clothes."

Kizzy was arrested on the street. He wanted to admit his terrible mistake.

"Everything's here. But her coat and hat are gone."

Marko wanted to vomit. Cold sweat ran down his exposed back.

"Where would she have gone?"

"I don't know!" Marko lied. "The hospital? She told me she wanted to see Duerr."

"And you let her?" Tsura shouted.

"Of course not! I told her to stay here. I left her at home, and I said I was heading to Charité and I'd be back. But you know Kizzy. She never listens!"

"What else?"

Tsura was buying his false logic. He pretended to think things through. He knew something went wrong on the street. Or maybe Kizzy had reached Charité Hospital and something had happened there. "Nothing else."

"Marko, get dressed."

He grabbed a thick sweater and fresh shirt. Alex should have been there. They should have been preparing to leave the city. "Sis, what about Broden? We've gotta do something. He was—"

"Forget him. I couldn't get him papers. They're rounding up the last of the Jews. And they're deporting us Romani next. I went to Marzahn last night. And I'm going back. But first we're finding Kizzy."

Tsura was talking, but Marko wasn't listening. His head was stuck on Alex. "We've gotta help him. Maybe he's hiding somewhere. Or if he was arrested, we'll get him out."

"What're you talking about?" Tsura shouted.

"You don't understand. I told Broden—"

"No! We have to find Kizzy. She's our cousin. She's a child!" Tsura was screaming now.

His sister's eyes looked panicked, but only for a second. "Get your coat, Marko."

Tsura turned up her collar and Marko followed her outside. He could hear Tsura's voice, but not her words. The street and the buildings and the sky were blurry and Marko's head jumped back and forth between the idea of finding Alex and the image of Kizzy pushing the wheelchair.

Kizzy

As soon as she heard a key rattling in the lock, Kizzy woke with a jolt. The door swung open and daylight from the corridor streamed in. It was Saturday morning. She'd been sleeping on the metal bed all night, its springs digging into her sides. Her coat was buttoned up all the way and her blue hat was pulled down to her neck, her curls sticking out of the sides. She'd slept badly, but she'd slept. Her face was still stinging and she remembered the policeman's slap. Kizzy's stomach growled and she thought about Marko's chocolate bar in her pocket. But Tsura had taught her how to wait. She'd eaten the whole jar of jam just hours ago. She didn't need to eat the chocolate. Not yet.

"Wake up, my dear." A nurse Kizzy hadn't seen before held a small pile of papers and a white cup. "Would you like something to drink?"

Kizzy snatched and gulped down the cool water. Receiving water was a good sign.

"Where—?" Kizzy stopped herself from asking the unnecessary question about Professor Duerr. There was a chance the policemen were gone. Perhaps the other hospital staff had finished their shifts. Perhaps this nurse had no idea why Kizzy was being detained.

"Where am I?" Kizzy asked, pretending to be disoriented.

"This is Charité Hospital. Someone is meeting you at the front desk."

A sense of imminent liberation pushed itself through Kizzy's stomach and up into her head, making her want to shout with relief. *Marko's come to get me. He's the only one who knows I'm here.*

"You're to be arrested," the nurse said in an apologetic tone.

As she heard the words, Kizzy felt as if she'd been clouted across the face again. She had to get out of there. If the nurse had brought her water, maybe she'd be sympathetic.

"I haven't done anything wrong. I need to get home," Kizzy said. Then lies poured from her mouth. "My parents are dead. My grandmother's ill. I look after her and I've gotta get home. She's all alone. She needs me."

The nurse closed the door, then sat down on the chair beside the bed. "Calm down."

Kizzy made her voice sound small and childlike. "What's the time? What day is it?"

"It's Saturday morning," the nurse explained.

"My grandmother needs to take her medicines. She'll die without them. Please. And she needs to eat. I have to make her breakfast. Why am I here? Why are they arresting me?"

"I don't know," the nurse said, furrowing her thin eyebrows and looking down at her chart. "What's your name?"

Kizzy unbuttoned her coat and handed her false identification documents to the nurse. "I'm Franziska. Fränzi for short. I can't remember coming here. Was I sick?"

The nurse checked her notes against Kizzy's papers. "I think I have the wrong file," the nurse said, handing back the identity documents. "I'll be back in a minute." This was Kizzy's chance.

"I need the toilet," Kizzy said.

"Oh, okay, my dear. Follow me."

The corridor was empty and the clicking sounds of their shoes echoed on the shiny tiles. The sunlight streamed in from the top of a staircase. *I should run.* But the toilet closet was only a few rooms away. "I'll wait for you out here," the nurse said.

Inside, Kizzy's breathing was quick. She reached for a lock, but there wasn't one. This was yet another room without windows. Kizzy took her time using the toilet. As she squatted down, she looked around. Next to her, a vent on the wall, close to the floor, was just large enough for her to fit into, although she had no idea where it led. She grabbed at the vent with her fingernails, but its edges were rusted solid. Standing at the sink, she used a bar of soap to wash her hands and face, careful not to get her hat or hair wet. *A wet head would make me ill.* Even though the water tasted earthy, she gulped some down. But drinking made her feel hungry.

"Are you all right?" the nurse called from outside.

"One second!"

Kizzy hated Marko right now. *If Marko was here, I'd punch his ugly face.* The thought of punching Marko gave her an idea. An idea she'd gotten from Marko. When out at night and feeling unsafe, he'd told her once, a key can be a weapon. She reached into her coat for Professor Duerr's key. She took it in her hand so the sharp point was poking out between her fingers and she made a fist. If she needed to, she'd punch the nurse in the neck. Or she'd swing at her face. With the key in her fist, Kizzy practiced jabbing forward. Just before the nurse opened the door, Kizzy grabbed the bar of soap and dropped it into her pocket along with Marko's chocolate. *Finders, keepers.*

Stepping into the hallway, Kizzy kept her hand and the key hidden. Her stomach growled, loudly. "I'm hungry."

Her hand on Kizzy's shoulder, the nurse led her along another corridor. As they passed closed doors, Kizzy wondered if Professor Duerr was behind one of them. She considered swiping the nurse with the key. *Not yet.* They arrived at a small seating area.

"Take a seat, my dear," the nurse said with a smile. "I'll get you something to eat. I'll be right back."

"Thank you."

The click-click of the nurse's shoes on the shiny tiles faded into light taps. This was Kizzy's chance. Once the nurse was out of sight, she dropped the key into her pocket and slipped off her shoes. Her stockings made no noise on the tiled floor and, with one shoe in each hand, she ran down the corridor as fast as she could toward the staircase she had passed before, toward the sunlight.

At the next floor, she passed a window that was barred and out of reach. She heard talking coming from around the corner. She kept going, up, jumping the steps two at a time. Without shoes, the marble steps hurt her feet. But she didn't care. She reached the highest floor, five, maybe six levels up. More voices came from her left. Checking the corridor was clear, Kizzy turned right. Her stockings glided against the polished tile and she almost fell, catching herself—a shoe in each hand—against the wall. Muffled voices behind her forced Kizzy to run to the closest door, hoping there was nobody behind it. She slipped into the room.

Kizzy was in an empty office. Books, files, a large green rug. Long green curtains around a large window. A sofa and two armchairs. A fancy desk to the side. She turned to check if there was a key in the lock. No key. She ran to the window and looked down. Dropping her shoes onto the floor and standing on tiptoes, she peered down at the street below. She could climb out, but the drop was too far. Kizzy could see across Berlin.

When voices from right outside the door became louder, Kizzy threw herself under the desk, crawling into the space between the chair and the desk's back panel. The door clicked open. "Take a seat," a man's voice said. The door clicked closed. Kizzy focused on taking breaths without making a sound.

From under the desk, she could see framed certificates on the wall. The office belonged to a doctor. A clock pointed to eight minutes after nine in the morning.

"How's everything?" The man's voice was smooth and soft.

The doctor, Kizzy assumed.

"Good news," a different voice, croaky and loud, announced. He coughed as he spoke.

Kizzy's heart stopped in her throat. *My feet! Where are my shoes?*

From under the desk, Kizzy heard the rustling of papers. "An older man had a heart attack," the coughing man reported. "We had an old woman come in with a stroke. She's in the basement now. And we had one birth—a girl. The mother is doing well. Oh, and one man with a broken arm." Kizzy could feel the swirling of blood in her ears. *Duerr had a stroke. She's in the hospital basement.*

"No complications?" the doctor asked.

The second man coughed again. "None."

"That'll be all," the doctor said to his coughing colleague.

The door clicked open and closed, and Kizzy listened to the dull sound of shoes on the rug. The doctor was still in the office. Without a sound, she turned to the side and pushed herself as far back under the desk as possible. The chair moved and she saw the doctor's polished black shoes and brown woolen trousers. The doctor sat and stretched out his legs. His shoe hit her coat. Kizzy wanted to disappear. She closed her eyes. *Professor Duerr's key.* But there was no time to reach for it. She opened her eyes to his face, gray beard, wire glasses.

He looked at her, almost smiling. "Well, hello."

Kizzy said nothing.

"What are you doing down there?"

"I got lost," Kizzy blurted out.

The doctor's face lit up with a grin and he let out a sincere laugh. He looked down at Kizzy's feet. "Are you looking for your shoes?" He pointed to the window.

A shoe in each hand, the doctor guided her to the soft green sofa against the wall. The doctor perched on the edge of the armchair.

"So, what's going on?"

A silly idea popped into Kizzy's head. "I was playing hide-and-seek."

He smiled until his eyes creased. "What's your name?"

"Franziska. Fränzi for short." She pulled her forged documents from her pocket and handed them to him.

The doctor glanced down at the papers. "I prefer Franziska. Have you eaten breakfast, Franziska?"

"I'm starving," she said.

"Let's fix that."

With her shoes back on, Kizzy followed the doctor out into the corridor. The doctor's kind demeanor made the pain in her stomach fade. But a wave of fear flooded her veins when she saw the nurse— the same nurse who gave her water—standing at the top of the staircase next to two young Nazi officers.

"There she is!" Without hesitation, one of the officers marched over to Kizzy and grabbed her upper arm. She tried to pull away, but his grip was too tight.

"He's hurting me!" Kizzy shouted to the doctor.

"What's going on here?" The doctor stepped forward.

Kizzy expected the officer to back away. But he responded with authority. "We have orders to arrest this girl."

"Why?" the doctor asked.

The officer glared at Kizzy. "*Zigeuner*," he said.

The doctor raised his eyebrows. He looked down at Kizzy's false documents still in his hand and nodded.

"Wait!" Kizzy shouted as the officer dragged her toward the staircase. "Please. The old woman. The old woman who had a stroke. Where is she? Her name is Duerr. Frau Professor Doktor Duerr. She's my guardian." As soon as she spoke, Kizzy felt light headed. She'd just incriminated Professor Duerr—the woman who had taken her in, used faked ration cards, and kept her safe for so many years.

The doctor took off his glasses, scratched his chin, and shook his head. Then, with Kizzy's false papers, he walked into his office, closing the door gently. A rush of nausea hit Kizzy's stomach. Her vision blurred. With the nurse leading the way, the Nazi officers dragged her down the stairs.

"Please, nurse, I need to eat," Kizzy said when they reached the reception hall.

The nurse walked away and appeared again, a few seconds later. She dropped two thick slices of bread into Kizzy's hand. In a daze, Kizzy put the bread in her pocket, along with Professor Duerr's key, the bar of chocolate, and the piece of soap.

Outside, a truck was waiting.

"Climb," one of the officers said.

Kizzy pulled herself up into the back of the vehicle. At least two dozen people, mostly men, stared back at Kizzy with pity in their eyes, and one woman began to cry. Kizzy was the only child among them. She expected to recognize a face or two, but all Kizzy could see were yellow stars.

G O L D

Tsura

For Tsura, the improbable was always possible. To those who checked her papers, she was Greta Voeske, an average Aryan woman waiting for the war to end. Yet she moved unnoticed through Berlin, living in the open while working in the shadows beneath the hanging Nazi flags. She had smuggled old men, children, and whole families, moving them from hiding place to hiding place. The stories she had heard. What she had witnessed. Families narrowly escaping falling bombs. Young boys pretending to be men in order to work. Grown women, pregnant women, crawling into suitcases and cupboards not big enough for dogs. Toddlers taught to play silent games, hidden in attics and cellars by their terrified parents. Kizzy was lost, but Tsura would find her.

As Tsura and Marko approached the Charité Hospital complex, a truck passed them, rattling along the road. In the morning light, Tsura could see the face of its driver—a young man, around her age—staring forward, concentrating on the road ahead, no thought to the misery of his cargo.

"I told you," she said to her brother.

"Rounding up Jews," Marko replied, as if reading her mind.

Marko's suggestion to check for Kizzy at the hospital felt like the right decision. Tsura couldn't think of a better idea. But as they approached the building, she saw that going inside would be risky. Except for the upper floors, bars masked most windows. The only way in and out, it seemed, was through the guarded entrance. If Kizzy had come to the hospital, Tsura thought, guards would have questioned her.

"Sis, what do we do about Broden? What if he was arrested?"

Tsura pictured Alex at the Fairy Tales Fountain the night before. Her brother was obviously concerned for his friend. But Tsura's head was stuck on her little cousin. "Maybe Kizzy was arrested, too."

Marko's red eyes were trained on the hospital building ahead. "Kizzy could be in there."

Marko is like me. Too many concerns at once. Tsura hoped he was right. Earlier, as they ran through the house searching for Kizzy, she could tell Marko felt responsible. Tsura felt responsible, too. From Duerr's place, they had walked quickly through the streets, the February sunlight brighter with each minute. All the way, Marko was visibly panicked. They'd find Kizzy, Tsura wanted to tell him. But moments like this, she believed, turned children into women and men, whether they were ready or not. Her brother needed this.

Tsura held out her arm for Marko to stop walking. They stood away from the hospital building.

"We need a story to get us inside," Marko said.

"I'll pretend to be ill," Tsura said. But it wasn't a great idea.

"No. We need something better than that."

Since they were children, Marko had always fought to be in charge. He would decide their games and races and competitions and then grumble when Tsura modified the rules. He was never happy when Tsura made their decisions. When Marko, Kizzy, and Tsura moved in with Duerr, Marko chose the bedroom with the least comfortable bed, leaving Tsura and Kizzy to share. It was a fair trade. When Tsura moved out, leaving Marko and Kizzy alone with Duerr, though Marko protested the unfairness of the situation, he seemed secretly happy to be the new oldest.

Marko was becoming a man. He had what would soon be a short beard. His eyes were bleary from exhaustion, but they were shining with life and ideas. Tsura noticed how he wasn't wearing his own clothes. She recognized the fancy buttons.

"Is that Alex's coat?"

Marko looked down at himself. "We swapped. I was supposed to wait for Broden outside and he thought I was cold, so he gave me his coat. He was coming back."

For a moment, Tsura was suspicious. She wondered if Marko had stolen it from Alex. But Marko's face—his desperation and dejection—made her believe him.

Tsura nodded toward the guards standing at the hospital's entrance. "Do you know them? When you came here with Duerr. Are they the same guards? Did anyone else see you? Anyone at all? Hospital staff? Any of the patients?"

Marko shook his head. "I've got an idea."

"What?"

"Just follow along."

He wants me to play his game. Tsura filled her lungs with morning air as if it could replace her lack of confidence. "You'd better know what you're doing. You have your papers, right?"

Marko sighed and tapped his trouser pocket.

As they approached the hospital building, Tsura could feel the weight of her gun against the side of her stomach. She prepared to present her papers. Years earlier, Tsura Lange had become Greta Voeske and assumed the role of an ordinary German girl who missed her dead parents. It wasn't so far from the truth. Marko was turned into Paul Voeske, Greta's brother, still a pain in the backside. And Kizzy was still their cousin. Marko thought it was hilarious that Kizzy was suddenly called Franziska Scholz and, just to wind her up, nicknamed her Fränzi. They were a new family—pretend orphans, living with their guardian, Professor Duerr.

Tsura learned quickly to use her false name in public. Marko and Kizzy were not as adept and so they practiced and practiced each night, every mealtime, each morning. Duerr started to call each of them by their false names, even at home. *Franziska, wake up. Paul, clean your room. Greta, go to bed.* But that lasted less than a week. Although amusing, it felt wrong to call each other by their false names. They were soon able to switch back and forth. Real names in private, false names in public.

As they approached the hospital guards, Tsura repeated the names Paul and Greta Voeske in her head, waking them up from their sleep. She smiled to herself, knowing she had no plan, but her gut told her to trust her brother.

The three guards, eyes wide open, uniforms pressed, looked as if they'd just started their shifts. All three were deep in conversation. Marko interrupted their banter. "We need to speak to the hospital manager."

"Why? Who are you?" one of the guards asked.

Marko ignored his questions. "We're looking for someone. Our uncle's tenant—an old woman. She was brought here. She owes us money."

Marko had a whole story mapped out. The guards squinted, looking at them up and down. Then Tsura's shoulders relaxed. "I'm his sister," she said. "And my brother's an idiot."

She sneered at Marko, who looked surprised at his sister's words, but not at her acting. "Stop calling me that," he whined. He was playing along, shaking his head, pretending to be embarrassed.

"It's his fault she left before paying up," Tsura said.

While Marko looked at his feet, Tsura took out her identity documents, unfolding the papers and holding them out for the guards to see. One guard groaned, as if they'd interrupted his fascinating job of guarding a doorway. "Follow me."

The hospital entryway was dimly lit with a strong smell of disinfectant. Tsura consciously blocked an old, frightening memory from playing out in her mind. Nurses and orderlies milled around, their shoes and voices echoing against the tiled floor and walls. Tsura checked for Kizzy among the small group of civilians who sat on chairs, waiting to be examined. The guard led Tsura and Marko to the reception area.

"Debt collectors. Looking for an old woman," he said to the young woman behind the desk.

"What's the patient's name?" the young woman asked.

Marko spelled it out. "D. U. E. R. R."

"She's in her late sixties. Do you need the address?" Tsura added.

The guard left them at the desk and headed back outside. The receptionist, with dark-red lipstick and her hair pinned up in a bun, thumbed through the large book in front of her. She muttered "Thank you" as Tsura handed over her false papers and helped her out by pointing to their address.

"Thanks for your help," Marko said, flashing his smile.

The receptionist checked the book and clicked her tongue. "Wait here, please."

Watching her walk through a door behind her, Marko and Tsura stood at the desk, now alone.

"What about Kizzy?" Marko said, as soon as the receptionist was out of sight.

Typical Marko. "I thought you had a plan," Tsura whispered with a snap.

Some of the waiting civilians were staring. In the hopes of finding Kizzy, Tsura surveyed the room and glanced down the corridor. The receptionist returned, followed by a short young man in a white lab coat.

"You're looking for an old woman?" the medic asked in a piercing voice. Fresh razor nicks on his neck made Tsura shiver. Knives frightened her, as did hospitals.

The receptionist snatched Tsura's papers from her hand and pointed out the stated address. Then she pointed to the page in the hospital book.

The doctor cleared his throat. "How do you know Frau Duerr?"

"She rents a room in our uncle's house," Tsura said.

Marko completed Tsura's explanation. "She didn't pay up. She owes us money."

"And where's your uncle?" the young doctor asked, coughing again.

"Stalingrad. Probably dead," Marko replied.

Tsura elbowed her brother in the arm. "Paul! Don't say that."

The doctor's questions stopped and his expression of distrust turned to empathy. As he turned away to cough again, Tsura gave Marko a quick smile. She'd underestimated her sly brother. Since the Nazis' defeat at Stalingrad earlier that month, it had become clear to the German people that scores of soldiers hadn't survived the battle. The news had had a profound effect. While those in support of the troops and of Hitler had grown despondent, the few fighting against the government had become empowered.

"Come with me," the doctor requested.

Immediately, the reality of their improvisation made Tsura worry. Seeing Duerr wasn't a good idea. Tsura tried to think through what she'd say if Duerr were awake and somehow gave them away.

"The old woman owes us five months' rent," Marko said as they followed the doctor along the corridor and down a staircase, into the basement. "A neighbor told us she was brought here. She said her granddaughter might be here, too."

Tsura was impressed at Marko's fabricated story. "My brother was supposed to collect her payment, but the old woman kept giving him excuse after excuse. I told him to get the money, but he didn't. Idiot," she snapped.

"We're here now, aren't we?" Marko shouted, smiling at Tsura behind the doctor's back.

"Idiot," Tsura repeated.

"Shut up, Greta!" Marko said with a grin.

The doctor began coughing again.

Marko had the gall to pat the man on the back. "What the hell's wrong with you? Aren't you a doctor or something?"

"Very funny," the doctor said, sounding mildly amused.

Tsura wanted to laugh at Marko's joke, but the smell of the basement filled Tsura's head. *This is the hospital morgue.* "The old woman. Is she dead?"

Marko shot his sister a wide-eyed stare. As they walked into the room, they looked ahead at four tables, each covered in a sheet, each hiding a fresh corpse. Tsura's eyes quickly searched the room, looking to see if one of the bodies might be a child. The idea disappeared as soon as she saw they were all adults. Tsura found herself speaking to her cousin in her head. *No, Kizzy—you're not dead.*

The doctor led Tsura and Marko to a body by the wall. "Frau Duerr died during the night."

A pain, like a cramp, twisted inside Tsura's stomach.

"What happened?" Marko asked, staying impressively calm.

"She had a stroke. She didn't respond to treatment."

He lifted the sheet. On her back, eyes shut tight, Duerr looked as if she were sleeping. Her skin had some color. Her brown and silver hair was brushed back, falling neatly beneath her neck. Tsura wanted to touch the woman's face. She found herself making a promise to the professor, a promise to remember her, and every woman and man like Duerr who risked their lives for the Romani people. There weren't many who had helped the Roma over the years and so Tsura supposed it wouldn't be difficult to make a list, to build a monument to their names. Tsura would always remember Professor Duerr. And, if she survived the war, she would make the world remember, she vowed.

"This is the woman you're looking for?" the doctor asked.

Tsura nodded while Marko groaned and turned away.

"Sorry. I've never seen a dead body before," Marko said.

Marko was lying. Tsura knew he'd seen the corpses in Marzahn, when they were children. Old men and women, and some not so old. Perhaps Marko had forgotten.

"Paul, are you okay?" Tsura asked her brother.

Marko shook his head. "I haven't slept. And this place is giving me the creeps."

The young doctor walked over to a table in the corner. He returned holding a small open basket containing Duerr's possessions—her watch, her eyeglasses, a necklace, a ring. "Take what you think is valuable."

Tsura reached inside and took everything, placing each item carefully in her pocket. "We appreciate this," she said.

"What happened to the girl?" Marko asked the doctor. "Her granddaughter."

"No idea, but my colleagues might know."

In her head, Tsura said a final goodbye to Professor Duerr. When they returned upstairs to the hospital reception area, the doctor knocked on the open door of what appeared to be a staffroom and gestured for Marko and Tsura to enter.

The room was bright. Two nurses sitting at a table looked up from their teacups and smiled.

"They were looking for that old woman. Stroke. Last night. She owed them rent," the doctor explained. "Now, they're looking for her granddaughter."

One nurse, seemingly more senior than the other, leaned forward. "You mean that Gypsy girl?"

Tsura almost screamed out. She held her breath. *Kizzy was here. Marko was right. And they know she's Roma.*

"She was held here overnight," the senior nurse said.

Marko looked at Tsura, saying nothing, his face drained of color.

"I don't know the whole story," the nurse continued, somewhat excitedly. "The night staff went home. I heard the woman was conscious at one point and she admitted to hiding the Gypsy kid in her home. For years! The kid wasn't her granddaughter, that's for sure." The nurse smiled, as if proud of herself and her colleagues for uncovering such a deception.

An aching swelled inside Tsura's stomach. Tsura kept her eyes on Marko, trying to appear both indifferent and intrigued. "Really? We had no idea."

"She seemed sweet to me," the junior nurse said.

The senior nurse shook her head and leaned toward them. "Gypsies are devious. Thieves, every one of them."

The common slur stung, but Tsura focused on remaining calm. "Where is she now?" she asked, trying her best to sound not too concerned about a conniving, little Gypsy kid.

"The poor girl tried to run, but she was caught," the junior nurse explained. "They put her on a truck. With a group of Jews."

Jews. "When?" Tsura asked.

The head nurse turned to the clock on the wall. "Maybe twenty minutes ago?"

When Tsura remembered the truck they'd passed on their way to the hospital, her stomach flipped. Marko turned to the side, groaned, and then, doubled over, vomited on the tiled floor. Both nurses rushed forward. Tsura focused on breathing and staying in control. She placed her hand on Marko's shoulder.

"I'm sorry. It was the morgue," Marko moaned.

Marko was terrified for Kizzy, Tsura knew. Tsura wanted to vomit, too. The room was spinning. She was exhausted. The white tiles were too bright and the fumes from the disinfectant being poured onto the floor filled her head.

"Here." The junior nurse tapped Marko on the back and passed him a cloth.

"Where did they take the girl?" Marko asked, now standing upright and wiping his mouth.

A smirk extended across the head nurse's face. "Straight to the camps in the East, I imagine."

Tsura swallowed hard and forced herself to speak. "I guess we can kiss our rent money goodbye."

"At least the old woman's jewelry will be worth something," the doctor said with another cough.

"Yes," Tsura said. She put her hand on Marko's arm. "Well, thanks for your time," she said and led Marko to the exit.

Marko in tow, Tsura walked away from Charité Hospital, stunned. Duerr was dead. Kizzy deported. That Kizzy had been arrested alongside Jews made the news all the more frightening and real. The Jews never returned, Wolf had once told Tsura. Kizzy was almost certainly on her way to a Nazi camp. *I'll never see you again.*

Tsura looked up to the winter sky and a question fell from her mouth. "Why did Kizzy come here? She knows better. It doesn't make sense."

Marko said nothing.

"It'll all be okay," Tsura said to him, but she didn't believe it.

Her brother seemed to be dragging his feet along the pavement. Finally, he spoke. "I haven't slept. We need to eat. What should we do now?"

Marko's question made Tsura pause. She had no strategy. She thought of Seraph and Wolf. "We'll find my friends."

Marko shook his head. "Me and Broden—we should've been out of Berlin by now." He ran ahead.

"Wait. Marko, where are you going?"

Marko led his sister through the city streets and over the river, headed south. She couldn't feel the cold. She couldn't feel her feet. Her chest ached, but she couldn't cry. As Marko traced a path through Berlin, walking fast ahead of her, Tsura remembered the Marzahn guard from last night. Wim. *I should've killed him.* She should have put a bullet in his head. She feared the moment her mother and Aunt Marie would hear that Kizzy had been taken. Forced onto a Nazi truck. Sent away with the Jews. *What'll they say, that I couldn't keep Kizzy safe?* For a moment, Tsura hoped Kizzy had been taken to the Marzahn encampment.

They walked close to Brandenburg Gate and along the eastern and part of the southern perimeter of the Tiergarten. As Marko led his sister south, in the direction of the Bavarian Quarter, Tsura made the decision to share her idea.

"Marko. In two days, my friends and I are going back to Marzahn. Maybe we'll find Mama before the Gestapo deports her, too. Maybe Kizzy was taken there." As Tsura said the plan out loud, she knew it would be impossible to pull off. Still, she continued. "You'll come, too. You'll meet Wolf. And Seraph. You'll like them. Marko, are you listening?"

They'd reached a building just north of Seraph's apartment. Marko led his sister into its empty basement.

"Where are we?" Tsura asked.

The morning light streamed in from the street above. This was some kind of wine cellar. Marko walked over to two mattresses in the corner.

"Marko?"

Her brother dropped to his knees, staring at the wall. "I thought, maybe—" His voice trailed off, then he spoke again. "I need to sleep." He fell onto a mattress in the corner.

"Marko, we'll go to Marzahn. With Wolf and Seraph. Seraph's father is a prisoner in Dachau. Did I tell you that? Seraph's mother— she's in Ravensbrück. And Wolf is Jewish. Their families are suffering, just like us."

Tsura couldn't be sure if Marko was listening.

Apart from wooden crates and an empty wine barrel, the cellar was empty. The concrete floor was bare. Patches of mildew covered the walls and cobwebs hung from the corners. The air was damp. Metal bars covered the small window close to the low ceiling. *What is this place?*

"Marko?"

"Sleep," Marko snapped and kicked the second mattress at her.

Tsura looked up through the window. The apartment across the street stood with its front door wide open.

"Marko—"

"Please, sis—"

"Let's go."

"I need to sleep." His voice was softer now.

"Why here? Where are we?"

Marko didn't reply.

Tsura had misjudged her brother. Marko couldn't accept that Kizzy had been arrested. On the mattress, he was now turned to his side, his head on his closed right fist and his left hand held up, between his fingers a small object he was using to scrape markings into the old plaster wall.

"Wake me in a few hours," he said with closing eyes, his voice becoming a whisper. "Then we'll keep looking."

"Marko. What're you talking about? She's gone."

Alexander

When Alex's name was called, he wanted to hide. A dull pain swelled inside his stomach as he jumped to his feet and joined the others against the wall. It made no sense. The selection seemed random.

"Where are you taking us?" an older man demanded.

The Nazi officer sighed. "There's nothing to worry about."

"I don't believe a word of it!" The old man was visibly shaking.

Another prisoner nudged the old man. "You'll get us shot."

Another man was in tears. Earlier, he'd been mumbling again and again that all this was happening on Shabbat, the Jewish Sabbath day. He was silent now.

Alex had spent the morning in the same overcrowded room. He was cold in Marko's thin coat. Huddled against the wall, his stomach turned, in fear and in hunger. There had been no breakfast. His mind raced through recurring questions. Had Marko, from the shadows, seen Alex forced onto the truck? Why had they risked returning home? And regrets. *I should've remembered the photographs*, Alex scolded himself. If only Father hadn't insisted Alex take his coat. For years, Father and Alex had talked about the risk of their arrest and deportation. *This is what it feels like.*

With the wretched image of his mother and Ruti in their nightgowns etched into his memory, the journey in the furniture truck had been short. They'd stopped along the way, picking up more Jews. With their fists and heels of their guns, the Gestapo had beaten those unable to climb up fast enough. Alex had counted thirty-four prisoners, including five children. Some had been taken with their family members. Others alone. All were strangers to Alex. One boy, no older than six years old, had been removed from his relatives. His aunt—she had no yellow star—was left screaming on the street outside her house.

One woman had noticed the absence of a star on Alex's coat. She'd asked about it as though Alex didn't belong. He was Jewish, as was his father, both born in Berlin, Alex had explained. His biological mother, born in Dresden, was Jewish, too, and had died when Alex was very young. Alex's response had caused the woman to cry. He had kept his step-grandfather's gold cross inside his shirt. When the truck had reached its destination, the sky was still dark. Guns at their heads, Alex and his fellow prisoners were marched into an old building with barbed wire across the windows. The men were separated from the women and younger children.

Alex had been held in the same crowded room for a few hours. A sea of yellow stars on coats and factory clothes was punctuated by some men still in their pajamas.

Following the Nazi officer's orders to march downstairs, Alex scanned the mass of frightened faces.

"Lea!" he called out.

Lea Federman was walking with her arm around her father, their faces sullen, yellow stars bright on their coats. Alex pushed through the line.

Lea's face brightened. "Alex!"

"It's so good to see someone I know."

Lea blushed at Alex's words. "I'm glad to see you, too." Her eyes were red, her hair tousled. At her desk in the brewery's office she had always looked so pristine. Mr. Federman remained silent, as if in a trance.

"Did they come for you at work?" Alex asked them. Alex was worried about his father, who had left for the factory in the west of the city, hours earlier.

"They picked us up at home," Lea explained.

"Same here," Alex said. He tried to shake off the memory of standing in front of Mother and Ruti with his underwear around his shins.

Outside, Lea grabbed hold of Alex's arm and stared ahead. The street was quiet. The building stood facing a small wooded area and Alex looked up at the treetops that swayed in the winter wind.

"It's the cemetery," Alex said. This was Hamburg Main Street, within walking distance from his home. The leafless trees stood at the edge of the old Jewish cemetery opposite the Jewish care home for the elderly and the building that, until recently, housed the Jewish school for boys. These Jewish buildings had been taken over by the government as makeshift holding centers. Alex looked through the trees, in the direction of the cemetery. He remembered the sad and confusing feeling of standing at his mother's grave as a young boy. To the Nazi officers pointing their rifles at their heads, Alex was already dead.

Through his boots, the uneven cobblestones felt familiar. But this feeling—of being swept away—was new; black and red waves swallowed him, undercurrents pulling him from his everyday life. His arms wanted to hold onto Lea and the people in front. He wanted to scream out. But he was sinking. For those few moments outside in the open, he looked around for Marko, hoping to see him hiding behind the trees across the street.

Alex helped Mr. Federman onto the truck. Some of the older men couldn't climb, even with some help. The prisoners pushed and pulled each other along. Three or four men fell. "I think my hand is broken!" one man yelped. A Nazi soldier took his whip to him. Grown men sobbed as if they were lost children looking for their parents. Two men, an older man and what was probably his even older father, gripped each other tight, terrified of separation. When the truck moved, the crowd surged together with a jolt.

Once they'd settled, the prisoners calmed and the truck filled with soft chatter. "Where are they taking us?" "I'm worried for my children." "This is the end for me." Alex tried to shut out their words. "They'll take us to a work camp." "We'll all be shot." "When Jews cry, the world turns away." Soon, except for sounds of weeping, the truck was quiet.

"It's just the two of you?" Alex asked Lea, looking at her father.

Lea nodded. "No siblings. My father is Jewish, but my mother isn't. I'm a *Mischling*." Lea was a half-blood—half-Jewish, half-Aryan. "But I don't see myself as Jewish. And because my mother is Lutheran, neither does the Jewish community. I'm Christian. I don't belong here."

Alex looked at Mr. Federman. Eyes shut, her father held Lea's hand. "What about your father's family?" Alex asked.

"My whole family on my father's side was deported to the East."

"My father's family, too," Alex said. "My stepmother and stepsister, Ruti, are Catholics. But I'm a full Jew."

Lea stared at Alex wide-eyed, as if they were the same, as if she suddenly understood everything about him. She squeezed Alex's arm and rested her head on his shoulder. Alex's shoulders stiffened, wanting to push her away. He could only think about Marko. *Lea doesn't know me at all.*

Five minutes later, the truck stopped. "Get out!" a guard ordered. Tidy buildings stood along the clean pavement. Alex could smell the frozen gutters. They were in the heart of the city. The neighborhood felt familiar, but still this feeling didn't. Alex looked up at the windows of what appeared to be apartment blocks surrounding them on both sides of the street. He tried to catch glimpses of who might have been watching, witnesses behind net curtains. The group moved quickly, led toward the doorway of another building, six or seven windows tall, a typical concrete Berlin structure with its pretty horizontal etched lines, pitched roof, small windows along the top, and larger windows on the lower floors.

"Where are we?" Alex asked Lea.

Mr. Federman pointed up to a sign above them that welcomed the crowd to Berlin's Jewish Community Center. A smaller sign read "Jewish Welfare Office." *We're on Rosenstrasse.* A rifle at his head, Alex shuffled along with the others, into the building.

"Women to the left," a guard announced.

Without protest, Lea let go of Alex's arm and kissed her father farewell. "I love you, Papa." Mr. Federman said nothing and a Nazi guard led the small group of women up a flight of stairs.

Once the women were out of sight, the men were led up the same staircase. Moving slowly, upwards, swept along by the crowd, Alex tried to block out the moans and shouts that echoed through the hallway. "We need water!" a woman screamed. Other voices called out family names. More people had been brought here before them. In one room, the sight of children—without adults, without their parents—made Alex want to cry out. *The government thinks these children are a threat?* Alex noticed one young girl sitting in the corner against the wall. She was a little younger than Ruti. Hugging herself, her hat was pulled down to her eyebrows. Other children—many were toddlers—huddled together. Some played. Others were asleep on the floor. In the next room along, young and old women were packed in tight, sitting, standing, holding each other.

"There's Lea!" Alex said to Mr. Federman when he saw her through the doorway.

"Lea! I love you, too!" Mr. Federman shouted out.

Surrounded by other women and girls, Lea smiled and waved.

"Keep going. Up the stairs," the guards ordered with their guns at the prisoners' backs.

On the next floor, Alex followed his group along the corridor and into a room already jam-packed with Jewish men. The space, which reeked of damp wood and body odor, was empty of any furniture, and the painted walls were peppered with vacant hooks and nails where paintings and noticeboards once hung. Daylight streamed in through the windows, highlighting parts of the wooden floorboards that, over time, had been scratched and worn by desks and chairs. Everyone was talking.

"Alexander?"

"Papa!"

Father ran toward him, with disheveled clothes and wide eyes, his arms out, and he fell against Alex, reaching for his son's face. "Why are you here?" his father shouted. "You should be out of Berlin by now!" Father began to weep and Alex wanted to cry with him.

"Papa, what happened? When did they arrest you?"

"This morning, at the factory. We were held on a truck for hours."

Mr. Federman still stood by Alex's side.

"Papa, this is Lea Federman's father. Herr Federman, this is my father, Samuel Broden."

"Sam." Father shook his hand.

"Everyone, be quiet. Listen," an older man announced. A young man, around Alex's age—no older than eighteen—was standing by the door. A yellow star sewn to his chest, he wore a thick red cloth band on his arm.

"I'm your assigned orderly," he said. He projected his voice so everyone could hear. "Food will be brought soon." He disappeared and the room erupted in chatter. Food was a good sign.

An account of his experience spilled from Alex's mouth. "Papa, they arrested me and took me to Hamburg Main Street. Then they separated us. We don't know why. There are hundreds of others, ten minutes away."

Another man, a notebook and pencil in his hand, overheard what Alex was saying. "Is your wife a Christian?" he asked Alex.

"I'm not married," Alex said, feeling embarrassed. He wondered what Marko would have said to that.

"This is my son," Alex's father said. He spoke with a sorrowful smile, as if Alex's arrival was both a gift and a burden. "Alexander, this is Herr Lessel. We work together at Siemens."

"My wife is Catholic," Mr. Lessel said to Alex.

"My mother— My stepmother is, too," Alex said. He pointed to Mr. Federman. "And his wife and daughter are Lutheran."

Father clapped. "We have a theory. There's a pattern. Everyone brought here is related to a gentile." He pointed to a group of men sitting by the window—a line of yellow stars. "All of us."

"Pay attention!" Mr. Lessel shouted to the room. He looked at the newcomers, those who had been with Alex in the truck. "If your wife or mother is Aryan, raise your hand." Every hand went up and Father's colleague laughed with delight. "This is a good sign."

"Not for the others," Alex said, thinking of the Jewish adults and children he'd left behind on Hamburg Main Street.

Father wasn't listening. He stared down at Alex's sleeve. "Why aren't you wearing the good coat I gave you?" he asked. His fingers studied the collar of the coat Alex was wearing. "This fabric is too thin. You'll fall ill."

"They arrested me at home," Alex told him, leaving out that he and Marko had switched coats. "I had to go back. My photographs were—"

Father gasped and pulled down on Alex's arms. "I made you forget your photographs! This is my fault!" He buried his head against Alex's shoulder and let out a muffled sob.

"Papa, don't say that," Alex said.

Father pulled away and wiped his wet face with his sleeve. "Are Ruti and your mother okay?"

"They were there when the soldiers came for me."

Father and Mr. Lessel made space on the floor for Alex and Mr. Federman. The room was bursting and they could hear more trucks pulling up outside. Four or five men stood on the window ledge, looking through the glass to the street below, providing a running commentary of what they could see. "Here's another truck." "More Gestapo with guns." "More Jewish men, one woman. They've got their hands up." "They're being brought inside." "They're beating a man who just fell down."

"Is there a toilet here?" Alex asked his father.

"You need to ask one of the orderlies—one of the men in the red armbands," Mr. Lessel explained.

Alex stood and walked to the room's open door. "Excuse me. Where's the toilet?"

"This way." The assigned orderly—a scrawny boy with floppy hair—led Alex downstairs, passing the room of children and the room where Alex had seen Lea earlier. But the doors were now closed.

"I'm Alexander."

"Simon."

"How did you get that?" Alex asked, pointing to Simon's red armband.

Simon shrugged. He was sickly thin with a greasy face and gray eye sockets. His red armband, the color of blood, bore a set of numbers. "I've got a special pass to come and go, as long as I report to them every morning."

"Why are you helping them?" Alex asked.

"It's not my choice."

A Nazi soldier walked by. He was also young—clean-shaven—and he looked familiar, but Alex didn't know why.

The ground floor was packed and chaotic. Simon joined Alex in the long queue for the toilets. As they waited, Alex listened to the conversations around them. The theory that the Gestapo had separated out Jewish people with non-Jewish relatives had spread through the building.

A beautiful Jewish woman in her late-twenties was sitting close to them. "My husband is Lutheran. He's an important businessman," she boasted. "Jews like me have always been promised protection. Until now."

A man in line was talking about two middle-aged Catholic women who had been forced onto his truck accidentally. "The women spoke with the officers in charge. They showed them their papers, and they were allowed to go home. Just like that!" The man nodded toward two Nazi officers by the door, both buttoning up their jackets, getting ready to step onto the street. "Incompetent swine," the man said.

"Oh no. They know exactly what they're doing," the attractive woman replied. "We've been brought here because the Gestapo haven't yet figured out how to get us onto the trains to Poland without causing too much of a fuss."

I have to get out. Alex turned to Simon and spoke in a lowered voice. "Listen. My father's on the second floor. If they let me go, tell him what happened. Here, take this." Alex took off Marko's coat and pushed it into Simon's hand.

In his shirt, Alex stepped out of the queue and walked toward the officers. He lifted up his chin and reached into his shirt collar to pull out the gold chain and cross. "Wait! Please," Alex called out.

"Stop!" A low-level guard held Alex back.

The officers, already on the street, turned around, their eyes squinting toward the doorway. Groups of soldiers on the street clutched their rifles. Alex had no chance to run.

"There's been a mistake," Alex said to the officers.

They walked toward him and nodded to the guard to let Alex pass. Alex stepped onto the pavement. In just his shirt, the February air made him shiver. His heart raced.

"What mistake?" one of the officers asked.

"My real parents. They're Aryans. I was brought here with my stepfather," Alex lied. He held out his gold cross.

"Papers," one of the officers sighed.

Alex held his arms out, palms open. "My papers are at home. They didn't let me bring my coat."

The officer stepped forward. "Your name?"

Alex's face burned with fear. "Broden. Alexander. My stepfather is upstairs. He's a Jew, but I'm a real German."

Alex's stomach hurt. When one of the Nazis produced a list from his pocket, Alex turned his eyes to the ground, his fist clutching the gold cross. When he looked up again, the officer's face was seething at Alex's insolence. The officer grabbed Alex's hand and pried his fingers away from the gold chain. Holding the cross in his right hand, he slapped Alex lightly on the face with his left.

"You think I'm stupid?" The officer said and slapped his face again, a little harder. "Greedy Jew."

Holding him by his gold chain, he pushed Alex hard and, as Alex stumbled, the chain snapped across the back of his neck.

"No—" Alex said with a gasp.

"Keep it," the officer ordered.

Alex held out his hand, but the officer dropped the chain and cross to the ground. Alex fell to his knees.

As the Nazi walked away, he called out to Alex. "Christ can't help you!"

Alex picked up the cross and broken chain from the pavement. A guard dragged Alex up and back into the Community Center.

After using the toilet, Alex found Simon and retrieved Marko's coat. Arms around himself, he trudged up the staircase, back to his father.

Ruti's idea hadn't worked.

Ruth

Ruth needed to feel useful. Itching for Mama to return, she wanted her to walk in with Papa and Alexander in tow. Papa would scoop Ruth up in his arms and kiss her forehead. Her brother would see Ruth upset and crack some jokes to cheer her up.

Yesterday evening, when Elise had helped her follow the first few treasure hunt clues, Ruth had brushed off Alexander's game as childish. But now, with her brother gone, Ruth felt compelled to read the puzzles, over and over again. Like playing cards, she fanned out the growing collection of riddles between her fingers. So far, she'd solved four of the puzzles, one was unsolved, and she had four words: *Freund, Unterwäsche, Nachthemd, Telefon.* She had no idea yet how a friend, underwear, a nightgown, and a telephone were connected. Staring at Alexander's handwriting, Ruth swallowed the urge to cry.

Ruth had been bursting into tears throughout the morning. When Elise had arrived, and hung her coat on the rack by the door, the sight of Elise's League uniform had made Ruth feel sick at the thought of Gestapo officers walking around her family's house, finding Alexander, threatening Mama.

Ruth was so glad Elise was there. She would've been frightened to be alone. The place was a disaster. Books across the floor, chairs and tables turned over, a vase and other ornaments smashed. The Nazi pigs had done a great job. Ruth couldn't bring herself to start tidying, so Elise had distracted her by making breakfast while Ruth sobbed. They'd chatted at the kitchen table until it was time for lunch.

While eating half of the leftover birthday cake, Elise told Ruth a story about Hackescher Market. She mentioned a young man she'd seen and how handsome he was. But Ruth wasn't really listening. Elise chattered away, as if she'd forgotten what was happening to Ruth's family.

"Why isn't she back yet?" Ruth asked for the hundredth time.

"I saw him last night," Elise said.

"Who?"

"Your brother."

"Alexander?" Ruth leaned forward, intrigued and confused.

Elise said nothing. She was being purposely vague and a little dramatic. Ruth knew her too well.

"Elise, what is it? Tell me."

"Last night. It was late," Elise said, with a hint of a smile on her face. She began to tidy the kitchen. "I saw him. Behind the garden. Behind my house."

"You saw Alexander? Last night?"

Alexander had told Marko he was meeting someone at midnight, Ruth remembered. A girl. Ruth couldn't recall her name now. And Alexander had given a small object to Marko. Ruth had seen them. Suddenly she remembered that Marko's little cousin was supposed to have been dropped off, first thing this morning. *Franziska.* Marko should have brought her by now. *Something must've happened.* Ruth worried that Marko and Kizzy had been arrested, too. She didn't say a word about Kizzy to Elise. Elise didn't need to know those details and she'd only make a fuss about the secrecy. It was best Elise didn't know about their plan to hide Marko's Gypsy cousin and pretend she was their family.

As she wiped down the countertop, Elise babbled away. But Ruth's mind was on Alexander. She pictured her brother forced to march down the staircase, humiliated with his trousers pulled to his ankles. She wondered where he was. *Still on the truck. Already in a Nazi prison camp.* Ruth's head was spinning. Papa's stories swamped Ruth's head. Stories about his family. Rumors of mass murder. They'd never heard from some of Papa's family again. Now Alexander had been taken away. Ruth didn't know what she'd do if the government killed him. Thoughts about losing her family took Ruth to questions about her biological father. Ruth wondered if he was dead, too. But Mama never spoke about him.

"Ruth!" Elise snapped.

"What?"

"You're not listening to me."

Standing with the kitchen rag in her hand, Elise scowled, as if Ruth should have been paying attention to her every word, as if Ruth had nothing important on her mind.

"I can't concentrate," Ruth said. Of all the people who should have understood, it was Elise. "I'm so worried for Alexander. And Papa." *You lost your brother, too,* she wanted to say.

Ruth pictured her father being forced onto a truck, just like Alexander. Her stomach and chest hurt. Again, she started to sob.

"Crying won't help," Elise said, wiping the table in front of her and pushing Ruth's elbows out of the way.

She's being so uncaring. Elise didn't seem to realize how nasty she sounded. Ruth stared right at her. "Elise, what's wrong with you? How did you feel when you heard Viktor was dead? And when your father left for the war?" The words spilled out and Ruth was immediately embarrassed, but also annoyed with her best friend.

From the look on her face, Elise was offended. It was unfair of Ruth to mention Elise's father and Viktor in that way. Ruth wanted to talk, to break the awkwardness, but couldn't think of anything to say. She didn't want to talk about Alexander's plan to escape. She didn't want to mention Kizzy. Or tell Elise about Marko, or the secret object Alexander had given him. Or the mysterious girl Alexander had met at midnight. Elise didn't need to know.

Ruth wandered into the hallway. She stared through the doorway at the mess in the living room. Her family's home had been invaded and she felt an urge to run outside. When she unhooked her coat from the rack, Elise's brown Girls' League jacket fell to the floor. Ruth shuddered.

All Aryan children were required by law to join the Nazi youth groups at ten years old. The boys had their club and the girls had the League. At age ten, Elise had signed up for the League associated with her school. But, with a Jewish stepfather, Ruth had a choice. Yet, despite Ruth's objections, Papa and Mama agreed that signing up would cause Ruth fewer problems with her teachers and schoolmates.

The League girls played sports and learned to sew and cook, but Ruth knew the club's true purpose. Ruth had received her uniform and showed up on the first day, just after her tenth birthday—exactly five years ago. Elise and Ruth attended different schools, so Elise had been excited to have Ruth for company. After some indoor games, they'd gathered in the main school hall. Ruth had felt like a fraud. A spy. The uniform choked her. The thirty or forty girls in the room began to sing the praises of their Führer and all Ruth could think about was how Hitler hated Alexander and Papa, just because they were Jewish. When the League leaders lectured the girls on their responsibility to bear children for the Reich, Ruth had pretended to feel unwell and asked to leave early.

At home, in tears, she'd torn off the uniform. She wouldn't return. Ruth's parents apologized for making her go. She'd never have to attend the League meetings again.

But the next day, Elise was angry Ruth had walked out. They didn't talk for two days, until Elise finally offered a small apology. Ruth had embarrassed her, she'd said, but she understood why Ruth had walked out.

Ruth put Elise's jacket back onto the rack and returned to the kitchen. Elise was at the sink. Ruth plucked up the courage to fill the silence. "Elise—" *I'm fifteen now*, she reminded herself. "Elise, I shouldn't have said that."

At first Elise didn't respond. Then she stopped scrubbing the plates. "You're upset," she said, without turning around.

Ruth walked back through the hallway and into the living room. She picked up a broken vase and photograph frames and pillows and a fallen lamp. She tidied some of the books and swept up the broken crockery.

Kneeling on the floor, Ruth noticed some kind of black or brown paste along the base of the wall, close to the fireplace. She removed her glasses and wiped the lenses on her blouse. When she put them back on, Ruth saw that what looked like black paste was actually a hole in the skirting board. Then she saw it. *Another note!*

Inside the hole was Alexander's folded notepaper. Reaching her fingers inside, she shivered at the thought of accidentally touching mouse droppings. Or an actual mouse. Ruth held the note's corners with her fingernails.

Across the front of the paper, in her brother's handwriting, were "Ruti" and the word "*Mausloch*"—mouse hole. Ruth unfolded it.

Dear Ruti
Hard boiled, please
Love, Mickey

Ruth let out a small laugh. Her brother was teasing her. For as long as Ruth could remember, they'd had a mouse problem. Ruth hated mice, especially when she heard the scratching at night. Alexander thought it was funny to call the intruder Mickey, after the Americans' Mickey Mouse.

When they were much younger, Alexander had owned a number of Walt Disney posters and postcards of Mickey Mouse and Pluto the dog. He would hide the cartoon pictures in places Ruth would be sure to find them. In her shoes, under her pillow. She'd shriek and scream when she found them, and Alexander would roar with laughter. Secretly, Ruth found it funny, too, but she kept up the shrieking for fun. Eventually, Papa became nervous that owning American drawings would be dangerous, and so he'd asked Alexander to throw them out. Ruth's brother still teased her about the mice, telling her that Mickey snuggled against her feet every night while she slept. Ruth pictured Alexander hiding the clue in the mouse hole, laughing to himself that she'd have to put her hand inside.

Ruth read the new clue again. *Hard boiled. Eggs!* Ruth jumped to her feet and ran through the kitchen and out the back door into the garden. She opened the wooden refrigeration box. With the temperature so low in the winter months, storing perishable foods outside kept them fresh. They risked having them stolen, Mama said, but nothing had been taken yet. Ruth rummaged through the butter and eggs and milk and pieces of hardened fish wrapped in paper. No note.

"I'm looking for eggs," Ruth said to Elise as she stepped back into the kitchen.

Elise said nothing. She pulled the timber chair legs across the tiled floor. She scraped the china teacup and saucer along the wooden tabletop. The sounds filled the kitchen so completely that Elise's silence gave Ruth a headache. Playing Alexander's treasure hunt game made Ruth want to cry again. *This is the worst birthday.*

"Is this what it felt like when Viktor died?" Ruth blurted out.

Elise's eyes widened. For a second, Ruth thought it was the worst thing she could have said. But then Elise lowered her shoulders, almost defeated.

"Probably." Elise's voice trailed off. Then she spoke again, softly. "It was terrible. And I was scared because my parents weren't talking about it. So I stayed out of their way."

Ruth was surprised to hear Elise speak so openly. She had never spoken to Ruth about Viktor.

Elise continued, "I remember how I didn't know what to do. I kept finding his toys around the house."

"That's it!" Ruth shouted.

Ruth pushed her chair away from the table and ran into the dining room. She threw open the doors of the sideboard. Pushing Papa's silver Kiddush cup aside, she reached to the back of the cupboard and pulled out the silver egg-shaped spice box she and Alexander had played with as children. The seal was tight, but Ruth managed to twist open the two silver cups that formed the egg. *I was right!* The air filled with the scent of cloves as she found another of Alexander's clues.

Beneath "Ruti," Alexander had written the word "*Eierschale*"— eggshell.

Fifteen
And nine months

162

This is getting easy. Ruth deciphered Alexander's puzzle right away.
She ran back to the kitchen, to the wall calendar hanging over
the countertop. Starting with February—Ruth's birth-month—she
flipped through the months, counting to nine.

There, on the second-to-last page, glued to the paper, was
another note, with "Ruti" and "November" written across it.
Carefully, Ruth peeled the note from the calendar and unfolded the
next riddle.

> *If you want to count to zero*
> *Spin the dial and listen*

Ruth was certain this clue would have led her to the telephone,
with its dial of numbers from one to nine, followed by zero. She
returned to her seat at the kitchen table.

"This is fun," she said to Elise.

Elise ignored her. *It's my birthday,* Ruth wanted to scream. She
wanted to remind Elise that Alexander had been arrested. The Nazi
pigs were looking for Papa, too. Instead, across the table, Ruth
spread out the treasure hunt notes she'd collected so far. The word
on the front of each note was important, she was sure. *Freund,
Unterwäsche, Nachthemd, Telefon, Mausloch, Eierschale, November.* She had
seven words now. Together, the words would lead Ruth to her prize.
But she was still missing some clues and had two dead ends—the
woman's place of birth and the riddle about the rose petals, white
piping, and the pickpocket in reverse. Ruth stared at her brother's
handwriting on each note. *If I solve every puzzle, everything will turn out all
right.* As soon as the thought filled her head, Ruth wanted to revoke
the pledge.

"We should tidy upstairs," Ruth said out loud.

Elise said nothing, but she followed her friend upstairs anyway.
Ruth stood in the doorway to Alexander's bedroom. His cupboard
door was open. His bed had been pulled away from the wall.

"He was supposed to leave this morning, but the plan all went
wrong."

Ruth turned toward her bedroom. Her sheets had been torn from the bed. Clothes spilled from her dresser drawers.

"No!" Ruth shouted.

No longer on her dressing table, pieces of her porcelain and bone china ornaments were scattered across the floor. She crouched down, careful where she stepped. Some of the pieces were undamaged. She picked up a china bear and a miniature bouquet of flowers. Other pieces were broken in half. A clay horse was missing two legs, her porcelain boy and girl in traditional German dress were missing one arm each, and some of her ceramic cats were missing their heads. The collection was ruined. As Ruth picked up pieces from under her bed, she remembered that it had been Alexander's hiding place, that morning.

"He was under—"

Ruth gasped when, on the floor beneath her bed, she saw her brother's face. She reached down to pick up two small copies of the same photograph. The repeated black-and-white image of her handsome brother looked back at her, his wavy hair in place, dark eyes, wearing a tie and jacket. Careful not to crease or smudge them, Ruth held the edges of the photographs between her fingers.

"We have to go," Ruth said.

Elise said nothing.

Ruth got dressed. Downstairs, she put on her coat, gloves, and hat. She placed the photographs of Alexander in her coat pocket. Elise put on her Girls' League uniform jacket and her thick, out-of-shape overcoat on top. In her coat and ugly hat, Elise looked horribly unfashionable.

Ruth left her mother a note to say they'd gone out to look for her. She couldn't waste time at home. Papa wasn't back. Kizzy hadn't shown up. Mama had been out for too long and there must have been a reason.

On the street, people went about their everyday chores, as if it was a normal Saturday. Ruth and Elise walked through the neighborhood, heading west. They checked the houses of family friends and other acquaintances. Most doors went unanswered.

Those who were at home admitted to hearing about the round-ups. "Your Mama stopped by earlier," one woman told Ruth, and she offered the girls tea and food. House to house, Ruth gathered a small collection of breads and jams in a paper bag. They approached another house, its front garden bare in the bright but cold afternoon.

"Mama's co-worker lives here," Ruth said to Elise as they walked through the front gate.

Ruth could see four people in the front room. She tapped on the window and waved at the people inside. The family jumped up right away and all four of them came to the door—the husband of Mama's friend and his two boys, both younger than Ruth, and a little girl, even younger.

"Your mother was here ten minutes ago," the man said before Ruth even opened her mouth. "If you run, you'll catch up with them. My wife went with her, to the Jewish Community Center on Rosenstrasse."

"That's close to Hackescher Market," Elise said.

It was the first thing she'd said to Ruth in over an hour.

"Thanks very much," Ruth said to the man.

"Good luck. Come back here if you can't find them, okay?"

"We will," Ruth called back.

Rosenstrasse was only a fifteen-minute walk away. As they approached the street, Ruth was surprised to see a small crowd of people standing in the road, all facing the same direction.

Mama saw them first. "Ruti! Elise!"

"We came to find you," Ruth shouted as she ran toward her. Ruth recognized one of the women as Mama's co-worker. "We were just at your house. We came right here." Then Ruth turned to Mama, who was staring at the building. "Is Alexander inside? What about Papa?"

"You should have stayed at home," Mama said.

The small crowd was made up of mostly women, a handful of men, and some children.

"Mama, what's happening?"

Mama let out a heavy sigh. "We think the Jewish men from the factories were brought here. Some people saw the trucks on the road. We don't know for sure." She paused, and Ruth knew Mama was about to deliver some bad news. "It was confirmed. Your father was arrested at work. I spoke to his colleagues at the factory. The Gestapo had their lists. They arrived early in the morning. There'd been a commotion and all the Jews were taken."

Ruth's heart pounded. She found it difficult to pay attention as Mama introduced Ruth and Elise to the other women, most of whom, Mama explained, were Christian Germans married to Jewish men. The women said their polite hellos, then turned their fearful stares back to the building. There must have been twenty or thirty people out on the street.

"Earlier, some of the women spoke to the guards," Mama said. "I tried talking to them, too. I demanded to know where your father and brother were."

Four Nazi guards—rounded metal helmets, long rifles, full uniform—stood at attention at the building's entrance.

"What did they say?" Ruth asked.

"They were polite but unhelpful. They denied anyone was in there, but, before I arrived, some of the other women saw them taking Jewish people inside."

Ruth watched as more women joined them on the street. The number of guards grew, too. A line of police, a dozen at least, formed across the center's doorway. The women whispered and watched the windows. Some ran over to purchase snacks from the café a few buildings away and quickly returned to the growing crowd.

Ruth stared—the whole crowd stared—as a woman approached the line of police, but the soldiers refused to speak to her. One of the women pointed to one of the guards. "I know him," she gasped. "He's my neighbor's son." Another woman, in a dark-green hat and matching coat, approached the policemen. After a few moments, one guard entered the building. The woman waited. They all waited. The crowd stood, whispering, watching the green-hatted woman at the entrance.

"Do you think they'll arrest her?" Ruth asked.

Before her mother could respond, the door opened and the guard appeared again. The woman held out her arm and the guard placed something in her hand. She walked away, quickly, back to her friends in the crowd. More whispered chatter broke out along the street. The policeman had given the green-hatted woman her house keys, proof that her Jewish husband was in the building.

"Ask for Papa's keys!" Ruth said to Mama.

Mama approached the police guards and one of them disappeared into the center. Ruth held her breath.

Elise

This is a waste of time. There was no chance Ruth's brother and father would be released, Elise knew. Ruth and Mrs. Broden would soon fall apart and Elise didn't want to watch all that. Not again.

Standing by the rows of police, Mrs. Broden looked back at them.

"I hope they're here," Ruth said and reached out for Elise's hand. Ruth's fingers were cold. Elise wanted to let go.

When the guard reappeared, he passed an object to Mrs. Broden. She ran back to Ruth and Elise with a set of jangling keys in her hand. "Look! Your father is in there," she said to Ruth.

"He's inside?" Ruth said. She sounded both relieved and devastated.

Elise expected their smiles to turn into a sob.

Mrs. Broden nodded. "Alexander is inside the building, too."

Ruth let out a yelp. "What? They told you that?"

"Ruti, hold out your hand." As she opened her fingers, Mrs. Broden dropped the keys into Ruth's palm. Wrapped around the key ring was a gold chain, broken, attached to a gold cross.

"No!" Ruth put her hand to her mouth.

Mrs. Broden put her arms around her daughter. "At least your father and brother are together."

Ruth nodded her head and took in a deep breath. "If I hadn't suggested the cross, we wouldn't know Alexander was here."

Elise was losing her patience again. *Ruth keeps making this about her.* Earlier, Ruth had been consumed by Alexander's silly treasure hunt. And without any care, Ruth had hurt Elise with harsh words about Elise's family. Ruth seemed oblivious that Elise was upset.

Elise pictured Viktor standing beside her in his hospital gown. As he sang softly, his fair hair brushed against her sleeve.

Ruth was lucky. Elise's parents didn't have the chance to negotiate for Viktor's release, to get proof he was still alive when they didn't know. Viktor had been alone in that hospital, detained by the government because he wasn't like normal kids. The letter had arrived without warning. Viktor had been a sudden victim of a typhus outbreak, it had said. There was no goodbye. She remembered walking home from the cemetery, clutching purple flowers, some weeks after his death. When he suspected the medical documents from the hospital had been falsified, Elise's father had taken her to see Viktor's grave. A kind of second funeral. There was a chance Viktor had been neglected by the doctors, Father had said. The thought made the skin on Elise's arm tingle. *Ruth should feel what I once felt.*

Viktor tapped Elise on the wrist. "She's frightened," he said.

Elise frowned. She looked toward the building. The policemen close to the Community Center's entrance had been joined by two Nazi officers in black uniforms. Elise found herself staring at one of the officers. He resembled Viktor, with his smooth blond hair. *Viktor would've grown up to look like him.* She couldn't look away. But when his blue eyes looked right at Elise and a hint of a smile appeared across his thin mouth, Elise moved her gaze upward to the windows of the Community Center. She saw little Viktor's face on one of the upper floors.

Ruth elbowed Elise in the arm and pointed. "Look. They're at the windows!"

The face Elise had seen wasn't Viktor's. It was a young girl, around twelve or thirteen. She had medium-length messy hair poking out from her blue-gray hat, her brown coat pulled up to her chin, and she was looking down at the crowd on the street. There were faces in the other windows, too. Hands waving. Mostly men, their mouths shouting, though Elise couldn't hear them. One or two people in the crowd screamed up to them. "I see my husband!" a woman shouted. The fair-haired Nazi officer who resembled Viktor rushed into the building. Moments later, the faces at the windows were gone. Viktor let go of Elise's sleeve and ran into the shadows the afternoon sun was making with the buildings.

"Did you hear that?" Ruth had been listening to some of the women who were cracking jokes. "She knew one of the guards as a boy. She said she changed his dirty underwear!"

Ruth was enjoying the drama of the protest and Elise found that infuriating.

More people, mostly women, arrived on the street. The news spread that those arrested during the round-ups had been separated into two groups. The Gestapo was holding those with full Jewish families elsewhere. Those with Aryan relatives—Jewish spouses and children of Aryan Germans—had been brought to Rosenstrasse. "Hitler's friends must be paying attention," one of the women said, referring to the high-ranking leaders of the government. "They're listening to us." The woman was a know-it-all. *She thinks she's important. A somebody. She thinks nothing could happen to her, or her husband.* The regime had stolen Viktor from Elise's perfect Aryan family. Nobody was safe.

They stood there for the rest of the afternoon. A woman walked through the crowd, passing out cups of hot tea. Some women left and soon returned with food, sometimes to share. Elise and Ruth finished off the bread and jam from Ruth's paper bag. Still, the crowd kept growing. As the winter sun began to set, the protestors chattered. A young woman approached Mrs. Broden. "What are you planning to do?"

"I have to take them home," Mrs. Broden said, pointing at Ruth and Elise.

The young woman looked up at the windows of the building. "I might stay out here for the night. Some of us should keep watch."

"We'll be back in the morning," Mrs. Broden said.

"Maybe we should stay, too," Ruth suggested to her mother.

Elise grimaced at the thought of standing out in the cold any longer, and she felt relieved when Mrs. Broden shook her head.

"Mama, do you want to stay? Elise can come home with me. Right, Elise?"

Elise kept quiet, waiting for Mrs. Broden to respond.

"I'm fifteen now," Ruth said.

Her mother nodded. "Okay. You can stay at Elise's house tonight. If I'm not with you by the morning, come back here to Rosenstrasse. All right? Just be careful."

Ruth seemed pleased by the compromise. "We'll be fine."

In other circumstances, Elise would have been excited by the idea of Ruth sleeping over. But with Elise's patience already thin, more time with Ruth wasn't going to be much fun.

Mrs. Broden continued, "Either way, we'll all be here tomorrow. Elise, tell your mother to come, too. We need all the people we can get."

Elise couldn't imagine her mother agreeing to join them. Besides, the demonstration would be over soon. The Jews would be sent to Nazi camps. As usual.

As Ruth hugged her mother goodbye, she whispered in her mother's ear. Elise let out a huff. *Ruth is being secretive.* Elise looked away in frustration. When she glimpsed the Nazi soldier—the young man who resembled Viktor, with his fair hair and square shoulders— Elise's grumpiness slipped away. The soldier walked between the protestors, heading toward Hackescher.

"I'm hungry," Elise said to Ruth. "How about the market?"

Ruth grinned. "Just like old times."

As they changed direction, Ruth linked arms with Elise. Elise wanted to shake her off. While Ruth reminisced, Elise kept her eyes trained on the soldier ahead and felt compelled to run up to him. To start a conversation. To hear his voice. Through Hackescher Market, Ruth browsed the fresh produce while Elise kept her eyes on the soldier. He walked alone, from stall to stall. Then he disappeared, out of sight.

When she saw the African boy, Elise couldn't move. She was frozen in place. He stood next to one of the stalls, picking up tins of food. Elise was afraid he'd see her. But she continued to stare. The boy looked hungry, his dark eyes sunken and small. Holding himself against the cold, he appeared smaller than he had on Friday, when he'd been fighting.

As she watched the African thief weave through the crowd, Elise wondered if she'd see the handsome young man, too. The idea was exciting. She would run up to him and Ruth would be impressed Elise was a friend of someone older and so good-looking. He would tell Ruth that Elise had saved him from the market thief. The thief rummaged through the market stall, figuring out how to steal, no doubt. Her pulse raced as he looked in Elise's direction. She turned away. *Did he spot me?*

Carrying cans of meat and a bag of potatoes, they walked away from the market.

"We'll have to take a detour. I need to check something at home," Ruth said.

"Why?" Elise asked.

At Ruth's house, Elise waited in the hallway while Ruth ran around searching for something. Elise didn't want to feed Ruth's behavior, but her curiosity won out. "What are you looking for?"

Ruth didn't reply until they were out on the street again. "One of our cousins, from Hamburg, was supposed to come stay with us."

"Which cousin?" This was the first Elise had heard of any such plans.

"It doesn't matter," Ruth said with a sigh.

Ruth is keeping secrets from me.

They arrived on Elise's street. When she saw a familiar woman standing outside her house, Elise's stomach flipped. *What does she*

171

want? Mrs. Unruh was balancing a sleeping baby on her hip. Her three other children, all young boys, were climbing up and jumping down from Elise's front step.

"Isn't your mother home?" Mrs. Unruh called out as Elise approached.

"She should be." *But she never answers the door.*

"She must be sleeping," Mrs. Unruh said, adjusting the position of her baby.

"Is everything all right?" Ruth asked.

Ignoring Ruth, Mrs. Unruh glared at Elise. "It's the tree in your back garden. One of the branches is broken and it's hanging onto our side."

Elise let out a heavy sigh. She didn't know what to say.

"You need to do something about it," Mrs. Unruh whined.

Elise was about to list the reasons for the state of the garden. "I'm sorry. My mother—"

"We'll take care of it," Ruth interrupted.

The woman scowled. "Was I talking to you?"

"Are you always this rude?" Ruth snapped back.

The woman's eldest son, no older than six, stared at Ruth with his mouth wide open. Elise wanted to laugh.

Mrs. Unruh's eyes looked like they were about to pop out. "Oh, how quickly little girls turn into their mothers," she said and led her boys home.

Elise's face flushed with embarrassment.

As the woman closed her front door, Ruth twisted her face. "What a cow!" Ruth said. Then she turned to Elise. "But don't take what she said to heart."

Ruth's words hurt more than Mrs. Unruh's comment. Ruth knew exactly what the awful woman had meant. Elise could picture her neighbors talking over their front garden walls. *Have you seen Elise Edelhoff lately? She's turning into her mother.*

"I remember her," Ruth said. "Is she always that horrible?"

Elise forced herself to speak. "Yes." Mrs. Unruh was the neighbor who had stopped talking to Elise's family because of Mother's endless screaming after Viktor's death.

"Elise? Is that you?"

"Yes, Mother."

She walked into the living room to find her mother in her armchair. "Where've you been?" Mother looked irritated and tired.

"The market."

"What's for dinner?"

"Ruth is staying over," Elise said. She didn't explain why, and Mother didn't respond.

In the kitchen, Elise stared at a pile of dirty dishes Mother had left for her. Ruth chattered away about the protest while Elise pulled down the blackout blinds and prepared a simple stew.

Mother ate her food in the living room, away from Elise and Ruth, and climbed the stairs to her room.

Ruth spent dinnertime chattering on and on about Alexander and her father, which gave Elise a headache.

In Elise's bedroom, Ruth helped to set up the spare mattress on the floor.

"What a day," Ruth sighed as Elise turned off the lamp.

Elise wanted to wish her friend a happy birthday, but she couldn't bring herself to speak.

Within minutes, Ruth was snoring lightly.

I'm a terrible friend.

In her head, Elise took Viktor's hand.

She climbed out of bed and followed him into the darkness of the hallway.

"Can we play?" Viktor asked.

He led Elise to the room that overlooked Berlin's rooftops.

Through the window, Elise noticed the broken branch hanging into Mrs. Unruh's back garden.

I don't want to turn into my mother.

"It's late," she said to Viktor.

She returned to her bedroom.

Marko

Waking with a jolt alone in the dark wine cellar, Marko wasn't sure of the exact time. The springs of the mattress dug into his back and his already forgotten dream was pierced with fresh memories of reality—*Alex is missing, Kizzy was arrested*—and Marko was wide-awake.

He could vaguely remember his sister kicking him while it was still daytime, and telling him she'd be back.

But that was hours ago. Marko had slept through the whole day. *It must be Saturday night.* By now, if everything had gone to plan, Alex and Marko should have been long gone. By now, Kizzy should have moved in with the Broden family.

Marko checked the street for guards and walked out into the icy night air. He strolled aimlessly, as if in a dream, through the side streets and gardens, avoiding the soldiers and checkpoints. Heading north, he walked close to the southeastern edge of the Tiergarten in Berlin's center. He remembered back to the spring of 1941, age fifteen. A young man had approached Marko and asked him to join him for a stroll through the park. Marko knew what the man wanted. Homosexuality had been outlawed for decades. The government would imprison two men for simply holding hands. Despite the enormous risk, Marko had agreed.

Later that summer, Marko met Alex.

His documents—Paul Voeske, not Marko Lange—were listed with the authorities and, when he turned sixteen, Marko was summoned to a factory close to Moabit that manufactured metal components for the German army. As a registered Aryan, Marko got paid. But he hated standing on his feet all day. When he asked to transfer, the manager happily obliged.

Marko was moved to a brewery just east of Gesundbrunnen and he couldn't believe his luck. Assigned to deliveries, he got to know the city. He even got to sample the beer.

One afternoon, a delivery error sent Marko to the brewery office. A young guy with a yellow star, Marko's age, dealt with

Marko's paperwork. He introduced himself as Alexander Broden. Alex was good-looking and focused on his work. Marko introduced himself as Paul Voeske.

After work, Marko waited for Alex by the brewery gate. They spoke about nothing important. Soon they were meeting every day. They discussed their co-workers and the war. Marko asked Alex about his yellow star. Alex's family had been sent to the East, he said. As Alex was Jewish, Marko felt comfortable telling him his real name and that he was Romani, living in hiding with his sister and cousin. They talked about Marko's mother and extended family imprisoned at the camp for Roma in Marzahn.

After a few weeks, Alex arranged to work the deliveries, too. Sharing a van, they talked and talked as Marko drove them through the city. They worked fast, staying on schedule.

On their fourth morning together, parked on the street with the risk of being seen, Marko kissed Alex and Alex, hesitantly at first, kissed Marko back.

And now, Alex was gone.

Marko arrived at Alex's home. He knocked on the front door but nobody came. At the back of the house, he tapped on the kitchen windows. He found pebbles and threw them against the windows upstairs. The house was empty. *Where are they?* "Broden! Alex Broden! Ruti!" he shouted. A face in the window next door startled him and Marko fled into the gardens. His mind wandered to Alex and stories of the Broden family, all sent away. *You accept the deportations*, Alex had told Marko once. *You move on because you don't have a choice.* Marko began to admit to himself that Alex—and his family, it seemed—had been arrested.

He made his way to the professor's house. After eating stale bread and scraps, Marko grabbed his bag, soap, food, and a change of clothes. He packed Duerr's jewelry and remembered his knife. Marko searched through Alex's suitcase, choosing to take his towel and shirts. And he found some of Duerr's vodka.

Lugging the bag through the side streets, he walked back to the cellar. Tsura hadn't returned. He checked the cellar's wall in the hope that Alex had been there to carved the letter "A" in the plaster. Nothing.

With the soldier's medal, Marko cut another letter "M" and opened Duerr's bottle of vodka. The vodka mixed with Marko's thoughts of sending Kizzy to the hospital. He would keep his secret forever.

Kizzy

Orange sunlight sparkled on the barbed wire across the windows, bringing to life the golden stars on the children's coats. Kizzy sat against the wall, her hat pulled down over her ears. She was the oldest in a room full of Jewish children. Most were asleep. Two or three were awake and quietly sobbing. Kizzy swallowed the last of the bread given to her by the nurse at Charité Hospital. She could hear vehicles outside. She jumped to her feet and stood at the window. On the street below, soldiers led a line of people down from trucks and into the building. The soldiers had separated the children from the grownups. Until the truck, Kizzy had never met Jewish people up close. She'd only seen them on the streets with their yellow stars sewn onto their clothes, bearing the word *Jude*— Jew. Professor Duerr had told Kizzy stories about them. Jews were ordinary people, the professor had said, like the Romani and Sinti peoples.

The door to their room swung open. Kizzy flinched and sat back down. Nazi soldiers led another dozen children into the room, each with a yellow star. When she noticed a boy and girl in the group, age ten or eleven, Kizzy kept her eyes on them. The boy appeared to be alone. The girl was holding the hand of a small boy with fiery red hair. The new children shuffled into the corner and the soldiers left, locking the door behind them.

"What are your names?" Kizzy asked the older children.

"Felix," the boy said.

The girl hesitated. On the floor, the toddler curled himself up in the girl's lap. "I'm Esther." She looked down at the little redhead. "This is Ari, my cousin. He's four." Esther paused, then continued to talk. "The soldiers came yesterday. They took my parents. And my aunt and uncle. Ari and I were at home on our own. Today, two nurses came to get us. Do you know if our parents are here?"

Kizzy shrugged. "Maybe." The rooms above and below them were filled with Jewish adults, she knew.

"My parents were with us on the truck," Felix said.

Many of the children had been talking about and crying out for their parents. It made Kizzy feel like an adult. Her father had been sent away. Her mother was captive in Marzahn.

Esther's cousin, Ari, was asleep now.

"He's got the right idea," Kizzy said and she pulled her hat to cover the back of her neck before curling up into the corner.

A few hours later, Kizzy woke up. Daylight poured over the children as they ate bowls of potatoes and raw cabbage. Esther was helping Ari eat the last spoonful. A bowl filled with the unpleasant food sat next to Kizzy.

"I saved you some," Felix said.

Kizzy forced herself to eat.

A while later, the door opened and the children looked up. Three women in uniforms surveyed the room.

"Let's start here," one of the nurses said. "Children, form three lines, please."

"What are they doing?" Esther asked.

"Sending us away again," was Felix's guess.

Kizzy watched the nurses as they examined the children's heads. "No. They're checking for lice."

The nurses were on their knees, inspecting the hair of each child. The thought of lice made Kizzy want to scratch her head.

When it was Kizzy's turn, because Kizzy was taller than all the others, the nurse at the head of her line stood up.

"Hat," she said.

Kizzy pulled off her blue hat and the nurse began to examine Kizzy's scalp by separating sections of her wild hair. The gentle pulling of her roots felt good and Kizzy's eyes began to fall closed. But she was startled when she noticed Esther crying.

"What's the matter?" Felix asked.

"I hate lice!" Esther said through tears. She held Ari's hand tight. Ari looked terrified but didn't make a sound.

"You're scaring your cousin," Kizzy said to Esther.

Kizzy was surprised by how frightened Esther seemed. Kizzy had had lice once. They were itchy and Professor Duerr had scrubbed Kizzy's head with awful chemicals, but the ordeal hadn't been that bad.

"What's your name?" Felix asked.

The doctor at the hospital had confiscated Kizzy's false papers. There was no need to pretend to be Franziska Voeske anymore. "Kizzy."

Felix looked down at her coat. "And where's your star?"

"I was living in hiding. Then I got caught," Kizzy told them truthfully. She didn't mention she was Romani.

THE FLEA

Tsura

Tsura hadn't needed more than a few hours of rest. On Saturday afternoon, she'd left Marko asleep in the wine cellar and walked to Seraph's apartment in the Bavarian Quarter. With the city swarming with Gestapo, Wolf and Seraph were nowhere to be found. In hiding, most likely. At the apartment, Tsura had washed and changed her clothes before returning to the wine cellar. When she'd kicked Marko awake, he'd groaned and told her to leave him alone.

She returned to the apartment. Kizzy had been caught—the hospital staff had confirmed it—and Tsura felt paralyzed. Wolf would know what to do. She fell asleep on the sofa, waiting for him and Seraph to return.

On Sunday morning, with still no sign of them, Tsura made herself a sandwich with cheese and stale bread, and set out for the train station.

Usually, avoiding the checkpoints wasn't too difficult, but sometimes it was impossible. Close to the U-Bahn station, Tsura became Greta. As the soldiers inspected her papers, Tsura's thoughts were stuck on Kizzy, leading her to picture Marzahn. Her mother. And baby Samuel, his lifeless body in Aunt Marie's arms. The

179

soldiers had watched from afar as Tsura's family buried the boy. *How could anyone hate a child?* She forced a smile at the station guards and they sent Greta Voeske on her way.

Underground, waiting on the platform with a few dozen others, Tsura heard the approaching rattling of a train. She disliked traveling on the city train lines, mostly because diligent police guards paid close attention to the commuters. But Tsura's false identity documents gave her access to the U-Bahn system, which cut her journey time across the city and kept her out of the cold.

Tsura jumped when a woman's scream echoed against the walls. It was followed by panicked shouts. "Help her!" Someone had fallen onto the tracks.

When she heard a baby's cry, Tsura pushed her way through the group of onlookers. "Move," Tsura shouted.

On the tracks, a woman was on her back, eyes wide, stunned by the fall, a crying baby in her arms.

"The train is coming!" someone screamed.

Tsura blocked out the panicked shouts of the frantic crowd and jumped down from the platform's edge. "Give me the baby," Tsura ordered. The clattering of the train grew louder. For a moment, the woman was motionless. "Now!" The woman raised the baby into the air. Tsura grabbed the swaddled infant. "Here." Tsura tossed the child toward the shocked witnesses. Two women caught the baby as Tsura spun around to reach for the woman's arms.

"Help me!" the mother screamed.

"The train!" a man shouted.

Tsura hauled the woman to her feet and, with her shoulder beneath the mother's thigh, pushed her up and onto the platform.

The people on the platform yelled. "Hurry!" "The train!" "Dear God!"

Tsura dragged herself onto the platform just before the train rattled by.

The crowd surged forward. "You saved her." "Are you all right?" "God bless you."

180

The train screeched to a halt. The baby, in its mother's arms again, continued to wail. Hands on Tsura's back pushed her toward the woman and child she had rescued. The woman was sitting on the platform, cradling her infant.

With tears in her eyes, the mother looked up at Tsura. "Thank you! You'll be rewarded for what you did. My husband is a senior government official. You saved his son." The woman smiled warmly, waiting for Tsura's response.

Tsura had nothing to say.

The woman continued, "Tell me, what's your name?"

Tsura's feelings of pride and relief for the woman and child's safety had transformed into a penetrating hatred that forced Tsura to clench her fists, to control herself. *I have to leave.* She turned away. Strangers in the crowd called out "Wait!" as she boarded the crowded U-Bahn train. Standing shoulder to shoulder with other commuters, Tsura held on as the train sputtered to life and pulled away from the station. *If I'd known she was a Nazi—* Tsura cut her thought short.

She exited the train and arrived at the professor's house. She checked for signs of Kizzy. Nothing. Tiredness was setting in, but Tsura couldn't stay there in that cold house filled with memories. Avoiding the train, she walked for an hour or so to Motzstrasse.

"Where've you been?" Marko asked as Tsura climbed down into the wine cellar.

Tsura sat on the mattress beside him. "We need to get to Marzahn."

The cries of the baby on the tracks repeated in Tsura's head. *I should have let the infant die.* Her hand on her lower stomach, she wanted to scream out. When Tsura was eleven years old, one year before the encampment at Marzahn was opened, Nazi doctors ordered her mother to bring Tsura to a clinic in the city. Tsura was sterilized on the spot, along with three Sinti girls. She would never bear children. Never know the feeling of her breasts swelling at the sound of her baby's cry. While Tsura had cried in pain, Mother had cried for the children Tsura would never have.

Alexander

Balanced on the windowsill, Alex put his head against the glass and looked down to the street below. In the early morning light, a dozen or so women stood in front of the Community Center. Alex almost shouted out when he saw his mother standing among them. He tapped on the glass. The women looked up and Mother waved and blew him kisses with her gloved hand. *Was Mama out there all night?*

"Papa, quickly, guess who's here," he said, gesturing for his father to join him on the ledge.

Father climbed up. "Annett!" he shouted through the glass. He turned to Alex. "She shouldn't be out there. She'll get herself arrested."

Alex's mother beamed and waved with delight. She was shouting something, but they couldn't hear her words.

Father climbed down while Alex kept watch at the window, his eyes fixed on his mother. As the sunrise beckoned another day, small groups of people walked onto Rosenstrasse from the side streets. The crowd was growing again.

"They're coming back," Alex announced to the room.

The men perked up. "They are?" "How many?" "Can you see my wife?"

Hope swelled in Alex's chest. He looked out for Marko's face, wondering if he'd heard about the demonstration.

The protest was heartening. Such a collective outcry against Hitler's regime was unheard of. Yesterday, when a Nazi police guard had walked into the room and ordered Father to hand over his house keys—because his wife had been locked out—Alex had almost laughed aloud. Immediately, Alex had entwined his broken gold chain and cross around the key ring, to signify to Mother that he was in the building, too.

"Roll call," Simon the orderly shouted from the doorway.

"Alexander, get down from there," his father said with panic in his voice.

Alex, along with the other men who had been standing at the windows, jumped to the floor.

Roll call was tedious and nerve-wracking. Breakfast would not be served until all prisoners had been accounted for. Alex stood between Father and Mr. Federman as the Nazi officers counted them and checked them off their lists.

Then they began to count again.

Mr. Lessel was jumping from foot to foot. "God, I'm bursting," he whispered.

Alex laughed and Mr. Lessel scowled, then smiled back.

"Breakfast is ready," Simon announced once the counting was complete.

Mr. Lessel ran ahead toward the toilet. Led downstairs, Alex and Mr. Federman looked out for Lea.

"Papa!" she yelled as the men passed the doorway to one of the women's rooms.

"Lea, are you all right?" Mr. Federman shouted back.

"I'm fine," she called out and locked eyes with Alex. Lea blushed and Alex gave her an awkward smile.

Downstairs, Alex stood in line with the other men. "Sauerkraut and potatoes today," the men at the front announced.

"Thank God," Father said.

"You can say that again," Mr. Lessel said, joining them in line.

Yesterday's lunch and dinner had been cabbage. A collective fear that supplies would run out had spread through the building. But the men were kind enough to allow those who hadn't eaten during the last meal stand at the front of the line.

Returning to their room on the upper floor, some of the men laughed as they listened through the floor to an argument amongst the women downstairs. But the quarrel settled down quickly and was replaced by pleasant singing. Alex was bored, as was everyone else. Some men had been telling stories. One man had created a chessboard out of a piece of mattress. Mr. Lessel had spent his time writing in what Alex suspected was his diary. Another man, nicknamed a know-it-all by some of the men, talked incessantly about history and politics, which Alex found interesting. Last night, the Gestapo had brought more Jews to the building, always Jews with non-Jewish families, which was a great sign, Father had said. The rooms were overcrowded now.

Three men, including Mr. Lessel, climbed up onto the sill and began providing commentary on what they could see. "There are at least a hundred people out there." The room filled with optimistic chatter. "Most are women. And there are a few men and children." Cathedral bells sounded in the distance. "They're missing Sunday morning services to be here," Mr. Lessel said.

Another hour passed. Again it was Alex's turn to stand at the window.

The sight of the crowded street amazed him. Through the glass, Alex could hear the muffled sounds of shouting from below. "I think the guards are telling the crowd to leave," Alex said to the men. An uneasy whisper spread across the room.

Father stood up. "What are the women doing?"

Alex watched for the crowd's reaction. "Nothing. They're staying put."

"Is your mother still out there?" Father asked.

When Alex saw Ruti's friend Elise in the crowd, standing close to his mother, his eyes searched for Ruti. But she wasn't there.

Ruth

Ruth pushed through the crowd. The protestors were waving frantically at the windows. Even though they couldn't hear one another, they still shouted the names of their loved ones. Then, like yesterday, all the faces disappeared.

"Mama!" Ruth called out. "Did you see them? Did you see Papa? Did you see Alexander?"

"We saw Alex," Elise told her.

"Where?" Ruth shouted.

"The same window," Mama said and pointed to the left of the building, three windows up. But the window was empty now.

This morning, when Ruth and Elise had arrived on Rosenstrasse, Mama had told them how she'd stayed awake all night and seen Alexander and Papa at the window, just after sunrise.

Ruth was about to cry. She took off her glasses and rubbed her eyes with her fingers, and scrunched up her face to stop the tears. "I can't believe I wasn't here." She'd chosen the wrong time to find a toilet. She'd been waiting in line inside the café up the street and missed the commotion. Ruth kept her eyes on the windows in the hope Alexander would make another appearance. Her thoughts led Ruth to Alexander's treasure hunt. *I need to find the woman's place of birth.*

"Elise, where were you born?"

"What?"

"Were you born here, in Berlin? And what about your mother?"

"Berlin. Both of us. Why?"

Ruth folded her arms and tapped her foot. There was a second unsolved riddle, too. "Rose petals, white piping, a reverse pickpocket," she said out loud.

It was lunchtime now and the protest was strengthening. Some people had walked from Bahnhof Börse train station. The protestors were coming from all over the city. More women had approached the Nazi guards to ask for their keys. Most of the time, the guards returned with proof the women's Jewish husbands were inside.

The crowd continued to grow. The church services were over and some of the women had brought along their friends and neighbors.

"Go home!" one of the guards shouted.

"We're not going anywhere," Mama whispered to Ruth.

They joined the crowd in a communal silent stare.

"Go home or we'll shoot," another soldier yelled.

Still, nobody moved. What was exciting to Ruth, but also frightening, was the sight of the soldiers on edge.

185

"It'll take more than threats to get us to leave," Mama said. "It's Sunday. We have nowhere else to be."

Without warning, the crowd was forced to stand back as trucks pulled up to the front of the Community Center.

"Look," Ruth said.

Soldiers dragged Jewish people—yellow stars adorned their coats and shirts and dresses—into the building. That Jews were being brought here was no longer a secret. One Jewish man turned and waved at a young woman in the crowd. She waved and called at him until a Nazi soldier kicked the Jew hard and he disappeared into the building. The protestors gasped.

"This must be the building's only entrance. Otherwise, they'd be taking them through another door," Ruth said.

"You know what, Ruti? You're right!" Mama clapped her hands at her daughter's shrewd thinking.

Ruth beamed.

More tea was passed around. More protestors joined the crowd, watching the windows. Waiting.

In the middle of the afternoon, some of the protestors began to chuckle. A woman had approached the Nazi guards with a cake, asking them if she could take it inside. The guards sent her away.

"It's Monday tomorrow," Mama said. As the evening neared on the second day of the protest, Mama approached some of the other women. She returned with an account of their decision. "We'll be missing work tomorrow and coming here instead."

Pride surged through Ruth's chest. They were refusing to give up.

"Will you stay out here again tonight?" Ruth asked.

"Not tonight, my darling. I'm exhausted. But some of the other women have volunteered. We're taking turns." Mama turned to Elise. "We'll take you home. We can pick you up in the morning, if you like."

"I have school tomorrow," Elise said.

Ruth laughed and poked her friend in the arm. "Don't be silly. We get to miss it."

They began their trek toward Elise's home.

A ball of sadness sat in Ruth's throat. "Did Alexander look all right?"

"He looked well," Mama added. She squeezed Ruth's hand. "I'm sure he was looking for you."

"I can't believe I didn't see him."

Elise

Viktor's voice woke her. It was still dark outside.

Today, Monday, was the Day of the Luftwaffe. Last week, in Girls' League, Elise had learned about the celebration. Hitler's head of the Air Force, Hermann Göring, had declared the first day of March a national thank-you to the fighter planes and their extraordinary power. Even though he hadn't flown planes, it made Elise think about Father, fighting on the front, risking his life for his people.

Elise washed and dressed. In the kitchen, another dirty cup sat beside hers. Mother had woken in the middle of the night. As the morning light appeared across the kitchen, Elise took a bite of hardened bread. But she wasn't all that hungry. She swept the floor and wiped the countertops.

Someone knocking on the front door made Elise's mother jump. "Who's that?"

"Ruth and Frau Broden."

"On a Monday morning?"

Until now, Elise had avoided talking to Mother about the demonstration on Rosenstrasse. "Ruth's brother and father were arrested. They're being held in the city. I'm going with them—"

Ruth and Mrs. Broden knocked again.

Mother held her dressing gown closed. "Don't let them inside."

With a heavy sigh, Elise walked into the hallway and opened the door.

"Good morning, Elise." Ruth was chirpy.

Mrs. Broden winked. "It's a perfect day for a protest, don't you think?"

Elise forced herself to respond. "Good morning. Good morning, Frau Broden. Did you eat?"

"We had a big breakfast," Mrs. Broden said.

"More birthday leftovers," Ruth added.

A feeling of impatience and resentment swelled in Elise's stomach. Since Alex had been arrested, Ruth hadn't been acting like a friend. Ruth still hadn't apologized for insulting Elise's family. And when Ruth had missed seeing Alexander at the window, rather than show gratitude that her father and brother hadn't yet been sent to a Nazi camp—as they should have been—Ruth had complained.

"Is your mother joining us?" Mrs. Broden asked.

"She's not feeling well," Elise fibbed.

What must Frau Broden be thinking? Mother and Mrs. Broden were once friends. They'd cooked together and gossiped over tea in their kitchens. They'd met at church when the girls were young. But after Viktor died everything changed.

Elise put on her thick sweater, heavy overcoat, hat, and gloves. She wouldn't only be missing school, she'd be missing the Girls' League meeting as well. Elise left her Girls' League jacket and beret hanging on the hook in the hallway. Mrs. Broden had brought them a bag of food and Elise ate a little cheese on the way back to Rosenstrasse.

Elise sighed while Ruth babbled away, again, about her awful treasure hunt.

They walked west. In his white hospital gown, Viktor dragged his feet beside them.

Hundreds of people stood on Rosenstrasse, shoulder to shoulder, facing the Jewish Community Center and the Nazi guards. Today was the third day of the demonstration and the government had closed Bahnhof Börse train station to make it difficult for people to congregate.

"Someone important is paying attention," Mrs. Broden said.

There was still a line of police guards, at least twenty of them now, in their metal helmets, holding their guns. Elise rolled her eyes as the women yet again hoped out loud that their husbands and children would be released.

"The soldiers are so frightening," Ruth said.

To Elise, the guards looked anxious and just as scared. She recognized the soldier she'd seen on Saturday—the young man who looked like Viktor, with pale skin and blue eyes, his fair hair flickering in the wind. Part of Elise wished she were wearing her Girls' League uniform. *That would make him look at me—make him notice.* Caught in her thoughts, Elise saw Viktor standing next to the guard, a metal soldier's helmet in his hands. He hadn't died after all. Viktor would have been twelve years old by now.

By mid-afternoon, the street was so full that Elise couldn't count the individual protesters. The crowd stared at the quiet building, whispering amongst themselves, some drinking tea, a few smoking cigarettes.

When the crowd became excited, Elise looked up to see faces at the windows again. Hands waved and tapped on the glass. People in the crowd called up, waving back, recognizing their relatives. Elise saw the same face once more, the same girl she'd seen on the first day of the protest, one level up, age twelve or thirteen, messy hair, brown coat and blue-gray hat. Then she disappeared.

Ruth stood on tiptoes. She looked at Elise. "I hope I see Alexander. I can't believe you saw him. I'm jealous."

Ruth was becoming more and more annoying. *If Ruth had seen Viktor at the window and I hadn't, I wouldn't be complaining.*

"But I think I figured out another riddle," Ruth continued. "I have to find someone's place of birth. A woman. Or a girl."

On Saturday, at Ruth's home, when Elise had told Ruth about Alex's girlfriend, Ruth had been too engrossed in her silly treasure hunt to listen. Elise wanted to repeat the gossip, but her irritation with Ruth kept her silent. On the other hand, Ruth would want to know, Elise knew.

Elise nudged Ruth on the arm. "I have to tell you something."

Overhearing Elise's words, Mrs. Broden looked at the girls with a curious stare. Elise took Ruth's elbow and pulled her aside, away from the adults.

"What's going on?" Ruth asked, looking down at Elise's grip.

"Remember I told you I saw Alex? Behind my house?"

Ruth nodded, listening.

"I think your brother has a girlfriend."

Ruth didn't smile as Elise had expected. "Why do you think that?"

"I saw him," Elise said, quietly, not wanting Mrs. Broden to hear. "He was kissing some girl."

"What girl?" Ruth said, her eyes bulging now. "When?"

She doesn't know. Elise was glad she knew something Ruth didn't. "On Friday night. I don't know who she was, but I saw them. From the window. They were definitely kissing."

"What time?" Ruth asked, a smile creeping across her face.

Elise shook her head, "Why?"

"Was it around midnight?"

"Maybe. I don't know. Yes."

Ruth said nothing, as if she knew more than she was letting on. *She knows about Alex. Why would Ruth keep that a secret?*

"Maybe she's here," Ruth said, standing on tiptoes again and looking across the crowd. "Do you think she knows my brother was arrested? Do you think the girl I have to find for my treasure hunt could be Alexander's girlfriend? Maybe I need to find her. No, that doesn't make sense. Alexander didn't tell me about her. But she must be so worried. Elise, what did she look like?"

So, Ruth has never met her, Elise realized. "I only saw the back of her head. And she was wearing a hat." Elise hadn't seen her face.

Mrs. Broden couldn't hear their words, but she was paying attention to their gestures. "What are you girls up to?"

"Nothing," Ruth said.

The protestors were still talking about seeing their family members in the windows.

"I think you're right," Ruth whispered to Elise.

"What?"

"Alexander was meeting a girl. On Friday, at midnight. I overheard him."

She was keeping things from me. Elise felt irritated by Ruth all over again. *We used to tell each other everything.*

A joke spread through the crowd. "If only we had a wooden horse, like the one sent by the Greeks," one of the women repeated. Mrs. Broden laughed. "Let's send the Gestapo a gift. We'll sneak inside the building and rescue our families."

Elise and Viktor listened to their fantasy.

"Did you try to rescue me?" Viktor asked.

If only I'd had a Trojan Horse, Elise wanted to tell her brother, *I would've climbed inside it myself.* Viktor would have believed the horse was real. His sickness made him think like that. He saw the world in a different way than other children his age. The Nazis saw him as untreatable. A mistake of nature, Elise's mother had called him.

Until now, the crowd had been largely silent, just whispering and praising each other for missing work, for choosing to come to the center instead. "The Gestapo has to listen. We're not asking for much," one woman said. "We just want our husbands back." Another woman repeated her phrase. "We want our husbands back." "We want our husbands back," Mrs. Broden joined in. The words spread quickly through the crowd. The chant surged along the street.

"We want our husbands back!" Ruth shouted along.

Elise listened as the women, and even the children and few men, shouted those same words. The Nazi guards looked at one another, not knowing how to respond. Elise watched the fair-haired soldier walk into the building, most likely to ask his superiors what they should do. The women continued to scream their words. As if it would make any difference.

"Look," Ruth said to Elise. She pointed to a man on the street standing amongst the women—a German soldier, around the age of Elise's father—shouting the same words as everyone else.

Elise listened to the commentary around her. The protest resembled the women's suffrage demonstrations years earlier, one woman suggested, before women could vote and before they'd even heard of Adolf Hitler. Another woman talked about an Indian activist who would have been proud of them. Ruth appeared to be listening carefully, as if taking notes in her head, as if the lessons from history would make any difference today. The truth, Elise knew, was that history only repeated itself and there was nothing anyone could do.

As the crowd chanted, one woman nudged Elise to join in, but Elise kept her mouth closed. Elise didn't know why she couldn't bring herself to shout along. Then she caught herself looking out for other members of the Girls' League. She was embarrassed to be there. *I'm a hypocrite.*

The day went on. The evening would come soon. Again, the women made plans for some to stay overnight and to congregate the next morning.

"Let's go," Mrs. Broden said and took Ruth's hand. "We'll come back tomorrow. We'll need our energy if this protest drags on."

Ruth and her mother walked Elise home. Mrs. Broden looked exhausted.

"I'll cook, if you like," Elise said as they reached her street.

"No, thank you, my dear," Mrs. Broden said.

Ruth gave Elise a half-smile. Things between them felt different. But it was Ruth who was acting like a self-centered child. Elise knew how to be an adult.

In her open doorway, Elise was about to say goodnight and close the door when Ruth jumped forward.

"Your coat! Elise, it's your coat!" Ruth ran into the house. She grabbed Elise's thin pink coat from the rack. "The white piping! And the color!"

Ruth checked every pocket. She huffed and stamped her feet.

Mrs. Broden walked inside, closing the door behind her. "Ruti, what is it?" she asked.

"A pickpocket in reverse," Ruth said, looking at her mother. Then she turned to Elise. "When my brother gave you the other clue—the one labeled *Freund*—were you wearing this pink coat?"

"Yes—"

Ruth grinned. "He must've planted a second clue on you, without you knowing. I know I'm right. A pickpocket in reverse. I figured it out!"

She always thinks she's right. Ruth checked the pockets of Elise's pink coat again. And again. She checked the hallway floor and behind the other hanging coats. She couldn't find anything. Defeated, her eyes became glassy. But she didn't cry.

Mrs. Broden sat herself on the stairs. "Actually, Elise, some dinner sounds good right now."

The sun was setting. Elise closed the small blackout curtain in the hallway and turned on the lamp. Mother was sitting in the living room, wearing an apron. It was clear, however, that her mother hadn't been cleaning, and Elise couldn't smell food cooking. Mrs. Broden started a conversation with her while Elise and Ruth headed into the kitchen. There were crumbs on the floor and milk, now warm and stinking, spilled across the countertop.

"Heat up some water," Elise said to Ruth, pointing to a pot.

With the chopping board and knife, Elise cut up potatoes and other root vegetables that were starting to mold. Ruth wiped down the table and Elise washed some bowls. When the stew was ready, they called their mothers to the kitchen.

At the table, Mrs. Broden talked about the protest. "The government is listening. We'll return to Rosenstrasse, every day, until every prisoner is released."

"I have a headache," Elise's mother said in response and climbed the stairs to bed.

A rush of shame swelled in Elise's throat. "I'm sorry."

"You have nothing to apologize for," Mrs. Broden said sincerely. "Are you okay, Elise?"

"I'm fine." Nothing had been okay for a long time.

"Thanks for dinner," Ruth said, filling the awkward moment.

Ruth and her mother put on their coats.

"See you in the morning," Elise said, forcing a smile.

Elise closed the front door. Having Ruth as a friend was draining. As she washed the pot and bowls, she heard her mother heading back downstairs. Elise left the sink and followed Mother into the dark living room. After checking that the blackout curtains were closed, Elise turned on a lamp.

"Turn it off," Mother said.

Elise had an urge to shout. Mother didn't need to behave like this. "You really should see what's happening in the city," Elise said.

"What's the time?" Mother asked.

Elise checked the clock in the hall. "Almost eight thirty. You should see the protest. The crowds. Hundreds of people, shouting for their husbands. It's astonishing."

"Are their husbands all Jewish?" Mother asked.

"Yes. They—"

"Why should I bother standing out in the dead of winter, protesting on behalf of Jews?"

Mother sounded like the leaders of the Girls' League, with their smug, parroted views about Jews and Poles. They squawked on about preparing for early motherhood in service of their Fatherland and beloved Führer.

"Why are you wasting your time on strangers, Elise? You should be helping me at home. What would your father say?"

Elise argued back. "Herr Broden. And Alexander. They're in there, too."

Mother closed her eyes. "Jews are Jews." She rested her head against the high-backed armchair.

Elise returned to the kitchen. She took a seat at the table, the dirty chopping board and knife in front of her. In his hospital gown, holding his metal helmet, Viktor swung his legs from the chair. His hair was wet. His skin was a kind of gray.

"What's wrong with her?" Elise asked him.

Viktor looked at the knife.

Elise rolled up her sleeve. The scratches on her arm had faded. She touched them. Scars, raised, rough. Viktor picked up the knife from the table, its handle heavy, its blade sharp, holding it out to his sister.

"Not too deep," Viktor said.

Before Elise could put the blade to her skin, a long and terrifying bellowing sound jolted her to open her eyes. *Oh God.* She dropped the knife. "Mama!" she screamed. Mother ran in from the living room. The air raid siren wailed and cried in waves, echoing through the house. Mother and Elise ran to the backdoor.

Mother stopped in the doorway. "I need my coat," she said.

"Mama, no!" Elise shouted.

She took Mother by the hand, dragging her into their back garden and through a gap in the hedgerow. They'd done this before. Last year. Because their basement was deeper, larger, and reinforced with more brick, their neighbors had offered them and their other neighbors to join them if ever the sirens went off. Elise opened the back door of their neighbors' home. They shuffled through their neighbor's kitchen, into the dark hallway, and down into the basement. Their neighbors were already there. More people rushed down the stairs, including the rude woman from next door, Mrs. Unruh, and her children.

Elise's mother screamed at the first sound of whistling. Then they heard a terrible crash, an explosion, close by. Everyone in the basement whimpered. There were a dozen of them in there, at least. Mrs. Unruh's boys were making a racket, fighting each other to sit next to their mother, who was holding her sleeping baby. When they heard the zooming of planes overhead, some people started to cry. *Ruth.* Elise pictured Ruth and Mrs. Broden running through the burning streets. More explosions. More whistling. The ground and walls shook. Mrs. Unruh's baby was awake and wailing now. Mother held on to Elise. It was the first time they'd hugged in a long time. Elise buried her head in her mother's lap and covered her ears. She could feel Mother's hand patting her on the back. The patting grew quicker, harder. Mother was trying to get her attention. Elise lifted her head.

"Elise—"

"Ruth!" Elise squealed.

Elise's best friend was standing, looking over her, with Mrs. Broden by her side.

The girls held each other tight.

"They're bombing Berlin!" Ruth yelled over the noise.

Elise let out a laugh. "As if I couldn't guess!"

Marko

When he heard the siren, Marko cheered. From the wine cellar, he enjoyed watching the Nazis scurry like rats toward the government bomb shelters and train stations below street level, terrified they'd be blown to pieces.

"Let's go." Tsura pointed to a Nazi car, black, shining, abandoned in the street. Bounding up the cellar steps, she called back to Marko. "The engine's on!"

Right behind her, Marko laughed. "Are you serious?"

They jumped in. As Tsura drove them south, they heard an explosion in the distance.

"Where are we going?" Marko asked.

"Stop talking."

Marko would never tell her, as it would only have gone to her head, but his sister made him proud. She was fearless and always had a clear goal. With the Gestapo's round-ups of Berlin's Jews well under way, they'd spent the day in the wine cellar. Tsura had talked about Kizzy, anxious they'd never see their younger cousin again. She'd fantasized about going to Marzahn, shooting the encampment guards dead, and finding their mother and aunt.

Within a few minutes they were in the Bavarian Quarter. Tsura parked the stolen car in front of an upscale apartment building. "Get out," Tsura said.

Marko followed Tsura into the building and up its iron staircase. A blast in the distance thundered through the stairwell. "Where are we? Is this where you live?" he asked.

"Be quiet."

Marko watched Tsura tap some kind of password on the door. The door was opened by a good-looking man, a little older than Marko, with a beard and dark hair. His white shirt was tucked into gray trousers that were held up by black cloth braces. His feet were bare. Marko and the young man exchanged guarded stares.

"Shouldn't you be in a bomb shelter?" the man said to Tsura.

Marko couldn't tell if he was kidding.

"This is my brother," Tsura said.

The man furrowed his eyebrows and Marko smirked.

Tsura grabbed a heavy coat from the rack and threw it at the man. "Get dressed. We're going to Marzahn. Right now."

Marzahn? Marko let out a laugh. "Sis, we're in the middle of an air raid."

"Where's Seraph?" Tsura asked, ignoring her brother.

"Basement," the man said, already putting on his socks.

"See you in the car. Two minutes," Tsura said to Marko, and she ran back into the hallway.

"I'm Marko." He held out his hand.

The man's handshake was strong. "Wolf."

As Wolf tied his boots, Marko checked out the expensive furniture and oil paintings. "I didn't realize my sister lived with rich kids."

Wolf half-smiled and led Marko downstairs.

There's no way Tsura would let him drive, but Marko tried his luck. As he climbed into the driver's seat of the stolen car, he heard the bombs approaching. Wolf sat in the back and rolled down the window. It felt as though Berlin was being liberated, but Marko's head swirled with fears for Alex, wherever he was. His hands on the wheel, he checked his watch. Tsura appeared with a young woman by her side. The woman had an angular face and short hair and she smiled at Marko, warmly, then she leaned through the back window, grabbed Wolf's face, and planted a kiss on his mouth.

"This is my baby brother. Marko, this is Seraph," Tsura said.

Marko ignored his sister's dig.

Seraph nodded. "Good to meet you, Marko."

"Same here."

"Seraph's driving," Tsura snapped.

Marko groaned and climbed into the back seat with Wolf. Tsura joined Seraph in the front.

"What's your plan, sis?" Marko asked.

Seraph slammed her foot down and the car took off, east, in the direction of the blasts. Finally, Tsura seemed to relax. "The Marzahn guards will be hiding from the bombs," Tsura explained.

When a blast close by made Marko jump, Seraph laughed. "I'm not scared if I'm killed," she boasted.

Wolf looked at Marko. "Good to know."

"Stop chatting. Drive faster," Tsura said.

"Don't worry, I'm more fun than my sister."

They were close to the park with the fountain and the fairy tale statues, Marko realized. *Broden lives near here.* Every part of him needed to know what had happened to Alex.

Marko tapped Seraph's shoulder. "Turn right. Friedrichshain."

"What? No. Stay on this road," Tsura instructed Seraph.

"We've gotta look for Broden."

"No, Marko. Not now. Alex was arrested."

"You don't know that. I'm serious. It'll take two minutes. Turn here, or I'm jumping out."

Seraph gave Tsura a stare. Tsura crossed her arms and looked away and Seraph steered the wheel right. Wolf stayed quiet. Behind them, bombs crashed into buildings between the river and Hackescher Market. They continued on the road along the riverbank.

"Turn left," Marko told Seraph.

"Be quick," Tsura said.

Marko rushed up to Alex's house and pounded on the front door. A loud whistling filled the air and a bomb landed streets away.

The ground and houses around him shook and the sky lit up bright with every blast.

"Marko! We have to go!" Tsura screamed from the car.

Seraph was shouting, too.

The blackout blinds on the windows had been pulled down. Ignoring his sister and Seraph, Marko found a rock and threw it through the window. The glass shattered and he used his boot to kick out an entry. *They'd be in the basement.* It was dark, but he could see around the furniture and into the hallway.

"Broden! Alex Broden!" he shouted down the steps, into the darkness. "Ruti!"

The basement was empty. Another bomb hit close and Marko bolted upstairs, into Alex's bedroom. He noticed Alex's map book on the floor. They'd looked through it on Friday night, side by side on his bed, planning their train journey to the border. Downstairs, he swung open the front door.

Tsura was screaming. "Get in, you idiot!"

Marko threw himself into the car. Seraph looked terrified. Wolf looked bored.

"What's wrong with you?" Tsura shouted.

An explosion lit up the night sky. There was a fire on the next street. Seraph took the car east, toward Marzahn.

"What's that?" Wolf asked, looking at the map book in Marko's hands.

"Nobody was home," Marko replied. *Broden's gone.*

Over the siren, an explosion lit up the buildings around them. Marko looked up at the sky. With the jets overhead, he couldn't see the stars. He felt sick. *Broden was arrested,* he knew. *Maybe his whole family.*

Every so often, Seraph looked at Wolf in the rearview mirror, the way Alex always stared at Marko. He remembered Wolf was Jewish, like Alex. Wolf's yellow star was gone, too. Marko gripped Alex's map book and made a plan in his head to search the city for Nazis, page by page, street by street. *Me and my knife.*

Watching the warplanes, Tsura hit her fist on the dashboard. "I hope they burn Berlin to the ground."

"It's retaliation for German bombs on London. The British want to destroy the Gestapo headquarters," Seraph guessed.

All Marko wanted was for Alex—wherever he was—to survive the war. *I'll go to London and find him there.*

They drove for fifteen minutes, heading northeast to the edge of the city.

"We'll only have until the sirens stop. Until then, the guards will be taking cover," Tsura explained.

The siren stayed steady. Minutes later, when Seraph stopped the car on an empty road, the whirring engine was replaced by bombs falling in the distance. The bombs sounded like thunder, but quick, one after another and another.

Tsura pointed into the night. "There's the camp."

The area looked familiar. Marko remembered himself as a boy. He could recall the adjacent refuse dump and his mother putting out their clothes, rinsed in dirty water, on the washing line by their hut. Broth boiled on the fire. People fell ill. He remembered baby Samuel, Kizzy's brother, screaming.

At the side of the road, Marko was startled when Seraph and Wolf pulled guns from their coats. *Real pistols.* Seraph showed off, aiming at planes in the sky, pretending to pull the trigger.

"Guns are for cowards," Marko said, but he was jealous.

Then Marko pulled out his knife, which made Wolf laugh.

"Go play with the kids," Seraph said.

Tsura let out a loud huff. "Enough."

Marko, Wolf, and Seraph smirked at one another, as if Tsura had reprimanded a group of kids.

But, when Tsura took out a pair of binoculars from her coat followed by a gun, she winked at him.

Marko laughed. "What the hell?"

"Let's go," his sister said, no longer smiling.

Kizzy

Every time a bomb crashed, the building rattled and the children's cries grew louder. Even the boys. One girl wouldn't stop staring at Kizzy. *She wants me to comfort her.* Kizzy crawled into the corner, covered her ears, and looked away. She told herself the air raid would stop soon. The bombs would kill the Nazi guards and they'd all run. *I'll find Tsura. And Marko.*

The loudest bomb yet made the children scream in unison. The room lit up. One little boy announced that the building down the street was on fire.

"Get away from the windows!" Kizzy shouted.

Kizzy had been in the same freezing building for two and a half days now. She made a mental note of the date. *The first day of March, Monday.* When the sirens had started, the guards had left and locked the door.

Right away, Kizzy had told the kids to stay away from the windows. She'd reminded them about the small air raid, around six weeks ago. For days afterwards, the streets were filled with glass. If a bomb hit close by, the glass would shatter.

Over the siren, Felix crawled to where Kizzy and Esther sat.

Felix was shaking. "If we're not killed, the soldiers will come back. They'll punish us for the air raid and send us to Poland. It's where they murder Jews. My Papa told me about it."

"Sshh! You'll scare the little ones," Esther said, holding her four-year-old cousin close.

"They're already scared," Felix replied.

As more bombs crashed close by, Esther covered her ears. Felix's warning didn't apply to Kizzy. *I'm not Jewish. They'll send me somewhere else.*

"If a window breaks, we should jump out," Felix suggested.

Esther disagreed. "And run into falling bombs?"

Kizzy sided with Felix, but his idea was flawed. "We still won't get through the wire," Kizzy said, pointing at the lattice of sharp and twisted barbs secured across the window frames.

As the bombs fell, Kizzy could hear the adults whimpering in the room next door. When one of the children opened the cupboard in the corner, the room filled with the stink of bathroom waste. There was no proper toilet; only a bucket in the cupboard. The smell was disgusting and Kizzy had tried to stop herself from needing to use it. In two days, she'd used the bucket three times.

Kizzy put her hand into her pinafore. She'd forgotten about Duerr's cigarettes—the ones she'd taken. *I could trade them for food.* In her coat pockets, she found her bar of soap and Professor Duerr's key. She held the soap to her nostrils and inhaled its flowery scent, blocking out the stench of the bucket. Kizzy wondered if Professor Duerr was all right. *I bet she's happy Berlin's getting bombed.* The war would be over soon.

Carefully, so the younger children couldn't see, she took out Marko's bar of chocolate from her pocket. She returned the key and soap to her coat.

She nudged Esther's arm. "Want some?"

"Yes!" Esther's eyes bulged.

Felix almost screamed with delight.

"Sshh!" Kizzy put her finger to her lips.

Kizzy opened the packet and broke the chocolate into sections, passing two pieces to Esther, for her and little Ari, and one piece to Felix, keeping most for herself. As the bombs fell and the little children screamed and cried, Kizzy ate. The chocolate helped Ari to calm down, and he rested his head of fiery red hair in Esther's lap. Esther watched the other children as she took a bite; Esther seemed to feel bad for not sharing. But Kizzy and Felix didn't care. Felix ate his piece in one go, stuffing the chocolate in without looking at it. Kizzy swallowed the chocolate quickly, too. The bitter taste led to thoughts of Marko.

The chocolate had been a gift from her cousin. *Marko sent me to the hospital. He got me arrested. And now I'm breathing in this stink and stuck with these annoying kids.* It made Kizzy smile that she was thinking of toilet waste and Marko at the same time. *I wish Marko was here right now.* Then she smiled even more for thinking about her stupid cousin like that.

More explosions. Kizzy wondered if Adolf Hitler could hear the bombs. Was he terrified of the explosions, too? As some younger children called out to their parents through tears, Esther patted Ari's red hair. His eyes closed and opened, fighting sleep.

"Oh God!" Esther shrieked.

Felix jumped. "What is it?"

Esther pushed Ari away and jumped to her feet. "Lice! He's got lice!"

Ari began to cry and Kizzy crawled toward him. "Esther, will you get away from the window?"

Esther crouched away from them while Kizzy leaned over Ari and, with her fingers pulling through his red hair, examined his scalp. "There's nothing here."

Esther edged closer and pointed to the floor. "What's that?"

Kizzy picked up what at first looked like a tiny speck of dirt. "It's a flea."

Esther screamed.

"It's dead," Kizzy said.

Esther was more terrified of the dead flea than the falling bombs. In her head, Kizzy laughed. Locked in the building with the Jewish children made her feel safer. If they were hit, she'd be killed with them. *Not in Marzahn.* Her life would end in the middle of Berlin. With the taste of chocolate between her teeth and along her gums, Kizzy felt content to be alone. She hoped Tsura and Marko were safe while Berlin burned.

D I R E C T   H I T

Tsura

Blacked-out Berlin her backdrop, binoculars in her hand, Tsura stood beneath a blanket of warplanes. Each screeching bomb and blast became a small revenge for Kizzy. Revenge for Duerr.

Tsura had outlined the simple plan. If the guards were taking shelter from the air raid, Seraph and Wolf would keep watch at the camp's perimeter. Marko and Tsura would run through the encampment, find their mother and Aunt Marie, and lead them to the car. Tsura inhaled the night air and prepared herself to witness the filth and illness. She dreaded to think how hungry her mother and aunt would be. *If they're even there.*

As they walked toward the field of caravans, Tsura updated Wolf and Seraph about Kizzy. "She was arrested. She was put on a truck with Jewish prisoners. What do you know about the round-ups?"

"We spent the weekend with our heads down," Wolf said.

"Our comrades will know more," Seraph told them. She looked at her boyfriend. "The last of Germany's Jews are slated for mass deportation."

"When was Kizzy arrested?" Wolf asked.

"At some point between Friday night and Saturday morning," Marko said.

"At Charité Hospital," Tsura added.

Wolf nodded and ran his fingers across his short beard. "There are holding centers for Jews across the city, but most prisoners are kept there for a day or two. No more. Then they're thrown onto the trains for the East." Wolf took in a deep breath and delivered the news Tsura had feared. "Unless she found a way to escape, your cousin was deported to Poland."

"Unless Kizzy was brought to Rastplatz Marzahn," Marko suggested.

The same idea had crossed Tsura's mind. It was improbable, but if the Gestapo had discovered Kizzy to be Romani, they might have sent her to the camp for Roma.

Wolf shrugged. "It's possible."

Bombs fell in the distance and Tsura pictured the prisoners of Marzahn cowering in their cabins, Kizzy among them.

"There could be a few hundred people. What do we do with them?" Seraph asked.

"We tell them to run," Marko said.

Wolf disagreed. "That'll create panic."

Tsura shook her head. "No, Marko's right. But whatever happens, we have to move quickly."

Wolf and Tsura signaled to Seraph and Marko to duck behind the hedges.

Seraph seemed unusually quiet. *The chatterbox is lost for words.* "Nervous?" Tsura asked her.

"I'm fine."

Keeping their heads down, moving fast, the four ran along the side of the hedgerow, toward the encampment. The air smelled of rotting waste.

Seraph nudged Wolf. "Is your stomach playing up again?" she joked.

Wolf brushed her away.

"The refuse dump is that way. And the cemetery is over there," Tsura said, pointing them out. The cemetery in one direction, the refuse site in the other, and the Marzahn encampment for her Roma family in between. *Nobody could say the Nazis lack a sense of humor*, Aunt Marie had once joked.

"Can I see?" Marko asked and snatched the binoculars from his sister's hand. "Look," Marko said, handing the binoculars back to Tsura.

Tsura peered through the lenses. Despite the sirens and explosions behind them, she could see a single guard, with his back to them, close to the camp's edge.

Marko tapped his knife. "One guard. We can do this."

Tsura pictured Mother asleep in her hut, close by. As a child, at bedtime, her parents would tell Tsura and Marko exciting Romani folktales and sing old lullabies. Marko would fall asleep first and Tsura would lie in bed listening to the comforting sound of her parents talking in the next room.

"Ready?" Wolf said.

Wolf was about to stand, but Tsura, with her binoculars covering her eyes, held out her arm. "Wait. It's him."

The police guard was the drunk from Friday night, Tsura was certain. *Wilhelm—Wim,* she recalled. She remembered how Wim had walked her to the cemetery and ordered her to undress. He'd shown Tsura the photograph of his wife and young son. As before, Wim held a bottle of branntwein in one hand, his rifle in the other.

Tsura jumped to her feet. "What're you doing?" Marko asked.

Marko is afraid for me. But Tsura knew what she was doing. She threw her binoculars at Seraph. "Follow me, all of you. But stay far back. Okay?"

The gun hidden behind her back, Tsura walked toward the encampment. She removed her hat and stuffed it into her pocket. As before, her dark hair fell below her shoulders.

"It's a lovely evening," she called out over distant blasts.

Wim recognized Tsura right away. "Greta?" He stepped forward, astonished to see her again. He laughed and looked up at the fighter jets in the western sky. "Nice night for a stroll."

"Why are you out here?" Tsura asked.

Wim shrugged and lifted his bottle of branntwein. The jar was almost empty. The man was wasted. "They won't be bombing Marzahn. They're aiming for the city center," Wim told her.

Tsura kept her gun out of sight. "Where're the other guards?"

"Hiding in Haupt's cabin," Wim said, gesturing to the caravans.

Haupt. Tsura remembered that a high-ranking police official had been stationed at the encampment for a while. "Too scared?"

Wim let out a laugh. "Terrified. But not me. I'm bored. I'd rather be working at the protest. Anything's more interesting than this stinking hole."

Tsura was confused. "What protest?"

"You haven't heard? Hundreds of people. In the city. Normal Germans want the Gestapo to let their Jewish families go. Some of the trains to Poland have been put on hold."

"They've stopped the deportations?" Tsura nearly shouted with surprise. She wondered what that meant for Kizzy. If the Jewish transports had been suspended, there was a chance Kizzy was still in Berlin. As the city shook from another blast, Tsura worried Kizzy would be hurt by a falling bomb, or even killed. She looked up at the planes over the city. "British?"

"Could be. Or Soviets. What difference? The bombs are bad. Bad for Germany. Bad for Hitler. Bad for all of us." He staggered back, swigged his last drops of branntwein, and dropped the bottle to the gravel ground. "Are you here to see the cemetery again?"

"No. I wanted to see you."

Wim smiled and dropped his rifle, too. "Kiss me," he said.

She held him back. "What about your wife?"

Staggering forward, reeking of alcohol, Wim fell onto her. "My wife—my wife's not as beautiful as you." He slurred his words. His hands were around Tsura's waist, his drunken breath in her face. She allowed him to hold her. "We could fall in love," he said. Her hand was on her gun, out of sight, her finger on the trigger. With her free hand, Tsura gripped his wrist, pushing his hand away from her chest. Behind him, in the distance, she could see Wolf and Seraph walking toward them. "Soon, you won't find me here," he said.

"You're being transferred?"

"This camp—it's being closed down," Wim told her. He kissed Tsura's neck, his rifle by their feet.

Tsura pulled back. "Closed down?"

"They started sending the prisoners away."

It's already begun. "When?"

"This morning," Wim said. Then he paused. "Why do you care?"

"I'm here for my family," she admitted.

Wim stared down and jumped back. Tsura pointed her pistol at his chest.

"Greta? No. Please, don't."

Tsura kicked his rifle hard. It skidded fast and far along the ground, out of his reach.

"Wolf!" she shouted. "Wolf! Seraph!"

Within seconds of her call, Seraph and Wolf were standing behind Wim, their arms outstretched, their guns aimed at his head.

Wim raised his hands. "No! Please! I'm a father. I have two boys."

"Where's Marko?" Tsura asked Seraph.

"No idea," Seraph said.

Tsura didn't need to worry about her brother. *He's always up to something.*

"What's your plan?" Wolf asked Tsura, his gun trained on Wim.

"They're clearing the camp. They started this morning," Tsura said against distant bomb blasts. She pushed away the possibility that her mother and aunt had been deported.

"Do you have the prisoners' names?" Tsura shouted at Wim. "Who have you sent away? Where are you sending them?"

Arms still in the air, Wim didn't reply.

"Answer her," Wolf shouted and stepped forward with his gun, Wim's mouth its target.

Wim gasped and stumbled. "Poland. To Poland. I don't have the lists."

Tsura was untrusting of his every word. She prepared to shoot. But she had more questions. "You said the deportations had stopped."

"Not all of them. Please, Greta, don't let them kill me."

Her stomach flipped. Then she thought of Kizzy. "Has anyone been brought here? A young girl? Thirteen years old."

"I don't know," Wim said. "But I can ask. Maybe there's a girl here. Want me to check?"

Tsura jolted her pistol forward, closer to his chest. "Wim, tell me the truth."

He stared at her gun. "I haven't seen any girls brought here. Please, don't shoot me. My children—I told them I'd see them soon."

Tsura surveyed the campgrounds. "Are there more guards inside?"

Wim was trembling now. "In the commander's cabin, hiding from the bombs."

"If you're lying, we'll kill you," Wolf said.

There were no more questions left to ask. Wim was crying now. Tsura's wrist trembled as she focused on the trigger begging to be pulled. She remembered the woman on the U-Bahn tracks. The screaming infant. And Samuel. Her father. Professor Duerr, dead in the morgue. *Kizzy. Aunt Marie. Mama.* As bombs fell over the city behind her, Tsura ran toward the encampment. Her eyes searched the area for Marko. But he was nowhere to be seen.

"Where's my brother?" she called out to Wolf and Seraph.

"Just be quick," Wolf shouted back.

As she ran, Tsura put her hat back on. Her boots sank into the muddy pathway that led into the barren field. The huts stood silent in the black of the night. She knew this place and her feet carried her fast, toward the towering trees at the rear of the encampment—

where she had once lived. The washing-line outside the familiar caravan was empty and broken. She climbed the wooden steps and pushed open the door. "Mama?" Inside, a damp stench of excrement hung in the air. The caravan was empty.

Tsura ran from vacant caravan to vacant caravan. *They're gone.* When she noticed a figure—a woman—disappearing into a doorway, Tsura's chest heaved with hope. "Wait!" Tsura reached the hut and climbed the steps. She peered through the door, and faces stared back at her. Four women and three children huddled on the beds and dirt floor with terrified stares. The air was rancid.

"I'm looking for my mother, Jaelle Lange. And Marie Lange, my aunt."

One woman's eyes glowed with acknowledgement. "They are Romani?" she asked.

"Yes."

These women were Sinti, Tsura gathered. Romani and Sinti families had been imprisoned together, just as Tsura had been sterilized along with three Sinti girls.

"We know them. Your mother and aunt were here."

Another woman added, "But they were taken. Hours ago. Marie was very ill. Jaelle wanted to go with her. She insisted."

Tsura ignored the swelling of discomfort in her chest. "What about Kizzy Lange? She's Marie's daughter. Thirteen. She would've been brought here at some point in the last few days."

The women shook their heads.

"Only deportations."

"There's been nobody new."

The pain in Tsura's chest grew outward, surging through her throat and down into her stomach. Despite the stench of the hut, she inhaled deeply, filling her lungs with the burning reality. *I'm too late.* Her mother and Aunt Marie were gone. Words masked in anger fell from Tsura's mouth. "They took my family. But you're still here. Why didn't they take you? Who—" Tsura's question was cut off by a dog's bark and muffled chatter outside. *Guards.* The air raid siren had stopped. *I can't be seen.*

"Officer Haupt," one of the women whispered, and they cowered against one another.

Pulling a blanket out from underneath one of the children, Tsura wrapped herself in it, as if wearing a shawl. Her coat and hat were covered, her face exposed. She fell to the floor in front of one of the women, who let out a small gasp. As the caravan door opened, Tsura pushed her shoulders backward, pushing the woman against the wall and blocking her from sight. The blinding beam of a soldier's flashlight filled the space, drawing Tsura's attention to the squalor of the cramped living conditions. Tsura's pulse raced and the women and children said nothing as a soldier counted them. Then he closed the door and the room was swallowed by shadows once more.

Tsura stayed still. She waited a while before standing. "I'm sorry," she whispered to the woman she had smothered, and she returned the blanket to the shaken child. When the door swung open again, Tsura almost screamed. She threw herself against the wall.

"Tsura?" Wolf whispered into the darkness.

"I'm here. Get inside," she said.

The women and children glared with fear as Wolf stepped into the caravan. "Come on, Tsura, we have to go," Wolf whispered. "The guards—"

Tsura addressed the women. "Come with us."

Wolf took hold of Tsura's wrist. "Are you crazy?"

"We have to try." Tsura signaled for the women and their children to stand.

One woman shook her head. "They'll beat us again. They'll ruin our daughters."

"That dog is trained to kill," another woman said.

"The government is sending you away. East. We can help you. Please, trust us." Marzahn meant only death.

"But where would we go? This is our home."

"It's okay—"

"Tsura. No. It's impossible."

She ignored Wolf's protests. "Come with us. Don't be afraid," she said to the children.

"You mustn't listen to her," the women said to their little ones. "It's too dangerous."

A distant gunshot marked the end of their debate.

"Hurry," Wolf said, his hand now pulling at Tsura's shoulder.

Outside, there were no guards in sight. The dog's faint bark signaled their opportunity to run. Tsura left the prisoners behind and followed Wolf through the camp. As they approached the boundary of the field, Wolf gasped and broke into a sprint. "Seraph!"

When Tsura caught up to them, she saw what Wolf had seen. Seraph was standing, gun in her hand. Wim was on the ground, face down in the gravel and dirt, motionless.

"What did you do?" Wolf shouted at Seraph.

Wim was dead.

Shouts and the barking dog echoed behind them through the night air. Tsura turned to see three soldiers moving between the huts in the distance. At that very moment, the air raid siren began to wail again and the soldiers disappeared, returning to their hiding place.

"We have to leave here," Tsura said.

The air raid siren whirled, as if crying for the dead man at Seraph's feet. Then Wolf turned around and let out a yelp, breaking Tsura's daze. Seraph was startled, too, and she spun in place, pointing her gun at something behind Tsura while Wolf stumbled backward. When Tsura turned, a face returned her stare—a man in uniform she didn't recognize. A Nazi officer, her father's age. He'd been standing behind her. Helmet and rifle. His sober eyes laughing, preparing to shoot. Tsura's gun was in her pocket. She held her breath, expecting the Nazi's gunshot.

"Drop it," a voice shouted.

Another face appeared from the shadows. Unshaven. Dark hair. *Marko.* Tsura couldn't breathe out. She took in more air.

Marko's hand and knife reached forward, his blade at the Nazi's throat. The officer dropped his rifle to the ground and Tsura could finally exhale. Tsura reached for her gun, training it at the Nazi officer as Marko stepped away from him. Seraph moved position and pointed her gun at the Nazi, too, while Wolf, gun in his hand, surveyed the area.

"What are you kids doing here?" the Nazi asked. His voice was harsh.

Wolf edged forward. "Shut up."

Marko stared at his sister, unsmiling. "I saw him earlier. I followed him."

He was no longer Tsura's baby brother. Marko's short dark beard contrasted with his pale skin. *My brother saved my life.* "Mama. Aunt Marie. They're not here, Marko." Her voice trailed off.

"What? You're sure? How do you know?" Marko's voice cracked. His stone face drained of all color.

Tsura strained to say the words. "They were taken this morning. We were too late." She turned to the officer. "You're Officer Haupt." Haupt was responsible for the camp and for the deportations, most likely.

"I'm not," he said.

"You're lying. Tell us what you know about the deportations," Wolf demanded.

The Nazi looked toward the fighter jets over Berlin. "Why do you even care about these *Zigeuner*? The transports will resume in the morning, as planned, with or without me."

Before Tsura could respond, Seraph fired two shots and the officer fell to the ground, his eyes open to the skies. Marko yelped in surprise.

"Why? Why, Seraph? Why did you do that?" Wolf shouted.

"He told us what we needed to know," Seraph said, her voice cold. She paused. "I did it for my parents."

Wolf kicked at the ground. Then he began to scream—a painful sound. Seraph had stolen his chance to kill. Wolf's cry faded into more explosions in the distance. Tsura couldn't take her eyes from Wim. He was face down, arms by his side, his right ankle twisted inward, fingers open. These men weren't the only people to die tonight.

Moving quickly, Seraph picked up the rifles of the dead men and began to search through their pockets. Keys. Crumpled bank notes. Cigarettes. Seraph kept what was valuable and discarded the rest. Tsura watched the photograph of Wim's family flip over in a light gust of wind.

"Help me," Seraph said to Wolf as she unbuttoned the Nazi officer's jacket. But Wolf just gawked. He was silent now while the air raid siren continued to cry.

Marko helped Seraph strip the Nazi down to his long underwear and under-vest. Seraph crouched over the corpse, clutching the bloodstained uniform—trousers, jacket, boots, and army cap. Tsura picked up the officer's identity card. "He wasn't Officer Haupt." He'd been telling the truth.

Wolf kicked Wim's body, twice, hard, and then spat on the almost-naked officer, as if killing them was not enough, as if his spit would make it so he was the one who had pulled the trigger. When Seraph reached up for Wolf's hand, he stepped away from her and ran toward the stolen car.

Behind Wolf, Tsura walked fast in front of Marko and Seraph. Seraph carried the Nazi uniform and guns. "I'll sell them. Or smuggle them," she told Marko.

Marko said nothing.

"Want one?" Seraph asked. Tsura turned back to see her offering Marko a rifle. "Go on. You earned it," Seraph said to him. But Marko shook his head and gestured to the knife in his pocket.

Tsura was tired of Seraph's chatter. "Stop talking. Please," she snapped.

With a huff, Seraph walked ahead of them.

As more bombs fell on the city, Tsura synchronized her steps with her brother's. They moved fast, together. Mud was caked onto their boots—evidence of Tsura's failed plan. As the planes flew above the city, Tsura implored the British to win this war.

"What now?" Marko asked her, his voice defeated.

Tsura choked on her anger, then swallowed it down, forcing her rage into the pit of her stomach. Hidden. Their mother and aunt had been deported. Nothing could be done. Kizzy hadn't been brought to Marzahn, but some of the trains had been halted. "When the air raid is over, back to the city. Kizzy might be there."

Marko squinted, as if trying to understand what his sister was saying.

"Alex too," Tsura said.

"What?" Her brother's face lit up.

"There's a demonstration. People are protesting for the release of the Jews."

"Are you serious?"

"That's what Wim said."

"Wim?"

"The guard. His name was Wilhelm."

When they reached the car, Wolf was sitting in the passenger seat. Seraph dropped the folded Nazi uniform and weapons onto his lap and took her place behind the wheel. She held out the binoculars for Tsura to take.

"I don't want them," Tsura said. She didn't need them anymore.

The thunderous explosions in the distance were beginning to sound ordinary.

Jaelle Lange. Marie Lange.

Marko was about to climb into the back seat when Tsura held out her arm to stop him. Then she tapped Seraph hard on the shoulder. "Move. Marko will drive us."

Alexander

When Noah built his ark and gathered the animals inside, his neighbors laughed. But as the rain began to fall, the men and women who had been given a chance to escape the impending flood panicked. If only they'd listened to crazy old Noah. If only they'd planned their escape. As the bombs fell, Alex knew how Noah's neighbors must have felt. The train that Alex and Marko should have taken out of the city was long gone. Perhaps Marko had caught it. Alex imagined him safe, already out of Germany. *Noah collected the animals two by two. Would Marko have boarded our train without me?*

With the exception of a short pause, the siren and bombs had been constant. The Nazi guards had allowed Simon and the other Jewish orderlies to leave. But before the Gestapo cowards had fled to their bomb shelters, they'd locked the hundreds of prisoners inside the building. Alex and his father were trapped.

Alex sat with his arms on his knees, chin on his hands. Taking his mind away from the bombs, Alex wondered what Marko would think to see him unshaven like this. Marko would have liked it, he was sure.

For the first time since Alex arrived at the Community Center, Rosenstrasse, from one end of the street to the other, was empty. Even those who had been holding vigil each night had scurried away when the siren began to cry. The protest was over now. *We'll be deported, as planned.*

As each bomb fell, the building shook. The room lit up as bright as daylight whenever a firebomb hit. They were in the heart of it, and the men jumped and shouted. The light and noise were spectacular. They could hear the women screaming from downstairs. Lea's father was scared for her while Mr. Lessel, Father's colleague, mentioned the children in the room below. Some of the men around Alex cried out in anger against their captors. Some recited aloud Hebrew prayers, asking God to forgive them. *As if we should be repenting,* Alex wanted to say to them.

The conditions in the Community Center were worsening. The toilets were now blocked and overflowing. It was hard to get used to the putrid smell. Now, instead, they were using buckets inside closets. And it was becoming harder to find somewhere to sleep. Some of them—Alex and the other teenagers—slept sitting up against the walls.

The whistling of a bomb so close to the building made many of the men scream even before it hit. Then the firebomb landed on the street, rocking the building and illuminating the room. One man began to recite the Kaddish, the Jewish mourners' prayer, for those who had already been killed that night. His praying reminded Alex of their first tragedy, earlier. An old man on the fourth floor, they had heard, died of a heart attack. And there were rumors of some people considering suicide.

As the bombs fell, Father covered his face. "I can't stop thinking about Ruti and your mother," he said.

"They'll be okay," Alex reassured him.

His thoughts led him to Marko, hoping he was safe.

Another firebomb landed so close to the building that the windows rattled. Lea's father hid his head in his coat. They were all afraid of the glass blowing in. The man reciting the Kaddish prayer began to repeat it. The melody was familiar, taking Alex to a memory from his childhood.

At age seven, soon after his father had remarried, Alex stood at the grave of his paternal grandmother. Father struggled to pronounce the strange Hebrew words and the rabbi instructed him to rip his shirt. Later, Alex had asked Father about the ritual of mourning. It was a Jewish custom, Father had said. By ripping their clothes, they accepted something had been forever broken, forcing the loss to sink in. Alex remembered his grandmother in the hospital, days before she died. Alex had asked if he could rip his clothes, too. Grandchildren were not permitted to mourn, the rabbi had said. But at home, in the privacy of his room, Alex had torn into his shirt and cried face down on his bed.

Another bomb hit and Alex hoped Mother and Ruti were safe. He imagined they were terrified, cowering from the bombs in their basement. Alex remembered Ruti's treasure hunt. He wondered if she'd followed all the clues to find her gift and its accompanying message written in white chalk. He smiled for a moment as he pictured Ruti finding her final clue, leading her to the hidden porcelain train.

Mr. Lessel was writing in his diary again. He appeared to be taking a tally of the blasts. As the bombs fell, he didn't jump or shout. He continued to write.

"This is the end of the protest," Mr. Federman proclaimed. "If only the British knew about the protesters."

Father smiled. "It's the Day of the Luftwaffe. They chose today especially, I bet." Today was a festival marking the strength of the Nazi Air Force. "The protest will end, but the bombs are sending a message to Hitler's immoral government. The end of the war is on its way." Another blast rocked the building and Father laughed. "The war could end within hours!"

Some of the praying men repeated Father's words as an imploration to God. "Let the war end, even if we all die," one man cried.

When an explosion illuminated every corner of their prison, Alex, for the first time, noticed the mezuzah, the encased Hebrew scroll, on the doorpost of their room. The ancient Hebrews, slaves to Pharaoh, marked their doorposts with the blood of a lamb so that God would take notice and ensure the tenth and final plague—the murder of the firstborns of Egypt—would not enter. *I'm a firstborn.* He wondered if God would notice the mezuzah, too.

Alex crawled over to Mr. Lessel, the diary keeper.

"Can I have some paper? Your pencil?"

At first, Mr. Lessel scowled at Alex as if he'd interrupted his greatest work. Then he smiled and carefully ripped out a handful of blank pages from the back of his notebook and pulled out another pencil from his pocket. "Keep it," Mr. Lessel said.

"Thank you."

As two bombs fell in the adjacent street, the room glowed bright. Alex's hand moved and, as if the words were escaping his fingertips, he began to write to Marko a poem, even though Marko would never read it. Each time he heard the crash of a building, the smash of bricks, glass, concrete, Alex was inspired to write more words, another line. He'd find something to tie his note to—one of his boots, maybe—and he'd throw it from the window. Marko would find it, after the bombs—a message that Alex was still in Berlin.

Alex finished the note and folded the remaining blank pages into the pocket of his coat. More bombs fell and explosions lit up the room. Then Alex scoffed at his ridiculous idea. *As if Marko could find the note in all the rubble on the streets.* He stuffed the note into his trouser pocket.

Another bomb crashed close by and Alex imagined Marko aboard his ark, Noah's drowning neighbors screaming while Hitler's capital burned. Alex hoped to God that Marko, Mother, and Ruti were all safe.

Ruth

The bombs are fireworks, Ruth told herself, *screeching and rocketing through the night.*

She was sitting on Mama's lap and Elise gripped her arm. Even though they hadn't talked much over the last few days, Ruth was so grateful that Elise Edelhoff was her best friend. Ruth was terrified for Alexander and Papa, and having Elise next to her—outside the Jewish Community Center and here in Ruth's neighbors' basement—had helped a lot.

Ruth's mind kept jumping to Alexander's girlfriend—the girl he'd planned to meet at midnight on Friday. The girl he'd been talking to Marko about. *Elise saw them kissing!* Alexander had kept his girlfriend a secret, but Ruth didn't know why. She'd overheard Alexander say her name, but Ruth couldn't remember it now. Ruth hoped Alexander's girlfriend was safe, for her brother's sake. She wondered if his girlfriend knew Alexander had been arrested.

Even in the middle of the air raid—or because of it—Elise and Ruth were back to their old selves, rolling their eyes at each other and trying to keep each other upbeat. The first few minutes of the bombings had been dreadful. Mrs. Edelhoff had gripped Elise's arm so tight that Elise had screeched at her in pain. The whistling and crashing of bombs had been unbearable. Then Elise's horrible neighbor—Mrs. Unruh, the impolite woman with her baby and three annoying sons—had started opening her mouth, cursing the British and the Soviets and the Americans for trying to destroy the Fatherland. The woman was a Nazi, and proud of it.

"She needs to shut up," Elise whispered.

There were fifteen people in the basement, all squeezed inside, adults sharing seats, children sitting on their parents' laps. The reinforced metal roof hung not far from their heads. Mrs. Edelhoff held her hands over her ears, trying to drown out the noise. Not sounds of the bombs, Ruth laughed to herself, but of Mrs. Unruh's remarks.

Mrs. Unruh's three-year-old kept running around the already cramped basement, kicking everyone in the shins with his heavy shoes. His mother, holding her baby brother, said nothing, leaving it up to everyone else to calm him down. "He's driving me crazy," Mrs. Edelhoff kept muttering under her breath.

"I was awarded the medal of motherhood," Mrs. Unruh announced.

Against the racket of the siren and bombs, Ruth adjusted her glasses and put her mouth to Elise's ear, trying not to laugh. "They gave the cow an award?"

Papa had told Ruth about the special medal. In their frightening wisdom, the Nazis had invented the medal to encourage German women to bear more children. If any German Aryan woman gave birth to four children, she received the honor. The children were needed to replace the soldiers killed on the front lines, Papa once told Ruth, only half-joking. Then he'd half-joked that, soon, Hitler would be sending ten-year-old Aryan boys to battle with toy helmets and real guns.

"I hope our house isn't hit, or the medal would be destroyed," Mrs. Unruh said.

"If we survive the cow and her awful children, we'll all deserve medals!" Ruth whispered.

Elise let out a loud laugh and the awful woman gawked and pouted at the girls disapprovingly. Embarrassed and amused that she'd been caught, Ruth couldn't help but smile before looking away. Despite the explosions, Ruth felt strangely chipper. Attending the protest each day had filled Ruth with hope that Alexander and Papa would be released. And she hoped they and the other prisoners had been allowed to take shelter from the bombs. After the British air raids last year and last month, Jews had been forbidden from entering the city's specially built air-raid shelters. So Ruth couldn't imagine the Nazis evacuating the Community Center. In her head, Ruth listed all the people she knew across the city—her teachers, friends at school, neighbors, familiar shopkeepers, Mama's friends at church. She thought about her brother's friend Marko, and his young cousin. Kizzy had never made it to their house. Ruth and her mother had been at the protest every day, so there was a chance Kizzy had shown up when they were out. But she would have left a note, Mama had said. Ruth said a prayer that Kizzy—*Franziska*—was safe. Then she said a prayer for Papa and Alexander.

Remembering the two small photographs of Alexander she'd found beneath her bed, Ruth reached into her coat pocket. She ran her fingers along their edges. Seeing her brother's face made Ruth scared for him, and she wished she hadn't looked. Ruth placed them back inside her pocket, along with Alexander's treasure-hunt clues. As more bombs fell, Ruth recited the riddles she hadn't yet solved. *The hidden rose. The woman's place of birth.* Ruth didn't know what they meant. She'd been going over and over them in her head. She turned to whisper in Mama's ear. "I said a prayer for Alexander and Papa."

"Me too," Mama said.

"It's rude to whisper," Mrs. Unruh snapped.

Ruth shot the woman a look to mind her own business. *Awful woman.* Papa would have called the woman a hypocrite. And worse.

Mama put her mouth to Ruth's ear. "Pay no attention. I've known her for years. She's trouble."

A bomb hit hard, closer than any of the others, and everyone screamed. Elise's nicer neighbors had been sitting with their eyes closed the whole time.

Mrs. Unruh continued her commentary. "They're trying to hit the Gestapo's headquarters. And important landmarks. The British and the Communists can go to hell. I hope their planes fall out of the sky." Then Mrs. Unruh addressed Ruth's mother. "Where's your husband?" As if she didn't already know.

Over the siren, Ruth couldn't help but provide an answer. "My father and brother are being detained. They're at the Jewish Community Center." Ruth placed emphasis on the word "Jewish."

Ruth knew what the woman had been getting at. *She's a Jew-hater. And an idiot.* Not a good combination.

"My husband is stationed in France. He just received another promotion," Mrs. Unruh boasted.

Mama nodded knowingly.

"So, he's a Nazi pig?" Ruth asked.

Elise gawked at Ruth. Mrs. Edelhoff gave Ruth a critical stare and Mama nudged Ruth in the ribs, but Ruth knew Mama agreed.

"You need to control your daughter!" Mrs. Unruh screamed.

Mama replied calmly, "She's fifteen. She's allowed to speak her own mind."

Ruth smiled. The Nazi woman clicked her tongue and looked away. Then she snapped her neck around again and looked right at Ruth. "Well, what can you expect from the daughter of a whore?"

The people in the basement, including Elise, gasped. Ruth felt mortified. Everyone knew that Ruth's mother hadn't been married when Ruth was born. Mama had never talked about it, but Ruth knew Mama was ashamed of the fact. Ruth stared at the cow, wishing she'd take back her remark. Ruth wanted to claw at her eyes. It was people like her, Papa had told Ruth once, that made him ashamed to be a German.

Elise gave Ruth an uncomfortable smile. Elise's father was fighting in Hitler's war, just like the woman's husband. But there was an enormous difference between fighting on the Eastern front— risking your life—and being a high-ranking Nazi, stationed in France.

When another bomb exploded nearby, they all closed their eyes and covered their ears. Then the sky was silent. Only the siren wailed. They sat there speechless, waiting for the sound of more fighter planes. They could smell smoke. *That was the last bomb.*

As the siren continued, Mrs. Unruh chattered away. "Well, I'm sorry to hear about your husband and stepson." She spoke in a mocking tone.

She's glad they've been detained. She'd have Mama and me arrested, too, given the chance. A feeling of pride surged from Ruth's stomach to her throat. "We've been going to the protest every day. And the government's listening."

"The protests will need to stop now there's been an air raid," Mrs. Unruh said, looking at Mama.

Mama sneered. "Oh, I have no intention of staying home. We'll be heading back to Rosenstrasse as soon as the sun is up. And we'll keep returning until they release every Jew."

For the first time, Ruth believed it.

The siren stopped. A veil had been lifted off the city. They could breathe again. Mama hugged Ruth tight, a kind of congratulations that they'd survived the bombing. At first, nobody moved, waiting for the all-clear. With a ringing in Ruth's ears, she sensed that everyone across Berlin was feeling the same relief at the same moment. But the wailing of the siren was replaced by distant screaming. Ruth tried not to imagine how many people had been buried and killed by the crashing buildings. Again, she prayed that Papa and Alexander were safe. *Maybe they found a way to escape.*

Ruth followed Mama up the basement stairs. Outside, people emerged from their homes. Some were crying. Many people were coughing from the smoke and fumes of burning rubber. The air was thick with gray smoke.

"Will you join us at the protest tomorrow?" Mama asked Mrs. Edelhoff as they walked into Elise's house.

Elise's mother shook her head. "Not after the bombs," she said and took herself to the living room.

"You'll join us, right?" Ruth asked Elise.

"I have to go to school. I'm sorry," Elise said.

Mama chuckled. "I'm sure school will be cancelled. We'll pick you up after breakfast."

"Goodnight." Ruth hugged her best friend tight, thankful they were unharmed. Ruth felt bad for Elise, with a mother like that.

Mama led Ruth outside.

Elise's street had been almost untouched by the bombs. The clouds of smoke, along with screaming, were coming from the next street down. As Ruth and her mother walked toward their home, the wails became louder. They turned the corner to see a pile of bricks and charred wood. The view was unrecognizable. Whole buildings gone. Women, men, and children walked over the glass that covered the pavement. Cats—domesticated pets, now strays—climbed and whimpered through the rubble. Mama took hold of Ruth's hand as they watched smoke pouring into the sky. The pavement was orange from the glow of flames that burned through a half-standing house.

Two boys around Ruth's age ran and shouted through the wandering survivors. "It's even worse that way," one boy reported, pointing east.

"St. Hedwig's Cathedral was hit," the other boy said.

Ruth held her hand to her mouth. "Our church."

"Father von Wegburg—" Mama said with a gasp.

Ruth remembered hearing how, after the first serious anti-Jewish violence, a year before the war had begun, Father von Wegburg had defied Hitler and encouraged his congregation to pray for the Jews of Germany. His decision to speak out led Mama to attend confession at St. Hedwig's. Ruth remembered her confession the day before her birthday. Father von Wegburg had been so patient with Ruth's childish jokes. She pictured him sitting behind the lattice of the confession box as the cathedral burned around him. Ruth's morbid thoughts were interrupted by the sight of an old man, on his knees, screaming on the road. As they approached, Ruth saw he was bent over a woman's charred body. *His wife*. She was dead. Ruth stared as the man howled.

By the time they reached their neighborhood, Ruth's glasses were covered in dust.

"We should expect the worst," Mama said.

As they turned onto their street, Ruth breathed a sigh of relief to see the rows of houses still standing. Some of their neighbors were outside, assessing the damage. At first, their home looked normal. But then, through the broken front windows, Ruth saw how its entire back had been blown out. A direct hit. Mama said nothing. "Oh God," Ruth whispered. They walked around whole pieces of roof and wall that had been blown into the road. Other buildings were on fire. Behind the façade of their home were piles of rubble, smoke rising from the ground. The sight of their basement exposed to the night sky made Ruth gasp. "We would've been in there!"

Ruth gasped again at what had been the house next door. "They must have been killed," Mama said.

"We were saved tonight," Ruth said, gripping Mama's hand.

Ruth's mother said nothing, wiping away the soot and tears with her sleeve. If Ruth hadn't seen Elise's rose-colored coat and rushed into her house, if Ruth hadn't overreacted and got herself upset over not finding Alexander's clue, then they wouldn't have stayed for dinner. They would have come home instead.

Ruth stared at the rubble and ashes and the space that, just over an hour ago, had been her family's home. They were lucky to be alive.

Mama wiped away tears. "We'll get through this. Objects are meaningless."

"My treasure hunt!" Ruth yelled.

Alexander's remaining clues were gone. Along with his gift. Ruth had promised herself everything would be okay—Papa and Alexander would be saved—if she figured out Alexander's puzzles.

When Mama reached into her coat pocket and handed Ruth a folded piece of paper, Ruth felt the urge to cry. "Ruti. Here. Your brother gave this to me. I was supposed to give it to you when you asked me for it."

Like the other clues, "Ruti" was written along on the top. Mama's name, "Annett," was written in larger handwriting, in the center. Ruth read the puzzle to herself.

The clue was from part of the treasure hunt that would have led Ruth to the mouse hole. Alexander had intended for Ruth to be repulsed by this riddle. Instead, Ruth felt a twinge of happiness, as if her brother were there with her. She wanted to walk to Rosenstrasse. She wanted to see if Papa and Alexander were okay. A sudden crash made Ruth jump. A burning house, four doors down, fell and crumbled to the ground. Ruth and her mother gasped and jumped back as more dust and smoke filled the air. Ruth's glasses were thick with soot. She could barely see, so she took them off.

"Who was my father?" The question fell out of Ruth's mouth.

Immediately, Ruth wished she hadn't asked. Ruth could tell Mama wanted to respond, but something was stopping her.

"It's okay," Ruth said, giving her mother permission to say anything or nothing.

Mama nodded and took in a breath. Ruth breathed in, too, the smell of burning filling her head.

"You were my birthday present, in a way," Mama said, as if giving confession.

"A birthday present?"

"It was my nineteenth birthday. June 1928. I went out for dinner with my friends from university. Then a wine bar in the city." Mama paused, and with the inside of her sleeve, she wiped the toxic smoke from her eyes. "I met a young man. He was an American, in his early twenties."

"Was he my father?"

Mama paused, then nodded. "At the time, selling alcohol wasn't allowed in the United States. The American was in Germany to drink for cheap. He spoke a little German; I spoke some English. I took him back to my friend's apartment. We threw him a party and we all drank too much." Mama was smiling as she talked. "In the morning, I woke up next to him. He was still asleep and I crept out. A few weeks later—I remember it was in the middle of the Amsterdam

Olympics—I realized I was pregnant. I've always meant to tell you all this."

At first Ruth didn't know what to say. She'd thought about her biological father from time to time. She'd asked Mama about him before, and Mama had promised to tell Ruth everything one day. With her glasses in her hand, without them on her face, hearing the truth, Ruth felt suddenly older. She looked through the remaining wall of their destroyed house.

"What did your family say?" Ruth asked.

Ruth's mother laughed. "Your grandparents were mortified. But eventually they calmed down. They kept it a secret for months, until the bump started to show. I was the talk of the neighborhood. 'Annett isn't married! How can she have a baby?' That's what they said. Martha Unruh—her name was Martha Petersen back then—was an old school friend of mine. When she found out I was pregnant, she stopped talking to me. Martha was always horrible, even as a girl." Mama's face filled with a grin and she squeezed Ruth's arm. "But you were my gift. The day you were born—it was such a sunny morning—it was the happiest moment of my life. You arrived a little early, which gave the doctors a scare, but you were healthy and perfect."

Mama's words made Ruth smile, too. "Does Papa know all this? And Alexander?"

"Papa knows everything, of course. Alexander has never asked."

"What did he look like?" Ruth asked, wanting to know if she resembled the American.

"He was nice-looking. Brown hair, fair skin, medium height. I never saw him again. All I know is that he lived in New York. Oh, and he was Catholic, too."

"I'm half-American," Ruth said and stared at the hot rubble. *The British did this, with the help of President Roosevelt.*

With her grimy glasses in her fist and her face and clothes covered in soot, Ruth walked beside her mother through the burning streets, back to Elise's home.

"The American. What was his name?" Ruth asked.

"William. That's all I know."

As they walked, another question appeared in Ruth's throat, as if it had been stuck there, waiting to be discovered. "Where was Alexander's mother born? His first mother."

"In Dresden," Mama replied.

Ruth wondered if Alexander's biological mother was the "her" of the unsolved riddle. "Dresden" could have been the answer to one of the missing clues. But the rest of the treasure hunt, along with Ruth's birthday prize, had been destroyed.

Elise

Ruth always gets her way.

"Please, can you wear it?" Ruth asked Elise.

Tired from a poor night's sleep, Elise was holding out her Girls' League uniform. *She should be grateful.* Ruth's clothes were covered in soot, and everything else had been burned, so she needed to borrow something. But Ruth was refusing to wear Elise's uniform.

"I don't have anything else for you. Your coat will cover it," Elise said.

Elise knew Ruth would feel uncomfortable wearing the League jacket, whether it was hidden or not. *I'm being horrible.* But Elise couldn't help herself. Elise wasn't happy having to attend the Girls' League. She hated having to spend her time learning about German motherhood. When Viktor was in the hospital, Elise had wanted to quit the meetings. She'd worried that the other girls would find out about her defective brother. But she'd heard rumors about those who'd stopped attending, identified as traitors. After Viktor died, Elise wondered what the League leaders would do if they knew that her dead brother had been mentally disturbed. Every time she wore the uniform, Elise thought about that.

Elise gave in and passed Ruth a dress and thick sweater. Over her stockings, Elise put on her Girls' League climbing jacket and skirt, covering them up with her warm old overcoat and scarf. She thought about the soldier on Rosenstrasse. *Maybe I'll unbutton the top of my coat so he'll see my uniform underneath.*

Last night in the basement, Elise had admitted to her mother that she was frightened. And Mother had whispered, in her bitter way, that this was war. As the bombs fell, Viktor had been with them the whole time. He wasn't afraid and he said everything would be fine. But he was talking to Ruth. If Elise hadn't offered to cook for Ruth and her mother, they would have gone home earlier. Ruth and her mother would have been dead, crushed by their house.

Parts of Berlin, especially near Elise's home, were devastated. The settling dust blurred the morning light as Ruth, Mrs. Broden, and Elise walked by destroyed buildings. Bricks and glass covered the streets and some structures were still smoldering. Four girls Elise's age, in their League uniforms, were talking to the injured and homeless. They walked together in their matching berets, just like the one in Elise's pocket, and their black neckerchiefs and brown climbing jackets. They were helping the poor people of Berlin. *That's what a good German would do,* they'd been told. Good Germans. Hundreds had died. Hundreds of good Germans. And hundreds, maybe thousands, had been injured. Viktor walked behind Elise, staring at the rubble and the girls in their uniforms.

"You think I'm one of them," Elise whispered to him.

Viktor looked down at his bare feet, as if embarrassed that Elise knew what he was thinking.

"Pardon?" Ruth asked.

"Nothing." Elise was mortified. Ruth had heard her speak to Viktor.

Ruth and Mrs. Broden had stayed over last night. When they'd returned, late in the evening, Elise's mother had caught a fright, wondering who was knocking on the door. Thieves, she'd guessed. Gypsies taking advantage of the air raid, trying to find some helpless women and children to steal from. Maybe Jews, like rats, trying to scurry away, Mother had said. When Ruth and Mrs. Broden said their house had been bombed, Elise's mother was surprisingly kind to them. *Misery loves company,* Elise's father would have said.

Elise had given Ruth a clean nightgown to wear. Ruth had slept on the mattress on Elise's bedroom floor while Mrs. Broden had slept on the couch downstairs. In bed, Ruth had kept going on about feeling scared for her father and Alex. But God had a plan for them, Ruth had reassured herself. *God ignored my family,* Elise had wanted to tell her. Mother had prayed for Viktor each day. Elise's father had taken them to church almost every week. But still Viktor had died.

Falling asleep, Elise had been glad Ruth's house had been bombed. Viktor had stared at his sister from the corner of her bedroom.

The morning wind threw dust in their faces. As they arrived on Rosenstrasse, Elise shielded her eyes with the sleeve of her coat.

"Oh no!" Mrs. Broden screamed at the sight of debris on the road. A building had collapsed into the street. On the opposite side, the Jewish Community Center was still standing, with a crowd outside.

"Thank God," Ruth said.

The protest was still going on, it seemed. The same Nazi police guards stood outside the entrance.

"The center hasn't been damaged. Everyone is still in there," a woman told Mrs. Broden.

Ruth's mother rushed over to a group of women to find out what they knew. Elise wished she were at school.

"I can't believe they still won't let them go," Ruth said to Elise.

What did she expect? Ruth was almost in tears, as if a little air raid would have persuaded the Nazis to surrender. *Nothing will persuade Hitler. Nothing.* When Elise's parents had received a letter stating Viktor had died of typhus, Elise's father had cried in his bedroom for days. Mother wouldn't allow Elise to comfort him. They were sent Viktor's ashes, and a small, sad funeral was arranged. People visited to watch them grieve. Ruth and her family invited Elise and her parents for meals and popped in with lunch baskets at the weekends or cakes in the afternoons. Alex invented all sorts of quizzes and games and riddles, trying to take Elise's mind off Viktor. Elise's father went back to work. At home, they didn't talk about Viktor's death. But the worst news was yet to come.

It was summertime, a weekend, a few months later. A married couple came to their door. Their daughter, Cecile, had been at the same mental facility as Viktor, they said—they were both nine years old. Viktor and Cecile had the same illness. Viktor's mind hadn't progressed beyond that of a five-year-old; Cecile acted as if she were three. Elise's father invited the couple in for coffee. Father should have sent Elise upstairs, away from the conversation, but she sat on his lap. The couple told them Cecile was dead, too. And there were others, they said. Other children who had died. And adults. There'd been an outbreak of typhus, Father clarified. But the couple explained how each death, each child, each adult, had died from different causes all around the same time. There was something wrong with Cecile's death certificate. The doctors had killed their daughter, they believed. That's when Mother screamed at them to get out. She called them liars. Elise's father tried to calm her, but Mother kept yelling. Elise's father saw them to the door.

Weeks later, one evening after dinner, Elise's father announced he'd spoken to the couple again. Cecile's parents were telling the truth. He had spoken to the relatives of other dead patients from the hospital. Elise sat quietly at the kitchen table, listening to the horrific news, while Mother shuffled in her chair. Doctors and nurses employed by the Nazi government were killing people who were deaf or blind, Father explained. The crippled, the epileptic, the schizophrenic, and the retarded. The doctors had been covering up the killings with death certificates stating how each patient had died of typhus or a heart defect or some other disease or infection. Viktor had been murdered.

In Girl's League, Elise had learned about the useless-eaters—the sick people who wasted government resources and precious food. Earlier, in 1939, when Hitler's government had encouraged parents to bring their ill children to special facilities, Elise's mother didn't hesitate. Viktor was damaged, Mother had complained. She said it as if Viktor couldn't be fixed, as if he should have been thrown away.

"Look!" Ruth was pointing at the debris from the bombed-out building across the street. Protesters were scaling the rubble, attempting to see into the Community Center. "They're trying to look through the windows. Let's climb up."

She thinks this will end well. Ruth was still hopeful about Alex and Mr. Broden. Just as Father had been hopeful the hospital would cure Viktor of his mental condition. Elise scowled at Ruth. Elise knew better. People thought the air raids would force the Gestapo to change its policies. But the British had bombed Germany before and those bombings hadn't changed a thing.

Ruth had reached the bottom of the debris. Elise stared at a young man standing on the highest point of the rubble.

"Ruth," Elise said, not moving.

Ruth turned and pulled on Elise's arm. "Elise, come on."

Elise was frozen in place. "That's him! From the market."

Right in front of them, on top of the debris, stood the scruffy young man from Hackescher Market, the man who said Elise had saved him, the young man with the knife. He had a short beard now. Without thinking, Elise waved, and he looked back at Elise with the same handsome smile, his face creasing at the sides of his eyes and mouth. Elise was smiling, too. Her heart raced.

Ruth gasped. "It's—Paul!"

"Ruti Broden!" he shouted.

Elise was stunned and baffled that they knew each other. *His name is Paul?* Elise said nothing, just repeating his name—*Paul, Paul*—in her head.

"Alexander's here!" Ruth called out to him, pointing to the center.

"What?" Paul's eyed widened and he leapt down the side of the rubble, right up to Ruth. "Your brother's here? Are you sure?"

Paul and Alex are friends. Elise was amazed at the coincidence.

"My father's here, too," Ruth said. She spoke extremely fast. "They're arresting all the Jews left in Berlin. We're protesting and we've been—"

"Is Broden okay?" Paul asked, interrupting her.

"Yes. I mean, we don't know. I hope so."

"Ruti, it's so great to see you," he said and put his arms around her, squeezing Ruth tight and lifting her off the ground.

Elise waited for Paul to throw his arms around her like that. She waited for him to thank her again for saving him in the market. She waited for Paul to tell Ruth how Elise had helped him, how he would've been stabbed by that African boy if Elise hadn't intervened.

"This is my friend, Elise. Elise, this is Paul. He works with Alexander, at the factory."

Paul and Alex work together? This was too strange. Elise beamed at Paul, delighted to see him again.

"Nice to meet you," he said.

Elise could feel her face turn bright red. *He doesn't recognize me.* She waited for Paul to figure it out. She wanted to remind him of how he knew her. *We ran together through Hackescher Market. We escaped the thief and took his knife.* Not wanting to embarrass herself, Elise smiled politely as Paul continued to chatter away to Ruth. *He has no idea who I am.* To Paul, Elise was just a silly little girl.

Marko

Thinking about Alex, knowing he was so close, made Marko feel dizzy, like drinking Duerr's vodka. In Marzahn, learning the news that his mother had been deported to Poland, Marko had felt entirely defeated. But now, with the news that Alex was here, Marko felt strong again.

"You sure he's in there?" he asked Ruti again.

"She saw him," Ruti said, nodding at her friend.

Ruti's friend pointed. "In that window."

Marko felt determined to find a way into the building, to climb the walls, smash the windows. *I'll smash every Nazi guard.* At Marzahn, he had held the knife against the officer's neck. *Except this time,* he told himself, *I'll have the guts to cut their throats.*

"The air raid. Our house was bombed," Ruti blurted out.

"What?" Marko pictured Alex's dining room, the hallway. And Alex's bedroom. All ash. Marko didn't tell Ruti he'd been there the night before. *I could've been killed.*

"Our whole house was destroyed."

"At least you're still here." Marko grinned and planted a light punch on Ruti's shoulder.

Ruth smiled, sadly. "I know."

"Wait here," Marko said and headed into the crowd.

"Where are you going?" Ruti called out. But he kept walking.

Nazis stood in line in front of the Community Center, black metal helmets, uniforms, keeping the crowd back, in rows like Nazi flags hanging from the buildings. Marko wanted to hang the bastards. Most of them weren't much older than him. Some might have been good-looking if it hadn't been for their Swastika medals. The crowd was growing. Children and men, but mostly women. One woman held a screaming baby. Nazis swarmed the area. Marko chose a spot against the open gate of a courtyard and kept his eyes on the guards, looking for a way to get inside. He made a plan in his head to kick open a window, crawl up a drainpipe, climb in through the roof. He'd find Alex and get him out. They'd run back to Seraph's place, take some food and Alex's map book. Tsura and Wolf would organize false papers for Alex. Then they'd take a train headed West, just as they'd planned.

Leaving Berlin had been Alex's idea. While Marko had been the first man—the first person—Alex had ever kissed, Marko was different. Before he met Alex, he'd kissed a couple of girls and a dozen men. But Alex was better than all of them. Alex had arranged for him and Marko to go out on deliveries together. They'd worked diligently and fast, so they could leave work early. That way, they had more time together.

Marko told Alex about the laws against homosexuals. Perverts, the Nazis called them. Alex knew a little about all that. The law had been written decades before Hitler came along. They were breaking the law and they had to protect their jobs and themselves. They had to keep their relationship a secret from their families. When Marko told Alex about men like them being sent to the Nazi labor camps, Alex became scared. More than ever, Marko wanted to escape Berlin.

Knowing Tsura could help, Marko told her he wanted to leave Germany. Tsura had called Marko selfish. He'd be abandoning Kizzy, she'd said. But Marko had argued that he had to leave before he was sent to fight Hitler's war. Risking death for the Nazis, the oppressors of their people—Marko put it in Tsura's words—wasn't something he was prepared to do. Finally, Tsura agreed. When Marko asked her to help his Jewish friend, Alex, as well, Tsura had agreed to obtain false papers for Alex and two train tickets.

Protesting for Alex's release, standing in the middle of a demonstration, felt strange. *People are speaking out.* Marko had been born in 1926. He could hardly remember what Germany had been like before Adolf Hitler became Chancellor. Standing close to the crowd made Marko want to be a part of the revolution. To do something. He continued to plot his way into the building, but he couldn't get close. *Too many guards.* For a moment, he had the crazy idea of going up to the Nazis and telling them he was Romani, to get himself arrested, just to be with Alex.

Since Marzahn, Marko had been thinking nothing good would happen. Tsura had allowed Marko to drive, as if it was some prize. But the car journey back to the city had been horrible. Marko had wanted to scream. His mother was gone. Seraph had talked about her parents, locked up in different Nazi camps, while Tsura and Wolf said nothing. All four of them—two women, two men, all young Germans—were lost in the middle of a horrific war. His hands on the wheel, Marko had stared at Berlin's burning streets. They'd gone to Marzahn too late.

At Seraph's apartment, they'd gulped down mouthfuls of schnapps. Seraph had sat on Wolf's lap and raised a toast. *To the dead*

Nazis, she'd said, proud of herself. Wolf had refused to drink to them. He'd pushed Seraph off and went to bed. Wolf was right. Celebrating their deaths was pointless. Wolf's family was still gone. Marko's, too. Seraph had headed to the sink to rinse off the drying blood from the dead Nazi's jacket, then followed Wolf to their room. Tsura slept on the sofa. Marko fell asleep on the floor, thinking about his mother, picturing her, black and gray hair, soft skin, mauve dress, and gray hat, on a train heading deeper into the Nazis' hell.

Marko pushed through the crowd on Rosenstrasse to find Ruti again.

Ruti waved Marko over. She was nicely put together, with neat hair in a braid that stuck out of her hat. Her friend was a mess, with spotty skin and broken hair.

"Where've you been?" Ruti asked.

Marko jumped over her question. "Any chance you've seen a little girl? My cousin. She was arrested—"

Ruti gasped. "Franziska? That's why she didn't show up!"

Marko described her. "She's thirteen, dark hair. She's skinny, probably wearing a brown coat that's too big for her. And a blue hat."

Ruti shook her head. "Sorry. Doesn't—"

"In the window," Ruti's friend interrupted. "A few days ago. I saw someone. A girl."

Marko took in a sharp breath. "Which window?"

Ruti's friend pointed. "There. She was probably about thirteen. She had a blue knitted hat. And dark frizzy hair."

"That's her!" Marko's heart beat faster, thinking about Kizzy in the building. *With Broden.* He looked around at the huge crowd. The protestors—mostly women—stood watching the windows of the building, determined. With hundreds on the street, Alex and Kizzy wouldn't be going anywhere. The guards in their helmets stared back. Marko's eyes searched for Tsura. He grinned at Ruti. "I can't believe I ran into you. Wait 'til my sister hears all this."

Kizzy

I'm not a yellow star, Kizzy wanted to tell the officer.

But the Nazi continued to shout, "Dirty Jews."

The younger kids were crying. The officer's dog was black and brown and showed its sharp teeth while pulling on its leash.

"Downstairs," the Nazi snapped at the Jewish orderly.

"Where are they taking us?" Esther asked.

"How should I know?" Kizzy said. *I don't even know where we are right now.* Tsura's words rang in Kizzy's head. *If a Nazi wants to take you somewhere, just run.* "We've gotta get out," Kizzy said to Felix and Esther.

Felix stared at Kizzy. He seemed too scared to talk.

"Where would we go?" Esther asked.

Ari, Esther's four-year-old cousin—with hair as red as fire—didn't let go of Esther's sleeve. *If we run and Ari's with us, he'll slow us down.* The guards would notice his hair. They'd be caught immediately.

"Ari can't come," Kizzy said to Esther.

"But we have to stay together," Esther protested.

"Fine with me," Kizzy said. *Fewer people, easier to hide.*

The orderly led the children into the corridor. Kizzy pulled down her hat, tight on her head. The doors along the hallway were open. The other rooms were empty, as if the whole building was being emptied. As the Jewish children walked aimlessly, slowly, steadily behind the orderly, Kizzy glanced back at the empty corridor. There were no Nazi guards. The orderly was up ahead of the group, Kizzy at the back. For a moment, the Jewish orderly turned around to look at them. A teenager, he was obviously upset by the younger kids who were crying. "It'll be all right," he told them and looked at the older children, in a sad way.

"Let's go," Kizzy whispered to Felix.

Felix tugged on Esther's arm. "Come with us."

Esther hesitated and looked at her cousin. "I can't leave him alone. He's only four." Then Esther slowed down.

"Are you coming or not?" Kizzy whispered at her.

With Felix right behind her, Kizzy rushed down the hallway to the door at the end.

"Esther!" Felix called out in a spoken whisper.

"Be quiet," Kizzy said.

The orderly watched them. Kizzy wondered if he would sound an alarm. But then he turned around, walking Esther, her cousin, and the other kids away. *He let me and Felix run.*

The door took them into some kind of storage room with shelves full of what looked like folded sheets, with mops and brooms leaning against the walls. The strong odor of chemicals and fresh paint hung in the air. There was more than enough space for them to hide, at least for a few minutes, while Kizzy could think through her next steps. Kizzy and Felix stepped inside and, before closing the door, Kizzy checked that the handle would open from the inside. It could. It was pitch black now. They couldn't see each other.

"They'll find us," Felix said.

"Will you shut up?" Kizzy snapped. But Felix was right.

In the darkness, Kizzy reached along the shelves, feeling around carefully for something to hide them. Her fingers touched tin boxes of bristles—paintbrushes—and a stack of rags and sheets—painters' sheets—folded in neat piles. There were loads of them. Careful not to knock anything over, Kizzy took two sheets from the shelf. She let one sheet fall open and then touched its edges and corners to figure out its size. *It's big enough.*

"Here. Get in the corner and cover yourself," she whispered and passed Felix a sheet. "Make yourself look like a box or something. And stay completely still."

Felix followed Kizzy's instructions. She could hear him get onto the floor, shuffling into the corner and covering himself with the sheet. In the pitch black, Kizzy ran her hands along the floor, making sure his feet weren't sticking out. Then she crouched on the floor, too, right next to Felix, and covered herself in the other sheet, trying to make herself as small as possible. She tucked her pinafore dress beneath her shoes and sat down with her back against the wall. The cold of the floor seeped through her stockings. She rested her elbows on her knees and put her arms over her head to change her shape. The strong smell of paint filled her head and she could hear Felix breathing lightly. She could hear footsteps in the corridor outside. "No breathing sounds," she whispered. Nazi guards would be searching for them. When the door handle rattled, Kizzy held her breath, hoping to hell Felix didn't move, hoping it wasn't obvious they were there. Suddenly, through the material, there was light. The storage room was open. *We've been caught!* Then it went dark. *They didn't see us.*

"Kizzy? Felix?" It was Esther speaking too loudly.

"Sshh!"

"They're all gone," Esther said through the darkness.

Kizzy pulled the sheet off her head, staring into the pitch black.

"This part of the building is empty now," Esther said.

Kizzy wanted to ask Esther about Ari. She was surprised she'd left her little cousin alone, though it was the right thing to do. But there was no time for chatter. The soldiers would be checking their lists. *We've gotta find a better place to hide.*

"Let's go," Kizzy said.

Standing up in the darkness, Kizzy could hear Esther stepping to the side. Kizzy moved to the door and opened it carefully. Squinting at the bright light, she looked out into the hallway. Esther was right. There was nobody around. She could hear voices coming from downstairs. She stepped into the corridor. When she turned to tell Felix and Esther to follow her, she saw Ari—the four-year-old, with his fire red hair and his yellow star—his hands gripping Esther's skirt. "What's he doing here? We can't take him. He's a baby."

Esther looked right at Kizzy, her eyes pleading, saying nothing. In the darkness, Kizzy hadn't seen Ari. *He's too young, but he knows how to stay silent,* Kizzy admitted to herself. "Fine." Kizzy scowled at the little boy. "But you've gotta be good."

Ari nodded. He seemed scared of Kizzy. She would've laughed if she weren't so angry with Esther.

As they passed the rooms along the corridor, Kizzy checked each one. They were all empty and led to nowhere. Close to the stairwell, she heard voices coming from the lower floor. The only option was up. Felix led the way up the stairs. But Kizzy remembered when she'd reached the top floor of Charité hospital and couldn't escape the building. *There's a way out of here, but it's not up.* "Felix. No. Come back down."

Felix listened to Kizzy's whispered instructions. Kizzy noticed a metal grate at the end of the corridor. "Stay here and keep watch," she told him.

Leading Esther and her little cousin to the other end of the hallway, right up to a vent close to the floor, Kizzy saw it was covered by a metal grate that had rusted along its edges. Kizzy pulled at the bars. They were loose, but the corners were screwed into the wall.

"Something sharp," Kizzy said out loud. *Professor Duerr's key.* Kizzy got onto her knees, her stockings against the hard floor. She pulled out the key, using it to turn one of the screws on the corner of the grate. *It's working.* The screw dropped to the floor and Kizzy started the next. The second screw wouldn't turn, so she tried the third, but it was also stuck.

Tapping of shoes on the hard floor made Kizzy look up. Felix was running toward them. He said nothing, but his eyes were bulging and told them there were soldiers coming up the stairs. *I need to run.* For a split second, Kizzy planned to leave Felix, Esther, and Ari in the hallway. *They'll be discovered, but I'll have time to hide.* But rather than deserting them, Kizzy lifted little Ari off his feet. To keep him calm, Kizzy made a shushing sound in his ear.

Esther and Felix followed them into one of the rooms along the corridor. Kizzy ran straight to the corner, to a cupboard. Swinging open its door, she was hit by the stench. But there was no time to pause and the four of them squeezed into the makeshift toilet. Felix moaned at the smell. Esther covered her mouth and nose with her hands. Kizzy continued to hold Ari tight, his feet off the ground and around her waist. He started to whimper.

"Sshh. It's okay. You've gotta stay quiet. We're gonna play a hiding game, okay? Sshh. Sshh." Kizzy remembered the professor, at nighttime, when Kizzy would wake up from a bad dream. The professor would sit on the edge of Kizzy's bed, stroking her hair.

Ari calmed and held Kizzy tight. Standing between Felix and Esther, the full toilet bucket by her feet, Kizzy listened for the sounds of soldiers in the hallway outside, expecting the Nazis to discover them. "Good boy," Kizzy whispered.

Voices in the room made Esther throw her back to the wall, which made Felix flinch. His leg banged against the toilet bucket. When she felt the wet, cold human waste splash from the bucket onto her stockings and shoes, Kizzy wanted to scream. Instead, she focused on getting away. *If they catch me, they'll send me to Rastplatz Marzahn.* As much as Kizzy wanted to see her family, being sent to Marzahn would be terrible. Marko had told Kizzy once that Marzahn was a one-way ticket to the grave. Her horrible cousin had made her cry.

The voices on the other side of the cupboard door disappeared.

Kizzy and the children stood in silence for at least five minutes. Soon, Kizzy's arms throbbed from holding Ari for so long. Felix and Esther were waiting for her to decide what to do.

"I'm putting you down," Kizzy whispered and lowered Ari carefully to the floor. Esther took his hand and Kizzy opened the door, just a crack. The room looked empty. The building was silent.

"Stay right here," Kizzy told them, and they gave Kizzy a look, as if furious she was forcing them to stay in the nasty cupboard for longer—or scared she was leaving them all alone. "I'll be back for you. I promise."

Kizzy walked over to the barb-covered window. She could see out to the trees across the street. The window muffled most of the noise, but she could hear shouting from below. Gestapo officers and guards yelled for people to get into a truck. Jews—women and men—cried, holding onto each other. She watched the guards beating the crowd of Jews with horsewhips. Climbing onto the truck, the people screamed. A guard held out his arm, signaling for the people in the queue to wait. Another guard slammed the truck's door and it drove away.

In every direction, the road was completely empty. It was broad daylight, but there were no witnesses to these deportations, only a pretty cobblestoned road, lined with trees on the opposite side.

Another truck pulled up and the Nazis pointed for the men and women to climb. Forty or fifty people in coats and suits and shirts and floral skirts and blue dresses and gray scarves and yellow stars. Then Kizzy saw the Jewish children, the little ones from their room. Some were crying, like they'd cried when the bombs fell last night. Some were held by adults, perhaps their parents, probably strangers. The Nazis lifted the littlest ones, almost throwing them inside the waiting trucks. Kizzy felt an urge to turn back to Felix and Esther and the little boy in the toilet cupboard. She wanted to make them look. *They should see this—see what's happening to their people.* But the sight would have terrified them. And they were already so scared.

A R I

Tsura

From one end of Rosenstrasse to the other, and spilling into the side roads, a dense crowd of civilians faced the guards and the silent building. Tsura stood shoulder to shoulder with strangers. All these people had done nothing while her family rotted away at the edge of the city. They had done nothing when her mother and aunt were deported, just yesterday. Regret and sorrow weighed Tsura down as she moved through the crowd of demonstrators and listened in on the conversations between groups of Christian women who were demanding the release of their Jewish husbands. There were some men also, waiting for their wives. Their friends and neighbors surrounded them in solidarity.

The knowledge that the Jewish Community Center was filled with hundreds of intermarried Jews and their children added to Tsura's doubts that Kizzy was in there. Without getting too close to the line of Nazi police, she walked part of the building's perimeter, checking for unguarded doors. The front door on Rosenstrasse appeared to be the only way in and out. Tsura suppressed a quiet rage that had been building inside her gut. Then she reminded herself of the Nazis' weaknesses. *The German Army lost at Stalingrad.*

When she spotted Marko in the crowd, he ran up to her. He was animated, beaming. "Broden's here! And his father. And Kizzy might be here, too!"

For a moment, Tsura's lungs felt lighter. "How do you know?"

He walked, pulling Tsura along. "That's Broden's sister, Ruti. The one with the braid." He pointed to a girl with light-brown plaited hair and color in her cheeks. "And we think her friend saw Kizzy at one of the windows." Another girl stood with her. Like Ruti, she was fourteen or fifteen, but this girl was withdrawn, arms wrapped around herself, shoulders high, shielding her body from the cold.

Grinning broadly, Marko introduced the girl. "Tsura, this is Ruti Broden."

"I'm Ruth," said the girl, with a smile.

Marko continued his introductions. "Ruti, this is Tsura, my sister."

"You're Marko's sister? You're Tsura!"

Tsura jabbed her brother in the arm. "Keep your voice down. Call me Greta."

"Greta. Got it," Ruth said, still smiling. Tsura was angry with Marko for using her real name, but entertained by Ruth, who seemed surprised that Marko and Tsura were related.

"Ruth," Tsura began her questions. "Have you seen our cousin? She's thirteen and—"

"Elise saw a little girl," Ruth interrupted. Ruth turned to speak to the girl behind her. "Elise, tell her. Tell her about the girl."

Immediately Tsura liked Ruth. She was quick and direct. The sickly girl next to Ruth—Elise, Tsura assumed—stood quietly.

Elise seemed unsure of what to say, and Ruth spoke for her. "In the window. She saw a girl like that, a couple of days ago."

Kizzy isn't here, Tsura told herself. "They're keeping Jews in there. Jews married to Christians."

"And their children," Ruth added.

"There's still a chance Kizzy's here," Marko said, unfazed by Tsura's cynicism.

"You mean Franziska," Tsura snapped at Marko. She glanced at the strangers in the crowd standing around them.

"It's all right, sis. She's Broden's sister."

But Tsura wasn't worried about Ruth. Tsura was wary of her quiet friend. "What exactly did you see?" Tsura asked Elise.

"I don't know," were Elise's first words.

To Tsura, Elise seemed uneasy, strangely introverted, and she just stared at Ruth, who stared at Tsura. *They're nervous. I'm older than they are.*

"The little girl you saw. What did she look like?"

Elise continued, "She was about twelve or thirteen. She had dark hair. Curly. She was wearing a black coat. Maybe brown. She seemed normal. She was staring out of the window, at the crowd, looking for someone."

Tsura was losing her patience. Elise was describing half the thirteen-year-old girls in Germany.

"What else?" Tsura asked.

Elise glanced to the sky, trying to remember. "She was wearing a blue hat. No brim."

Tsura ignored the feeling of hope bubbling to the surface. "Did you see her again?"

"She saw her twice," Ruth responded. "Right, Elise? We think the children were separated."

"What do you mean?" Marko asked.

"There've only been children in that window," Elise said, pointing at a window on the first floor up.

"And she saw Alex over there," Ruth said.

"You mean that one?" Marko was pointing, over the heads of the protestors, at another window on the other side of the building, higher up, and Elise nodded along.

Tsura watched her brother. Last night had changed everything. Marko had saved Tsura's life. He'd proven himself. If Marko hadn't been there, Tsura could have been killed. *If my brother could do that, if he could be that brave, then he's capable of much more.* Seraph had killed Wim and the Nazi officer, but Marko had made that possible.

"What should we do?" Tsura asked her brother.

"I say we find a way in," Marko said.

Tsura was intrigued. "How?"

"I don't know." Marko lowered his voice so Ruth and Elise couldn't hear. "Seraph's got the dead Nazi's uniform."

Tsura knew what Marko was suggesting and it wasn't a bad idea. "You'd have to shave," she told him.

Marko smiled and scratched his jawline. "I've seen soldiers with beards. Seriously, sis. Should we do it?"

Tsura weighed the risk. She remembered jumping onto the train tracks to save the Nazi woman and her infant. The crowd had taken Tsura for a German hero. She imagined Marko in the dead Nazi's clothes, talking his way into the building, fooling them with a false story, checking each floor for Kizzy. Tsura shook her head at him. "Too dangerous," she whispered.

As they talked, Tsura could hear Ruth and Elise chattering beside them, arguing.

"You ask her," Elise muttered through her teeth.

"No, you," Ruth said, glancing at Tsura.

"Ask me what?"

Elise and Ruth stopped, stunned into silence by Tsura's bluntness. Tsura frowned at Elise. Tsura hated shyness. If there was anything she'd taught Kizzy, it was that girls had to speak up.

"Elise," Ruth said, prompting her to speak. But Elise said nothing. She was intimidated and Tsura was enjoying it.

"Spit it out," Tsura snapped.

Elise's eyes widened.

Tsura turned up the corner of her mouth to soften her expression. "Honestly, you can ask me anything."

Still Elise was silent.

"Okay, fine," Ruth said, unfolding her arms. "We want to know, are you Alexander's girlfriend?"

It was the last question Tsura had anticipated.

Marko let out an odd laugh.

"Why do you want to know?" Tsura asked.

Ruth elbowed Elise, nudging her to talk. "Tell her!" Ruth said.

"I saw you," Elise said to Tsura, her face now red.

"You saw me?"

"Around midnight," Ruth added, encouraging Elise to explain. Elise nodded. "From my window. Outside. On Friday night."

Tsura said nothing, letting Elise talk.

"I saw you with Alex," Elise continued.

Tsura didn't flinch. She didn't nod. *Elise is confusing me with someone else.* Tsura went through the events of Friday night. She had met up with Marko and Alex at the Fairy Tales Fountain in Friedrichshain Park, just after midnight. Marko and Alex had arrived late. They'd walked through the back gardens. Tsura looked at her brother in his flat cap and long coat. She laughed to herself at how much she and Marko looked alike. *She thinks Marko was me.*

"How did you two meet?" Ruth asked.

Tsura frowned. "How did I meet Alex?"

Before Tsura could answer, murmurs and gasps spread across the crowd. Tsura looked toward the building. A young girl, no older than ten years old, had approached one of the guards with a loaf of bread in her hands. When the Nazi guard took the bread and disappeared inside, the crowd began to buzz.

Minutes later, a woman in the crowd yelped, "The window!"

The little girl, now standing with her mother, waved at her father and, from inside the building, he held up the loaf. The crowd cheered. Then the people began to shout.

"We want our husbands back!" Ruth shouted along.

Tsura watched Ruth pull Elise forward, encouraging her to join in the chant. But Elise stood there with her mouth shut. Tsura's stomach knotted in distrust. Elise had a kind of wretchedness about her. Tsura and Marko stood back, watching the excited crowd.

A minute later, a woman approached Ruth and Elise. She stood with her hands on Ruth's shoulders. The woman's hair was pinned neatly in a bun beneath an elegant hat.

"That's Broden's mother," Marko clarified.

Mrs. Broden looked strong as she shouted along with the crowd, screaming at the Nazi guards, spitting her words toward the windows of the building. Mrs. Broden turned to survey the crowd around her, clearly happy that so many people were out there, demanding the release of the Jewish people inside. There were hundreds of people on Rosenstrasse. Women handed out cakes and coffee. Children took turns warming themselves in the café across the street. These were Germans. Aryans. Full citizens of the Reich. Such a demonstration was unprecedented. Berlin, at least since the Nazis took power, had never seen anything like this. A seed of resentment took shape within Tsura's core. The crowd screamed, defiant, at the Nazi guards. *While Marzahn is emptied in silence.*

Ruth tapped her mother on the arm, whispering to her, pointing at Marko and then Tsura.

When Mrs. Broden approached Marko, she put her hands on his face. "Marko, I'm so glad to see you!"

Tsura watched Elise turn to Ruth. "I thought his name was Paul," Elise said with a frown.

"Frau Broden, this is Tsura, my sister," Marko said.

Greta, Tsura wanted to say. But before Tsura could speak, the smiling Mrs. Broden embraced Tsura, too. "Call me Annett," she said and held Tsura close. "Alex will be released. I'm so glad you're here. Alex didn't tell us he had a girlfriend."

For a moment, Tsura felt uncomfortable at Annett's use of their real names. But Annett could be trusted, she sensed. Tsura was amused by the confusion that Alex Broden was her boyfriend and she wanted to tell Annett the truth. She didn't want to mislead her, but Annett seemed so happy. *She can believe what she wants to believe.*

Annett grabbed Marko's arm. "Help me fetch some tea," she said and pointed to the café across the street. Marko looked back at Tsura as Alex's mother led him by the arm through the demonstrators and out of sight.

Again, excitement spread across the crowd. Tsura watched as a woman approached the building. She held some kind of package and began to argue with the Nazi guards. Chanting was replaced by chatter when the guards stood aside to allow the woman into the Community Center. With anticipation in her eyes, Ruth looked back at Tsura. People around them whispered and speculated. "Will they let her leave?" someone in the crowd asked. "Maybe they'll release her husband," a woman suggested. Tsura could feel the spirit of the protestors. The women on Rosenstrasse were invested in every occurrence, each consequence; Tsura was a mere spectator.

Five minutes passed. The door opened and the woman emerged, her hands empty, smiling and also crying. Others rushed toward her and the crowd started to chant again. The word spread quickly that she was not only able to deliver her package of food, but she'd spoken to her husband, too. Tsura's mind shifted into focus. *If that woman found a way inside the building, so can I.*

Alexander

When the air raid had ended and the Nazi guards had returned, with the street empty for the first time, the prisoners had expected immediate deportation. An officer had walked into the room and ordered three men to stand. Mr. Federman had been one of them. He'd stared back at Alex's father, terror in his eyes, as he was marched from the room.

In the morning, the orderlies had spread good news throughout the building. Not only were the protestors returning to Rosenstrasse, Simon had told them, but a number of men—all fathers of baptized children, which included Lea's father—had been given release papers. Mr. Federman was free to go. When Simon had told them the reason for their discharge, Alex's father had laughed. Ruti was baptized, too, but she wasn't family by blood. It was preposterous, Father had said mockingly, that a prayer and a splash of holy water could save people in that way.

When Alex was twelve, Father asked him if he wanted to celebrate his Bar Mitzvah. As a Jewish boy about to turn thirteen, he'd be responsible for observing the Jewish commandments. When Alex pointed out to his parents that nobody in the family kept the Jewish laws, Father smiled and told his son to make up his own mind. Alex chose to skip the rite, embarrassed about the idea of celebrating the start of puberty. But, to both the Jewish community and the Nazi government, Alex and his father were—and would always be—Jewish. Even though they'd never kept the religious food laws, or attended Synagogue, or observed Jewish practices. Yet they still faced deportation.

In the morning, when Alex had approached Simon to ask if Lea Federman had also been released, Simon said he'd check. He'd returned some time later with confirmation that Lea had been permitted to leave with her father. The news made Alex feel both relieved and unsettled. Lea, a baptized *Mischling*, was now free, but he worried what that meant for him and the hundreds of full-blooded Jews that remained.

The Community Center continued to fill. Speculations about how everything would end continued to circulate, but for now they waited, taking turns to watch the still-growing protest outside. Everyone was restless.

It was the middle of the afternoon on Tuesday and Father was fast asleep. At lunchtime, Alex had tried to wake him, but his father said he wasn't hungry and wanted to rest.

Alex had passed the morning writing on the blank pieces of paper he'd been given by Mr. Lessel. In the smallest handwriting, up to the paper's edges, Alex had described the conditions inside the center and the protest outside. Sleeping on the floor. The terrible food. The buckets of human waste in the cupboards. The young men standing on the windowsills. The release of Lea and her father. Every hour or so, he'd added a few sentences. His daydreams blurred into thoughts of Marko. Only last week, running deliveries across the city together, Alex and Marko had stolen kisses whenever they knew they wouldn't be seen.

At sunrise, the men had taken turns to stand on the window ledge and provide a rundown of the bomb damage. The building across the street had burned out and collapsed during the night, scattering bricks and glass across part of Rosenstrasse.

Now, a man a few years older than Alex stood on the sill, balancing on the tips of his shoes to get a better look. "The crowd is chanting again."

Alex turned to Father, but he was snoring away.

Alex stood up to take the man's place at the window. On the ledge, he rested his forehead against the fingerprint-covered glass. Rubble from the destroyed building spilled out onto the cobblestones like the carcass of a dead animal. Looking down at the protesters, he wondered how many had lost their homes in the air raid. Alex hoped to see Mother and Elise again. He searched the crowd for Ruti's face, too. The protesters began to move.

"Something's happening," Alex said to the room.

The men sat alert and ready to listen to Alex's commentary.

"The crowd's moving back. Away from the building. I don't know why."

Below, Alex could see the tops of the guards' metal fighting helmets. *What a joke.* They appeared to be wearing full military apparel while the crowd was made up of mostly women and children. The guards' rifles pointed out from under their helmets, forcing those at the front of the crowd to step backward.

"They're threatening them. The guards have guns. The women are holding out their arms. They're shouting not to shoot."

The men gasped and began to chatter.

Alex was astonished at what he saw. "They're running, now. They're running away from the center."

He watched as the crowd scattered. Avoiding the debris in the road, they flooded into the side streets. When Alex saw Ruti looking up and back at the building, he wanted to scream out her name. Elise was next to her. He couldn't see Mother. Alex waved then banged his fist on the glass. But they couldn't hear or see him. Then he saw Tsura's face. It was her, in her cap and long coat. *The girls are with Tsura.* The three of them ran into a side street and out of sight. *If Tsura's here, Marko must be here, too.* Holding his breath, Alex's eyes jumped back and forth from one face to another of the shrinking crowd. If Marko was out there, Alex had missed him.

"What's happening?" Mr. Lessel shouted.

"The street's clear. They all ran," Alex announced to the room.

"They'll deport us now," one of the men cried out.

"No, they're still here. They're standing in the side streets. I can see some of them."

Excited that he'd spotted Tsura and Ruti, Alex jumped down from the ledge. He tapped his father on the arm. "Papa, wake up." Beads of sweat covered Father's forehead. Alex reached his hand beneath his father's head, touching the back of his neck. "Papa, you're burning."

With his eyes still closed, Alex's father whispered, "I feel cold."

Ruth

The crowd seemed even stronger. Ruth stood with Elise and Tsura in a courtyard, just off Rosenstrasse. Everyone was shivering and, for a moment, Ruth wished she were at home. But her house was no longer standing. Despite the bombings, Ruth was glad she was staying with Elise. Elise seemed happier with Mama and Ruth around.

After Mama and Marko had left to fetch hot drinks, a Nazi police guard at the front of the building had shouted at the crowd. Rather than protesting illegally, the women would be better to divorce their husbands, he had said. Some of the women had jeered. One woman had shouted back that she'd tell his mother about his behavior. The women's comments had made Ruth feel less frightened. The Nazi guards were local boys.

But then the door of the center had opened and a high-ranking Nazi pig had walked out. More women heckled that they wouldn't be going anywhere. A guard had shouted that they were prepared to shoot. They'd been given orders. From his voice, he'd seemed not to believe what he was saying. But as he'd said his words, the line of Nazi guards had raised their guns. The pig was serious. The women with younger children had turned back into the crowd, which started a wave of pushing and shoving. Ruth had looked for Mama and Marko. But there'd been too many people around her.

When Elise and Ruth ran into the alleyways along Rosenstrasse, Tsura had stayed close to them. From the relative safety of the courtyard, one woman had suggested they dare the guards to shoot, because they never would. Others had disagreed. They couldn't take that chance. One man had speculated that the Gestapo officers were purposely clearing the streets so they could empty the building, which started a wave of people proposing they return to the street immediately.

This was the fourth day of the protest. Hundreds were out there, despite the weather, and the Gestapo appeared to have no way to respond effectively.

Packed into the courtyard, Tsura stood ahead of Ruth and Elise, surveying the street.

"So, his name is Marko—not Paul?" Elise whispered to Ruth.

"Right. Marko," Ruth replied.

Elise screwed up her face, as if baffled. "And he's Jewish too?"

Marko and Tsura's family was Romani, but Ruth remembered Papa's insistence that they tell people that Kizzy was their cousin from Hamburg. When Tsura walked back over to them, Ruth was saved from replying to Elise's query.

"The women need to calm down. They're asking for a bloodbath," Tsura said, referring to the Nazis' threats.

Ruth disagreed. "They'll never shoot at German women. We're Christians."

Tsura let out a stilted laugh and Ruth felt embarrassed by her simpleminded comment.

Ruth was so happy to meet Tsura. She couldn't believe Marko's sister was Alexander's girlfriend. It all made perfect sense. *Tsura is so pretty.* She had a slim frame and a perfect face, like a film star. Unlike most other girls approaching twenty, Tsura was wearing no makeup, which made her beauty even more striking.

Tsura was entirely focused on the protest, engaged with what was happening around them. She and Alexander were a perfect match. She was mature and intelligent, just like him. Ruth imagined them talking and debating for hours about politics, about the war. She wondered why they'd been so secretive. *I hope they get married.* Ruth pictured the wedding, the dancing, the food. Her parents would toast the happy couple, wishing them health and children. She would be Aunt Ruth. *Or Auntie Ruti. I wouldn't mind that.*

Remembering the photographs of Alexander, Ruth reached into her pocket. "Here."

Tsura took the photograph. She seemed hesitant.

Ruth grinned. "It's okay. I have another one."

"Thanks," Tsura said. She paused, wanting to say something else.

"I bet Alexander's thinking about you," Ruth said.

Tsura didn't smile. "Ruth, you've got it wrong. I'm not Alex's girlfriend."

Ruth couldn't understand why Tsura and Alexander were trying so hard to keep their relationship a secret.

"Tell her," Ruth said with a smile, staring at Elise. "Tell her what you saw."

E*lise*

Elise was choked by an upwelling of embarrassment. Paul, or Marko, or whatever his name was, hadn't recognized her. And now this.

"What did you see?" Tsura asked Elise.

Ruth had put Elise in the most awkward of situations. But Elise couldn't find the words.

Ruth jumped in. "Elise saw you. Behind her house on Friday night. She saw what you were doing."

Tsura stared at the girls, obviously wanting a full explanation. Ruth elbowed Elise's arm, wanting her to tell Tsura everything.

I hate Ruth right now. "I— You and Alex—" Elise stuttered, trying to find the right way to say it.

"She saw you kissing," Ruth said impatiently.

Tsura said nothing, her eyebrows furrowed, her mouth slightly open.

Ruth continued, "She saw my brother kissing you. Around midnight on Friday. The night before he was arrested."

"You did?" Tsura didn't seem amused.

Elise's embarrassment hadn't worn off. "I'm sorry. I wasn't spying. I heard something. I thought you were robbers, maybe. I don't know. It was really late. I saw you and Alex. I'm sorry. I really am."

I'm acting like an idiot. Elise's arms were pulsating in time with her heart.

Viktor stood next to her now, holding her sleeve. "Are you okay?" Viktor asked.

Elise didn't respond to him. Not in front of Ruth and Tsura. *They'll think I'm crazy.*

"It's okay," Tsura said and looked down at the photograph in her hand. "Just don't tell anyone."

"We won't," Ruth said and paused. "But, you should know, I already told my mother about you two."

Tsura's frown hardened. "What did you tell her?"

"That you're my brother's girlfriend. But it's okay. She's happy for you."

Elise stood in the courtyard and looked at the crowd around her. She felt an urge to break the awkward silence. "Tsura, it's funny, I saw you and your brother on the same day."

"You know Marko?" Ruth asked. Elise enjoyed Ruth's puzzled reaction. Ruth had lied about Marko's name. She'd called him Paul. *She thinks I'm stupid.* Elise wanted Ruth to know she had secrets, too. Elise had met Marko before. *I saved his life.*

"On Friday. I met him in the market. There was a boy. He was trying to steal Marko's bag."

"Steal his bag? What boy?" Tsura asked.

"He didn't tell you?" Elise said, proud to know something Tsura didn't. "The boy had a knife. He almost stabbed Marko with it."

Ruth leaned in, seemingly amazed by Elise's story.

"I saved him. I distracted the thief and Marko got away."

"You did?" Tsura said.

Ruth jolted backward. "You didn't tell me that!"

Elise wanted to tell Ruth that she had already told her, the day after it happened. It's just that Ruth hadn't been listening. She'd been obsessing over Alex's pointless treasure hunt. But Elise kept her mouth closed.

Excitement broke out around them and the protestors spilled back onto Rosenstrasse.

Tsura took Elise's hand. "Stay here," she said to Ruth.

Tsura guided Elise toward the front of the crowd. "You saved my brother from a thief?" she asked as they walked.

"Yes. An African boy," Elise explained. As she followed Tsura, she felt simultaneous waves of fear and excitement. "Where are we going?"

"Just play along," Tsura whispered. "And, if anything happens, my name is Greta."

Greta. Tsura. Paul. Marko. They were a Jewish family, Elise had figured out, living under false names. She'd learned about these kinds of arrangements at the League meetings—Jews pretending to be Aryan, camouflaged, sneaking around with fake German identities. Elise couldn't catch her breath as Tsura led her toward the line of Nazi guards in front of the building. As they walked, Tsura took off her cap. Her long hair fell down her back and Elise could see the guards turning their heads and paying attention, smiling at Tsura as they approached.

Tsura addressed the guards. "Please, you have to help us."

"Sure." The guard closest to Tsura grinned, as if to say she could ask him anything.

Some of the other guards smiled, too. Then Elise saw him—the soldier who looked like Viktor—standing in the doorway, behind the row of police guards. Up close, his eyes were a piercing blue and he was thin and his face was lightly freckled. *Just like Viktor.*

Tsura continued, "We're looking for two little girls. They were seen at the window." Tsura gestured to Elise. "She's their friend."

Two girls? Startled by Tsura's confidence and confused by the lie, Elise nodded, saying nothing. She prayed they wouldn't ask her any questions. The guards looked down at Elise. She was visibly anxious, which, Elise assumed, was Tsura's plan.

"Kizzy Lange and Franziska Voeske. Are they here? Can you check?"

Franziska. Kizzy. Tsura's cousin had a false identity, too.

"I'll see what I can do," one of the guards said, and he disappeared into the building.

Elise was still staring at the soldier who looked like Viktor. When the soldier stared back and smiled, Elise blushed.

Less than a minute later, the guard returned. "I'm sorry. We're not allowed to give out any more information," he explained.

"You can't help us?" Tsura said. She looked down at Elise. "She just wants to know her friends are safe."

Elise nodded and looked at the soldier who resembled Viktor. "Please?"

He shrugged, implying that he wanted to help but couldn't.

Tsura led Elise back to the crowd. Ruth, Mrs. Broden, and Marko were watching them. Seeing Marko made Elise nervous all over again.

Marko held his cap, his dark hair falling over his forehead. "What did you find out, sis?"

"Nothing," Tsura said.

Stuck in place, words trapped in her throat, Elise wanted to tell Marko how she'd tried to find out about his little cousin. And she wanted to remind him of who she was. She was about to ask Tsura about the names Kizzy and Franziska. Which one was their cousin's real name? But again the police guards began to shout.

"Leave the area. Or, this time, we really will shoot." The guards raised their guns and the protestors ran back to the side streets and courtyards.

"We have to go," Tsura said, looking at her brother.

"Go?" Ruth said. "Will you be back? We'll be right here."

As Tsura led Marko away, Elise felt humiliated. *How can he still not remember me?*

Marko

Marko followed Tsura away from Rosenstrasse, suddenly consumed by his crazy idea. He'd fetch the dead Nazi's uniform from Seraph, return to the protest, and find a way inside the center. But Tsura wouldn't have approved of his plan. Marko kept his mouth shut and put his hands in his coat pockets, allowing himself to think about Alex.

Marko's time with Alex's mother had been surreal and a little sad. He'd wanted to tell Mrs. Broden how worried he was for Alex. Instead, their conversation had been a prolonged lie. When the guards had threatened to shoot at the crowd, Mrs. Broden had grabbed Marko's hand, as if he were family. In a side street, surrounded by the frightened protesters, Mrs. Broden had asked about Kizzy. When Marko had told her that Kizzy had been arrested, she'd put her arms around him. He'd wanted to tell Mrs. Broden his secret—that he'd messed up and sent Kizzy with Duerr—but he kept the truth to himself. Walking back to the crowd, Mrs. Broden had asked Marko about Tsura and Alex. She'd wanted to know how long they'd been together and how they'd met. Marko shrugged. That she thought Tsura was Alex's girlfriend was amusing, but frustrating, too.

On foot, Marko and Tsura headed west.

"Elise said she's met you before," Tsura said.

"Who?"

"Ruth's friend. She met you in the market."

"The market?"

"She said she saved you. From an African boy. You didn't find that bag," she snapped.

Marko laughed. *Ruti's friend was that girl?* "Beethoven. I thought I recognized her." Ruti's friend had been his savior that day. And she'd been bragging about it, telling all his business. *Little girls and their big mouths.*

"You stole it, didn't you? You lied to me."

"What? The bag? No. I found it, I told you." Marko was bending the truth. For a moment, he felt ashamed for starting the fight. "But that's where I got the knife."

Marko pictured Hackescher Market, picking up the knife from the ground—holding the blade to the Marzahn guard's throat.

They walked fast, passing bombed buildings that weren't burning anymore. People were clearing the rubble, searching for the dead, digging out their belongings, salvaging furniture and family treasures.

Marko shook his head. "This war is crazy."

"Elise saw something else," Tsura said.

Just east of the Tiergarten, with nobody else around, Tsura stopped on the pavement, making Marko halt.

"What?" Marko asked.

"On Friday night, behind her home. Elise saw you and Alex," Tsura snapped. "She thought I was you."

"So?"

Tsura gave him a sharp stare. "She saw you two messing around."

"What?" Marko felt like he'd been hit in the face. *She knows everything.* At the same time, he found it almost comical. "What're you saying?"

"You know what I'm saying!" she shouted.

"No, I don't," he lied.

"Marko, she saw you kissing." Tsura spat her words and grimaced.

Marko ignored the look of disgust on his sister's face. They'd been caught. *Broden would be mortified.* The last thing Alex would have wanted was for people to know about them. "Come on, sis. The girl doesn't know what she's talking about."

"I'm not stupid, Marko!"

He let out a nervous laugh. There was no point in denying the truth. "She thought you were me?"

"Yes!" Tsura barked. "They think I'm Alex's girlfriend."

Marko bit down on his smile. "That's good."

"Good? Why didn't you tell me? Why did you lie?"

Marko stopped smiling. "Why d'you think?"

"Oh, I see," Tsura said, mocking him. "That's why you didn't want Kizzy with you."

"What the hell?" Marko shouted. But he knew what she was getting at.

Tsura folded her arms across her chest. "You and Alex. You didn't want Kizzy leaving Berlin with you. You two wanted to be alone."

"Don't be stupid. We couldn't have taken her. It would've been too dangerous."

"You can tell yourself that."

"I'm serious," Marko snapped, trying to convince himself. "It wouldn't have worked."

"Did you take him to that wine cellar? Those mattresses on the floor. Is that where you and Alex mess around?"

"Shut up."

"It's sickening, Marko!" Tsura continued to walk ahead.

Marko couldn't speak. *Sickening. Sick.* It was a slur he'd heard before. A stranger he'd met once and fooled around with had introduced Marko to the forgotten history of homosexuals in Berlin. Before Adolf Hitler became Chancellor, there'd been cafés and wine bars and dance halls for men and women like them, he'd told Marko. And organizations, and petitions, and a political climate that would have led to changes in German law and more tolerance. At the same time as the infamous book burnings, the new Nazi government had destroyed a research institute where German scientists had collected evidence that homosexuality was natural. Normal. *I'm not sick.*

Marko stayed a few steps behind his sister. Then she turned and stopped again.

"What about our family, Marko?" she yelled. "What about our people?"

"What about them?" Tsura was always going on and on about the Romani, as if she could fight the government by herself.

"Marko, don't you care? Don't you care they're trying to kill us? We're responsible for our family's future. And here you are messing around with boys like Alex Broden. Without us, Marko, our people will die off!" Tsura spoke as if Marko hadn't considered these ideas before. As if he had a choice. "It's sickening," she repeated.

I'm not sick.

"Don't you know what they do to men like you?" Tsura continued to shout.

Marko clenched his fists. "Yes, Tsura. I know what they do to men like me!"

Marko reached his hands up to his head and closed his eyes. He wanted Alex. He needed him. He could almost hear Alex's voice, saying it would all be okay. Marko took a deep breath and walked away from his sister.

"Where are you going?" she shouted.

Marko didn't need Tsura. He walked south. Fast. He pushed his hands deep into the pockets of Alex's coat and spun the soldier's medal between his finger and thumb.

Kizzy

The Gestapo had finished loading the trucks of Jews. From the room upstairs, through the bars and barbs on the window, Kizzy saw the street below was deserted. As if nothing had happened. Felix, Esther, and little Ari were hiding in the toilet cupboard behind her, waiting for her instructions.

Locked in the room during the air raid, Kizzy had tried to guess where they were. Through the window, she had seen a sealed-off courtyard. For days, except for the Nazi trucks bringing more Jews to the building, the surrounding streets had been quiet. Now, in a room on the other side of the building, overlooking the main street, she could see they were in the center of Berlin. The street was empty. This part of the city had been completely closed off.

I've gotta get out. Kizzy was prepared to leave Felix and Esther and the boy behind if she had to. She didn't care about them. The trucks had gone, but from the window, she couldn't see if the building was being guarded.

"Come on," Kizzy whispered as she opened the toilet cupboard door.

Felix jumped out first, gasping for fresh air. Esther started to cough.

"Sshh!"

It was only Ari who stayed quiet and calm.

Kizzy checked the corridor. She led them out to the staircase. There were no sounds, no soldiers. The building was empty.

"Let's go." Without thinking, Kizzy kept Ari close. She held her finger against her mouth and Esther and Felix followed, slowly, soundlessly, downstairs.

When they reached the ground floor, Kizzy heard voices. *Soldiers.* "Quickly," Kizzy whispered and pointed at the stairway that appeared to lead into the basement.

With her heart racing, she led the children down. On the bottom step, Kizzy held out her arm and checked the dark passageway. Again, she put her finger on her mouth, even though the children were silent. Kizzy edged along the damp corridor and through an open doorway. Boxes and crates stood stacked in shadows, covered in piles of blankets, in front of a small window. *Daylight!* Kizzy ran over to the barred window—without glass, without barbs—close to the low ceiling, below street level at the front of the building. This was their way out.

A wooden trunk stood against the wall. "Gimme a hand," she said to Felix and Esther.

They dragged the trunk over to the window and Kizzy climbed on top. Assuming there were no guards on the street, they'd be able to squeeze through the bars. Kizzy tried to pull herself up to the windowsill, but it was too high. She jumped down to the floor and crouched at Ari's level.

"I'm gonna pick you up again. You're gonna look outside and tell us if you see any soldiers. Okay?"

Ari nodded. The yellow star on his coat was as bright as his red hair. Kizzy grabbed at the star with her fingernails, trying to rip it off. But it was sewn down, as if it were part of the coat fabric.

"Let's get your coat off." Kizzy spoke with a fake smile, trying to keep the boy calm. "Your coats, too," she said to Esther and Felix.

Ari was in just his shirt now. She saw he was shivering.

"The blankets," Kizzy said.

Esther pulled a blanket from one of the crates and wrapped it around her little cousin.

Felix grabbed a blanket for himself. "Here." He passed an extra to Esther.

Again, Kizzy climbed onto the trunk. Felix jumped up, too.

"Come here," Kizzy said to the little boy.

Kizzy and Felix helped Ari up. They held him at the waist, the gray blanket rough and scratchy around him, and lifted him toward the window.

"Put your head through the bars. Look out for any soldiers. Can you do that?"

Tilted sideways, Ari's head fit through the bars easily, stopping at his chest. He looked left and right. They pulled him back inside.

"Soldiers?"

He shook his head.

"Well done," Kizzy said with a real smile.

"You're being such a good boy," Esther said softly, as if reading Kizzy's mind.

Still on the trunk, reaching up to the bars, Kizzy was sure she could fit through. *I could get myself out right now.* Tsura's voice echoed in her head. *Just run.* But she felt compelled to help the others first.

"We're climbing out," she said to them. Kizzy looked at Ari and Esther. "You two first."

In her mind, Kizzy jumped two steps ahead. Once outside—with her Jewish friends without their yellow stars—they'd pretend to be Aryan, orphaned survivors of last night's air raid.

Again, they lifted Ari, still wrapped in his blanket. He climbed through the bars and into the street. Kizzy's heart was beating fast. *We did it.*

"Good boy," Esther said.

"Hide behind that tree," Kizzy said to Ari. She pointed through the bars toward a wooded area across the street. "Keep quiet and wait for us, okay?"

From the street, Ari looked down at them through the bars of the window, as if he were visiting them in prison. Kizzy grabbed the hat from her head. *It'll hide his red hair.* But before she could pass it to him, his little legs ran across the empty road. The blanket over him like a cloak, Ari disappeared behind a tree, just as Kizzy had instructed.

Kizzy put her hat back on.

"You're next," she said to Esther.

Esther's coat with its yellow star was already on the basement floor. A blanket was draped over Esther's shoulders. Felix helped Kizzy to lift Esther up. Her head cleared the bars, but her shoulders were stuck.

"I can't do it," Esther said.

Kizzy gritted her teeth in frustration. "Turn on your side."

Half of Esther's body was out of the building, her legs on Kizzy's shoulders. Then she started to kick.

"Esther, be careful," Kizzy whispered.

"No! No!" Esther shrieked, suddenly squealing like an animal, and kicked her legs hard.

"What're you doing?" Kizzy tried not to shout.

Esther's shoe hit Kizzy's head. "Fleas!" Esther screamed and kicked and thrashed between the window's bars.

"Stop!" Kizzy yelled.

Esther wouldn't stop shrieking. The three of them tumbled against the crates and onto the basement floor. A crate toppled over, almost striking Kizzy's head as her knee landed on Esther's shoulder, and they both yelped in pain. Felix pulled off Esther's blanket and Kizzy saw handfuls of dead fleas fall to the ground.

"Esther, they're dead. Be quiet!" Kizzy pleaded.

But still Esther wouldn't stop screaming.

The sound of a whistle made Kizzy leap up. *Soldiers.* Through the bars of the window, Kizzy saw a face, a Nazi, black uniform, shining medals.

"Jews in the basement!" the man shouted.

Kizzy ran to the doorway, leaving Felix and Esther behind, and bolted up the stairs. She could hear guards' voices on the ground floor. Shouting and boots behind her. At the next level, Kizzy rushed out into the corridor and toward the room she'd hidden in earlier. She opened the cupboard, the toilet bucket at her feet, and slammed the door closed. Her heart was pounding.

The soldier's voices grew louder. "Where did she go?" The soldiers were shouting and getting closer. "I'll check in here."

Kizzy reached into her coat pocket, a bar of soap in one hand, Professor Duerr's key in the other. Putting the key through her fingers like Marko trained her, Kizzy waited. The stench of the bucket filled her nostrils. She tried to catch her breath.

The cupboard door swung open. "Found her!"

Kizzy threw her fist and key forward, trying to stab and punch the Nazi guards. Holding back a growling dog, the soldiers took hold of Kizzy's arms and the ends of her hair that stuck out from the bottom of her hat. Kizzy dropped the soap, kicking, swinging her arms. *The key!* It was gone. She scratched at them with her fingernails. One soldier cried in pain and let her go. Kizzy fell back, hitting her head on the cupboard wall, and then she was falling. Her hand landed on the floor and her shoulder smashed into the bucket. She slipped, without time to scream, and her hand slid into the cold human waste.

Sprawled across the floor, she was covered—from the left side of her face and down her arm, thigh, leg—in putrid muck. The stench was unbearable and she let out a gasp of disgust.

The guards stood back. One burst into laughter. The soldiers stared at her. She was on the floor, the bucket spilled over, cold excrement mixed with urine and vomit all over the floor, all over her. Her mouth opened and her eyes bulged and she started to screech, uncontrollably.

The Nazis, four of them, howled with amusement, with their guns all aimed at her head. "Look at this filthy Jew," one of the soldiers said.

At his words, Kizzy yelled, "Romani! I'm Romani!"

Kizzy's admission caused the soldiers to laugh even more.

"Get away from me! Go to hell! All of you, go to hell! You're gonna lose the war. I swear it!"

Another guard started a joke. "What's the difference between a Jew and a Gypsy?"

He didn't get to the punch line. An officer, higher ranking, had walked into the room.

Kizzy stopped shouting at the guards and, from the waste-soaked floor, gazed up at the officer. "They're gonna hang you!" she shouted. Then she reached for the waste bucket and, with all her strength, swung it at the officer. But the officer was too quick. He jumped out of the way and what was left of the sludge sprayed across the wooden floor.

The officer looked down at Kizzy with disgust. "Get her cleaned up," he told the guards. "The protest on Rosenstrasse is growing. We'll have more Jews arriving soon."

A protest?

"Stand," one of the guards said, without touching her.

The muck dripping from her sleeves and rolling down her neck was cold and made her want to retch. As they led Kizzy into another room—tiled floor, bright white, a washroom of some kind—the guard had a chance to finish his joke. "A Jew rolls in money while a Gypsy rolls in shit." Then he kicked Kizzy toward the wall.

Before she could think, Kizzy was being soaked with cold, dirty water. Some splashed into her mouth. More cold water, thrown from buckets, soaked Kizzy's pinafore through to her underwear. It washed off some of the excrement. More water, over her head, her legs, down her back. Soaked to her skin.

Shivering, embarrassed, Kizzy was led downstairs. A guard held her by the wrist. As they reached the ground floor, she kicked at him. Then she saw Felix and Esther standing against the wall by the building's entrance, holding their coats. Esther was sobbing. Felix's face was completely white. A Nazi stood with his rifle pointed at them. Kizzy kicked the guard again hard on his shin.

"Do that again and I'll shoot your friends dead," he shouted. He turned to another guard. "Mark them off the list. Two Jews and a Gypsy girl."

The guards marched them outside. The street was empty. *Nobody to help. Nobody watching.* She watched the trees opposite the building. *Is Ari waiting there for us?*

Crying her eyes out, Esther was looking out for her little cousin, too.

The Jewish orderly who led the children earlier—his red armband gone now—was in the back of the waiting truck. The Nazis were calm, waiting for Kizzy to climb. The truck was empty, except for the four of them: the Jewish orderly, Felix, Esther, and Kizzy.

"Did we get you in trouble?" Kizzy asked the orderly.

"No. They arrested me before they knew you were missing."

"Where are we?" Kizzy asked him.

"Hamburg Main Street," he said. "At the old Jewish home for the elderly."

"They were talking about a protest," Kizzy said.

"We're not far from Hackescher Market," he explained. "There's a huge anti-Nazi demonstration happening, ten minutes away. It's been going on for days. It's a mass protest against the government."

"That's good news," Kizzy said. *Maybe we'll be released.*

"I'm Frank," the orderly said.

Kizzy remembered her false papers—the ones that said Franziska Scholz. *Fränzi.* "I'm Kizzy."

The engine sputtered to life. Frank sat on the truck's hard floor and nodded for them to sit, too.

"Where are they taking us?" Esther asked.

"I don't know," Frank said, but Kizzy didn't believe him.

Esther burst into tears again. "Ari can't look after himself."

The journey took less than half an hour. Kizzy climbed out of the truck. The afternoon sun was shining. Kizzy shivered through her wet clothes. Rail tracks and trains surrounded them. *A freight yard.* Nazi rifles pointed at their heads as they walked toward a table in the open air.

"Sign your full name here," a seated soldier ordered. With his gloved hand, he pushed a piece of paper in front of her.

"What's this?" Kizzy asked.

"Permission for relocation," he replied, boredom in his voice.

Frightened to disobey, Kizzy scrawled her name on the document. *Relocation.* As she was led away, Kizzy touched her drenched woolen hat—the blue one Professor Duerr had knitted, the one Tsura had worn as a young girl.

Another soldier guided Kizzy, Felix, and Esther toward a waiting freight train, the kind that transported cattle and horses.

"I've never been on a train before," Felix said with a smile on his face.

A door of the train was open and, from the inside, men and women stared down at them. Yellow stars. The carriage was packed. Grown Jewish men and women. Shoulders against shoulders. A woman was held upright by the group. Blood trickled down her leg, her hand at her stomach. She'd been shot, it seemed.

"Climb," a Nazi guard instructed.

Felix and Esther were pushed up first. Kizzy followed.

"Where are we?" Kizzy asked the adults, as she squeezed in. "Where are they taking us?"

The people around Kizzy turned away. They could smell the muck in Kizzy's clothes and skin. *If I was them, I'd do the same.*

Two men—more Jews—were marched along the platform. The soldiers pointed for them to climb into the carriage. They struggled to force their way inside. People next to Kizzy told others to move into the gaps. Kizzy couldn't see Felix anymore.

"There's no more space," a woman shouted.

A man at the back screamed out, "We're being crushed!"

Kizzy could no longer see the platform. Just people. It was the second of March, she told herself. *Tuesday.* She wanted to remember the date. The sound of water on the floor took her eyes to a puddle at her feet. Urine. She looked up at Frank and his face turned red and he looked away.

Esther was still sobbing. "I need to be with Ari."

Kizzy felt sorry for her. *Where are my cousins right now?* Kizzy had been so young when they'd moved into Professor Duerr's home. She wondered where Marko was. *Is Tsura looking for me?*

Darkness swallowed them as the freight train door slammed shut.

RADIO

Tsura

Marko likes men. In other circumstances, Tsura wouldn't have really cared. She wouldn't have been concerned that he and Alex were planning to leave Berlin together. What made her furious was that Marko had lied. He and Alexander Broden were colleagues, he'd said. Good friends. The truth was jarring. There were strict laws against men like Marko. *My Romani brother.* Double points for the Gestapo.

But something else, a deeper fear, was taking hold. Marko was homosexual. His bloodline would stop with him. Tsura would never have children. *The Nazis are murdering our people.* Who would continue the future of their family?

After their quarrel, Marko had stormed off. Tsura was concerned for him, but her brother could take care of himself, she knew.

The freezing air filling Duerr's house made the stench of rotting food bearable. Tsura climbed upstairs to Duerr's bedroom. She remembered the old woman in the morgue, just as she remembered Wim and the Nazi officer on the cold ground. Tsura forced herself to picture Kizzy and her mother and Aunt Marie alive. Duerr's bed was unmade, as they'd left it, days ago. She rummaged through the piles of photographs and documents on the bedside table. Tsura found the photograph she was looking for and returned to the hallway downstairs. She took Marko's stolen bag—heavy with bottles, tins of good food, packets of cigarettes—and stepped outside, heading south.

Tsura tapped out the code on Seraph's apartment door. She hadn't seen Seraph since the morning after Marzahn.

"How are you?" Seraph put her arms around Tsura.

She allowed Seraph to hold her for only a moment before she gently pushed her away. "I need false documents."

"That's Wolf's department. He'll be back soon," Seraph said.

Tsura jumped when Marko walked out of one of the bedrooms.

"It'll fit," Marko said. He was wearing the dead Nazi's army cap.

To see her brother in the enemy's hat filled Tsura with disgust. "Marko! What are you doing?"

"Leave me alone, Tsura." Still wearing Alex's coat, Marko was holding the gray uniform jacket against himself, silver piping on the collars. Stripes and medals. A dark stain surrounded a rip close to the jacket's collar. A bullet hole. But most of the officer's blood had been washed out of the fabric and the uniform had been ironed.

"Take off the hat," Tsura snapped.

"I told you she'd act like this," Marko said to Seraph.

Seraph stayed quiet and Tsura realized her brother's intent. "Marko, don't be ridiculous."

"Leave me alone."

Tsura inhaled to calm herself and stepped forward with open hands. "Let's talk it through. I might have a better idea." Tsura reached into her pocket and passed Marko the photograph of Alex, the one Ruth had given to her.

Marko looked down at the image. He took off the Nazi cap and placed the pressed uniform on the armchair. Dropping to the floor, now sitting on the rug in front of Seraph's couch, Marko's eyes were glassy, close to tears. "Where—?" his voice trailed off.

Tsura sat on the floor beside her brother. "Ruth gave it to me."

"Are you hungry?" Seraph asked as she poured three glasses of schnapps.

"Something hot would be good," Tsura replied.

Marko couldn't take his eyes from the small photograph of Alex. He ran his fingers around its edge. He stared at the image as if the picture were alive.

"It's not to keep. We need to get Alex out. And Kizzy, too. If she's even in there." Tsura picked up the Nazi hat, feeling its rough fabric. As she remembered the dead Nazi officer, she could see Wim, face down on the gravel. For a moment, she felt sorry for the drunk police guard, but the image of Duerr on the table in the hospital morgue erased Tsura's pity. She recalled the crying infant at the train station. She had saved his life, yet he'd grow up to wear a Nazi uniform.

Seraph returned with a bowl of hot meat stew and a plate of bread and real butter. As Tsura updated Seraph about the protest and the possibility of finding Kizzy, Marko helped himself to the food but said nothing. Tsura observed her brother tuning out of the conversation. He reached for a book on the coffee table—the map book he'd taken from Alex's home. Turning its pages as if hypnotized by its contents, he continued to glance at Alex's photograph.

A few hours passed. As nighttime came, Tsura craved the outdoors. She was at her best when she could move through Berlin's shadows.

Keys against the wooden door jolted them alert. *Wolf.* When Seraph stood to kiss him, he avoided her, grabbing the bottle of schnapps and trudging into the kitchen. They could hear him turn on the wireless. The radio crackled. Tsura stood up, shook the cramp from her legs, and picked up Marko's bag.

Marko followed Tsura into the kitchen. Still in his coat, Wolf sat at the kitchen table, drinking, the sounds of the BBC news announcer filling the room. Tsura placed Marko's bag on the table. "It's all yours," she said to Wolf, opening the bag in front of him.

"Tsura!" Marko crossed his arms and frowned. He had wanted to sell the bag's contents for cash, Tsura knew.

But Tsura had a different idea. Her hands on the back of a chair, she leaned over the table. "Wolf, we need false identity cards. Two sets. And some Gestapo release papers, with the same two names. All by tomorrow morning."

Wolf shook his head. "Not possible." He turned up the volume on the radio.

Tsura prodded the bag. "You can keep what you want. Take a look."

As Wolf opened the bag's main compartment, the BBC announcer, in clear German, began talking about war ships from the United States headed over to save Europe from Hitler's grasp. Wolf inspected the wine bottles, tins of caviar, boxes of cigarettes. Marko glared at Tsura. But still Wolf seemed undecided.

Tsura softened her voice. "Please. We need your help with this. The papers aren't for us."

Wolf pushed the bag away and took a gulp of schnapps. "I'm too busy."

Marko reached across the table to turn off the wireless, and the kitchen fell quiet. "It's for a Jew," Marko said. To Tsura, Marko suddenly resembled their father, his beard, his eyes, the way he spoke.

Wide-eyed, startled by Marko's insolent tone, Wolf scowled at him.

"For Kizzy, too. We have their photographs," Tsura added.

Marko looked at Alex's photograph one last time before passing it to Wolf, and Tsura pulled out a small photograph of Kizzy. She couldn't bring herself to look at her cousin's face.

Wolf no longer protested. "Okay."

"Papers for each of them," Tsura said.

Kizzy already had false documents, but Tsura suspected they'd been taken when she was arrested. Rummaging through the bag, Wolf took out two bottles of wine. He didn't take the tins of food, cigarettes, or the fancy cheese. "I'll have the papers by the morning," he said. "But I need more to trade."

"The side pockets," Marko said to him.

As Wolf opened the bag's side compartments, pulling out Duerr's jewelry and watch, Seraph entered the kitchen. "What are you three up to?"

"Give me your gun," Wolf said to Tsura, ignoring Seraph.

"Why?" Tsura asked.

"You want the documents immediately? You have to pay more," Wolf explained.

The idea of giving up her weapon made Tsura nervous. "Give them your own gun," she said.

Wolf let out a sigh.

Reluctantly, Tsura removed her pistol from her coat pocket and dropped it into Wolf's open palm. "The people you work with— You'll get the papers, right?"

"If not, Wolf will kill them," Seraph joked.

Wolf slammed his fist on the table. "Shut your mouth," he said without raising his voice.

Tsura had never heard Wolf speak that way—not to Seraph.

Seraph let out a nervous laugh. Arms crossed, Seraph turned to Marko and Tsura. "He's angry at me because he wanted to kill those soldiers."

Without a word, Wolf pushed his chair from the table.

Tsura followed Wolf into the living room. "I'll come with you," she said.

Wolf smiled softly. "Stay here. Get some rest."

"The names," Tsura said to Wolf, referring to the false names on the documents. "They need to be believable. And the dates of birth."

"I'll take care of everything," Wolf assured her.

He closed the door quietly behind him. Tsura felt naked without her weapon.

In the kitchen, Seraph was slouched at the table, upset. "I don't know what's wrong with him," she whined.

But dwelling on Seraph's boyfriend troubles was a waste of Tsura's time. "We need to put together a package," she said to Marko.

Tsura found a small woven basket and a clean cloth. They wrapped the cheeses and expensive spreads, the tinned food, cigarettes, and, from Seraph's kitchen, a stale loaf of bread. Before they packed the loaf, Tsura scooped out some of its insides. In the morning, they would hide the papers inside the bread.

"What about this?" Marko asked, holding out his knife.

Tsura laughed at him. "Definitely not." *My brother, always going to extremes.*

Marko clapped his hands together and grinned. "Fine. I'll get the uniform."

"That's not the plan." In her head, Tsura laughed at her brother's juvenile ideas.

Marko looked skeptical. "So how're we gonna get the papers inside?"

Tsura raised her eyebrows and twisted her mouth sideways, waiting for Marko to figure it out.

"Ruti," Marko said, smiling.

My brother and I are the same.

Seraph joined Marko and Tsura on the living room floor. "Did you hear about the Gestapo executions?" she asked Marko. "Three students—one woman and two men—old-fashioned guillotine, just weeks ago. The White Rose." Seraph was trying to frighten him and Tsura was amused.

"Beheaded?" Marko gulped down more cheap schnapps. A little while later, he was asleep on the soft rug.

Seraph jumped up to use the toilet and Tsura reached over for the map book on the coffee table. Browsing the maps and charts of German towns and cities, a small piece of paper fell into her lap. Written on the outside was the name "Ruti" above the word "Dresden." Inside the folded note was a short, strange message in neat handwriting.

When Seraph returned, Tsura dropped the note in her pocket.

"You're my closest friend," Seraph said and rested her head on Tsura's shoulder.

Tsura didn't know how to respond. *I'm her only friend. And she's mine.* The realization was disconcerting.

Seraph continued, "I'm losing Wolf. He's so distant, isn't he? He hasn't touched me since I shot those soldiers." To Tsura, Seraph's complaints were trivial. Seraph offered her a cigarette.

"We should get some sleep," Tsura said.

"I guess," Seraph said. She stood up and called out "Good night" before closing her bedroom door.

Tsura dropped onto the sofa, her mother's name—*Jaelle Lange*—repeating as she drifted to sleep.

In the morning, Tsura woke on the sofa to someone standing over her, touching her arm. She jumped and saw Wolf's face. Tsura brushed him away. "You have the papers?" she asked, forcing the sleep from her throat.

"Marko has them," Wolf said and nodded toward the kitchen. Wolf held out Tsura's gun. "I didn't need it."

Dropping the weapon back into her coat pocket felt satisfying.

It was now Wednesday morning. Kizzy had been missing for four days. Seraph was still asleep. Tsura found Marko in the kitchen, struggling to fold the documents into the bread loaf.

"I'll do it," Tsura said. She checked the false papers for Kizzy and Alex. The false names sounded authentic. The documents looked real. Dog-eared at the corners. Small stains and worn folds.

Wolf pointed at the official stamps on the paper. "They look good, right? Two sets of identity cards and matching release papers."

Tsura folded the documents long ways and slid the papers one by one into the loaf, careful not to make the opening in the bread too wide. Then she squeezed the loaf closed. "Not perfect, but it'll work."

"Coffee?" Marko asked them.

Wolf turned on the wireless, twisting the dial, making the radio crackle. Tsura listened as Marko poured coffee. On Monday, the BBC announcer explained, tens of thousands of American Jews had gathered at Madison Square Garden in New York. They had come together in opposition to the Nazi regime and to demand that the international community give its support to the millions of Jews struggling to survive across Hitler's Europe.

"Those Jews in America—do they know about the protest here in Berlin?" Marko asked.

"Maybe," Wolf said.

Marko continued, "But the Jewish protest in New York—The world will listen to them."

"The world will do nothing," Wolf snapped, his eyes on the radio. "Nobody ever helps the Jews."

"The same for the Roma. The BBC doesn't even talk about us," Tsura said. The exclusion of the Roma from the news reports had angered Tsura for some time. She'd listened to many BBC broadcasts about the Jewish community in the United States, applying pressure on its government to save Jewish lives. But she'd heard nothing about actions to help the European Romani. "They're killing us too. But the world doesn't care."

Wolf let out a sigh. "The world doesn't know. And the Jews have their own battles."

"No, Wolf." Tsura's voice was raised. "The entire world, those Jews in America included, couldn't care less about us *Zigeuner*—you know that."

Wolf became quiet. Tsura continued the argument in her head. *He knows I'm right.* The Jews had done nothing when the Nazis threw her family into the encampments. They'd done nothing when the Nazis sent her father away to a work camp. Nothing when, as a child, Nazi doctors sterilized Tsura and other Roma children. *I'll never give birth. I'll never be a mother*, Tsura wanted to scream. The Nazis wanted to cut off the bloodline of her people. They wanted the Romani, as well as other so-called Gypsies, including the Sinti people, to die out. The Jewish people had their own problems—the same problems—but Tsura had never heard of a Jew helping her people. "Those Jews. They only speak out for their own."

Wolf leaned back in his chair and kicked the table hard, spilling their coffee and almost sending the wireless crashing to the floor. "You should think before you speak." He stood and pointed his finger at her, mouth open, about to talk, but instead he walked into the living room.

"Wait," Tsura called out, running after him.

He slammed the front door and Tsura followed him into the hallway.

"Wolf!" Tsura's voice echoed down the marble and iron staircase.

Wolf stopped and looked up at her from the landing below. "Get away from me!"

"Keep your voice down."

Wolf ran back up the stairs and joined Tsura on the landing. With both hands, he gripped the back of his neck. "The Jews have no choice. The world isn't listening to us. Throwing the Roma into the mix—it'll only make things worse."

"You're wrong." *We'd be stronger together*, she wanted to tell him.

"No, you're the one who's wrong. I just travelled across the city to get those papers."

"You did that to help a Jew."

"I went to Rastplatz Marzahn."

"You—"

"I got papers for your Kizzy."

"That's not what I'm saying—"

"I risked my life for your Romani people. I was nearly killed!"

"No. You wanted revenge."

"No—"

"You wanted to kill them for your own family. For yourself."

"I wanted to murder them for you." Wolf pressed his mouth onto hers. His rough hands held her face.

"No," she said and pushed him away. She could still feel the pressure of his lips. She wanted to kiss him, but she stepped back. "I'm sorry. For what I said."

Wolf and Tsura walked back into the apartment. When Wolf closed the door to Seraph's bedroom, Marko stared at Tsura, knowing she and Wolf had been arguing.

"Are you all right?" Marko asked.

"Let's go."

As Marko and Tsura packed up their things, Tsura could feel her face burn, as if Wolf's touch had seared her skin.

Marko carried his bag. Tsura clutched the basket with its foods and hidden papers. As they closed the apartment door, Tsura felt as though she'd never see Wolf or Seraph again. With the memory of Wolf's kiss on her cracked lips, she wiped her mouth with her sleeve and bit down hard until she tasted blood.

They walked across the city, saying nothing.

Rosenstrasse was bustling.

"There they are," Marko said. Ruth and Elise were in the middle of the crowd.

Across the masses of people, Tsura gestured for Ruth and Elise to walk into the courtyard, away from the Nazi guards.

Ruth was eager to speak. "They threatened us again, but we didn't run this time."

Tsura focused on Ruth's words. She tried her best to push away thoughts of Wolf. The Gestapo was becoming weaker by the day.

"Where did you stay last night?" Tsura asked Ruth, remembering that her house had been bombed out.

"With Elise." Ruth pulled on the collar of her coat and laughed sadly. "I'm wearing Elise's clothes."

Elise wasn't listening. She was talking to Marko.

"Sorry I didn't recognize you," Tsura heard Marko say to Elise, who couldn't stop smiling at him.

Then Marko cut off Elise's words and turned to Ruth. "Where's your mother?"

"Fetching food for the crowd."

In many ways, Tsura and Ruth's mother were alike. Annett was strong. Assured.

"It's better your mother isn't here," Tsura said. In the empty courtyard, Tsura held out the small basket of food. "Take it," she said to Ruth.

"Food for Broden and your father," Marko said with a wink.

"Food?" Ruth said, sounding worried.

"And for Kizzy, if she's in there," Tsura added.

"Kizzy?" Elise asked. "That's your cousin's real name?"

Tsura nodded reluctantly. She kicked herself for using Kizzy's name so freely. Tsura gripped the handles of the basket. Ruth had to be calmed. "Don't worry. Just listen to us. Take the basket to the guards. Explain it's for your father."

Marko jumped in. "But, if they try to take it from you, refuse. Tell them to let you inside."

"What?" Ruth said, her eyebrows raised toward the gray skies.

Tsura continued her instructions. "Demand it. Cry. Scream like a baby if you have to. You have to take it in there yourself. You must give it to your father."

"What is all this?" Ruth asked, looking down at the basket in her hands.

"Listen to me." Tsura made her voice serious and quiet. "There's something hidden inside."

"False documents. And release papers. For Broden. And for Kizzy. Hidden inside the bread," Marko said.

Ruth listened, her mouth open.

"And one more thing." Tsura lowered her voice. "Your father must find out about Kizzy and tell us if she's being held here. Either way, we need to know. Understand?"

Tsura liked the look in Ruth's eyes. She was focused and on board with the plan.

"Elise," Ruth almost shouted. "Take off your coat."

Elise stared at her friend. Tsura watched them. *What is she doing?*

"Take it off," Ruth repeated and walked to the corner of the empty courtyard, pulling Elise along with her.

Ruth placed the basket at her feet and removed her own overcoat. Hidden by the wall, out of sight from the crowd, Elise began to unbutton her large heavy coat. When Tsura saw that Elise was wearing a Girls' League uniform, she had an urge to scream out.

"What the hell?" Marko said, half laughing, stealing his sister's words.

While Marko seemed amused by the revelation, Tsura felt only fear and anger. When she'd first met Elise, Tsura knew the girl couldn't be trusted. A wave of recent memories flooded Tsura's head. Wim, his guard's uniform, drunk, the empty bottle at his feet, the photograph of his family. The Nazi officer, on the ground by the edge of the Marzahn encampment. The Nazi woman on the train platform. *She's one of them.*

"It's okay," Ruth said to Tsura, as if sensing her shock and discomfort.

Tsura kept her eyes on the sickly girl who had been wearing the hidden Hitler Youth uniform beneath her coat all along. That Tsura felt frightened by Elise, who was four years younger, made Tsura even more uneasy. She thought of the papers in her pocket marked with her alias, Greta Voeske. *She knows my real name. Marko's real name, too. She knows about Kizzy and our plan.* Her eyes searched the courtyard, up to the windows and back out onto the street. For a moment, Tsura expected an ambush, organized by Elise. Tsura prepared to take Marko's arm and run with him back onto Rosenstrasse. To Tsura, even the protesters were suspicious now. She wondered how many were supporters of the regime. *Hypocrites.* They cried out for their Jewish husbands, yet they kept silent on every other Nazi policy.

With her coat and sweater already off, Ruth hit Marko with a string of questions. "What does Kizzy look like? What should I tell my father?"

Ruth listened attentively as Marko described his little cousin.

Elise unbuttoned her brown Girls' League jacket. Apprehensive and self-conscious, she passed the jacket to Ruth, along with her Nazi neckerchief and beret, which she pulled from her overcoat. Tsura was amazed, as if witnessing a tasteless magic trick. *What else is this girl hiding?* Both girls were standing in their thin blouses in the winter air. Elise's face turned red, either from the cold or from the embarrassment of being exposed.

"Turn around," Ruth ordered Marko. "Take off your skirt," she said to Elise.

Elise gasped. "No, I won't!"

"Listen to Ruth," Tsura said.

Elise glared at Tsura and nodded.

Marko turned away from the girls and watched the street. *He's not interested in women.* Tsura didn't know him as well as she'd thought.

The girls' shoes tapped on the cobblestones as they undressed below their waists. Explanations for Elise's Nazi membership spun in Tsura's head. Either Elise really was an enemy, or she was simply following the law that required all girls to attend the League meetings.

"Ready," Ruth said.

Marko turned back around and let out an awkward laugh at the sight of Ruth transformed. The uniform's jacket was a little too big, the neckerchief was tied poorly below her chin, and the black beret sat on her head in an awkward way, not quite fitting, certainly not keeping her warm. But Ruth looked convincing with her plaited hair and glasses, and she picked up the basket to complete the ensemble. Tsura was impressed. Ruth's disguise would fool the guards, there was no doubt.

"She's our spy," Marko whispered to Tsura.

Tsura remembered the fountain. *Red Riding Hood.*

"Wait," Ruth said.

Elise was holding Ruth's coat and Ruth reached into one of its pockets. She pulled out what looked like a small pile of notepapers and tossed one of the papers into the basket. Tsura watched her, baffled and intrigued.

"What're you doing?" Marko asked.

Ruth gave him a wink. "It's my back-up plan. If the soldiers check the basket, this will confuse them."

Tsura was impressed. While Ruth folded the remaining papers into the uniform jacket she was now wearing, Tsura saw that Ruth's nickname was written across the note in the basket. *Ruti.* Tsura reached into her own pocket. "Ruth, this is for you."

When Ruth saw the note in Tsura's hand, she appeared to hold back a shriek of excitement. Ruth placed the basket at her feet, grabbed the note, and threw her arms around Tsura. "Did Alexander give this to you? Did he tell you to pass it along to me?"

"No. I found it," Tsura replied.

In the borrowed Nazi uniform, reading the mysterious note, Ruth beamed. "It'll all be okay," Ruth said, picking up the basket, and she walked out onto Rosenstrasse and toward the building.

Tsura couldn't take her eyes off Elise. Elise was looking at Marko. "You lost a button," she said to him, filling the awkward silence, and pointed to a loose thread on the front of his coat.

Marko shrugged.

"It must be difficult being Jewish," Elise said.

She thinks we're Jewish. Tsura shot Marko a stare to make clear they shouldn't trust the girl, to keep quiet about their Romani family.

"That's right, Beethoven," Marko said and glanced back at Tsura. He'd got the message.

Alexander

Alex had been staring at the same faces and the same walls for days. In the space remaining on his few sheets of notepaper, he wrote about his family and the deportations, about his ruined plan to escape Berlin with Marko. How Tsura had helped them. He wrote about needing Marko. He couldn't shake the hope that Marko was outside, protesting with their sisters.

A Jewish doctor from the upper floor had been allowed to move through the building to check on the prisoners.

As soon as the doctor entered their room, with his scraps of paper in his pocket, Alex approached him. "Could you take a look at my father?"

"What's the matter with him?" the doctor asked.

Alex led the man to Father, who was sleeping on the floor. He watched the doctor examine Father with his stethoscope.

"He has a high fever, boy. He needs medicine. Find the orderly."

Alex ran to the doorway. Simon was standing at the top of the stairs, listening to a complaint about the blocked toilets.

"Simon," Alex called out.

Simon sighed, seemingly tired and bothered by so many requests.

"It's my father. He needs something for his fever. The doctor said so."

Simon escorted the doctor out of the room. Alex felt grateful but also sorry for Simon. There was little he could do. The building was a mess. The prisoners were unable to wash properly. Alex was getting used to the smell. And the building was still filling up with more Jews—all with Christian relatives. Another truckload of men had arrived in the early hours of the morning. Even after the air raid, even when they should have been clearing the streets and helping the new homeless of Berlin, the government was unwavering in its hunt for Jews. *The government is obsessed.* Like the ancient enemies of the Jewish people, Hitler with his hardened heart wanted them dead.

As Alex returned to his father's side, a Nazi officer walked into the room. "Samuel Broden."

Instinctively, Alex stood. "He's sleeping."

"Then wake him."

"He's ill. I'm his son."

The Nazi paused then gestured for Alex to follow him. Alex's mouth was suddenly dry. He didn't want to leave Father alone, but he had no choice.

Led down the staircase to the ground floor, Alex passed Simon on the way.

"Wait in here." The officer guided Alex into a room close to the building's entrance—an office. Two Nazi guards stood against the wall. The bright, clean room and the sounds of the crowd outside made Alex feel both hopeful and uneasy. "Take a seat."

Alex half expected to be offered coffee. He watched the higher-ranking officer turn to leave the room. As the door swung closed, Alex saw a girl in her League uniform. She turned and, just for a moment, Alex saw her face. His sister was standing in the hallway, looking down at the floor, in an ingenious costume. Alex held his breath, suppressing a joyful scream. *Ruti is here!*

Ruth

"Wait there," the officer told Ruth. Ruth's heart raced with excitement and she leaned against the hallway wall. *Papa is so close right now.*

When Ruth had approached the guards outside the building, wearing Elise's uniform and holding the basket, she didn't have to say a word. One of the guards had smiled and asked Ruth whom she was there to see. Ruth had given them Papa's name and right away the guard had walked inside while another had asked Ruth if she had any food for him. Ruth had grinned as sweetly as she could, trying to act bashful and childlike. A guard had led her inside the building. She stood in the vestibule, waiting.

Five years earlier, on her first and only visit to the League, the brown uniform had made Ruth shiver; with the cloth around her neck and the skewed hat, age ten, she felt and looked like a traitor to her Jewish father and brother. But now, in Elise's uniform, all she felt was pride. She was proud for thinking to take Elise's uniform and proud that she'd fooled the Nazi guards.

Ruth held the new note passed to her by Tsura. *Alexander's girlfriend is wonderful.* Ruth's nickname was written across the top. "Dresden" was written in the center. She read the message again.

Made in Hamburg

Dresden. I was right! Alexander was referring to his Jewish mother, who was born in Dresden. And the clue would have led Ruth to Mama, who was born in Hamburg. Ruth pictured the notes in her pocket. The treasure hunt had come back to life and she could recite each clue and each puzzle word by heart. *Freund, Unterwäsche, Nachthemd, Telefon, Mausloch, Eierschale, November, Annett, Dresden.*

Her birthday gift had been destroyed along with her house, but she was still desperate to solve the puzzle. *If I figure it out, Alexander and Papa will be released.*

Voices echoed through the hallways. Papa and Alexander were so close. Another Nazi officer appeared. From the medals and ribbons on his coat, he was obviously more high-ranking than the guards outside. *Another Nazi pig.*

The pig reached for the door handle to the room. Then he stopped. "Why are you here?"

"For my father."

The pig furrowed his eyebrows. "You mean your stepfather?"

"Yes."

Ruth hated his question. It was upsetting when people reminded her how Papa was not her father by blood, as if he hadn't raised her, as if he hadn't comforted her when she cried or when she was ill, or made her laugh with his bad jokes and thrilling stories.

"What's in the basket?" the Nazi pig asked.

"Food." Ruth pretended she wasn't scared.

He shook his head. "Why are you protesting with these desperate Jew-loving women? A nice member of the Girls' League like you."

He thinks I'm one of them.

"What food do you have?"

"Bread." As soon as she said it, she found it difficult to breathe. The bread contained the false documents. *Why did I say that?*

"What else?"

"My mother packed it." She was trembling.

The Nazi lifted the cloth that covered the basket. He pushed the items around, prodding the bread, picking up a jar of jam. "I'll keep this for my wife," he said. Ruth wanted to slap him, just as Mama had slapped the Nazi pig in their home after they arrested Alexander. The Nazi spoke again. "Such fancy jam for a greedy Jew."

"And you must have a fat wife!" Ruth blurted out.

Why did I say that? Ruth couldn't believe what had just come out of her mouth. This had all gone horribly wrong.

But the Nazi laughed a deep, loud laugh. "My wife is fat indeed." He pinched Ruth's cheek. "But she'll hate Jewish jam." He dropped the jar back into the basket. "You have a lot to learn, girl," the Nazi pig said. Then he opened the door.

"Ruti!"

"Alexander?" Ruth threw her arms around her brother. "Where's Papa?"

"Sleeping."

Ruth's head was spinning. They were standing in an office. Alexander looked dirty and he was unshaven, but he looked well, considering. The Nazi pig and two other guards remained in the room.

Alexander asked Ruth question after question. "Have you seen Paul? How's Mama? How are you? Where were you during the bombings?" It was wonderful to see him, to hear his voice.

"We're okay. But hundreds are dead, across Berlin."

Ruth decided not to tell him that a bomb had destroyed their house. She didn't tell him that Mama and she were now staying with Elise and her mother. He didn't need to know all that.

"Is Paul okay?" Alexander asked again. "Have you seen him?"

Ruth nodded.

"You have?"

"And Paul's sister is here, too," Ruth said.

Alexander was beaming. *He's so relieved his girlfriend is outside.*

"I saw you all from the window. Did you see me waving?" Alexander asked.

Ruth felt incredibly happy for her brother and Tsura. "Greta's waiting for you," she said.

"Give him the basket and leave," the Nazi pig said.

Ruth was suddenly aware of the Girls' League uniform she was wearing. But Alexander was acting as if he hadn't noticed.

"I brought you and Papa some food," Ruth said, handing Alexander the basket. "There's some food for Franziska, too. And your favorite bread. Share some with Franziska. Okay?"

"I will," Alexander said.

Ruth's brother locked eyes with her, nodding along, following her clues.

"Have you seen her? Have you seen Franziska?"

Alexander shook his head.

"If you see her, tell her to wave at us. Okay? Through the window."

Alexander nodded. "I promise."

Ruth was glad he understood what she was telling him.

The Nazi stepped forward. "Get going."

"Shouldn't we check the basket?" one of the guards suggested.

Ruth felt ill. "And something else," she said, trying to distract the soldiers. "In case you're bored, there's a puzzle for you." Ruth reached into the basket and pulled out a folded note, the first of Alexander's clues to his birthday treasure hunt. Alex was about to take it from her.

"Stop. What is that?" The pig grabbed the paper and unfolded it. "It doesn't make any sense."

Ruth let out a loud, impatient sigh. "It's a riddle. It's not supposed to make sense."

The Nazi pig refolded the paper and dropped it into the bin by the desk.

"That's not fair! I worked hard on that," Ruth whined.

The Nazi stepped forward. "Say goodbye."

"Not yet," she snapped and narrowed her eyes at him. For a moment, he backed off. She turned to her brother. "Are you okay? Is Papa okay?"

"We're fine. Did you figure out your treasure hunt?"

"No."

"You will," Alexander said with a grin.

Again, Ruth decided not to tell him their house had been destroyed along with his birthday gift. She reached forward to put her arms around her brother.

"Look for me in the window. I'll give you a thumbs-up for Franziska," Alexander said. He put his mouth close to Ruth's ear. "And give this to Marko," he whispered.

As they hugged each other, Alexander dropped something into her jacket pocket.

"Tell Papa I love him," Ruth said.

"We love you, too."

As the guards marched Ruth out of the office, she wondered what Alexander had passed to her. It was some kind of message or document for Marko, a message her brother had already prepared.

Elise

Viktor tugged on Elise's arm and her stomach flooded with guilt. On the fifth day of the protest, there were still hundreds of people on the street. Wearing Ruth's clothes made every part of her itch.

"You didn't come to see me," Viktor said.

"I wasn't allowed," Elise whispered.

"Liar," he replied. He crouched down and picked at the frozen weeds between the cobblestones. His feet were bare. His legs so thin.

Elise turned her attention to Marko.

"Ruti can handle the guards," Marko said to Tsura.

Marko remembers me now. But he seemed more concerned about Ruth. She'd been in the building for ten minutes, at least.

"Where did you get that uniform?" Tsura asked Elise, finally. Elise knew what Tsura was thinking. Tsura had been visibly shocked to see Elise in her League jacket and had been glaring at her every few seconds. *She thinks I'm a Nazi.*

"I'm forced to attend the meetings. For fives years now."

Tsura said nothing. Tsura was Jewish and so she was against the government, Elise knew. Her face said it all and, if Tsura didn't act carefully, she'd get herself into trouble. Tsura had obtained false papers for Alex. Elise had been listening to her every word. *If I wanted to, I could report her.* The League leaders always reminded Elise and the others to keep their eyes open for Jews and traitors. On the other hand, if she wanted to, Elise had a chance to tell Tsura the truth about Viktor's death and how she hated Hitler's government, too. But Elise kept her mouth shut.

Elise tried to ignore the crowd's tired chant. She paid no attention to the same women wandering the crowd, asking if anyone had seen their husbands. The same policemen protected the building, staring forward. And the same protestors laughed at them. But Elise's soldier guarding the center's entrance—the one who resembled Viktor—gave her a wink. Elise smiled back. She was about to lift her hand to wave.

"There she is," Tsura said.

Ruth exited the building. Without the basket. Tsura led them into the middle of the crowd, out of sight of the guards.

"I saw Alexander!"

"You did? Is he okay?" Marko said, eager to hear everything Ruth had to say.

Perfect, wonderful Ruth. Elise crossed her arms and gripped at her sleeves, digging her fingernails hard into her elbows in frustration. But the thickness of Ruth's coat blunted the sensation.

"My father was sleeping, so they called for Alexander instead," Ruth explained.

Ruth was nauseating. Elise never had a chance to smuggle in false papers for Viktor, or to wear a clever disguise. Elise didn't get to sweet-talk Nazi guards into letting her into Viktor's hospital room. Ruth didn't know how lucky she was, dressed in Elise's clothes, making Marko smile, thinking she was important.

"What did he say?" Marko asked.

"My brother seemed fine," Ruth said, looking at Tsura. "He was—"

"Is Kizzy in there?" Tsura interrupted in a whisper.

Ruth fidgeted with the Girls' League neckerchief around her throat, then took it off. "Alexander will wave from the window, if he finds her. And I told him I was delivering his favorite bread. And to share some with Franziska, too."

"Good." Tsura smiled, clearly impressed by Ruth's quick thinking.

"Did he mention me?" Marko asked.

Ruth nodded. "He asked if you were out here." Then Ruth turned to Tsura. "And he asked about you. I told him we're all out here, waiting for his release."

Elise watched Tsura, who was keeping her eyes on the windows.

Marko gave his sister a light punch on the arm. "If Kizzy's in there, Broden will find her."

They moved closer to the front of the crowd, eyes on the building, looking for a sign from Alex that he'd found Kizzy. Mrs. Broden called out to Ruth. When she approached and saw what Ruth was wearing, she fell silent. Mrs. Broden was flustered and, from her grimace, quietly outraged. Ruth whispered to her mother what had happened—the basket, Elise's uniform, the false papers hidden in the bread, seeing Alex.

Mrs. Broden was astonished. "What if something had gone wrong?"

"And what if this protest amounts to nothing?" Tsura retorted.

Mrs. Broden kissed Ruth's forehead. "I'm proud of you."

Elise pictured her mother at home, moping around in her apron, drinking tea, complaining. *She wouldn't be proud of me right now. "Jew-lover," she'd call me.*

"Elise, let's get changed," Ruth said as she removed the League hat.

Ruth was obviously still uncomfortable wearing Elise's uniform. While Tsura and Marko stood staring at the building, Elise followed Ruth to the courtyard. Mrs. Broden kept watch while Elise and Ruth exchanged clothes again.

Back in her League uniform, her heavy coat in her hand, Elise's gaze returned to the soldier by the center's doorway. When she saw him leave his post and walk toward the café, Elise wanted to follow. "I need the toilet," Elise said to Ruth and pushed her way through the protesters, placing the League hat on her head as she walked.

The café was bustling. Women stood huddled, sipping at cups of hot drinks to keep warm. The soldier stood at the counter, looking at the pastries on display. In her uniform, Elise fought her paralysis and stepped forward. She stood beside the soldier and looked up at his pale face. His fair hair poked out from his black soldier's hat. *Viktor.*

"Hello," she said.

When he didn't reply, Elise wanted to run.

Then he spoke. "How are you today?"

"I'm fine." Elise's skin was burning up. *I sound so stupid.*

"Can I get you something?" he asked, pointing at the cakes and pastries.

"Okay."

The soldier had been paying attention to her. Why else would he be offering to buy her food? Elise pointed to a slice of lemon cake.

All the tables were taken. The soldier led Elise to an open space against the wall.

"Thank you," she said, as he put the slice of cake wrapped in thick baking paper into her hand.

"I'm Dieter." He bit into the pastry he'd bought. "And you are?"

"Elise."

"Good to meet you, Elise."

"My father's in the army," she blurted out.

Dieter turned toward her, as if interested in what she had to say.

"Stalingrad," she continued.

"Sorry to hear that. I was almost sent there. Have you heard from him?"

"My father? No. But I think about him all the time." Elise felt as though she could say anything to Dieter, as if he were family.

"You're here with your friend, right?" Dieter asked.

Dieter had been paying attention to her. A feeling of comfort filled Elise's core. "Yes. Her stepbrother and stepfather are being detained." Then she lowered her voice, so the women in the café wouldn't hear. She placed her hand on her uniform jacket. "But I'm not part of the protest. I don't have Jews in my family."

"Your friend—that girl. What's her name?"

Elise said nothing. It didn't feel right to tell him.

He leaned in. "It's okay. Maybe I can do something," he whispered.

He wanted to help. If Alex and his father were released, Elise would be able to go home. *No more standing in the cold. No more stupid chanting.* "Ruth. Ruth Broden."

"Broden," Dieter repeated. "And what about that man? The one with the beard. And that young woman."

He was referring to Tsura and Marko. Dieter had been watching them, too. Elise felt nervous. Breathless. Her face was burning again. *Did he see me give Ruth my uniform?* Ruth had smuggled papers into the building. *Does he suspect me as a traitor?* "I don't know them," Elise said.

"Who are they? I saw you all talking."

Marko. Tsura. Paul. Greta. Elise couldn't speak.

Dieter let out a laugh. "Elise, it's okay. I'm curious, that's all. I can help." Dieter smiled at Elise with his eyes. He took the last bite of his pastry. "I'd better get going now."

Elise didn't want Dieter to go. "They're looking for someone," she said.

"Who?"

Elise paused. She didn't want to get Marko into trouble. Dieter was waiting for her reply. His resemblance to Viktor was striking. She could trust him. "A Jewish girl. I think she's thirteen. Her name's Kizzy." Dieter listened and Elise continued to speak. "And Ruth's brother is Alex. He's seventeen. Alexander Broden."

"Broden," Dieter repeated again. "They all know each other?"

"Yes."

"Broden." He looked out to the street. "I should get back."

"Oh. Okay." Elise didn't want Dieter to leave, but she couldn't think of anything else to say.

"Are you eating that?" Dieter asked, looking at the slice of lemon cake in Elise's hand.

"I will."

Dieter stopped in the doorway of the café. "Elise, if you need anything—if your friends need information—come speak to me. Okay?"

As Elise returned to the street, she took a bite of the lemon cake and felt a surge of happiness—an old feeling she'd forgotten. The shouts of the protestors were drowned out by the echo of Dieter's words. It was as if Elise had spoken to Viktor in real life. As she approached her friends, she prepared to tell them about Dieter—that one of the soldiers was on their side.

"There you are!" Ruth shouted, running toward Elise. "Did I leave my puzzles in your jacket?"

Her silly game. Elise put her hand into her pocket and pulled out Ruth's small stack of crumpled treasure hunt notes. If Elise had known she was carrying them, she would have thrown them away.

"Oh, thank God. I thought I'd lost them all." Ruth ran back into the crowd, toward Marko and Tsura.

From a distance, Elise watched Ruth pass one of the notes to Marko. He took the paper from Ruth and put his arms around her. Tsura looked on.

Elise walked over. "What was that?" Elise whispered to Ruth.

"Nothing."

She's keeping things from me again. If Ruth wasn't prepared to be a friend, then Dieter would remain Elise's secret.

Hours passed. Elise and Dieter exchanged glances and smiles and, for the first time, Elise didn't mind standing out in the cold for so long. Again, some of the protesters volunteered to hold vigil through the night. Rumors spread. More bombs tonight were likely. Toward the end of the protest's fifth day, Alex still hadn't appeared at the window.

Tsura sighed. "Kizzy's not in there."

"There's still a chance," Marko said.

As the sun set, the building's windows turned into mirrors. There was no way to see inside.

"We should go," Mrs. Broden said.

Elise looked over at Dieter and nodded her goodbye. Dieter smiled.

"See you here tomorrow?" Ruth asked Marko and Tsura.

"It's a date," Marko said with a small laugh.

Mrs. Broden put her hand on Elise's back, encouraging her to walk. "Will you join us for dinner?" she asked Tsura and Marko.

Elise's body stiffened. Part of her wanted Marko to visit her home. But she didn't want him to meet her mother.

"Another time," Tsura said.

Elise felt relieved as Mrs. Broden led Ruth and Elise away from Rosenstrasse.

"What did you give to Marko?" Elise asked Ruth, referring to the crumpled note.

"What?"

"You gave him something. A piece of paper. Earlier."

"Oh, it's nothing important."

"Tell me," Elise snapped, irritated by Ruth's secrecy.

Ruth paused. "It was a love letter for Tsura. Alexander gave it to me."

Ruth is a liar. If it was a love letter for Tsura, why did Marko take it? Ruth was supposed to be Elise's best friend. As they walked, Elise resented that Ruth's house had been bombed. She wished Ruth didn't have to stay over.

Elise's mother hadn't bothered to prepare dinner. Mrs. Broden threw something together while Ruth took a bath. When she returned to the kitchen in another of Elise's sweaters, with her hair pulled back and her face washed clean, Elise felt an urge to slap her.

While they ate, Ruth spread out her treasure hunt clues on the table, reading them over and over again. "What do you think this means?" Ruth asked.

Her stupid game. Elise took in a deep breath, trying to control her temper.

"The crowds are growing, every day," Mrs. Broden said. She chattered on and on about the protest while Elise's mother said nothing.

Elise wanted to tell Mrs. Broden not to waste her words—that her mother couldn't care less about the Jews in the Community Center. And Elise was starting to feel the same.

All this time, Elise had been watching them. Ruth. Mrs. Broden. And Alex's Jewish girlfriend, so quick to judge Elise, with suspicious looks and squinting eyes. Elise knew what Tsura had been thinking. Elise was like all the guards, Tsura had wanted to say. A Nazi. Like Dieter, with his hair like Viktor's. *Tsura doesn't understand. We're more than what we're forced to wear.* At the Girls' League meetings, that's how Elise felt sometimes, standing there in her beret and brown jacket, mouthing the words to songs she was forced to sing. *I'm more than this.* The other girls stood at attention in their uniforms, reciting their pledges to the Fatherland, sounding like a swarm of insects buzzing empty hopes for a collective future. In a way, they had no choice. *We pretend to be what our parents wished for themselves.* Actors, in their neckerchiefs and tilted berets, all in disguise. Not believing, just watching.

All week, Elise had been watching Ruth, following her like a shadow. Watching the protestors, listening to their chants. Elise hadn't joined in. She hadn't repeated their words. She'd watched them. Just as she'd been frozen in the market with Marko. Stuck in one place. Watching him fight off the African boy. *Marko.* Handsome Marko. Jewish Marko. Elise had helped a Jew—saved him from that thief. Elise hadn't been acting then. Unlike his sister, Marko seemed genuine. *I'd help him again, if I had the chance.*

After dinner, Elise cleared the dishes and wiped the table while Mrs. Broden made up her bed in the living room and Mother headed upstairs.

"I need to sleep, too. Are you coming?" Ruth asked.

"Not yet. Good night," Elise forced herself to say.

Alone, Elise took a seat at her father's desk. Viktor sat next to her, with his bare feet and skinny legs protruding from his hospital gown.

"Elise, I waited for you. It was my birthday."

"The hospital scared me," Elise admitted.

The sad truth was that Elise couldn't take the smell. It was Viktor's birthday. He'd been at the hospital for months and their parents had taken Elise to visit him often. Elise couldn't bear to see him in that place, with its stark rooms and disinfectant stench. She didn't want to see him like that. She'd wanted to remember him as a happy little boy. Elise had locked herself in her bedroom and refused to come out. From her bed, she could hear her mother on the stairs screaming at her father, calling Elise a selfish brat. For days, Mother punished Elise with her silence.

From her father's desk, lifting up the blackout shade, Elise stared out of the window, into the back garden, into the darkness. She remembered last Friday night. Tsura and Alex, lost in their kiss, hiding away from the world. *What's it like to be in love like that?* Something like running with Marko in Hackescher Market, Elise imagined. Viktor had been by her side, cheering them on. The thief. The bag. The knife. Elise was holding a pair of scissors. She pulled up her sleeve. The scratches on her skin were faint now.

"Not too deep," Viktor said.

"I know."

The edge of the dull scissors almost touched her arm.

"They killed me," Viktor said.

"How?"

Viktor opened the top drawer of their father's desk. The scissors still in one hand, Elise reached for a pile of papers, looking through them for Viktor's name. Bills, receipts, old letters. She checked them all. Viktor pushed the checked papers aside, passing Elise more documents to search through. They opened the second drawer, and the third.

"What are you looking for?"

Then Elise found it. Viktor's death certificate. The typed letters made her shiver.

NAME: Edelhoff, Viktor
CAUSE OF DEATH: Typhus

Along the side, in her father's messy handwriting, clear and underlined, Elise read Viktor's true cause of death—the Nazis' method for murdering her father's little boy.

Suffocation by gas

Father had left to fight in Hitler's war, crushed by the knowledge that his son had choked to death.

From her pocket, Elise pulled out another piece of paper. Unfolding it, she stared at the words in Alex's handwriting—"Ruti" written across the top—one of Ruth's treasure hunt riddles. Elise hated the idea of Ruth solving Alex's pathetic childish game. Ruth would have gloated. She would have been so happy to find it, in a boastful way.

On Monday evening, before the air raid, when Ruth had figured out Alex had hidden the riddle in the pocket of Elise's pink coat, Elise hadn't told her how she'd already found it, that morning. Ruth had been right; Alex had planted it there. Even though Ruth was upset and frustrated she couldn't solve the treasure hunt, Elise had kept it from her.

Viktor stared at Elise, upset his sister was being nasty to her friend. *My best friend who thinks she can wear my clothes and flirt with Marko and so easily pretend to be someone else. It should be me.* There was something wrong with Ruth. She didn't care about Marko like Elise did. She only cared about herself. The leaders at the Girls' League were right. *Those Jews and Jew-lovers deserve what they get.* With the scissor blade on her arm, making new wounds over old scars, Elise watched the trickles of blood paint patterns on her skin.

Marko

Marko woke up in the wine cellar, still holding Alex's note passed to him by Ruti. It was Thursday now. Marko read Alex's words again, scrawled on scrap paper.

> NOAH'S ARK
> *Our glass train, on fragile tracks*
> *Beneath bombs that fall like the flood*
> *To wash away the shards*
> *—But all this sorrow will recede*
> *And we will leave*
> *Two by two*
> *And until then, I will only think of you.*

Broden the poet! If Marko hadn't been missing Alex so much, he would've laughed. Their train should have taken them from Berlin. Out of Germany, toward London.

The night before, Marko and Tsura had returned back to the cellar. Out on the street, Tsura had been angry with Elise, shocked that the girl was an active member of Hitler's youth organizations. Tsura had asked Marko if he'd known that Elise was one of them. Nearly a week before, in the market, when Marko and Elise had been running from the black kid, Marko had no idea she was a Nazi. Most Aryan girls were. They walked on the streets, small gangs of them, in their brown uniforms and stupid hats. *They don't know what they're doing.* They simply copied what the adults said. Elise was one of them, but Marko didn't care. Joining the Girls' League was the law. She didn't have a choice. Elise had attended the protest every day. She wanted Alex to be free. She was Ruti's best friend.

When Marko realized he'd left Alex's map book at Seraph's apartment, he tapped the back of his head against the wall. Marko sat there, awake, using the mid-morning light to read Alex's poem again and again. He looked at the wall, at Alex's one carved "A" and his own list—"M—M—M—M—M—." Marko held the place on Alex's coat where he'd ripped off the button. He wondered if Alex had found it yet, hidden in the basket. Marko couldn't write poetry, not like Alex. The button was his way of sending Alex a message.

Tsura opened her eyes. "We have to get going," she said with a yawn.

"I'm hungry," Marko groaned.

He looked down at his watch. It was after ten a.m.

From the mattress, Tsura stared out through the window to the street above. "Kizzy's not in the center. I have this feeling."

"Where else do we look?"

Tsura sighed, as if she were giving up.

"We should get back to Rosenstrasse," Marko said.

"I keep thinking about Kizzy. It doesn't make any sense. Why did she go to the hospital?"

Marko's eyes traced the cracks on the ceiling. He wanted to tell Tsura the truth, that he'd made all that up. *I sent Kizzy to the hospital in my place.*

"Duerr," Tsura said. "Where did you leave her?"

"What?"

"Inside or outside the hospital?"

"No idea."

Tsura squinted her eyes. "You don't know?"

Marko was silent. His pulse raced.

"Marko?" Tsura sat up.

"Outside. I left her outside."

"You're lying!" Tsura eyes were bulging.

"No, I'm not." Marko needed to keep up the pretense.

"Marko. Where did you leave the professor?"

His head was spinning. *I didn't take the professor,* he wanted to say. But his sister deserved to know the truth.

"Marko!"

"Kizzy took her," Marko blurted out, surprised by his own honesty. "I didn't tell you. Kizzy took Duerr."

Tsura shook her head. "Kizzy?"

"On her own. I'm sorry. I sent her alone. I was—"

"What? Alone?" Tsura screamed, leaping forward. "Why? Why would you do that?"

Marko wanted to tell Tsura that he didn't know why he let Kizzy go on her own. He should've gone himself. Like Tsura had told him to. "Something must've happened. Kizzy must've said something. To the hospital guards."

Tsura's mouth was wide open, saying nothing.

"I had to find somewhere safe for Kizzy. Broden was—"

"Broden? You sent Kizzy with Duerr and you went to see Alex?"

"I told Kizzy to leave Duerr on the street. I told her to go home. She must've said something wrong. She screwed up. It was her fault. I had to speak with Broden's parents."

"Traitor!" Tsura screamed.

"Wait—I—"

"You're sick!"

The cellar walls felt as if they were crashing in. "Calm the hell down." *I'm not sick.* Marko hated Tsura for calling him that.

Tsura lunged forward. "You're a liar, Marko. All you do is lie. Kizzy's our blood. Alex is nothing to us. You care more about your Broden than your own family. It's sickening. You're sick, Marko!"

Marko wanted to scream back. He wanted to tell her that, yes, Alex was more important than even her, his own sister. He wanted to shout in her face. *We're not sick!* To Marko, Alex was more important than anyone.

"Hypocrite," Marko snapped, his finger pointing at her eyes. "It's got nothing to do with family. He's a Jew. And a man. That's what you don't like. You wouldn't be saying all this if I was in love with a Romani girl."

"Yes I would, Marko! I don't care that he's a Jew. I don't care you like men. Kizzy is your blood. Your blood, Marko. She's a kid. You were supposed to protect her. She's a kid!"

Marko couldn't breathe. "Why? Why's that down to me? You left me with Kizzy, for years. She was safe with me while you disappeared for weeks at a time, with your stupid missions and secret friends. Kizzy missed you. Did you ever think about that? You hardly knew her."

"Stop changing the subject," Tsura shouted. "You sent her alone, Marko!" With her teeth closed, she let out a growl of rage. She reached her fists toward him, then she seemed to hold herself back. She dug her knuckles into her forehead. "Our parents would be ashamed of you!"

"No, Tsura. You're the one who's ashamed. You're ashamed of me. You don't know anything. You don't know what it's like."

"Kizzy only had us. Alex has his own family."

It was as if Tsura was mocking him, as if she thought Marko and Alex had some kind of childish crush. *She thinks we're sick.* "You don't understand." On his feet, Marko put Alex's note back in his pocket. He pulled up his collar, swung his bag over his shoulder, and walked to the doorway.

"That's right, Marko! Go back to Rosenstrasse. Wait for Alex. Forget Kizzy. Forget me!"

Marko couldn't look at her. He needed to forget his sister and her absurd way of thinking about everything. He stepped outside. Tsura was demented. *There's something wrong with her, not me. She's sick— not me.* Tsura was a loner. She had a sad soul. She hated the idea of Marko and Alex being happy. Marko's boots hit the ground. *I'll find Kizzy. I can care about my family and Broden at the same time. I don't need to choose.* He was running now, feeling the knife in his pocket. It tapped at his chest. *I'll prove Tsura wrong.*

The cobblestones tilted. The buildings spun and Marko couldn't focus.

In the courtyard, out of sight, he opened his bag. He took off his coat and trousers and put on the uniform that had belonged to the dead Nazi officer.

Yesterday morning at Seraph's apartment, with Tsura and Seraph still asleep, he had folded the officer's uniform into his bag.

Dropping his knife to the ground, he stuffed Alex's coat into his bag's main compartment. Then he buttoned up the Nazi jacket and smoothed it out, crisp and clean. He secured the belt. He positioned his bag strap over his shoulder to cover the bullet hole and small bloodstain. With the Nazi army cap on and the knife hidden in his sleeve, Marko stood at the back of the crowd and watched the line of Nazi guards. In full uniform, Marko would find his way inside the center, find Alex, find Kizzy, and get them out. Marko moved toward the guards. Confident. *I'm one of them. I belong.*

People in the crowd shouted as an empty truck pulled up outside the building. Marko couldn't see the entrance. The crowd started its usual chant. Some women screamed out that the Gestapo had started to clear the building. *They'll send Broden away.* Marko watched a Jewish woman exit the center, her yellow star for all to see. She cried as a guard led her onto the empty truck.

"Let her go!" the protestors screamed. "We want our husbands back!" The protestors' shouts were all around him.

The Nazi guards formed a line.

This is my chance. Marko stepped forward.

"Marko?"

It's that girl. "Get away," he said to Elise. *She'll ruin my plan.*

Ruti and her mother were shouting at the truck, looking the other way.

"What are you doing?" Elise gasped. She seemed surprised to see Marko in the Nazi uniform.

Marko kept walking.

"No, it's too dangerous," Elise said, pulling on Marko's sleeve.

Marko shook her off.

"I can help," she said.

Marko stopped and turned to her.

"Let me come with you," Elise said.

"What?" *Stupid girl.* Marko turned away.

"Him," Elise said, grabbing Marko's wrist. She pointed to a Nazi guard with fair hair, standing near the entrance. "Talk to him. His name is Dieter."

Elise stayed in the crowd. As Marko approached the line of Nazi guards, two more Jewish women were thrown onto the truck. Marko walked up to Dieter, his shoulders back and chin forward.

"I was sent here," Marko told him, his voice strong, loud, like he was a somebody.

The Nazi saluted and stared at the medals on Marko's jacket. Dieter led Marko into the building. "How can I help?"

Marko was in and he wanted to laugh. He could feel the knife inside his sleeve. *I should slit the throat of every Nazi in sight.* The building's hallway was cold. Marko could hear voices echo in the corridor. *Alex is close. Kizzy, too.* Marko was anxious, but he couldn't show it. He could hear shouts from the crowd outside as another two Jewish women were led out into the street.

"What's going on?" Marko asked the Nazi.

"Some women are being relocated," Dieter explained.

Marko nodded, as if he knew what the soldier was talking about.

"I'm looking for two people," Marko said.

"Wait, please," Dieter said. He returned seconds later, holding a stack of papers. A list.

"We're looking for a girl. Age thirteen, maybe fourteen," Marko said. "And a boy. A Jew. Seventeen. Broden. Alexander Broden. They're both to be questioned. Connected with a robbery. Can I see your list?"

"Broden," the Nazi repeated and nodded, obeying Marko's rank.

Marko took the stack of papers and thumbed through the pages of names. "They're to be questioned," he explained.

Dieter smiled. "An interrogation? Yes, I'm sure you want to question them." The Nazi laughed and grabbed Marko's jacket. "Your fake interrogation, in your fake uniform."

"Take your hands off me!"

Then it hit Marko. Who he was. Blue eyes, white-gold hair. Marko should have recognized him, the Nazi who had seen them last week—he'd seen Marko and Alex kissing out on the street. He'd chased them through the city center. Dieter's eyes were swelling, smiling; he remembered Marko, too. The Nazi grabbed his rifle. "I've been watching you for days."

Slamming the guard's chest with his fists, Marko raced through the door and smashed into another guard. Back out on the street, the truck was driving off. The crowd was still chanting. He caught Elise's gaze and ran, in his stolen uniform. The protestors let him through. Turning back, he could see the Nazi behind him. Marko couldn't think. His shoulder and bag hit the protestors as he forced himself through the crowd. Faster. Marko's army hat fell from his head. The Nazi was still on his tail. *I've gotta lose him.* Marko scrambled into a courtyard. Dieter followed. The courtyard turned right into an alley and a tall brick wall. *Dead end.* The Nazi was walking now. Marko was trapped. Aiming his rifle, Dieter stepped forward, smiling. Marko backed up against the wall, breathing quickly.

"Get away!" Marko shouted.

Out of breath, Dieter laughed. "I saw you days ago. In the crowd. You were looking for your boyfriend, right?"

Marko looked for a way out of the alley.

"I knew it. Pervert. And your boyfriend. Broden. A perverted Jew!"

Marko wanted to cut the bastard's throat.

Dieter stepped forward and spat. Saliva landed on Marko's uniform. The Nazi's eyes were shining, excited. Gold hair covered his forehead. He was sweating, one hand on his rifle. His other hand grabbed his belt buckle.

"I'll teach you a lesson," Dieter said and he unbuttoned the top of his black army jacket. Ironed. Silver medals. Stepping closer.

Marko let the knife slip out from his sleeve. "Get away." He jumped forward and swung his arm quickly, forward, right, left, almost cutting Dieter below the shoulder.

The Nazi reached out and grabbed Marko's arm, pulling him down. Marko dropped his bag. Every part of Marko was filled with anger. This Aryan and the other Nazi bastards had taken his family away. And kept him from Alex. Ruined their lives. He remembered the black kid in the market. They'd turned Marko into a desperate runaway. A thief. *Zigeuner.*

The Nazi grabbed hold of Marko's arm.

A sound, almost a growl, came out of Marko's throat. "No!"

Swinging his elbow away from Dieter, Marko kicked him hard in the stomach. He took another swipe and cut into the Nazi's hand. Dieter screamed and dropped his gun. Marko flung himself at the wall and started to climb. Needing both hands, Marko let go of his knife. He clambered up and swung himself over, falling to the ground. His wrist hit the path, hard.

Marko raced through the side streets in the uniform, like a stray Nazi dog, heading east through Hackescher Market. Passersby moved out of his way. His feet carried him as if he were flying. Suddenly he couldn't breathe. He stopped on the street. Buildings towered over him. Then he was running again. No thoughts. Friedrichshain Park. In and out of the trees. Standing. Stone statues all around. Red Riding Hood. Gretel. Hansel. *Kizzy. Broden. Holy hell, holy hell. I should've killed the Nazi bastard. Should've cut his throat.* Marko's wrist burned from the fall. He pulled up the sleeve of his Nazi uniform. His watch was crushed, smashed. *I sent Kizzy in my place.* Falling to his knees, with his forehead on the fountain's wall, Marko slammed his fist into the stone, again, again, again, again, until his knuckles were covered in blood. *I told him Broden's name.*

Kizzy

Two days. In this train. In and out of sleep. Heading to a work camp, someone said. *They'll feed us there.* No food since Tuesday. No water. Kizzy's stomach hurt. Hunger was worse than winter. Her clothes were almost dry. Dirt seeping into her skin. On the tracks. Rocking. Jolting. Some light. Sunlight from the small window. Darkness, as night came. Trying to sleep. Standing. Felix and Esther. Frank. *Packed in here.* A hundred Jewish men and women. Morning. Taking turns sitting. Crying. On each other. Taking turns to lean. Esther was quiet. Felix was asleep. Standing. Leaning on Frank. Esther had stopped crying hours ago. One man, sobbing. Praying. *In a Jewish language.* He couldn't stop. Coughing. The corner was the toilet.

Trying to sleep again. In the dim light, Kizzy saw a piece of bread. In a woman's hand. Kizzy reached out. The woman took a bite. *Give it to me.* Kizzy fell against Esther. *She pushed me. That woman. Give it to us kids.* Nothing.

Daylight. Kizzy felt more alert now. The filth on her clothes and in her hair had dried. The smell was worse.

"Where are we?" Kizzy said to an old man standing next to her.

"We haven't moved for a few hours," he said.

"The train broke down," someone added.

The engine was off.

"There are fields all around us," a woman close to the small window announced. "We'll die out here."

Kizzy pulled the hat over her ears, blocking out the cold and their words.

THE TRAIN

Tsura

Tsura loved her brother, but she couldn't forgive him, or trust him any more. He'd stolen the bag from some poor kid. He'd pretended not to know Elise. Alex was only a friend, he'd said. But all those lies were nothing compared to what he did to Kizzy. All this time, Tsura had thought Kizzy had visited Charité Hospital without thinking about the consequences. But Marko had sent her with Duerr. Their little cousin, their little Kizzy, frightened, alone. Tsura would never know what had happened. Marko should have gone to the hospital, just as Tsura had asked. This was all his doing. Tsura would have gone instead, had she known.

Tsura made her way toward the old antique shop. As she walked, the distant familiar clattering of a train on the railway tracks beckoned a moment from her childhood. As a child, she'd held Mother's hand as little Marko deliberately took his time behind them, examining every stray pebble and fallen leaf. As children, their parents scolded Tsura for any missteps. She was the oldest. They expected her to know better. Marko got away with his misbehaviors, his disobedience, his jokes and pranks. Their parents put up with it, encouraged him by saying nothing. He was the baby. He was the boy. They made his excuses.

When their parents sent Tsura, Marko, and Kizzy to live with Duerr, it toughened Marko up. But he was still wild and brazen, doing whatever he wanted. He and Kizzy never got on. Marko resented having their cousin around, as he'd often be required to watch her. Marko and Tsura were different in that way. To Tsura, family was everything. To Marko, family was an inconvenience. He had better things to do. That he and Alex were lovers was no surprise to Tsura. It was what Marko did. Tsura wished she had such luxuries, time to fall in love. Wolf loved her, Tsura knew. He talked to Tsura and Seraph in different ways. Seraph—his girlfriend, always his shadow, hanging on his arm—meant nothing to him. Tsura could have been everything. *But Wolf is too broken.* The Nazi regime erased his family. Murdered them, most likely. In another time, Tsura could have been his.

When Tsura saw the rubble and shards of broken glass spilling out into the street, a sharp pain hit her chest. *The antique shop was bombed.* But as she walked closer, she saw that it was another building, two doors down, that had been hit. The shop looked the same as it always had. As Tsura opened the door, bells announced her entrance. She breathed in the familiar smell of dust-covered antiques and timeworn fabrics. The shopkeeper appeared from the back.

"Tsura Lange?"

Tsura smiled widely. "Uncle!"

His eyes looked aged, his skin weathered. He rushed forward, throwing his arms around her. "You need to leave soon, Tsura. It's too dangerous for long visits." Quickly, the old man led Tsura to the backroom, filled with more furniture and cabinets stuffed full with ornaments and camera equipment.

"How've you been?" Tsura asked.

Taking a seat in an old leather armchair, Tsura's great-uncle shook his head. "There was an air raid," he said. He recited political events from over the last few months, the significance of Stalingrad, the news of executions of dissident groups, as if Tsura had been living on the other side of the planet and had only now returned. Still, she listened to his every word.

Tsura's great-uncle, her grandmother's brother, had travelled from Dusseldorf to Berlin years ago. In 1936, when Hitler's government rounded up the Roma into makeshift camps, her uncle had disappeared. Tsura's family thought he might have escaped overseas, but it turned out he'd been in Berlin all along, running the antique shop under a false name. He'd made contact with Professor Duerr—his old friend—and, because Tsura was the oldest, Duerr trusted her with his address. Now and again, Tsura had visited him, to check in on his wellbeing and to pass along updates about Marko and Kizzy and their family in Marzahn.

The week beforehand, when Marko had asked Tsura to help Alex escape, she thought of her favorite shopkeeper right away. Alex needed photographs. The old man had his camera and darkroom. Tsura gave Marko the address to pass on to Alex, not telling her brother that she was sending Alex to see their great-uncle.

"Thanks for helping that boy last week," Tsura said to him.

Her old uncle nodded and pushed his glasses onto his face. "He bought an ornament from me. The porcelain train."

Tsura remembered the old train from when she was a child. It had belonged to her mother and it sat high up on a shelf in her parents' living room, away from little hands.

"The boy was arrested," Tsura told him.

"That's too bad."

"Kizzy was taken, too."

The color faded from the old man's face.

"And Rastplatz Marzahn," Tsura said, aware she was delivering him one blow after another.

"Jaelle? Marie?"

Tsura forced herself to say it. "Mama and Aunt Marie were deported."

He stood and stepped toward his great-niece and put his cold hand on her face. "There are few Romani remaining," he said. His

313

eyes were concerned, expecting more terrible news. "What about Marko? And Frau Duerr?"

"Marko's fine." Tsura hesitated. "But at the weekend, Frau Professor Duerr fell ill. She died."

Tsura's uncle dropped back into his chair. With his shaking, thin hands at his mouth, he began to weep. He closed his eyes, taking in quiet, deep breaths. Tsura tried to imagine Professor Duerr as a young woman, but she could only picture her slumped in that broken wheelchair.

Tsura's great-uncle wiped away his tears. "Tsura, it's not safe. You should go into hiding. Leave Berlin. Marko, too. Leave Germany, if you can, for the sake of our people."

"Yes, Uncle."

He led Tsura to the front of the shop. "It's always good to see you." Then he smiled and touched her face. "You'll be married soon. Your children will be beautiful, like you." He began to cry again.

"Look after yourself," Tsura said, embracing him goodbye. Tears collected in her eyes, but she refused to let them fall.

As the shop doorbells jangled, she could hear her uncle sing from the back room. It was a familiar Romani song she recognized from her childhood. She paused in the doorway and took in the old melody. *If only the world were different.*

She returned to the cold. Tsura wondered whether she and Wolf would have married. If his family hadn't been deported, if her family hadn't been sent to Marzahn, they would never have met. With Wolf's family gone, he was incapable of becoming close to Tsura. *Perhaps I'm also like that.* Tsura wished she were brave enough to immerse herself in ideas of carefree romance, to be pursued and persuaded. But there would be no point. She could never become pregnant. Her energy and focus would be wasted on frivolities. There were more urgent matters. Kizzy. Her family.

Marko was different. While Tsura tended to evaluate her surroundings and plan ahead, Marko didn't care about anything beyond his world. He was oblivious. Impervious. Always the optimist. He could think on his feet and take advantage of dire circumstances. In that way, her brother and Tsura were similar. Marko knew what to say, how to blend into the background, to keep his head in the shadows. His unruliness was not entirely bad. *At Marzahn, Marko saved my life.*

Tsura couldn't blame Marko completely. Perhaps Kizzy's arrest had been inevitable. Tsura should never have sent her brother to take Duerr to the hospital in the first place. Marko saved himself. Deep down, he must have known the hospital would be a trap. Tsura began to admit a cruel truth. *We should have left Duerr to die peacefully at home. Marko isn't to blame. This is my fault. I'm the oldest.*

Alexander

Alex placed his wrist against his father's forehead. *Still burning.*

Father opened his eyes. "Alexander?" he mumbled.

"Papa, go back to sleep."

"What day is it?"

"It's the fourth of March. Thursday."

"Where are we?"

"Still in the center. The protest is still going on."

Alex was astonished. Never before had German civilians objected to the round-ups of Jews. Some of the men attributed the rebellion to the Nazis' recent defeat at Stalingrad. Others had complained that only friends and family were outside; this was not a public demonstration but a personal one. They had a point. There'd been no crowds of Christians when Alex's uncles and aunts and grandfather had been deported. No chanting for them. No evening vigils, even when the weather was warm. Whatever the outcome, whatever was to happen at Rosenstrasse, history would remember this moment.

Yesterday, clutching Ruti's basket, Alex had returned upstairs. Seeing Ruti had filled Alex with hope. That Father had fallen ill was fate. If he'd been awake, Father would have been led downstairs. He might not have understood Ruti's hints about Kizzy. And Alex wouldn't have passed on his note to Marko.

The men around the room, their eyes hungry and desperate, had watched Alex return with the basket. Some of the men had wished aloud that Alex would share whatever he'd just been given. It had been difficult to ignore them. Alex had rummaged through the basket items. He'd made an exception for Mr. Lessel, Father's colleague who had given Alex the blank notepaper, and shared with him some cheese. The cheeses had been soft and ready to eat. Alex had examined the labels on small jars of spreads, jams, and canned foods. At the sight of the packets of cigarettes, he'd recognized the items from Marko's bag.

Alex had turned toward the wall and pulled out the loaf of bread. Ruti had told him that the bread was his favorite and to share it with Franziska. He'd got the hint. Something important was hidden inside. Carefully, he'd opened the bread along a narrow cut already along its side. His heart had jumped when he found a small stack of folded papers, two documents with photographs, and two without. He'd looked at his own image in his borrowed tie and jacket, taken by the antique dealer last Friday. Marko and Tsura had arranged everything. He'd lost the photographs at home, before his arrest. Ruti and Mother must have helped. He'd wanted to wake Father, to show him his new forged identity. Alex had release papers, too.

He had stared at the second photograph. The young girl was age eleven or twelve with brown curly hair and dark piercing eyes. Kizzy. Immediately, the false papers had made Alex feel unbeatable yet vulnerable. He'd find Kizzy. They'd leave the building. He had looked down at Father, realizing they'd need to say goodbye. There were no papers for him.

Alex had untied his laces. Checking nobody was watching, he placed his own papers in his right boot, Kizzy's in his left, against his revolting socks.

Alex had whispered to Father that Ruti had been there. Father had opened his eyes and smiled. He'd looked around for her. She was outside, on the street, Alex had explained. She'd brought them some food.

After his father fell back to sleep, Alex's chest had felt tight with nerves. There was no guarantee the Nazi guards would believe the false documents. He would need to find a way to explain their sudden appearance. He'd worried that the papers would appear obviously fake. On top of that, he needed to find Kizzy. He would keep his eyes open for Simon. Alex would ask for Simon's help.

But there'd been no sign of Simon all day. Alex had stayed awake into the night and woke up late on the sixth day of their incarceration. He could hear the crowd's chants outside.

"How are you feeling?" Alex asked Father.

"The same."

Alex held some bread and cheese to Father's mouth, but he pushed Alex's hand away.

"Papa, please, you need to eat."

Alex could hear Simon's voice in the corridor. Quickly, Alex slipped off his left boot and took out Kizzy's identity papers.

"What are you doing?" Father whispered.

"Nothing." Alex put his boot back on and held the documents inside his coat. "I won't be long." He stood up and walked to the doorway.

"Simon," Alex called out.

Simon walked over. "How's your father feeling?"

"Still not good. Where were you yesterday?"

"They let me take the day off. But I had to return today. Did you hear the screaming, earlier?"

Alex nodded. Earlier, the quiet of the room had been disturbed by the sounds of women screaming and Nazi officers shouting downstairs, as if the women were being dragged through the hallways. Everyone had listened. And they'd heard the crowd's shouts and chants. "What happened?"

"The Gestapo arrested five women. They accused them of throwing a note through the window," Simon explained.

"Did they?" Alex asked.

Simon shook his head. "All the windows are nailed shut."

"What'll happen to them?" Alex asked, already knowing the answer.

"Poland. I think they're planning to send us all away like that, eventually. In small groups."

Simon had a point. Sending them away one by one sounded entirely feasible.

"My sister was here, yesterday," Alex said.

Simon nodded. "I heard."

"And I have something to ask you."

Simon sighed and Alex was sure he wasn't the first person that day to ask Simon for a favor.

"Can you give me your armband?" Alex asked.

Simon laughed. "What?"

"I'll give it back to you, I swear. You can trust me. I need to check the building. I need to find someone. For ten minutes, no more."

"Not a chance." Simon said.

"Hold on." Alex ran back to Father. As he reached into the basket, Alex noticed something tucked into one of the packets of cigarettes. A black button. *Marko!* It was Marko's message that he was outside. The discovery felt as sustaining to Alex as a full meal. He kept the button in his hand and returned to Simon in the doorway with items from the basket. "What do you want? Cheese? Cigarettes?"

Simon shrugged. "I can't give you my armband. I trust you, but we can't take the risk."

Alex understood. He trusted Simon, too. Making sure nobody could see them, Alex took out Kizzy's false identity papers and release document from his coat. "Kizzy. She goes by Franziska, too. She's Romani. I have to find her. Have you seen her here?"

Simon stared at the photograph glued to the paper. "I don't recognize her. But there are so many people here. I haven't been into the rooms with the children. Anyway, I don't think there are any

Gypsies being held here. But I can check." Simon stared at the photograph again.

"Thank you. If you find her, bring her to me."

Simon hesitated.

"Or take me to her," Alex added.

"I'll try." He took one last look at Kizzy's photograph and Alex put the papers away. "Can I have some cigarettes?"

Alex smiled, passing him a packet.

Alex walked back to Father. He took off his boot and, still holding Marko's button, he put Kizzy's documents back inside.

"I have a way to get out," Alex whispered to Father.

Eyes closed, Father nodded. He didn't ask Alex any questions.

Alex broke off a piece of soft cheese. Tasting the rich food, Alex closed his eyes. The taste took him to their dinner table at home, to Ruti's birthday, with Marko on Friday night. Father had stood with his Shabbat wine while Ruti and Alex rolled their eyes at his recital of the Kiddush prayer. Marko's button felt good in his hand.

When Alex opened his eyes again, Simon was in the room. *He already found Kizzy?* But a Nazi officer was standing next to him. Dark hair, middle aged. Gestapo. High-ranking. Simon pointed to Alex.

"Stand," the officer ordered.

Is Ruti here again? Or Marko? Alex realized what was happening. *Simon betrayed me.*

The officer stepped toward him. "Alexander Broden?"

"Yes," Alex said, standing, Marko's button in his fist.

"You're under arrest," the officer said.

Alex looked at Simon. *He told them about Kizzy and the false papers.* But Simon's face was full of concern. Simon hadn't betrayed him. *Did someone overhear us? Will Simon be arrested, too?*

Grabbing Alex's shoulder, the Nazi dragged him to the hallway.

"Sit down or receive a bullet," another guard snapped at someone behind them.

Alex turned to see his father standing in the doorway.

"Where are you taking him?" Father shouted, his hands shaking.

"Papa. It's okay."

"This is your son?" the officer said.

"Yes."

"Your son is sick. A homosexual."

Alex felt a rush through his chest and up to his face. *This can't be happening.*

The Nazi continued, "Your son will stand trial. He'll be sent to a hard labor camp for many years."

"Alexander?" Father stared with an expression of confusion.

As the officer pulled him along the corridor, Alex wanted to call out to Father, but an intense embarrassment prevented him from making a sound. *They found Marko.* That was the only explanation. *That's how they know.*

The Nazi dragged Alex down the stairs and into the ground floor office, the office where Alex had met with Ruti. Through the walls and covered windows, Alex could hear the crowd on the street, shouting, chanting. Two other Nazi officers, different men than the day before, were also in the room. One of them had his arm in a sling, his hand bandaged.

"Is this the right man?" the Nazi asked the wounded officer.

"That's him." The wounded man looked at Alex. "I chased him and that other pervert last Friday night. I saw them kissing and touching each other."

Alex stared at the young Nazi's face and light blond hair. *The Nazi who saw us!* The white bandage on his hand was stained through with fresh blood. He took out a pistol.

"No!" Alex pleaded. *They're going to kill me.*

"Sit down."

He followed their orders, slumping onto a wooden chair. Alex stared at the floor. Marko's coat button was still in his fist.

"Face forward. What's your boyfriend's name?"

"There's been a mistake," Alex said.

"Your boyfriend's name."

"I don't know why I'm here."

He showed Alex his bandaged hand. "Three fingers gone. Your pervert boyfriend did this."

"You have the wrong person."

"It's him," the wounded Nazi said and, with his better hand, he slapped Alex across the face. The chanting of the crowd outside drowned out Alex's cry. "If you don't give us your boyfriend's name, we'll beat it out of you."

Grasping Marko's button as tight as he could, Alex's eyes filled with tears. From his stomach, he let out a sob. "You're confusing me with someone else. I swear to you!"

The Nazi put his hand below his belt. He'd done that on the street, Alex remembered, when he'd caught Alex and Marko kissing.

"I'll make you pay," the Nazi said. Then he pointed to the desk.

At first Alex didn't know what the gesture meant. Then he saw it. Marko's knife. *They found Marko.* Marko had wounded him.

"I'm German. I'm German. Like my mother. And my sister." Alex cried each word.

"You're no German." As one of the men swung the back of his hand across Alex's jaw, another fist smashed into his shoulder. "You'll be deported." Another strike. "As a Jew." They hit him again. "As a Jew or homosexual." A harder blow crashed into his teeth. "Or both. Nobody cares." Alex tried to scream.

They locked the door.

Alex remembered the notepapers in his pocket. Everything he'd written. His plan to escape Berlin. How much he missed Marko. *Every word will incriminate me. And Marko. Ruti and Tsura, too.* Alex pictured Father upstairs. *Papa knows.*

"What's your boyfriend's name?" the Nazi asked.

Alex's tears stung his swelling face. Blood poured from his mouth.

The Nazi brought his face close and Alex could smell the soldier's rotten breath. He picked up Marko's knife. "Your pervert boyfriend cut me. So he was executed."

Executed? The Nazi picked up a bag from the floor. *Marko's bag.* From the bag, he pulled out Marko's coat. *My coat. Papa's coat.* Blood across the collar. One button was missing. The black button in Alex's hand matched those that remained.

"We'll shoot you, too."

"No!" *Marko can't be dead.* Alex could taste blood pouring from his gums. His side teeth were broken. *They're lying.* Alex pictured Marko outside, waiting for him, with Mother and Ruti.

The Nazi officer stood over him. One of the other officers grabbed Alex by the collar and pushed him onto the desk, face down, holding him in place. A stream of blood poured from his mouth. The flash of Marko's knife appeared in front of his face. *They'll cut my throat.* Instead, they dropped the knife onto the desk.

"Pervert," the Nazi said, his mouth against Alex's ear.

Alex didn't want to be thinking about Marko. He opened his fist and dropped the coat button to the floor.

Ruth

We'll be out here until we're all old women. Ruth laughed to herself.

When the five Jewish women were thrown onto the truck, Ruth had shouted so loudly it hurt her throat, only thinking about Papa and her brother. At first, Ruth had thought they were clearing the building. Mama's beautiful eyes were filled with tears, clutching the front of her neck as if trying to hold in a scream. The Nazis were heartless pigs, Ruth had said to Elise. They were murderers, Elise had replied.

The protest returned to its strange normalness.

"It's getting dark," Elise said, looking up at the sky.

Mama nodded. "We should head home soon. We'll come back tomorrow."

Ruth wanted to stay, but she didn't argue. As they walked through the crowd, Ruth overheard that while St. Hedwig's Cathedral was mostly destroyed, Father von Wegburg—the kind man who listened to their confessions—was alive and well.

"Can we see it? The cathedral." Ruth felt as if she'd asked a strange question.

"I want to see it, too," Mama said.

Mama led Elise and Ruth west, toward Berlin's grand museums. As Ruth stared up at the beautiful stone structures, she couldn't stop thinking about her treasure hunt and the clue that Tsura had given to her. Ruth's grandfather—Mama's Papa—had told Ruth stories of the construction of those incredible museums, last century. They'd been built with such care, each stone block, each archway, each pillar bursting with German pride. Like the architects of the magnificent buildings, Alexander had spent so much time and effort on his treasure hunt riddles. He'd asked Elise to hold onto one note. He'd given Mama another. And, it seemed, Tsura had one, too. But Ruth didn't understand. Ruth had never met Tsura, and Alex had been keeping her a secret. *How did she get it?* Tsura had told Ruth that she'd found it. It didn't make sense. *I guess it doesn't really matter.*

As they approached what was once St. Hedwig's Cathedral, Mama and Ruth gasped. Elise said nothing. The dome had been demolished. Parts of the walls were still standing, but sections of the building had collapsed in on itself. Fragments spilled out onto the street in piles of gray stone and burnt wood.

Ruth expected to find a crowd of people mourning the cathedral's destruction. But they were the only people there. Last week, the day before her birthday, Ruth hadn't repented for her sins. And now the confession box was ash.

"Should we say a prayer?" Ruth said.

"Go ahead," Mama said through tears.

"We pray for Father von Wegburg and we thank God he was saved," Ruth said. She stared at the smashed stone and broken glass. "And for Papa and Alexander and all the Jewish people and all the Romani people and everyone else the Nazis want to kill."

"We pray for our dead neighbors," Mama said, holding Ruth's hand. "We pray for the German people."

"And all of Europe," Ruth said.

Mother whispered, "Amen."

Ruth stared back at her best friend. "And for Elise's father, fighting in this war."

Elise

There's no point in praying, especially for the already dead. Elise's father had told her that. Yet Ruth, her pathetic friend, was reciting useless prayers about Jews. *And, for some reason, even dirty Gypsies.* But as soon as she'd seen the cathedral's ruins, before Ruth and Mrs. Broden had begun their performance, Elise had prayed for Marko. And for herself. When she saw Marko sprint out of the Community Center in that Nazi uniform, her heart had almost stopped. Dieter had raced after him. She'd trusted Dieter, the soldier who looked like her dead brother. But Marko had taken an enormous risk. Elise prayed that Marko was all right.

On the way back from the cathedral's ruins, Elise followed Ruth and Mrs. Broden through Hackescher Market. They'd be staying at Elise's home indefinitely. Mrs. Broden was planning to cook soup and Elise was pretending to be excited. The stalls and smells of raw fish reminded Elise of running with Marko away from the thief, almost a week ago.

As Elise rummaged through the produce in the market, as if her thoughts had summoned him, she caught sight of the African. He stood on the other side of the street, talking to an Aryan woman and her little boy, both in old clothes. Their pale white skin contrasted his dark hands and face. The little Aryan boy was seven or eight, Viktor's age when he had died. The woman looked a little like Elise's mother, but thinner. The African thief was trying to swindle them.

Elise watched as the child reached up to the African boy, as if asking to climb onto his back. The woman swung a bag of clothes and blankets on her shoulder. To steady herself, she held on to the African boy's arm. *They know each other. Are they a family?* Yet the woman and the little boy had white skin. *Real Aryan Germans.* The family approached the merchants, offering the fabrics in exchange for food. When one man offered the woman a can of food for free, she seemed embarrassed but thankful. The younger boy began fussing. While the African boy knelt down to calm his brother, their mother took a biscuit from her pocket, breaking it in half.

Elise lost sight of them and continued to follow Ruth from stall to stall. By one of the market stalls, Elise almost screamed to see the African boy right in front of her.

He stared at Elise. "I know you, right?" the boy asked.

Elise couldn't speak. She was frozen in place. He squinted, as if trying to figure out why Elise was familiar. Elise shook her head.

"Nikolaus!" the Aryan woman called.

Elise found the guts to speak to him. "Is that your mother?"

"Yes," Nikolaus said and walked away.

"Who was that?" Ruth asked.

"No idea."

Elise's head was dizzy with questions and realizations. *When the African boy stole Marko's bag, was he trying to feed his family? Would I steal to save my parents? To save Viktor?* When Viktor was ill, Elise had done nothing.

At home, Elise's mother was unusually talkative. The four of them sat at the kitchen table. Mrs. Broden talked about the protest and the arrest of the four Jewish women. Elise's mother changed the subject. "I spent the afternoon walking around the neighborhood," Mother said. Elise was surprised she'd left the house. "I went to see the bombed-out buildings. The newspapers are calling the British air raid a terror attack. The royal palace was destroyed. And the opera house. Some people are still buried under the rubble."

It was the most Mother had said in a long time. *Only Mother would be happy to report destruction and death.*

Mrs. Broden looked angry. "Those guards at the center should be helping to dig them out. The government is rounding up our families when it should be helping the survivors of the bombings."

"Well, you should be helping, too, Annett," Mother snapped. "You're wasting your time. The Gestapo will never let the Jews go."

Elise waited for Mrs. Broden to argue back. But she kept her mouth closed, took in a deep breath, and bit her lip.

Scraping the legs of her chair across the wooden floor, Elise's mother walked out of the kitchen and into the living room. Mrs. Broden followed.

In silence, clearing up the dishes and wiping down the counters, Ruth and Elise listened to their mothers. "How dare you... You're talking about my husband and son." Mrs. Broden was doing most of the talking. They couldn't hear all her words, but she was furious.

"Ruth—" Elise said, about to talk about Marko.

Ruth shook her head. "You don't need to apologize."

"I wasn't going to," Elise snapped.

Ruth sighed and dropped the rag in the sink. "I need to sleep."

Elise wanted to ask Ruth to sit with her. She wanted her to suggest they play a board game. Marko was on her mind. She was worried for him. She wondered if Ruth knew something she didn't.

"Good night," Ruth said coldly.

At her father's desk, Elise picked up his letter opener. She climbed the stairs and walked into the dark room that overlooked the city. From there, she had seen Alex and Tsura last Friday night. Elise took a seat on the chair, gazing at the furniture and familiar objects.

"I'm here," she said to Viktor.

Viktor rested his head in her lap. Elise's fingers became entwined in his blond hair.

"Sing me a song," he sobbed.

I can't.

Quietly, Viktor cried. "Do you remember me?"

Elise couldn't remember what Viktor looked like. She knew he had straight, soft hair. She imagined Dieter chasing Marko through the cobblestone streets, dragging Marko to the ground, covering his face, forcing Marko to breathe poisonous fumes until he no longer moved. Like Viktor, Marko would visit Elise soon. Part of her looked forward to it. Viktor had been murdered. *By gas.* That's what her father had scrawled on Viktor's death certificate. Elise wasn't sure what that meant. She remembered Viktor's thin legs and arms, but she couldn't picture his face. The only face Elise could see was the African boy—*Nikolaus*—and the hungry pale face of his little German brother. *I could have helped them.* Marko lay at Elise's feet. Viktor took hold of Elise's hand, guiding the letter opener against her skin. *Marko is dead because of me.*

Marko

With the Nazi uniform and broken watch still on, Marko headed to Duerr's home in Moabit. His wrist was badly bruised, knuckles covered in drying blood. He changed into a shirt, sweater, and an old, tattered coat. He washed the raw scrapes on his hand.

Back on the street, he walked south to the Bavarian district, to Seraph's apartment. Climbing the staircase, he tried to remember the entry code. Marko tapped on the doorframe. Nothing.

He was about to leave when Seraph opened the door. "Wrong password. Get inside," she said.

"I left my map book," Marko said.

He found the book next to the armchair. His smashed hand held Alex's book against his chest.

"I should go," he said to Seraph.

A key in the lock made Marko jump.

At the sight of Marko, Wolf scowled. Marko still didn't feel welcome.

"Don't worry. Tsura's not here," Marko said.

"We have to leave this place," Wolf said to Seraph. His voice was panicked.

"Why?" Seraph asked.

"My friends. They were arrested."

Seraph ran around the apartment, grabbing clothes, documents, throwing everything into a bag. Wolf walked out of the kitchen with some stale bread and cheese in his fist, the wireless pressed against his side.

Marko couldn't help laughing. "You're taking the radio?"

Wolf smiled. "Not all radios receive British reports." Then he spoke seriously. "The war's turning. Some German planes fell behind Soviet lines."

Marko wanted to tell Wolf about the Nazi guard, how he'd messed up and given him Alex's name. And his argument with Tsura. Marko wanted to talk about Kizzy, how he was responsible.

Instead, he held out his hand, bleeding. His knuckles were crushed. "I think it's broken," Marko said.

"Untuck your shirt," Wolf said. Wolf put the food and wireless to the side. He took the bottom of Marko's shirt, ripped off a strip of fabric, and bound Marko's hand. "What happened?"

"A fight."

Wolf broke off some bread for Marko. He ate it right away.

Seraph, in her coat, was ready to go.

"We shouldn't be together," Wolf said.

"Fine, where should I meet you?" Seraph asked.

Wolf stared at her. "Nowhere." He opened the door.

"What?" she cried out. "You have to stay with me. Wolf! Come back!"

Gripping Alex's map book, Marko followed Wolf outside. It was getting dark.

"Warn your sister about the arrests," Wolf said and he took a bite of bread. With the radio tucked under his arm, he disappeared into the side streets.

Kizzy

The rocking and shaking stopped, forcing Kizzy awake. Poland, someone said. The news was jarring. She was still standing. *They must've fixed the engine.* They'd arrived. Their destination. Relocation. Kizzy wanted to breathe. *Let us out.* The freight train doors slid and crashed open. Some people fell onto each other. Others fell hard onto the ground. Screaming. People pushing for air. At the front, they tried to push back. Scrambling. Hands around Kizzy's arm. Fingers scratching. Her face. Shouts and threats. Then the pushing stopped. The sun, so bright, made her squint. Now she could breathe. *Let me out.* It was morning. Or afternoon. She didn't know what day it was. *Where are we?* Dogs around them. *I'm awake, I'm awake now.* A Nazi shouted. Screaming at them to climb down. Being pushed. Almost falling. Someone's hands under her arms. Her feet hit the ground. The men, the women—they had to separate. More sobbing and wailing. Women were to stay with their children. The men were pulled away. Women screeching, like they'd gone insane. Frank disappeared into the crowd with the men. *He's gone.* Kizzy stood with the kids. Tugging. Esther held on to her coat. Felix too— young enough to stay with the women. It was good they could stay together. Shoving. Screaming. Crying all around—middle-aged women wept with dread, toddlers sobbed with hunger. Forced into lines. Men in strange uniforms, dirty blue stripes, matching hats. Words Kizzy couldn't understand. Another language. The sky was perfect. Through the freezing air, she moved. Forward. The sun beat down on her back. *Feels good.* Crying turned into talking, guessing. *Where is this place? What's happening?* Pushing from behind. Guns pointing. Shouts to stay in line. A loud wail. An older woman begged to stay with her son. Gasps in the crowd, and then the wailing stopped. *I'm gonna run.* Guards in front, checking everyone. Kizzy remembered the cigarettes in the pocket of her pinafore. She pulled them out. They were damp but intact. Kizzy faced the soldiers. They wanted to know their ages. Esther and Felix spoke first. They were pushed along. *My turn.* Kizzy was ready to talk. She held out the cigarettes. A gloved hand pushed her hand away. The smokes fell to the ground. A hand grabbed her, pulling her aside. Two Nazi officers, looking at a list—*Zigeuner,* whispered. The noise, the screaming, it faded as an officer dragged Kizzy away, faster than she could walk, away from the mass of Jews, her shoes scraping on the bright gravel. Her wrist hurt. He was gripping too hard. *Stop. Slow down, please. Let me stay with my friends.*

329

DARK SKIES

Tsura

It was Friday. Tsura waited on Rosenstrasse with the protestors. She hadn't seen Kizzy for almost one week. When a hand touched her shoulder, she jumped.

"Follow me," Marko whispered, pulling on her arm.

Tsura had been standing with Ruth, Elise, and Annett, close to the front of the crowd. They didn't seem to notice Tsura slip away.

Standing behind the protesters, Tsura's fingers folded into fists. An urge to scream at her brother filled every part of her. *Marko sent Kizzy in his place.*

But Marko's face seemed different. His eyes didn't smile as they usually did. His words and tone were solemn. "Wolf told me to find you. You've gotta get out of the city. His friends were arrested. It's not safe."

Tsura had no interest in leaving Berlin. "I'll be fine." She noticed a ripped piece of fabric tied around Marko's hand. "What's that?"

"I messed up."

He seemed genuinely sorry. In her head, Tsura accepted his unspoken apology.

Marko kept talking at rapid speed, panicked. "I tried to find out about Kizzy. She's not here. But the guard—he knew me. He saw me once. And Broden. He knows about us. They know everything."

Along with Marko's words, Tsura's pulse quickened. "Slow down. What happened exactly?"

"Kizzy's not here. Broden's in serious danger."

"Marko—"

He continued, in a whisper at first. "I told him Broden's name. I used my knife. I should've killed him!" Marko stared down at the crude bandage around his hand. He was close to tears.

Marko wounded a Nazi solider. Tsura put her hand on his arm. Her brother's eyes looked dead. He was delirious. Broken. His hair was tangled, his beard unkempt. He was accepting that Alex couldn't be saved. Tsura tried to find the strength within herself to apply the same idea to her hopes for finding Kizzy. Tsura had to stop dwelling on fantasies of finding her little cousin. Her efforts were needed elsewhere. As Marko's words sank in, Tsura acknowledged the truth. *She's not here. It's confirmed. Kizzy is gone.*

"I should've killed him," Marko repeated.

Tsura spoke over him. "We can help our people. Marzahn might not be empty yet. There are other Roma encampments."

Marko didn't respond. He stared forward and nodded at the protestors. "They deserve medals."

Tsura's brother was wrong. "No, Marko. We're not like them." The women had come to the center to cry for their husbands. When the Roma had been locked in encampments on the outskirts of Berlin, these women had done nothing. When Tsura had been forced along with Mother to submit to the Nazis' surgical knives, rendering them unable to conceive children, these women of Rosenstrasse had gone about their everyday lives. When the Roma men had been sent away, when Father had been sent to Sachsenhausen, when Nazi soldiers had begun to empty Marzahn, these people had held no protest. Tsura despised them. *They stand with Nazi uniforms beneath their overcoats.* "They only care about their own."

"That's not fair. They're here for the people they love."

Tsura watched the crowd, chanting in unison, determined to free their husbands, brothers, fathers, neighbors, friends, in-laws. When she saw Annett scream at the guards, a pang of shame flooded Tsura's face. *Maybe Marko's right.* Just as Annett demanded the release of her husband and Alex, Tsura would have done anything to free Kizzy. And Mother and Aunt Marie. And Father. She would have sacrificed a million strangers to have them back. Now, Tsura only had her brother. And he was in danger. Marko needed to escape Germany, as they'd planned. "If you wounded a guard, they'll be looking for you. You need to leave Berlin. I'll get you a train ticket."

"I'm staying here," Marko said.

Marko's eyes were fixed on the doors of the Community Center. He needed to stay close to Alex, just as Tsura needed to stay close to ideas of Kizzy being in there, too.

"Marko, stay out of sight. I'll be back in a moment."

"Why? Where're you going?"

Tsura prepared herself to tell Ruth and Annett the truth, or at least part of it. It was time to say goodbye. Tsura practiced her words as she returned to the chanting crowd. *I'm not Alex's girlfriend.*

"We want our husbands back!" Ruth and Annett screamed at the guards.

The women called up to the empty windows, muttering to each other in disbelief that this was the protest's seventh day. Tsura was about to speak when she heard a different scream.

Vehicles on the road. More trucks. The guards driving them seemed to be aiming for the people. The protestors ran toward the side streets. They screamed again to find the gates of the courtyards locked. The crowd surged. People would be crushed. Ruth held on to her mother's coat, Elise in tow. When Annett grabbed Tsura's arm, Tsura gasped. To avoid a truck, they rushed toward the building's entrance.

"Give me back my husband! Release my son!" Annett screamed.

Another guard jumped forward, almost tackling Annett to the ground.

"Let her go!" Ruth shouted.

As Annett screamed and pushed the guards away, Tsura remembered the gun in her pocket.

Elise cowered by the wall.

Hands pulled down on Tsura's shoulders. Her wrists were restrained. Like Mother, dragged from her home. Aunt Marie pulled by her hair. The guards marched Tsura and Annett toward the truck.

"No!" Tsura twisted her hands and kicked backward against the shins of a Nazi. Her hands were free and she screamed. Swinging clenched fists. Her elbows against their metal helmets. They surrounded Tsura. Her boots dragged along the cobblestones and they threw Tsura and Annett into the truck as other women were pushed in with them.

The crowd screamed for the guards to release them.

In the truck, watched by two soldiers and their rifles, Tsura counted ten women, including herself. They were already calming each other down with sensible words and a few jokes.

Annett laughed. "You're making an example of us," she said to the soldiers who sat quietly with a sympathetic glance.

"We'll be questioned," one woman said, sounding terrified of what would happen.

Annett sighed. "Who cares? What do we have to hide?"

Fear rose in Tsura's throat. *They'll find my pistol.*

At the Nazis' Labor Bureau on Fontane Promenade, a dozen minutes south of Rosenstrasse, a guard checked their identity papers. "Greta Voeske," he read.

Annett nodded knowingly at Tsura's false name. She held onto Tsura's arm, and Tsura breathed a sigh of relief when they weren't searched.

In the hallway, the soldiers stood close by.

"I hope we're fed," one woman wished aloud.

"Indoors is better than out there in the freezing cold," Annett said, staring at the guard. "But I'm worried about Ruti," she whispered to Tsura.

Tsura pictured Ruth in Elise's League uniform. "Annett, your daughter can take care of herself."

One of the soldiers led the ten women through the building, into a kitchen. "Get to work." He pointed to bowls and cutting boards, then to sacks of potatoes.

Some of the women laughed.

Annett was angry. "You've got to be joking. You can peel your own potatoes!"

"Raw potatoes are better than nothing," Tsura said and took a bite.

As Tsura spat the mouthful back out, coughing at the chalky taste, the women laughed at her, in a kind way. Then Annett took a bite and dared to chew it. The women roared with delight. The soldier in the corner laughed along. The potatoes reminded Tsura of Seraph's van. And Wolf.

Potatoes and peelers in their hands, the women began to work. The women were cooperating so easily. "What're you doing?" Tsura said to them. She lowered her voice so the soldier couldn't hear. "We're holding knives, for God's sake!" *And I have my gun.*

Annett smiled. "There's no point in provoking the Gestapo. We'll be released soon enough." She sounded certain. "Hitler's leadership is confused. They don't know what else to do. This pointless arrest of ten women is the best development all week. They're desperate. If we fight, if we provoke them, they'll act in the only way they know how. Our efforts would have been for nothing."

Annett was right. Tsura set aside the idea of using her gun. She picked up a potato.

After thirty minutes of peeling, another Nazi soldier walked into the kitchen. "Come with me," he said and pointed to one of the women.

"Interrogations?" Tsura whispered to Annett.

"We have nothing to be afraid of," Annett said.

She was wrong. "My family—we're Romani," Tsura whispered.

Annett squeezed Tsura's hand. Tsura's eyes searched the room for somewhere to hide her gun. But the soldier was watching their every move. No more than four minutes later, the woman returned.

"Well, that was a waste of time," she told the others.

Moments later, Tsura was being marched down a dimly lit corridor. The pistol in her pocket felt heavier. *I can't let them find it.* Led into an office, Tsura was guided to a chair in front of a desk. A government official, a middle-aged woman in an ugly suit and pulled-back hair, sat with her shoulders square.

"Remove your hat, girl."

Fury rushed to Tsura's fists. She wanted to reach over the desk and take a swing at her head. *I'm not afraid.* Tsura obeyed.

"Your name? Age?"

"Greta Voeske," she lied and offered the Nazi her identity papers. "I'm nineteen."

The woman examined the forged documents. "And why were you on the street?"

"You've detained my family. And now you're arresting patriotic Germans."

"Watch your words, girl." She spoke calmly, unperturbed by Tsura's outburst. "I'm sure I don't need to tell you what we do to government defectors."

Tsura wanted to laugh in her face, to tell her she was a proud dissident, that she'd kill her without hesitation, on behalf of her people. She remembered the train station and the crying infant and his Nazi mother. Tsura had chosen to jump onto the tracks. *I could have let the woman die.*

The interrogator pushed toward Tsura a piece of paper. In her long coat, holding herself and pretending to be cold, Tsura leaned forward. She had seen the illegal newsletter weeks earlier. What she couldn't tell the official was that she agreed with every word.

"You've seen this before, yes? The White Rose. Those pathetic students distributed this illegal flyer and now they are dead. Executed just weeks ago. Beheaded. Do you understand, girl?"

"So I'm a traitor? Is that what you're suggesting?" Tsura shouted with pretend outrage.

The Nazi shifted in her chair. The questioning was over. The interrogator knocked on the desk and a guard in a pressed uniform, clutching his rifle, appeared in the doorway. "We're done here. Take her back to the other women." Tsura stood and the Nazi spoke again. "And with what you've been doing, this embarrassing protest, yes, we might very well call you a traitor."

The interrogation had been quick and easy. Tsura walked along the hallway, head held high. She imagined the voices of her family, of her people, of Kizzy. *I'll find you*, Tsura swore.

"Wait, bring her back," the government official called out.

Tsura held her breath and fear filled her stomach. *They'll search me.* Possible explanations for possessing the pistol spun through Tsura's head. *I found it. I carry it with me to feel safe.*

In her coat, Tsura stood in front of the desk, waiting to be instructed to empty her pockets.

"Tell me, girl, what do you think about this protest? Why are so many civilians returning to the street every day?"

"To be honest, I'm surprised, too," Tsura said.

The Nazi sat back in her chair, gesturing for Tsura to keep talking.

Tsura forced a smile. "It's amazing out there. The energy. The determination of the women to save their husbands and children."

"What would you do in my position?" the woman asked.

Tsura was astonished. She chose her words carefully. "After Stalingrad, after Monday's air raid, if we don't act carefully, if we don't consider the attitudes of the public, German morale could drop even further. I want the people I love to walk free. But I also love my country."

Taking a deep breath, the government official nodded. "Thank you for being honest," she said.

No other women were questioned. As they peeled potatoes, the ten detainees took bets on how long they'd be held. They chattered and laughed. One woman sang to them. She was a trained performer, she said. But she wasn't very good and Annett and Tsura rolled their eyes. Annett remained next to Tsura, telling her what she'd cooked before the war, before the rationing. She told Tsura about her work as a civil servant of the Weimar Republic. Annett talked about meeting her husband, Alex's father. "How long have you and Alexander been together?" Annett asked.

Tsura hesitated. "I met him through Marko."

Annett smiled. "I'm so glad you're here—that you joined the demonstration."

"Of course."

"I'm proud of you, Tsura. And I'm glad Alex found you. Are you two planning to marry?"

She deserves the truth. "I can't have children," Tsura said.

Annett seemed taken aback by the comment. "Doctors often get these things wrong," she said.

"They sterilized me," Tsura whispered.

One hand to her mouth, Annett took hold of Tsura's arm. "Tsura. My God. I'm so sorry to hear that."

Tsura wanted to tell Annett the full story. The hospital as a child, the forced sterilization, the pain. Tsura was sterile and Marko was homosexual. *My mother will never have grandchildren.*

"Does Alex know you're barren?" Annett asked.

"I've never told anyone."

Annett shook her head and narrowed her eyes. She became quiet, disengaging from their conversation. *Annett thinks Alex has a right to know. She thinks I'm being selfish.*

"Annett, don't worry. Alex and I won't be getting married."

Annett seemed surprised but placated by Tsura's declaration. Again, she held Tsura's arm. "Alex is lucky to have you. I'd be proud to have you as my daughter-in-law."

A sense of embarrassment surged through Tsura's body. *This pretense is unnecessary.* "Ruth was confused. I'm sorry I played along."

A soldier entered the kitchen. "Get comfortable, ladies. You'll be staying the night."

"I don't understand," Annett said, ignoring the soldier. She held a peeling knife in one hand, a potato in the other.

"Annett, I don't know what Ruth told you, but Alex and I weren't kissing. I'm not Alex's girlfriend. I never was."

Alexander

Alex woke on the office floor. Alone. His shoulder to the wall. His eye was swollen and it throbbed. His jaw may have been broken; his side teeth were cracked. He'd been there since Thursday, and all day Friday. The room was dark again. It was late. The middle of the night. No sound of the crowds on the street.

Marko was dead. Alex would never see him again. Or tell Marko his stories. Or kiss him. *What were our last words to each other?* He couldn't remember.

The three Nazis had left Alex there with his mouth full of blood. When he had recalled his father's expression of shock that his son was to be arrested and deported as a homosexual, tears streamed down Alex's face. Then, throughout yesterday, the Nazis had returned, again and again. To teach him a lesson, they'd said. Every time they'd left the room, Alex cried himself to sleep. The Nazis had kicked Alex in the face to wake him. Whenever they'd forced Alex to stand, Alex had forced his mind away from their voices and laughter.

Alone now, Alex took out the notepapers from his pocket, thin wilted pages. With no light, he held the papers close to his swollen face, trying to read his written words. He ripped them to pieces. *Why did I write them?* Shards of notepaper scattered to the floor. *Why did I take the risk?*

When the door opened, Alex crawled as close to the wall as possible. They were back.

"Time to go," a soldier said.

Still in pain, Alex buttoned up his trousers. He was led to the hallway, his false identity papers in one boot, Kizzy's in the other. An unfamiliar Gestapo officer, older, with rows of medals, gray and black hair sticking out of his hat, was waiting. As if he weren't there, as if he were invisible, they talked about Alex.

"I'll testify against him during the trial," the officer with the bandaged hand said.

"There's no need to trouble the courts," the senior Gestapo officer replied.

Alex trembled.

It was the middle of the night. No big crowds. Across the street, a group of women huddled together, flasks in their hands, watching.

"Help me!" he called out to them.

A soldier brought his rifle down hard on Alex's head and pushed him toward a waiting truck. "Get into the vehicle, pervert, or we shoot you right here."

This was the end. Alex had an urge to fight, to throw his fists at them, to give them a reason to murder him there outside the Jewish Community Center. But an overwhelming sense of restraint ran through his core. Alex wanted to live. These men, with their pressed uniforms and ignorant slurs. These men were the enemies of the Jewish people, like Pharaoh, Amalek, Haman. Each year, at the reading of *The Book of Esther*, Alex had learned, whenever Haman's name was read aloud, praying Jews shouted and stamped their feet to render him unheard. These men, who stood over Alex, accused him of perversion—*I'll blot out their names. I swear.*

It hurt to climb. The truck burst to life. Alex listened to the wheels on the road. The journey took just minutes. Anhalter Station. Marko and Alex would have taken their train from Anhalter. By now, they would have been far from Germany.

This is how it feels. Alex had expected to be terrified. In a way, he was. But, with most of Father's family deported before him, this had become a family rite. *A new Jewish ritual.* Toward the work camps. Or worse, if the rumors of mass murder were true.

Alex was kept at Anhalter for a number of hours. The entrance and any possible exits were guarded. In the cold, he was wide awake. On the floor, Alex stared up at the bare trees that swayed in the winter wind. The branches against the dark skies looked like dancers on a stage. Synchronized and beautiful. Waving goodbye.

The sun would rise soon. He'd been awake all night. Alex was startled by the rattling of metal on metal in the distance. As a train pulled closer along the rail tracks, Alex thought about his false papers in his boot, Kizzy's papers in the other. Alex had never met

Kizzy. He wondered what she was like. Kizzy was just a child. Alex didn't know what he'd do if Ruti went missing.

Last year and the years before, Ruti had needed help solving Alex's puzzles. She'd always asked him for extra hints. Sometimes his clues were too cryptic. Alex would offer her tips and he'd help her out with words and phrases. But she was older now. His baby sister had grown up. He wondered if she liked her birthday gift. *Did she quickly solve the clues?*

Last Friday afternoon, just before leaving home, Alex had taken a piece of white chalk from Ruti's art box and a shovel from the pile of garden tools by the kitchen door. He hid Ruti's birthday gift and used the chalk to create a message that would ensure she would find it. Here at this train station, Alex smiled as he imagined Ruti discovering the hidden word within the ten she had found, following the final clue, carefully retrieving her gift box, and finding her porcelain train. Ruti would have noticed how the train engine had been repaired and that the first and fifth carriages had cracks along their sides. But Ruti wouldn't have minded, Alex knew.

Last week in the antique shop, Alex had been looking for an object related to travel. He remembered the oil paintings of ships. He'd looked for a London guidebook or map. As he'd written in Ruti's goodbye letter, which he'd placed inside the gift's wrapping, the porcelain train was both a reminder that he was leaving their home and a promise that they'd see each other again, one day.

Alex would find a way to escape to London. The British and Americans would win the war. He'd return to Ruti and his family. Or they'd join Alex in London as soon as they had the chance.

The train cars rattled closer along the tracks. Several railway lines, side by side, pointed toward the platform. The metal rails, joined by wooden planks like ladders, crossed and connected and overlapped. One could have mistakenly assumed that each train could choose its own destination. But there was no choice. The Nazi operator sat in the station booth, his hands on levers and switches, forcing each train along its given path.

I'll find a way to run. Marko will—

Alex stopped himself in his thought.

"Marko."

He remembered the graveyard where as a child he'd watched Father rip his shirt—the Jewish ritual of mourning from which children were barred. Alex gripped his collar. He moved one hand left and one hand down, snapping the stitches and splitting the fabric of Marko's coat.

Ruth

Ruth put on her glasses and tiptoed across the creaking floorboards, careful not to wake Elise.

Yesterday, when the trucks had driven toward the crowd, Ruth had held onto Mama. But the soldiers had still pulled Mama away and onto the truck. Ruth had screamed for her, but the Nazi pigs wouldn't listen. They'd taken Tsura, too. A dozen or so women had been arrested. Many of the protesters had surrounded Ruth. Her mother would be okay, they'd told her. The arrests were an attempt to scare the crowd. Some women had offered Ruth somewhere to sleep. She thanked them and explained she was staying with her friend. After midnight, with still no sign of Mama, two women— strangers—insisted on escorting them home. Mrs. Edelhoff was already sleeping. Ruth and Elise had grabbed something to eat. Upstairs, still in their clothes, they crawled into their beds. Elise fell asleep right away. Ruth's mind was racing.

The sun would be up soon. Ruth went downstairs and sat at the kitchen table. Another Saturday. *I'm fifteen and one week.* She wondered what she'd do if the Gestapo wouldn't release her mother. She wanted to cry. She stood and walked over to a desk by the back window. Piles of papers covered the surface. As Ruth's bleary eyes skimmed the pages, a sound outside startled her. She pulled the blackout shade aside and almost screamed when she saw a face staring back at her. *Marko!*

Ruth ran to unlock the back door.

"Ruti—"

"What're you doing here?"

"I had nowhere to go," he said.

It was good to see Marko. But he had dark circles around his eyes. He was shivering. His hand was bandaged with torn fabric.

"What happened to you?" Ruth asked, closing the door.

"I'm fine."

But Marko didn't seem fine. Ruth turned on the heat beneath the kettle on the stovetop.

"How did you find us?" Ruth asked.

"Your brother brought me here once."

"He did?"

"Last Friday night. After your birthday dinner, I was here, behind that garden wall."

Pieces were starting to fall into place. Ruth played through the events. At midnight on Friday, Alexander had headed out to meet Tsura. *Alexander and Tsura met here and Elise saw them kissing.* Marko met up with them, too. Tsura had been planning to leave Berlin with Alexander. *And Marko was helping them.*

"Marko, Tsura was arrested."

"I know."

"My mother was taken, too."

"I was there. I saw everything."

Tears fell down Ruth's face and Marko put his hand on Ruth's shoulder.

"Alexander and Papa were taken. And now Mama." Ruth spoke through sobs. She looked up at Marko, who stared back blankly. "And Kizzy. And now Tsura," Ruth added.

Ruth and Marko were the same. *We both have nobody.* Even with Elise upstairs, Ruth felt alone. Marko's presence was comforting. He reminded Ruth of Alexander and her birthday dinner, when things felt normal.

Orange light streamed in from the hallway. The sun was rising. Another day.

"Wait here. I'll wake Elise."

Ruth left Marko in the kitchen and climbed the stairs. She remembered back to one week ago when, on her birthday, Alexander had been arrested. She'd met Marko the night before, eating cake, blowing out her candle. But Ruth's birthday wish was broken—the wish for her brother to leave Berlin safely.

As she approached Elise's bedroom, Ruth could hear her talking. She stopped at the doorway, watching.

"It's okay. Don't cry," Elise said quietly.

Elise was on her back, talking to herself, eyes closed. The dim light of the sunrise fell on her hair. Ruth stepped into the room.

"I wanted to... I wasn't allowed... I'm sorry." Random words and phrases and pauses. Sleep-talking.

"Elise," Ruth said.

Elise sat up, startled. She jumped out of bed and ran past Ruth and onto the landing.

"Elise—"

Ruth followed her into one of the other bedrooms. Elise sat on a bed in the corner of the dark room. Its window looked over the back gardens rather than the sunrise at the front of the house. Elise was crying. Ruth looked around the unfamiliar room. A teddy bear and a toy car sat on a shelf. Wooden building blocks and a stack of books rested in the corner on the floor. *Viktor's bedroom.*

"Elise, what's wrong?" Ruth asked. Ruth sat on Viktor's bed, next to Elise. "You were talking in your sleep."

Elise leaned toward Ruth and rested her head on her shoulder. Ruth couldn't be sure, but she had a feeling Elise was crying.

She smoothed down Elise's coarse hair. "It's okay. It's okay."

Ruth remembered when Viktor had died. Her family brought Elise's family cooked meals every other day. Elise's parents couldn't deal with Viktor's death. Ruth and Alexander had talked about it, once, and they'd promised each other that, if the other ever died, they'd make sure their parents remembered all the fun memories of their birthdays and trips out of the city.

Elise wiped her eyes and sat up straight. "This is yours." Elise handed Ruth a folded piece of paper. "Ruti" was written at the top; "Elise" in the center.

Ruth gasped. "Wow! Where did you find it?"

"In the lining of my coat. You were right."

Alexander will be okay. If Ruth could solve the treasure hunt, the protest would work out. Ruth put her arms around her best friend.

"Come downstairs. Marko's here."

Elise gawked at Ruth. "Marko? Is he all right?"

Elise was suddenly flustered. She found fresh blouses for both of them. While Elise combed her hair, Ruth took her brother's notes and laid out the clues on Elise's bed: *Freund, Unterwäsche, Nachthemd, Telefon, Mausloch, Eierschale, November, Annett, Dresden.*

Ruth picked up the newest folded paper with the final word, "Elise," across the front. Slowly, she opened it to read Alexander's riddle written so neatly inside.

Words connect
Like carriages of a train

Ruth remembered Alexander's first riddle, suggesting she count to ten. There were no more clues. She had all ten words: friend, underwear, nightgown, telephone, mouse hole, eggshell, November, Annett, Dresden, Elise. Together they made no sense. As much as Ruth tried, she couldn't see a pattern. No obvious connections. She couldn't see how they would've helped her find her birthday prize.

Downstairs, Marko was asleep at the kitchen table, his head resting on his folded arms, an empty plate and cup beside him.

"Look at his hand," Ruth said to Elise, pointing to the bandage. "What do you think happened?"

Elise stared, saying nothing. Elise prepared some breakfast and they ate, quietly, letting Marko sleep. They put on their coats. Ruth placed the treasure hunt clues in her pocket.

Ruth tapped Marko's shoulder. "Marko—"

He woke with a jolt.

"We're going back to the protest," Ruth told him.

Marko walked with them, bleary eyed.

As they approached Rosenstrasse, Marko pulled back. "I can't be here. I've gotta look for Tsura."

"Marko, wait—" Elise said.

But Marko walked away. Ruth was worried for him.

Because it was Saturday or because the word had spread, the crowd was larger than ever. As Ruth and Elise approached the Community Center, Ruth searched for her mother. But she was nowhere to be seen. Ruth was frightened for Alexander, too. She hoped the smuggled documents hadn't put him and Papa in danger.

By late morning, the street was heaving. News spread through the crowd. The Gestapo had arrested more Jews across the city. And there was another protest now, on Hamburg Main Street, close to the old Jewish cemetery. *This is a revolution! I'll stand out here every day, all spring and summer, if I need to.*

As Nazi guards walked out of the Community Center, Ruth stared in disbelief as they set up machine guns.

"We have to leave," Elise said.

"Be quiet," a woman next to them snapped. "We won't be going anywhere."

The crowd started to chant. Ruth joined in. "We want our husbands back!" Ruth stared at Elise, who seemed so terrified she couldn't make a sound.

The guards pointed their machine guns at them and a new chant began.

"Murderers. Murderers!" Ruth shouted along.

Nobody ran. Ruth could see in the guards' eyes that they wouldn't shoot. *We're their people.* The women were their teachers, their neighbors. They knew their families.

An officer walked out of the building to give instructions to the guards, and the men took apart their machine gun stands. Everyone was talking, cheering, shouting. *They're giving in.*

By mid-afternoon, even more people packed onto Rosenstrasse, spilling onto the side streets. But still no sign of Mama.

Then they heard the news they'd been waiting for. The prisoners would be released. People in the crowd shrieked. Some of the women were crying. The woman next to Ruth laughed that her tears were freezing to her face.

The first Jewish prisoner stepped out of the Community Center, his yellow star sewn to his shirt. Everyone cheered as he looked out at the enormous crowd. Then more people behind him. More yellow stars. Exhausted, but delighted. People shouted names. Many were crying. Christian women ran toward their Jewish husbands, embracing, disappearing into the crowd. Ruth could barely contain her excitement. She searched the faces for her brother and father and kicked her feet against the cobblestones, almost dancing on tiptoes. When Ruth saw a young girl with a knitted blue hat, her heart leapt.

"Is that Kizzy?" she said, grabbing Elise's arm.

Elise stared and nodded, then broke out into a wide smile. "That's the girl I saw. Marko will be so happy!"

The girl fit Kizzy's description. Curly hair, around thirteen years old. Ruth searched the crowd for Marko or Tsura. She couldn't see them. Ruth turned back to the girl in the blue hat.

"It's not Kizzy," Elise said.

A yellow star was sewn to the girl's coat. She held the hand of a Jewish man. The woman in the dark green hat and coat embraced her husband, then fell to her knees to smother her daughter with kisses and tears. *It wasn't Kizzy after all.*

When Ruth saw her mother pushing through the crowd, she felt giddy. "Mama! Over here! Mama! Mama!"

"Ruti!" Mama's smile was wide across her beautiful face.

Ruth ran forward and squeezed her mother tight. "They're letting them go!"

"It's wonderful," Mama said with a laugh.

"Where's Tsura?" Ruth asked.

"I don't know. But she was released, too."

Everything would be okay. They waited, staring at the Jewish men and some women exiting the building, Ruth with her arms around her mother, Elise by her side.

"Papa!" Ruth shouted as she saw his face.

"Sam! Samuel!" Mama called out.

Ruth felt as if she were floating. The protest had worked. *The government caved!* Walking toward them, Papa beamed. But as he approached, Ruth could tell from his face, from his eyes that were bloodshot and small, that he was only trying to smile. His hair looked grayer. Inside Ruth's chest, her heart dropped. *Where's Alexander?* She couldn't swallow. Mama put her arms around her husband.

"Alexander— Papa, where's Alexander?"

Papa stared at them, his bottom lip hanging open.

"Where's Alexander?" Ruth shouted again, her voice lost in the screaming crowd.

"We need to go," Papa said, his eyes closing.

Ruth took hold of her father's hand. "No. Alexander. He's in there!"

Her father looked down at the ground.

"Sam? What's happened? Sam. Tell me."

"He was arrested. On Thursday."

"What?"

Papa continued, "They took him—"

"Thursday? What are—"

"Alexander was deported. An officer confirmed it."

Mama shrieked.

"Why? Why?" Ruth screamed. She had been standing on the street all that time, thinking Alexander was inside. But he was already gone. Ruth didn't understand. Everyone was being released.

"Why?" Mama repeated.

Papa closed his eyes, tight. "I don't know why," he said.

Ruth took hold of his hands. "We have to find out. We'll keep protesting. Papa, we can make the listen. They'll listen. They will. They'll have to." Then a wave of guilt made Ruth's face burn. If Ruth hadn't smuggled in the basket, Alexander would have been released. *The Nazis found the false papers. I'm to blame.*

Papa let go of Ruth's hand. "Let's go home."

"Our house was bombed," Mama said through her tears. "Everything was destroyed."

Ruth expected Papa to collapse with grief. But he nodded, as though he already knew. He put his hand on Ruth's face, his cold fingers against her cheek.

Mama's eyes were streaming.

Ruth looked at Elise, who had been watching in silence.

"Alexander was deported," Ruth said to her in disbelief.

Elise's eyes were vacant. "That's what happens in wartime."

Ruth felt the urge to cry, but she kept it inside. *Crying won't solve anything.* Ruth's head was a haze. Papa was now talking to some people in the crowd—a Jewish man and woman and their daughter. "This is Herr Federman," Papa said. As Papa and Mr. Federman talked, his daughter approached Ruth.

"I'm Lea," she said. Lea was pretty. She was tall and had dark, neat hair. "I'm so sorry about your brother. I liked Alex, very much."

Lea spoke as though Alexander had died.

"Tsura!" Ruth blurted out, grabbing Mama's arm. "We have to tell her about Alexander."

Wiping away tears, Mama shook her head. "No. No."

"Mama, she needs to know."

"No, Ruth. Tsura wasn't Alexander's girlfriend after all."

Ruth's head raced through everything she knew. *Elise saw Alexander and Tsura kissing. Alexander and Tsura were going to leave Berlin together. Marko was in the back gardens, too. He told me.* Ruth pictured the three of them behind Elise's home.

"We'll be staying with the Federmans tonight," Papa announced.

"You're not staying with me?" Elise whispered.

Mama put her hand on Elise's arm. "Elise, we're very grateful for everything, but we've taken advantage for too long."

Elise looked down, obviously disappointed.

As Papa led them from Rosenstrasse, Ruth's head swirled with facts and theories. "My brother, Tsura, and Marko," Ruth said to Elise, trying to figure everything out. "The false papers. And the note. It wasn't for Tsura; it was a message for Marko. And Alexander gave Marko something else." Ruth remembered Alexander passing Marko something when they'd joined for her birthday dinner. She wondered again how Tsura found one of Alexander's treasure hunt clues. "And Kizzy," Ruth continued, knowing Elise probably wasn't following along. "Do you think Kizzy even existed?"

"Existed?" Elise said, narrowing her eyes.

"Maybe Kizzy was some kind of code word."

Elise stared at Ruth as if she were crazy.

"Well, I never met her. Did you?"

Elise shook her head.

Ruth was confused. "Oh, I don't know." She wanted to sob. Elise said nothing and, for a few moments, they walked in silence.

"What about the kiss?" Elise asked.

"Who knows," Ruth said as they arrived at Elise's front step. "I guess I'll see you soon."

Elise nodded and turned to walk inside. Then she turned back to face Ruth. "I'm so sorry. I'm sorry about everything." Ruth's best friend put her arms around her. Ruth returned the hug.

Lea and her parents led Ruth's family to their house, just streets away from where Ruth's home once stood. Passing bombed-out buildings, Ruth walked with Lea, the adults behind them.

"Your brother was trying to leave Berlin," Lea said. "I saw him the day before we were arrested. I can't believe he was sent away."

Ruth didn't know how to respond.

Lea continued, "I'm sorry about your house. You can have my old clothes. You'll share my room."

"Thank you."

While Ruth got ready for bed, she could hear sounds of talking through the walls. She dropped her glasses on Lea's nightstand and walked out into the hallway. Through one of the bedroom doors, she could hear Papa crying.

Ruth knocked before stepping into the dark room. Her parents were sitting up in bed. When he saw Ruth, Papa wiped his eyes with the sleeve of his borrowed nightshirt and turned on the bedside lamp.

"Come in, Ruti."

"I think I know what happened," Ruth said.

With her hand, Mama patted the edge of the bed. "Come."

Ruth sat down and took a breath. "Tsura and Marko. I think they're working against the government."

Mama's eyes widened.

"And I think Alexander was, too."

Papa listened, saying nothing.

"Why do you think that, darling?" Mama asked. "Alexander would have told us."

"Last week, when Marko stayed for dinner, Alexander gave him something."

"What?" Mama asked.

"I don't know. But, later, in the middle of the night, Elise said she saw Alexander and Tsura together, in the gardens behind her house. Well, Marko was there, too. He told me. And the other day, when I took the basket of food into the building, Alexander passed me a note to give to Marko. I didn't read it, but—it's—I just have a feeling. I think Tsura and Marko are involved in an anti-Nazi group. I think—"

"You're probably right about most of that," Mama interrupted. "But Elise was wrong. Alexander and Tsura weren't kissing. Tsura said so."

"Tsura told you that?" Ruth asked.

"Yes. Well, unless she was embarrassed about being seen." Mama sighed a deep sigh and kissed Ruth on the head. "We're so proud of you. My little girl isn't so little any more. Right, Sam?"

Papa dropped his face into his hands and sobbed.

"It'll be okay, Papa," Ruth said, reaching out for his arm.

Mama smiled. "Thank you, darling, for telling us everything. I'll sleep better now."

Ruth kissed both of them and turned off the lamp. In the darkness, Ruth could hear her father weeping.

"I'm proud of him," Mama said. "Our son, working against the regime."

Ruth held back her tears. *Me too.*

As she walked into her new bedroom, Ruth saw that Lea was already asleep. Ruth's throat and chest burned and her stomach was in knots, but she felt strangely better about her brother. She'd figured it all out. She knelt by Lea's bed, about to say a prayer. The room was dark, but she could see the yellow star on Lea's coat, hanging by the door. She remembered Alexander's yellow star that Elise had found. Ruth's coat rested on the back of a chair. Taking out Alexander's clues from her coat pocket, she set the notes out on the cold wooden floorboards. Then she gasped. *I've been thinking about the words in the wrong way.* She had been arranging the words in the order in which she'd found them, not in the sequence Alexander had intended.

Ruth put on her glasses, reordered her brother's notes, and into the darkness of the unfamiliar room she whispered Alexander's ten words. In their correct sequence, they moved through her head.

Freund, Unterwäsche, Nachthemd, Dresden, Annett, Mausloch, Eierschale, November, Telefon, Elise.

Then she saw it. It was so simple. *Words connect. Like carriages of a train.* Immediately, Ruth knew exactly where Alexander had hidden her prize.

Her heart beating fast, Ruth put on her stockings. She buttoned up her coat and crept down the staircase.

She rummaged around the kitchen and found a candle and a box of matches, then put them in her pocket. At the front door, she slipped on her shoes and walked out into the night.

The neighborhood was deserted. Within minutes, she was on her street. The smell of burning had almost disappeared.

With tears behind her eyes, Ruth faced the ruins of her family home. Stepping over the smashed brick and glass, she approached the building's remaining façade. The front door hung from its hinges. Through the broken front windows, Ruth gazed at piles of rubble. This was where she had lived her childhood. This was where her family had celebrated, said goodbyes, comforted one another, teased

352

and laughed with each other. Fighting the urge to cry, Ruth fixed her thoughts on Alexander's game.

The house had been blown backward and to the left. To her right, part of the floor above the basement had been ripped away. She used a stray piece of wood—the leg of a dining chair—from the front garden to break and clear the remaining shards of glass attached to a window frame. As she placed her hands on the front sill, she inhaled dust. Taking the chair leg with her, she climbed into what was once her family's living room, expecting to find books and more broken furniture. But the debris was charred and unrecognizable. She scrambled over and between the heaps of wreckage. The blackened bricks shifted and caused her to stumble. With the smell of burnt wood in her nostrils, she used the broken chair leg to steady herself and made her way toward what once was the hallway. Although covered in soot and exposed to the sky, the basement seemed mostly untouched. Its stairs were intact.

With care, using the chair leg as a walking stick, she climbed downward into the shadows.

Again, with each step, Ruth recited Alexander's clues in their intended order.

Freund, Unterwäsche, Nachthemd, Dresden, Annett, Mausloch, Eierschale, November, Telefon, Elise.

It couldn't have been a coincidence, she knew, that the first letter of each word, strung together, spelled out a location.

When she stepped down onto the basement floor, she reached into her pocket for the candle and matches. The sound of the match catching fire filled her core with expectation. But as the basement filled with flickering candlelight, her heart sank. Aside from small pieces of debris and part of the upper floor hanging inward, the basement was empty. *I was wrong.*

But when she turned to climb out again, with the burning candle in her hand, Ruth almost squealed with joy.

On the front face of each basement step, written in white chalk, was a single letter, spelling out the hidden ten-letter word she had already discovered.

FUNDAMENTE

In the darkness, written clearly before her eyes, beginning at the top of the staircase, was Alexander's final clue, an explicit signal that Ruth had indeed found the location of her birthday gift. *Fundamente*—foundations.

Breathing quickly, Ruth spun around to look closely at the basement's floor. She spotted an uneven patch of dirt by the far wall. With the broken chair leg, she brushed away the loose earth. The blunt wood hit a flat object. Ruth fell to her knees. She pushed the lit candle into the ground and used her fingers to pull out a box. *I solved the puzzle. I saved my brother! When this war is over, he'll come home.* Tucked into the paper wrapping, she found Alexander's birthday note. With fresh dirt beneath her fingernails, holding the letter close to the flame, she inhaled his every word—his promise. They would be reunited. Looking up at the night sky, she remembered the falling bombs. Tonight, the sky was silent. As Ruth unwrapped the box, she tried to imagine her brother's return. Yet she couldn't. Tears dropped onto the lenses of her glasses, blurring her view of the beautiful porcelain train in her trembling hands, and Ruth accepted, finally, that finding Alexander's birthday gift would never make up for his deportation. He hadn't escaped. He would never reach London. Her brother's game was meaningless now.

Elise

Now, at last, Ruth is like me.

Years earlier, when Elise was told that Viktor was dead, she didn't cry. Not straight away. The weeping coming from her parents' bedroom had sounded alien. Her father had cried all day, all night. He'd cried on behalf of his family. Mother hadn't allowed Elise to see him.

On the third night after the news, while her parents were sleeping, Elise crept into Viktor's bedroom. She sat on the chair in the corner. She spoke to Viktor in her head. She told him about her day.

Weeks later, Viktor began to talk back. One night, Elise had the urge to reach up to the toys on his shelf. On tiptoes, she knocked over a small photograph frame, a photograph of her family—her parents and Elise and Viktor, from when he was very young. It fell to the floor and the glass smashed. Elise was terrified she'd be found out. Quickly, Elise picked up the shards of glass. At the sight of blood on her hand, Elise wept. It had been more than one month since Viktor's death and that had been the first time she had cried. It had felt good to let go of her tears. She returned the frame to the shelf, its glass gone. Her mother never noticed.

Again and again, Elise had returned to Viktor's room. She started to make scratches in her arms. She dug her nails into her skin. Releasing the blood was soothing. Elise knew it was a bad thing to do, but she couldn't stop. Over time, rather than her fingernails, she'd used sharp bottle tops, desk scissors, kitchen knives. In Elise's head, Viktor encouraged her, warning her not to go too deep.

Crying into Ruth's shoulder that morning was the first time Elise had cried without making herself bleed. She didn't tell Ruth the real reason for her sobbing. Elise had woken up thinking about Marko's cousin. She'd never met little Kizzy, but somehow Elise cared about her. Part of her had expected Kizzy to be found. Elise had wanted to show Ruth the cuts and scars on her arm.

The protest was over now. The Jewish prisoners had been released. Elise fell asleep in the living room, still in her coat.

She was jolted awake by a sharp sound. *Somebody's trying to break in.* She should have sounded an alarm. She should have screamed. Instead, Elise crept into the hallway. The tapping was coming from the kitchen.

"Elise! Ruti! Are you there?"

Marko is here again. For an instant, she pictured Marko in his pressed Nazi uniform. Elise ran to the kitchen door. He was still wearing the badly fitting civilian clothing. His beard and hair were a little too long. His gaunt face was sweating and his eye sockets were dark, his hand still wrapped in cloth. When she'd seen him, hours earlier, sleeping at her kitchen table, she'd felt relief mingled with deep regret. She had wanted to say sorry. Sorry that she'd led him to Dieter. Sorry that he was hurt.

"Where's Broden? Is he here?" Marko asked, panic in his voice.

"No—"

"What about Ruti?"

Elise felt ashamed that Ruth and her family weren't staying at her home. Frightened away by her awful mother. "Ruti's father was released. But Alex—" Her words wouldn't come. Viktor stared up at Marko.

"Broden's gone. Isn't he?" Marko's voice cracked.

Elise's pause was her reply. "He was deported. And Kizzy wasn't there. The girl I saw—she was someone else." *They murdered my brother, too*, she wanted to say.

Marko said nothing. He clawed at the back of his neck and let out a small yelp, almost soundless, as if in severe pain. Elise expected questions. She expected Marko to cry. He turned to leave.

"Wait. Are you hungry?"

Marko nodded.

"It must be hard to be a Jew," Elise said to him.

Marko gave her a puzzled look. "My family—we're not Jews. We're Roma."

Roma? Marko is a Gypsy. His confession was startling, but Elise liked him all the same. "It doesn't matter to me," she blurted out and immediately felt embarrassed.

But Marko wasn't listening. He was looking over her shoulder. Elise turned to see Mother in the doorway of the kitchen.

"*Zigeuner!*" Mother screamed. "It doesn't matter to you? You want to share our rations with a thief?"

"Mama—"

"It's okay," Marko said to Elise. He turned to her mother. "I'm sorry. I didn't mean to bother you."

Her mother pointed her finger at Marko and continued to shriek. "Get out! Filth! Get out of our house!"

Elise wanted to shut her up. "No! Stay. Marko, please." Elise spoke with open palms, her scratched arms reaching toward him.

Marko stepped back into the darkness.

Trembling, Elise stared up at the sky above the gardens and alleyways and closed the door, turning to face her mother. Her palms closed into fists. "Why did you do that?" Elise yelled.

Viktor stared at Elise from the kitchen table. His sickly legs swung from the wooden chair. Hiding behind his hands, he seemed frightened that his sister was shouting.

"You let a strange man into our house?" Mother screamed. "*Zigeuner*, Elise! The *Zigeuner* are thieves! A naïve little girl—that's what you are."

"He's Alex's friend."

Mother wasn't listening, just shouting insults and squawking like a crazy woman.

"Where's Papa?" Viktor asked.

Somewhere in this war. Maybe Papa was dead, too.

"Ruth's father was released," Elise said.

"I couldn't care less about that Jew!" Mother yelled.

"Elise," Viktor said, tapping her arm. Elise couldn't look at him.

Mother was still making a racket. "*Zigeuner! Zigeuner!* People like you will cause the collapse of our Fatherland. Jew-lover— "

"What the hell's wrong with you? You make our lives miserable. I'll never be like you." Elise trembled as she screamed.

Viktor stepped away from his sister.

For a moment her mother's face was unrecognizable. "No daughter should ever speak to her mother like that!"

Elise stepped forward. "Everything's your fault. Everything. You sent Papa to war. You sent Viktor away. You took him to the hospital yourself. You wanted him dead."

Viktor stood by the kitchen doorway.

Elise's mother began to screech, the way she screeched when Elise's father told her that Viktor had been murdered by the government. She fell against the kitchen wall. "Leave this house! Leave!" she wailed.

Elise pictured her life without her mother. Without the constant draining.

"Get out, Elise, and never return!"

Elise felt strangely calm. "Then who will you have?" Elise said, looking right at her.

As he walked toward the front door, Viktor looked back.

Elise climbed the stairs to her room.

"The government is already falling apart," Mother called out. "It's because of people like you. I bet you're happy about your Jew protest. What a success!"

"No, not for Alex. Not for Ruth's family."

Behind Elise, in her head, Viktor reached for the door handle.

"Why? What happened to Alex?" Mother asked, her voice bitter, almost pleased.

The front door snapped closed.

"He's gone."

Marko

Marko woke to footsteps on the wine cellar stairs. It was the middle of the night. "Who's there?"

"Marko?"

In the dark, Marko could hear his sister's voice. He sat up on the mattress as Tsura knelt down and put her arms around him.

"We were at the Labor Bureau," Tsura said.

Marko forced himself to say the truth out loud. "Alex was sent away. Kizzy, too."

"Here," Tsura said, as though she already knew. "The train leaves tomorrow." In the near darkness, Tsura held what Marko assumed were two train tickets.

"You're coming with me?" Marko asked.

"Yes."

The idea of Tsura leaving Germany with him filled Marko's chest with hope. He imagined living with Tsura in London. Tsura would own a shop. Or she'd attend university. Marko wanted to be a mechanic, to work hard and save to buy a car, become an engineer. He pictured them driving through England, far away from his childhood.

Tsura moved the second mattress away from the damp wall. Minutes later, she was asleep. Awake, Marko stared at the walls. He pulled up his shirtsleeve. Ripping off his smashed wristwatch, his hand fell down to the mattress, touching Alex's map book. Swallowing the embarrassing, burning feeling of wanting to cry, Marko reached for his medal. *Broden, Broden.* A pain pierced his throat, as if he'd swallowed a bullet.

He forced his mind to Kizzy, sent in his place. Tsura was right. He and Alex could have taken Kizzy with them, out of Germany. They would have made it work. But Marko had been shamefully self-centered, wanting Alex to himself.

Marko stared at his sister as she slept. Marko's head—and his whole body—burned with agonizing regret. Disgrace. Kizzy was gone. *Maybe she's dead.* And it was all his fault, everything. Alex, too. *That bastard Nazi.* Marko hadn't recognized him. Marko was usually one step ahead. The Nazi had figured it out. *I told him Broden's name.*

Marko touched the markings he'd made on the wall. He would forget about Alex. He didn't need to remember. He wanted to forget how it felt to look at him, how it felt with his mouth touching his, his hand on Alex's back, in his hair. He wouldn't talk about him. Or think about him ever again. He'd erase every memory. It would be easier that way.

Earlier, after dark, weaving in and out of the side streets and courtyards close to Rosenstrasse, afraid to be seen, Marko had returned to the Community Center. The protest was over. The building appeared to be empty. The guards were gone. A dozen or so people—the remaining protestors, women and men and children—were still out on the street. Marko asked a group of them what had happened. Most prisoners had been released, they told him. But a few had been deported, it seemed. They spoke with tears. In shock. Then Marko had run through the gardens, to Elise's kitchen door. She had confirmed what he'd known deep down.

Broden was sent away.

In the cellar, with Tsura now close by, clutching his medal, Marko drifted into the beginning of a dream. He saw himself with his sister, on a train preparing to leave Berlin. His head touched the windowpane. Reflections on the grimy glass merged the black platform with the blue sky. Marko's hand was healed, his wristwatch fixed. The train started to move and Marko could see him. His yellow star. A crowd in the distance. Stone statues. Fairy tales. From the carriage, Marko watched him run to catch the train, shouting for the driver to stop. A girl with wild hair ran, too, calling out to him. The train slowed down and it stopped, just for them. Marko's sister jumped onto the platform and lifted up the girl, their hair glowing in the sunlight. Alex Broden climbed aboard. His hands reached for Marko's face. He leaned in. And Marko waited for his kiss.

Kizzy

Kizzy drifted in and out of sleep.

Yesterday, the Nazi officer had led her to a group of adults and children without yellow stars. Women and children. Roma, like her. Sinti, too. All strangers. Some without shoes. Women's heads covered with scarves. Old men had been talking together, quietly. Kids playing on the dirt ground. They'd shared Kizzy's train. In another carriage. The Nazi soldiers had marched them along an outdoor corridor, between fences, rocks covering the ground, barbed wire tall around them. Toward a large wooden barn.

The sounds of babies, voices, chatter, had made Kizzy feel safer. This was the *Zigeunerlager*, the Gypsy compound, a young man had told her, speaking in broken German. This was Birkenau, he'd explained, built in Oświęcim—Auschwitz—a Polish town close to Kraków.

Women had stood in rags. Others in what once were their best clothes. A German man in a striped prisoner uniform had given Kizzy a bowl. Bowls were for food only, he'd said.

Inside the barracks, more children. Whole families. The air heavy with a sickening smell. A young woman had approached Kizzy and had led her to a place where she could sleep. A wooden bunk. The woman was pregnant, due in a few weeks, she had said.

Kizzy drifted into sleep, picturing Professor Duerr slouched in her wheelchair with her mouth dripping with saliva. Spooning tea into her mouth, falling back out. The nurses and doctors stripping off her clothes. Berry jam on her lips. Kizzy wanted to call out. But other names were stuck in her throat. *Tsura. Marko.*

Awake now, Kizzy's stomach ached with hunger.

"Kizzy?"

Kizzy opened her eyes.

"Kizzy. It's you. It's you! Kizzy. Our Kizzy!"

In the darkness of the barracks, Kizzy pulled herself up onto her elbows. "Mama?"

"No, Kizzy. It's me."

"Auntie?"

"Yes. I'm here, Kizzy. I'm here. It's you. How can this be? How can this be? Kizzy. Our little Kizzy!"

Aunt Jaelle—Tsura and Marko's mother—looked gaunt and ill. A patterned scarf, tied beneath her chin, covered her long, graying hair. Aunt Jaelle held out her hands and Kizzy climbed into her embrace. She led Kizzy to her bunk. Under her scratchy blanket, she held Kizzy in her thin arms.

Aunt Jaelle whispered her questions. "My children—are your cousins here? Have you seen them? Are they well?"

"I don't know. Where's Mama?"

"It'll be all right. Sleep, child. It'll be all right. Your mama—she's at peace now. She was very ill. She passed away in the train car. It was a long journey. Sleep, little Kizzy. I'm here." Aunt Jaelle whispered an old song, a familiar lullaby.

An hour or two later, Kizzy woke again.

"Kizzy, we must get up now," Aunt Jaelle whispered.

It was the middle of the night, Kizzy was sure. "Not yet."

"We have to be counted."

Leaning out of her bunk, her blue hat and brown coat still on, Kizzy watched the adults and children climb down from their bunks. The barn-like structure was full. Arms around shoulders, hands gripping hands, the crowd filed toward the door.

"Auntie, I'm hungry."

"We'll eat soon. At sunrise, I promise. Coffee. And bread."

As they walked out into the bitter night, they joined more crowds, more families. Speaking in whispers. Shoes on gravel.

Kizzy looked for Esther and Felix.

A boy, also Romani, not much older than Kizzy, tapped her arm. "You're lucky you've got a hat."

"My friends," Kizzy said to her aunt. "A girl and a boy. Jews. Are they here, too?" Aunt Jaelle squeezed Kizzy's hand.

The boy had heard her question. "Your friends are dead. After the gas, they burn the bodies." Kizzy tried to absorb his words as the boy continued, "It'll be us Roma next. In the same ovens. The same chimneys. Same smoke. Can you see it? There. Look."

Through the barbed wire fences, billowing black smoke covered the dark skies. Kizzy didn't understand until she saw tears falling from Aunt Jaelle's black, smiling eyes.

"Little Kizzy, you give me strength. You look like my Tsura."

EPILOGUE

In the early hours of another day, Tsura sat up in the darkness of the cellar. Her brother was still asleep. At the window, she watched the street.

The protests were over now. The Community Center was left empty and, as she'd suspected, Kizzy was never there. She must have been sent to the East, with the others. All those years, Tsura had seen such terrible things. Forced sterilizations. Her family forced from home. The hunger and muck in Marzahn. Father taken. Leaving her mother. Those events changed the course of each life. They shattered Tsura's understanding of the world and her place in it. They toughened her. They toughened Kizzy, too. Tsura had built armor for herself, except the thought of losing Kizzy had filled her with dread. She didn't worry about Marko. He was already grown, with his own ideas and ambitions. Kizzy was different.

Tsura had thought she'd break if she lost her little cousin. She had thought she'd never recover. But Tsura was wrong. Kizzy's disappearance had become another episode in their family's shared suffering. Tsura now knew where Kizzy belonged on the timeline of her survival. Without Kizzy, she could go on.

Tsura grabbed the hat from her head, her fingers running down her face, and it was only then she realized she'd been crying. She let out a sob, an embarrassing hollow sound that made her lungs burn. She felt an urge to run through the bombed-out city, to set fire to every standing house, to turn on every streetlight, to wake up every person, the city ablaze, to make them—every one of them—stand in the streets, and to yell Kizzy's name. They would stare with hate into the burning skies and scream until their throats tore open, howling, enraged. *How could the world allow this?*

Tsura's face dried as daylight streamed into the wine cellar, bathing her and Marko in their reality. Tsura wondered what would become of them. Marko planned to settle in Britain. Tsura preferred the idea of the United States. A new start, where people stood together, demanding their government listen. Tsura would go to Madison Square Garden in New York. Organize a rally. Force the world to remember the Roma—her family. *Kizzy, we'll remember you.* Such a commemoration, she knew, wouldn't bring Kizzy back, but the world would be forced to face its indifference, its inaction.

Tsura knelt by her brother. "Marko, wake up."

He was fast asleep. On the cellar floor, next to Marko's open hand, Tsura saw a small coin. She remembered how Marko had used it, almost a week ago, to engrave something into the cellar wall. In the darkness, she could make out the initials scraped into the plaster: "A" and "M." *Alex. Marko.* "M" had been repeated a number of times, a message for Alex that Marko had been looking for him. She wondered if Wolf was looking for her. Shaking away thoughts of Wolf, Tsura leaned over her brother and, with the edge of the metal coin, she pushed against the crumbling plaster. With care, she wrote the word "London" and then placed the coin into Marko's coat pocket.

In his sleep, Marko let out a small cry of pain.

"Marko, it's okay. Wake up. It's me. It's me."

With enough time before their train was scheduled to depart, they rushed to Professor Duerr's old house.

They washed in ice-cold water and dried themselves with cold, hardened towels. Tsura wandered into Kizzy's room, as if she might find her there. Tsura searched the house, rummaging through cupboards and drawers, finding clean clothes and anything of value. There wasn't much. Tsura and Marko had their forged papers and their tickets for the train. Marko took Alex's suitcase of clothes. The map book, too.

Aboard the train, they took their seats, their suitcases beside them.

"Promise you'll never talk about all this," Marko said.

Without thinking, Tsura nodded.

She remembered her promise to Professor Duerr when she looked down at her corpse in the hospital morgue. She had sworn to tell her tale, to make her name famous—the woman who saved them. How Tsura's great-uncle had wept for her. He'd told Tsura to flee, for the sake of their people. Tsura swallowed her sadness. A life of remembering awaited her. And memories wouldn't bring Kizzy back.

Berlin was awake now. The intermarried families of Rosenstrasse were waking on this Sunday morning, gratified and vigilant against the strange silence of bombed and broken church bells. They'd won their fight. They'd been permitted to live together a little while longer. Tsura had resented the protestors' apathy toward the Romani. They hadn't spoken out, yet they couldn't be blamed. They didn't care about Kizzy any more than Tsura cared for them. Like the protestors on Rosenstrasse, Tsura was selfish. She put her people first, placing Kizzy before anyone, and she would do the same again. Kizzy had been the sweetest child, like Samuel, her brother. How much they all loved them both. But the world was silent. Their family had been forgotten. Tsura couldn't allow herself to leave. She needed to stay in Berlin, to fight. She stood, picking up her coat and hat.

"What are you doing?" her brother asked.

It was hard to look him in the eye. "Find London."

"No, don't leave." Marko jumped from his seat. "Come with me. Forget about this place."

"Marko, I have to stay."

She couldn't forget. She wanted to cry again. But this time, not for Kizzy. Tsura wanted to cry for Marko. Marko blamed himself. He loved both Kizzy and Alex more than he would admit out loud.

"Hell, I'm staying, too." Marko stood up and reached for his belongings.

Tsura hit her arm against his shoulder, pushing him back down. "You have to go."

The engine shook to life. The train would depart at any moment. Marko stood again. "We need each other. We're the same," he said.

"You'll be fine, Marko. Go to London. Please."

As Tsura put her arms around him, their dark hair became entangled. He was right. Marko and Tsura were the same. They shared the same history, the same way of thinking. They shared the same blood.

"Promise you'll find me, after the war," she said softly.

Marko held her close.

"Tsura, don't leave."

"Promise me."

"I promise."

Marko slumped back into his seat.

She walked fast along the carriage, jumped down onto the platform, and tucked her hair into her hat. Behind Tsura, the train screeched along the tracks, carrying her brother and his memories west toward safety. The rattling of the wheels on the rails transformed into false echoes of gunfire and the voices of her family filled her head. With the weight of the gun in her coat pocket, beneath her gray German sky, the winter air froze in Tsura's throat as she walked back into the city. To return to the side streets and shadows. To sidestep the light. *They'll never know we were here.*

AUTHOR'S NOTE

The historical events described here are fact: The forced sterilization of Roma girls and the systematic murder of German children with disabilities, administered by Nazi doctors; The deportation of homosexual men and the sexual violence perpetrated against them; The round-ups of Berlin's remaining Jews; The Rosenstrasse protest; The establishment of the compound for Roma and Sinti at Auschwitz-Birkenau in Nazi-occupied Poland.

Historians have yet to determine the precise dates of the Nazi deportations of Roma from Marzahn to Auschwitz, but it is quite possible that those deportations began on the first day of March in 1943—hours before the air raid on Berlin—as represented here.

Historical details in this novel are documented through witness and survivor testimony, including: Christian women telephoning their friends for information about their Jewish husbands; Women tricking the Rosenstrasse guards into handing over their husbands' house keys; The arrest and release of ten protestors.

Certain scenes in this novel are inspired by true stories, including: Attempted escapes from the Nazi encampment for Roma at Marzahn; Notes hidden inside gifts of food smuggled into the Jewish Community Center on Rosenstrasse; And a teenager who donned a Nazi uniform in an attempt to rescue his boyfriend.

Visit www.unsilence.org to access educational programming created to accompany this novel.

Acclaimed artist and poet Ava Kadishson Schieber is a Jewish survivor of Nazi-occupied Yugoslavia. After the war, she trained as a theater set designer. She is the author of *Soundless Roar*, a collection of drawings, poems, and stories about her experiences as a teenager in hiding during the Holocaust.

THE AUTHOR

Danny M. Cohen is a learning scientist, fiction writer, and grandson of Maurice Ziekenoppasser, a Jewish survivor of Nazi-occupied Amsterdam.

Danny is an author of human rights fiction for young adults, including the short story DEAD ENDS, the interactive mystery THE 19TH WINDOW, and the forthcoming contemporary thriller HIDE OR SPEAK.

TRAIN, which is Danny's first novel, grew out of his doctoral research on educators' perceptions of Holocaust victimhood.

A professor at Northwestern University's School of Education and Social Policy and The Crown Family Center for Jewish and Israel Studies, Danny teaches about the design of Holocaust education, Holocaust fiction, and marginalized narratives of human rights. He is a Governor-appointed member of the Illinois Holocaust and Genocide Commission and sits on the editorial advisory board of the journal The Holocaust in History and Memory. He designed the pedagogical track of the inaugural docent training program of the Illinois Holocaust Museum and Education Center and was a faculty fellow of the Auschwitz Jewish Center.

Born and raised in London, Danny lives in Chicago with his husband and their daughter.

www.dannymcohen.com

Made in the USA
Lexington, KY
08 April 2018